EVERYMAN'S   LIBRARY

EVERYMAN,
I WILL GO WITH THEE,
AND BE THY GUIDE,
IN THY MOST NEED
TO GO BY THY SIDE

E. M. FORSTER

A ROOM WITH A VIEW

WHERE ANGELS FEAR TO TREAD

WITH AN INTRODUCTION
BY ANN PASTERNAK SLATER

EVERYMAN'S LIBRARY
Alfred A. Knopf   New York   Toronto

340

THIS IS A BORZOI BOOK
PUBLISHED BY ALFRED A. KNOPF

First included in Everyman's Library, 2011
Where Angels Fear to Tread: Copyright © 1920 by Alfred A. Knopf, Inc.
Copyright renewed by Edward Morgan Forster.
Originally published by Edward Arnold, London, 1905.
A Room with a View published in hardcover by Alfred A. Knopf, Inc.,
in 1923.
Originally published by Edward Arnold, London, 1908.
The two Appendices, E. M. Forster's 'A View without a Room' and an
exchange of letters between Forster and R. C. Trevelyan, are published
with the permission of The Provost and Scholars of King's College,
Cambridge and the Society of Authors as the Literary Representative
of the Estate of E. M. Forster.
Introduction Copyright © 2011 by Ann Pasternak Slater
Bibliography and Chronology Copyright © 2011 by Everyman's Library
Typography by Peter B. Willberg

www.randomhouse.com/everymans

ISBN: 978-0-307-70090-2

Library of Congress Cataloging-in-Publication Data
Forster, E. M. (Edward Morgan), 1879–1970.
[Room with a view]
A room with a view, Where angels fear to tread / by E.M. Forster; with
an introduction by Ann Pasternak Slater.
p.   cm.—(Everyman's library)
"This is a Borzoi Book."
Includes bibliographical references.
ISBN 978-0-307-70090-2 (alk. paper)
1. British–Italy–Fiction.   2. Young women–Fiction.   3. Florence
(Italy)–Fiction.   4. England–Fiction.   I. Title.   II. Title: Where
angels fear to tread.
PR6011.O58R6   2011   2011023542
823'.914–dc23   CIP

Book design by Barbara de Wilde and Carol Devine Carson
Typeset in the UK by AccComputing, North Barrow, Somerset
Printed and bound in Germany by GGP Media GmbH, Pössneck

C O N T E N T S

INTRODUCTION

─────

Cover-ups and the Unspoken

It is 1901.

E. M. Forster, a young man of twenty-two, has just arrived in Florence, and is deeply shocked. 'How flagrantly indecent,' he writes to a friend, 'are the statues in the Uffizi with their little brown paper bathing drawers.' Even Catholic fig-leaves are preferable. Rubens is unacceptable 'because he paints undressed people instead of naked ones'.[1] Forster, wayward maiden aunt of the Modernists, is affronted by the cover-ups of conventional propriety.

The excessive decorum dominating the turn of the last century is barely conceivable today. It's hard to imagine Michelangelo's David politely wrapped in paper pants. In *A Room with a View* Forster signals his amused dissent, when Lucy escapes from the Pension Bertolini 'to do something of which her well-wishers disapproved', and buys an armful of art reproductions. An innocent rebellion? No. They are all nudes: Georgione's 'Tempesta', the 'Idolino', Botticelli's 'Birth of Venus'. At which point Forster's narrative blandly slips into the voice of his times:

Venus, being a pity, spoiled the picture, otherwise so charming, and Miss Bartlett had persuaded her to do without it. (A pity in art of course signified the nude.)

That shift in voice is one tiny example of Forster's delicate ironies. Often his delivery is so successfully deadpan, it's hard to tell where he stands. The difficulty is compounded by his own inarticulate uncertainties.

Where Angels Fear to Tread and *A Room with a View* fall neatly within the Edwardian era (1901–10). This was the period when audiences rioted nightly against the word 'shift' in *The Playboy of the Western World*; when gentlemen's trousers were euphemized as 'ineffables' or 'unmentionables'; when one of Forster's Cambridge friends congratulated him on flouting linguistic decorum by calling Gino's newborn son a 'baby' rather than a 'child'. It is the time when Forster's fictional alter ego, Maurice, seeks the help of a doctor, shamefacedly introducing himself as 'an unspeakable of the Oscar Wilde sort'.[2] Forster was six-teen years old when Wilde was condemned to two years' hard labour on a charge of gross indecency. Wilde died in 1900, just before the Edwardian decade began, and Forster was coming to a slow understanding of his own homosexuality.

Unspeakable, unmentionable, ineffable: social taboos impose and are created by linguistic blackout; they are mutually reinforcing. The unspoken doesn't cease to exist. But it becomes unrecognizable, unknown, dimly sensed, feared, reviled. In Forster's case, initial innocence was compounded by his un-usually protected and protracted upbringing by a myriad maiden aunts and a young mother who was widowed at twenty-five, when he was a year old. On his own admission, he only 'understood how copulation took place' when he was thirty.[3] This bred fruitful ambiguities. In his early work, his inherent sexual ignorance, and an ingrained disinclination to offend, combine with deliberate literary occlusion, and a mocking adoption of Edwardian euphemism – as in Venus being 'a pity'. Consequently, in his work it's often difficult to distinguish the consciously ironic from the unconsciously acquiescent. The English *muddle*, which Forster's novels combat so energetically, often reflects his own half-articulated and imperfectly recog-nized confusion.

Take Forster's first piece of fiction. In 'The Story of a Panic', a group of English tourists are terrified by a visitation from Pan whom they sense but cannot see. Eustace, a boy in their company, is liberated and transformed. His instinctive percep-tion of nature disturbs the rest of the group who try to imprison him; his kindred spirit, a low-bred Italian waiter, helps him escape into the woods. Charles Sayle, a Cambridge fellow-student, deliberately misread the story in the basest sexual terms, wryly recounted by Forster many years after the event.

B— by a waiter in the hotel, Eustace commits bestiality with a goat on that valley where I had sat. In the subsequent chapters, he tells the waiter how nice it has been and they try to b— each other again. [To others, the travestied story] seemed great fun, to me disgusting. I was horrified and did not want to meet Charles Sayle. In after years I realized that in a stupid and unprofitable way he was right and this was the cause of my indignation. I knew, as their creator, that Eustace and the [goat's] footmarks and the waiter, had none of the conjunctions he visualized, I had no thought of sex for them, no thought of sex was in my mind. All the same I had been excited as I wrote and the passages where Sayle thought something was up had excited me most.[4]

With age, Forster admitted, such ambiguous passages grew rare in his work, as he left behind him 'that enchanted valley where beauty is lust, lust beauty, and neither has nor needs a name'. Forster's adaptation of Keats's insoluble aphorism ('Beauty is Truth, Truth Beauty') is at once straightforward and ironic. The relationship between beauty and lust isn't a conundrum, but an unspoken truth. Wilde's love that dare not speak its name is Forster's lust that neither has nor needs a name.

The unsaid and the unspeakable throw their shadow over Edwardian married life too. Forster's friend, J. R. Ackerley, was brought up in a seemingly normal well-to-do London household. Ackerley only discovered after his father's death that he had also raised an alternative family nearby, visiting them regularly while walking the dog. To take another example, Forster wrote a tart memoir of his aptly named Uncle Willie, a member of the Northumberland landed gentry, whose house Forster frequently visited. Uncle Willie married a woman eight years his senior, the unfortunate Aunt Emily, while maintaining in his household sparkling Leontine Chipman, thirteen years his junior. So much Forster tells us directly: the unspoken inference is that Leontine was Uncle Willie's live-in mistress. However, 'the proprieties were strictly observed', Forster observes sardonically. Uncle Willie forbad his unloved wife to take trips away from home unless young women could be found 'to keep dear Leontine company . . . during the hours when copulation is possible in Northumberland'. Such plans invariably fell through, and drove Uncle Willie 'half out of his mind'. He sounds very like Edward Ashburnham in Ford Madox Ford's *The Good Soldier*.

In spite of Uncle Willie's insistence on public form, sex played a large part in his life. There was 'the youthful feminine trash that thronged the house as years went on . . . Little girls he took an interest in too, and would pay for their school: indeed in the end he was interested in nothing but little girls ...' His well-trained wife and aging mistress made no objection. Forster himself, and his secret desires, were something quite other. Note the hiatus in Forster's manuscript. 'I [*one-word blank*] was outside his vision, and though he once referred to "the worst thing in creation" he was not illuminating about it. It never struck him as it did me that the groom was alone during hours that are possible in Northumberland'.[5] Like the brown paper shorts on Florentine statues, Forster's shorthand draws attention to what it hides. These are the great unanswered questions: what is the worst thing in creation? When *is* copulation possible in Northumberland?

Forster's reminiscences of Uncle Willie, as well as his account of 'The Story of a Panic', were written in the 1920s. It was easier to recognize the hypocrisy of the Edwardian era after it ended. J. B. Priestley's *An Inspector Calls* (1945) is an attack on Edwardian double standards. In it the members of a rich mill-owning family discover that each of them has, secretly and independently, taken advantage of the same working girl. Their carefully sustained veneer is gradually scraped away as revelation follows revelation. The father dismissed the girl from one of his mills for involvement in a strike. The daughter got her sacked from her next job on a false charge. The daughter's fiancé set her up as his kept woman, and then abandoned her. The son (whose alcoholism is another unspoken family secret) raped her and then stole from his father's business to pay her off. The mother convinced her women's charity not to support her in pregnancy and destitution. All the social and sexual cover-ups of underhand Edwardian respectability packed into one facile play.

Forster cleared the way for Priestley. *Howards End* (1910) urges its characters to 'only connect' – the prose with the passion, of course, but also the double standards endemic in such a secretive period. Margaret Schlegel forces Henry Wilcox to recognize the connection between his affair with Jacky Bast, and Helen Schlegel's one-night stand with Jacky's husband, Leonard. If Helen's unmarried pregnancy is to be condemned by Henry, his own adultery is equally culpable. Or both must be forgiven. By *Howards End* Forster had the strength to extend his social range and intensify the sharpness of his attack. In *Where Angels Fear to Tread* and *A Room with a View* he was still feeling his way. Like Philip Herriton, Caroline Abbot, and Lucy Honeychurch, he was a confused but obedient participant in a society whose values he found increasingly suspect.

1901–1908

In 1901 Forster left Cambridge with a mediocre degree and set out for Italy with his mother. For a year they drifted from pension to pension on the Baedeker trail, following the leisured, genteel life of the well-heeled Edwardian tourist. We may be surprised to find the middle-class and not obviously rich Caroline Abbott, in *Where Angels Fear to Tread*, also coolly embarking on a year's Italian travels in the company of the irresponsible Lilia Herriton. Who could contemplate such an extensive holiday now? A century ago, apparently, it was nothing special. Forster's early fictions are peppered with English tourists enjoying the middle-class equivalent of the aristocratic grand tours of the nineteenth century. He and his mother returned to England late in 1902, only to set out again on another continental trip in the new year.

Two instalments of his first novel, tentatively identified as *Old Lucy* and *New Lucy*, were begun during his travels abroad. They predate Forster's first published novel, *Where Angels Fear to Tread*, which came out in 1905. *The Longest Journey* followed in 1907. In 1908 the two halves of *Old* and *New Lucy* finally coalesced in the polished text of *A Room with a View*.

Though this chronology is convoluted, both novels benefited from it. *Where Angels Fear to Tread* is spontaneous and energetic, profiting from Forster's literary apprenticeship in the drafts of *Lucy*, and the short stories he was accumulating in this early period. The best of them, 'The Story of a Panic', epitomizes most memorably the emergent dualities that were to dominate all Forster's subsequent work. They can be summarized very simply as a neat alignment of conflicting values: suburbia versus nature; Sawston versus Italy; propriety versus passion. Dryads, fauns, Pan and the ancient gods battle with Miss Bartlett,

Mr Beebe, Mrs Herriton and the 'vast armies of the benighted'. It is one of Forster's great weaknesses that this recurrent template is too easily identifiable for the reader's sustained suspension of disbelief, and encourages an over-schematized reading of the novels.

Where Angels Fear to Tread

Two gossipy English ladies overheard in an Italian hotel were the trigger to *Where Angels Fear to Tread*. They were picking over the marriage of another Englishwoman to a young Italian who was both her junior and her social inferior. 'This sorry bit of twaddle stuck in my mind,' Forster says. 'I worked on it until it became alive and grew into a novel of contrasts.' On one hand were 'the English suburbs with the grey inhibited life that I knew only too well'.[6] On the other was the fictional Monteriano, based on San Gimignano, a recent stop on Forster's tourist trek. However, the novel is more subtle than Forster's impatiently schematic summary.

The novel is subtler, because Forster takes care to turn the contrasts typical of his recurring template into living particularities. Take the first chapter, which draws to an easy close as Mrs Herriton and her spinster daughter Harriet are planting vegetables.

They sowed the duller vegetables first, and a pleasant feeling of righteous fatigue stole over them as they addressed themselves to the peas. Harriet attached a string to guide the row straight, and Mrs Herriton scratched a furrow with a pointed stick . . .

All Sawston is implicit in this memorably dull scene. Its punitive self-imposed morality over trivia. Its scratchy, straitjacketed values. Its futile attempts to tether liberal nature to the straight and narrow. They are interrupted by the midday post with unwelcome news. Mrs Herriton's widowed daughter-in-law, Lilia, has kicked loose and got herself engaged in Italy. The letter is irritably ripped up and the uncovered peas are forgotten. Later Mrs Herriton remembers them and goes out in the dark, to find the sparrows have eaten them all. Only the letter's litter remains, 'disfiguring the tidy ground'. Sawston can't control libertine instinct. Lilia will find another mate; sparrows will peck up peas; even Harriet and Mrs Herriton will lose control in their passion for propriety.

Forster's problem is that from our present, seemingly liberated perspective, the impulses driving Harriet and her mother are altogether too extreme to be convincing. In England, they successfully interrupt Lilia's burgeoning flirtation with Mr Kingcroft. Then they attempt to stop her Italian marriage, and fail. Yet Beatrix Potter provides an illuminating parallel to such selfish restraint. Between 1902 and 1905, when she was in her late thirties, her parents obstructed her wish to marry the youngest of the Warne brothers, her publishers. Invitations to visit the Warne family in Surbiton were refused because, as Beatrix tactfully put it, her mother was 'exacting'. So much is left unsaid. Suburban Surbiton was beneath Mrs Potter. Warne was notionally in trade, while the Potters' wealth came from cotton mills. Beatrix's unspeakable heresy, 'Publishing books is as clean a trade as spinning cotton,' was uttered to a cousin 'in confidence, scarcely above a whisper'. Sadly, Warne died before the couple had been disobediently engaged more than a few months. The Potter parents continued intransigent till Beatrix, at forty-seven, rebelled and married a Westmorland solicitor well beneath her parents, but not her.[7]

So is the Herritons' interference that improbable? Once Lilia has conveniently died in childbirth, they pointlessly prevent her daughter, Irma, finding out about her half-brother, and fail. Then they switch to the contrary scheme of rescuing the baby from his socially undesirable father – and fail. They are incapable of conceiving that Gino might love his baby. Their obsessive attempts at control are self-deceptive and self-defeating. Unremittingly unsympathetic and unimaginative, they self-righteously misread their low urge to have their own way as high morality. For Forster, it is a typical English *muddle* with tragic consequences. However, their confused machinations also serve a fictional imperative. The conflict central to the novel's climactic finale depends on Forster's getting Philip Herriton and Caroline Abbott to Italy. Philip and Caroline vacillate near the fulcrum of a seesaw with repressive Sawston weighing down one end, and flighty Italy up at the other.

Harriet and Mrs Herriton's malign meddling is the necessary
mechanism to catapult Philip and Caroline over the Alps to
Monteriano, and into the arms of Gino.

Once he escapes to Italy, Forster is at ease. He's enchanted
by its warmth, culture, and beauty. He also knows it can be
messy, mercenary, ignorant and vulgar, and he loves that too.
Three times we're told that Philip, Forster's alter ego, has a
sense of beauty, and a sense of humour. Italy satisfies both.
Forster's presentation of Sawston is one-sided; his presentation
of Italy shifts to modulated dualities. They are neatly, and
indeed emphatically epitomized by a repeated phrase from the
Baedeker entry on Monteriano: 'The view from the Rocca
(small gratuity) is finest at sunset.' They are symbolized by the
city's towers, recalled by Caroline at the novel's end: 'That
tower in the sunlight – do you remember it, and all you said
to me?' An authorial nudge, referring us back to a conversation
fifty pages earlier:

'It reaches up to heaven,' said Philip, 'and down to the other place.'
The summit of the tower was radiant in the sun, while its base was
in shadow and pasted over with advertisements. 'Is it to be a symbol
of the town?'

Monteriano isn't short of symbols. When Philip and Caroline
first meet Gino, he quotes the opening lines of Dante's *Inferno*,
with the self-satisfied air of an Italian who knows his classics.
'*Nel mezzo del cammin di nostra vita / Mi ritrovai per una selva oscura, /
Ché la dirrita via era smaritta*' ('In the middle of our life's journey
I found myself in a dark wood, where the right road [or 'direct
way'] was lost'). The zigzag road climbing up to Monteriano
passes through a dark wood, but in springtime, as Philip later
remembers, it is awash with violets.

Gino perfectly embodies such dualities. He's first presented
through the suspicious eyes of the English – ill-bred, ignorant
and sublimely complacent. Forster doesn't gloss over the stubborn clash of cultures in Gino and Lilia's unsatisfactory marriage. Yet Gino is untainted by English hang-ups and Sawston
mendacity. As Caroline and Philip are thawed by Italian
warmth, Gino's cordial frankness endears him to us and to
them. Everything Forster relishes in Italy is celebrated in the

absurd ovations for the diva singing *Lucia di Lammermoor* in Monteriano's provincial opera house. Gino emerges from the audience's hilarious hullabaloo like a Venus Anadyomene *musculoso*, rising from the waves in a gale of flowers and cheers. 'I saw him mixed up with music and light,' Caroline says.

There are no difficulties in Forster's affectionately amused picture of Gino and Italy. But this is also where Philip and Caroline are tested, and the novel begins to bite. Until this point the opposing values of Sawston and Italy have created conflict but no dilemmas. For the reader, the good and the bad are too obviously distinct. The fundamental ethical conflict that emerges in the novel's climax is clarified by its title, a half-quote of Pope's dictum: *For Fools rush in where Angels fear to tread.*[8] The title was suggested by a friend, late in the novel's composition. Forster then appears to have inserted some slightly awkward references to 'fools' and 'angels' in the earlier chapters, to prepare for the central dilemmas facing Philip and Caroline. Should they interfere in Gino's life, or not? They have to recognize, and reject, Harriet and Mrs Herriton's moral code, whose perversity seems so obvious to us. They also have the harder problem of their own response. Should they do more than leave Gino in peace? Should they step in, and stop Harriet's mad crusade?

Harriet, invading Gino's house and rushing off with the baby in his brief absence, is very obviously the intemperate fool implied by the novel's title. Her ill-judged precipitancy is underlined by the headlong career of the fast hired carriage hurrying her downhill to the railway station with the stolen baby. Her foolishness is emphasized by the village idiot who accompanies them. And yet even this symbolic fool is ambivalent. As the villagers say, 'He understands everything, but he can explain nothing.' He has visions of the saints, but Philip, a true Englishman, finds him disgusting. Forster orchestrates his grim climax with emblematic precision. The carriage crashes in mid-journey, *nel mezzo del cammin*, in Dante's wood of error, to the grotesque accompaniment of the burbling idiot, the silently crying baby, and Harriet's hysterical laughter in the dark. It is only at this point that we can see, in retrospect, the full monstrosity of what Harriet and her mother have

E. M. FORSTER

undertaken. They are against nature: they are bent on robbing a father of his child. In direct antithesis, Gino has been simply, sensibly seeking another wife as mother for his son. From the very first, Herriton meddling flouted the laws of natural decorum, and the virginal, twenty-three-year-old Caroline Abbott was improperly expected to act as a chaperone to Lilia – married, widowed, and ten years her senior.

If Harriet is the novel's fool, Caroline, equally obviously, is its angel. She hesitates to enter Gino's house on her mission to save the baby. She pauses outside his open door, and hears him talking, incomprehensibly, to an apparently empty room. (Gino is asking his baby's advice about lottery numbers – a scene at once mysterious and absurd, and another image in little of Italy's charm.) She finds she can't barge in. When Gino discovers her, he co-opts her into bathing the baby, and Forster creates a charming update of the staple Renaissance topos: Virgin and Child – with dusty washing-up bowl and tablecloth standing in for bath and towel, and handsome, fallible Gino as Donor. Caroline is won over, falls for Gino, realizes his rights – and this could have been the happy ending Forster denies us.

Even in his earliest work, Forster is – not always successfully – at pains to avoid simplistic moral judgments and simple resolutions. To counterweigh the balanced alternatives of the novel's title he introduces another charged icon: the frescoes illustrating the authentic but ludicrous story of Monteriano's patron saint.* Santa Deodata achieved sanctity on her back, refusing to rise even when tempted by the devil throwing her mother downstairs. She is, to put it baldly, a mediocre angel with little get up and go. She's not an interfering fool either, but 'in her death, as in her life, Santa Deodata did not accomplish much'. She points us to Philip's questionable virtues. Like Caroline, Philip comes to see they probably shouldn't interfere in Gino's life. Yet he's reluctant to restrain Harriet. His inaction is neither angelic nor even morally neutral: it allows Harriet to

---

*She is based on Santa Fina (Seraphina dei Cardi, 1238–53), who achieved sanctity by lying on her back for five years till her death at fifteen. The Collegiate Church in San Gimignano has Ghirlandaio's frescoes of her death and burial.

abduct the baby. His complicity in her crime carries him headlong downhill with her and the idiot, and leaves him in the dark
wood with Gino's baby dead in his arms.

Caroline is the golden mean between these interfering
idiots and dubiously inactive angels. It's telling that while
Philip and Harriet take the fast cab down to the station, and
crash, Caroline has gone ahead, cautiously, in the slow coach.
Caroline rightly hesitates to intrude on Gino, but she is also
courageously honest in thinking her way through many
changes of mind, which merely irritate Mrs Herriton and
Philip. Once firm in her own mind, she's equally courageous
in her frank attack on Philip's passivity, and her pained criticism of his mother. Her first action is to try and get Philip
not just to withdraw from, but proactively halt the Herriton
campaign. In vain.

In *The Longest Journey*, boys are heard singing in the school
chapel. Their pauses for breath give the old hymn a new
meaning:

Fight the good . Fight with . All thy . Might.

When Harriet vanishes with Gino's ill-fated baby, Philip finds
her prayerbook on her bed, open at the text: 'Blessed be the
Lord my God who teacheth my hands to war, and my fingers
to fight.' This is the 'good' that Philip and Caroline must
oppose with all their might. Philip fails, and when he returns
to Gino with news of the baby's death, well aware of his own
guilt, he offers himself up to Gino's mercy. Gino has no com-
punction in trying to strangle him. Caroline's active virtue is
seen at its most highly charged when she separates them ('This
thing stops here.') At just this moment Perfetta enters, painfully, 'hilariously', with the baby's supper. And here Forster
creates a second iconic scene, at once prosaic and sublime, as
Caroline makes Gino and Philip share the dead baby's milk.
It is the milk of human kindness, *Liebfraumilch*, and once again
Caroline figures as Virgin and peacemaker.

For Forster, Gino, and Philip, the fight is good because it is
justified, natural and physically liberating. Yet in his reminiscence about the unintentional implications of 'The Story of a
Panic', Forster admitted that writing this scene had also excited

him, even though he was unaware of its homoerotic subtext.* It was his practice to allow instinct as well as craft to carry him, and here the novel's unconscious sources of energy are most evident. In the novel's finale, the unrequited loves of Philip for Caroline, and Caroline for Gino, are bloodless and unconvincing. They come from nowhere. Conversely, Philip's growing delight in Gino is vividly realized and completely compelling. Forster seems not yet to be fully aware of his own nature.

Consequently, there is a tangle of overwritten authorial manipulation complicating and confusing the novel's ending. When Caroline confesses her love for Gino, Philip thinks of Pasiphaë. Pasiphaë's mythic love of a bull certainly was aberrant, and their offspring was the monstrous Minotaur. Yet it is grossly disproportionate for both Caroline and Philip to reject her physical attraction to Gino as comparably taboo. He's a lower-class Italian, nothing more. But Caroline appears to concur with Philip's instinctive sense of fearful revulsion. When she watched Gino with his baby, and hesitated to intrude, a ring of his cigar smoke floated towards her like 'a breath from the pit'. This infernal image explains its enigmatic predecessor, Philip's comment, quoted above, that Monteriano's sunlit tower symbolizes the town because 'It reaches up to heaven, [...] and down to the other place'. Released from Gino's stranglehold, Philip refers to him as 'the foul devil'. On the novel's last page, Philip finally recognizes that 'This woman was a goddess to the end. For her no love could be degrading; she stood outside all degradation.'

Both extremes, revulsion against the abnormal as infernal, and its apotheosis, are in excess of Forster's declared subject. Caroline's love is neither degraded nor sublime. Yet the motivating force of the novel, Forster's suppressed homosexuality, was outlawed by the society of his time. Half-strangled himself, he found his voice in an attack on the xenophobic and social taboos of middle-class Edwardian England, and located aberrancy in two English women's love for the son of an Italian dentist.

*It pre-empts by fifteen years Lawrence's 'Gladiatorial', the chapter describing Birkin and Gerald's wrestling in *Women in Love*.

A Room with a View

Forster's next novel, the ambitious, unsuccessful *Longest Journey*, brings together many of his most pressing themes in an inchoate form, bundled together by an intricate and obscure symbolic structure. Their extended articulation appears to have been cathartic, enabling Forster to rework the unfinished *Old* and *New Lucy* with a lighter touch. 'I shall scarcely write another *Longest Journey*,' he notes, 'for it vexed people, and I can with sincerity please them.'[9] In the sunny *Room with a View*, Sawston's repressive conformity dwindles into the comic absurdities of Pension Bertolini and the milder proprieties of Summer Street. The symbolic leitmotifs are simpler and more persuasive. The template explored in *Where Angels Fear to Tread* is deliberately redeployed, and once again Forster's suppressed hunger for homosexual friendship is reconfigured in a safely conventional heterosexual love-story. In both novels Edwardian homophobia is placated by its convincing relocation in the two acceptable fictional barriers to romance, differences of social class and nationality. Throughout 1907–8 Forster's attitudes to the novel in progress fluctuated with characteristic uncertainty. It is 'clear and bright and well-constructed. But so thin.' 'Bright and merry and I like the story.' 'Toshy, but one trusts inoffensive.' 'Bilge.' Significantly, Lucy 'and Mr Beebe have interested me a good deal'.[10]

Forster was, by now, more aware of the kind of novel he wanted to write, and took pains to enlighten his readers accordingly. Like Jane Austen, he is ironically self-referential. *Northanger Abbey* played off the silly Gothic novels of contemporary lady novelists against the mundane charm of Austen's radically unremarkable heroine. Comparably, Forster clarifies the innovative nature of his own fiction through the counter example of Miss Lavish's *Under a Loggia*, an overheated version of Lucy's Florentine experiences. 'Love, murder, abduction, revenge, was the plot', Forster drily informs us, in an ironic nod towards *Where Angels Fear to Tread*. He mischievously makes Miss Lavish add: 'There will be a deal of local colouring, descriptions of Florence and the neighbourhood, and I shall also introduce some humorous characters. And let me give you all fair

xix

warning: I intend to be unmerciful to the British tourist.' It all sounds remarkably familiar.

How, then, does Lavish's Florentine Loggia differ from Forster's unexotic rooms, local colour, and mockery of English tourists? Further discreet hints follow. Miss Lavish, boldly unconventional as ever, claims that the murder Lucy witnessed in Piazza Signoria is 'a tragedy', and 'I repeat and I insist ... not the less tragic because it happened in humble life'. Miss Bartlett is overwhelmed by the brilliance of Miss Lavish's platitude; she is 'a really clever woman ... that last remark struck me as so particularly true'. Forster, for his part, locates truth elsewhere. He chooses Cecil as the unexpected spokesman for his single most important direction to the reader:

'I, even I, have won a great victory for the Comic Muse. George Meredith's right – the cause of Comedy and the Cause of Truth are really the same...'

Later, Mr Beebe walks Miss Bartlett home, conversing 'on indifferent topics: the Emersons' need of a housekeeper; servants; Italian servants; novels about Italy; novels with a purpose; could literature influence life?' On the next page they find Lucy at the piano, her mother and brother gathered beside her, reminding Mr Beebe of another Renaissance topos, like the Virgin and Child of *Where Angels Fear to Tread*. This time it is 'the *Santa Conversazione*, in which people who care for one another are painted chatting about noble things – a theme neither sensual nor sensational, and therefore ignored by the art of today'.

So: Forster uses the same materials as Miss Lavish, but his novel differs from hers, and those of his popular contemporaries, being neither sensual, nor sensational, nor even tragic. It is a comedy with a serious purpose, promoting Truth. And we can be pretty sure that Forster wanted it to influence the attitudes of his times.

The central theme of *A Room with a View* is Lucy's denial of truth. She lies to herself about her feelings for George; commits herself to an engagement with Cecil, and then lies again in her attempts to disentangle herself from Cecil without admitting the cause. Forster details Lucy's self-deception with amused understanding. 'She loved Cecil; George made her nervous; will the reader explain to her that the phrases should have been reversed?' Once she has broken off the engagement, she still wants to keep running further and further away: from her home, from herself, to Greece – to Turkey! – with the spinster Misses Alan, their mackintosh squares and digestive bread. For us, the fortunate outsiders, her self-deception is painfully funny:

She did not acknowledge that her brain was warped, for the brain itself must assist in that acknowledgement . . . She only felt, 'I do not love George; I broke off my engagement because I did not love George; I must go to Greece because I do not love George; it is more important that I should look up gods in the dictionary than that I should help my mother; everyone else is behaving very badly.'

Finally, Mr Emerson sums it all up for her. 'Beware of muddle,' he says. 'Do you remember in that church, when you pretended to be annoyed with me and weren't? Do you remember before, when you refused the room with a view? Those were muddles – little, but ominous – and I am fearing that you are in one now . . .' At this point he falters, but the reader has had the assistance of Forster's preceding chapter headings. Their ominous crescendo – *Lying to George*; *Lying to Cecil*; *Lying to Mr Beebe, Mrs Honeychurch, Freddy and the Servants* – summarizes the rest of Lucy's story, a descent into darkness which ends here, with *Lying to Mr Emerson*. He, however, sees through her self-deceit, and bursts out, 'You love George!' True love is vindicated, and the novel's romantic parabola completes its expected course in the traditional comic closure of marriage.

Lucy's story is essentially the same as Philip and Caroline's in *Where Angels Fear to Tread*, and Rickie's in *The Longest Journey*. All of them try to belie what Keats called the holiness of the heart's affections, and sacrifice genuine feelings to social shibboleths. It was, obviously, a theme intimately close to Forster's own embattled heart. As a writer, however, he also felt bound by the literary demands of his time, and maintained a covert counter-attack against them. In *Aspects of the Novel*, the lectures delivered in Cambridge after his novel-writing was over, he lamented the imperatives imposed by a popular readership. 'Yes – oh dear yes – the novel tells a story,' he concedes, 'in a sort of drooping regretful voice'. The story is the primitive bait which keeps us reading. What's more, *Homo Fictus*, unlike *Homo Sapiens*, has an unnaturally impoverished life. 'He wants little food or sleep, he is tirelessly occupied with human relationships'.[11] The weary novelist, in his turn, must satisfy his readers' insatiable appetite for romance. Hence the love triangle of Lucy, George, and Cecil, as the novel's ostensible centre. Yet, as Mr Emerson emphatically concludes to Lucy, 'we fight for more than Love or Pleasure: there is Truth. Truth counts, Truth does count.' The novel's real concern is Lucy's troubled journey into her self-deceiving denial of love, and the impact of those around her, pushing her on, or dragging her back from her descent into the underworld. That is why the central myth of this novel is the story of Persephone.

Persephone, the Roman Proserpina, daughter of the harvest goddess Ceres, was abducted by Pluto, god of the underworld. When she was rescued from Hades, her return brought spring to the earth. Since she ate four pomegranate seeds in Pluto's kingdom, she is doomed to return to the underworld for four months every year, and with her absence winter returns. The time cycle of *A Room with a View* takes two years, from the first spring in Florence, culminating in George and Lucy's kiss in the Tuscan hills above Fiesole, and Miss Bartlett's dragging Lucy off to winter in Rome. There she meets Cecil and begins an uncertain and reluctant relationship with him. Part Two opens in aptly named Summer Street, where her engagement to Cecil is disrupted by the reappearance of George. As summer ends, the increasing darkness of the lying chapters suggests Lucy's struggling descent back into the underworld. The novel ends with the lovers united in Italy in the following spring.

The myth is established at the beginning of chapter 6, when Lucy and her friends *Drive out in Carriages to See a View*, as Forster's chapter title has it. They are driven by two god-like young Italians, 'Phaethon in Tuscany driving a cab'* and his girlfriend

---

*Phaethon borrowed the chariot of the sun from his father Helios, couldn't control its horses, and when he endangered the burning earth by flying too close, was killed by a thunderbolt from Zeus. In mourning for his death, Helios refused to drive his chariot and plunged the earth in darkness for days. Forster makes no further overt use of this myth, but this link to Persephone's story is significant.

'Persephone, tall and slender and pale, returning with the spring to her mother's cottage, and still shading her eyes from the unaccustomed light'. The vegetation myth, a universal metaphor for seasonal birth, death, and rebirth, is capable of embracing many embodiments. In Forster's handling, Lucy, George and Cecil, Miss Bartlett and Mr Beebe, in their various ways, partially replicate the roles of Persephone and Pluto.

In Miss Lavish's *Under a Loggia*, the lovers' embrace in the hills is a null cliché ('He simply enfolded her in his manly arms'). Forster lavishes a richer rhetoric on the episode. Lucy tumbles out of the woods to find herself on a terrace covered with violets, a torrent of blue running downhill 'in rivulets and streams and cataracts, irrigating the hillside with blue ... collecting into pools in the hollows'. Lucy is another Persephone, releasing the melted snows of spring; the lovers' terrace is 'the well-head, the primal source whence beauty gushed out to water the earth'. As George steps forward to kiss her, they're interrupted by Miss Bartlett, a wintry Pluto, standing 'brown against the view'. The lovers are separated, a thunderstorm breaks, Lucy is driven back into the town, and George makes his way downhill, on foot and alone. Darkness envelops them both.

Forster's symbolism is well-sustained and relatively discreet. The Emersons 'have a view'; Miss Bartlett is 'against the view'. She is narrow-minded, constantly closing the pension shutters – just as Harriet Herriton wanted the train windows shut to protect her from smuts. When we first meet Miss Bartlett, Forster describes how 'her long, narrow head drove backwards and forwards ... as though she were demolishing some invisible obstacle'. On the very next page she asks Mr Beebe whether he thinks her 'narrow-minded and suspicious' in rejecting the Emersons' offer of their room with a view. The same sentence is repeated verbatim many chapters later, in Summer Street, after George kisses Lucy for the second time. Upset by her own repressed feelings, Lucy takes offence and orders him to leave, calling on Miss Bartlett as witness. George turns to Miss Bartlett, begging her sympathy:

'You wouldn't stop us this second time if you understood,' he said. 'I have been into the dark, and I am going back into it, unless you will try to understand.'

Her long, narrow head drove backwards and forwards, as though demolishing some invisible obstacle...

George is banished into the shadows of depression, and Lucy feels the summer dying around her. 'The evening brought her odours of decay, the more pathetic because they were reminiscent of spring ... the earth was hastening to re-enter darkness.' As the lying chapters run their course, the darkness grows, and a storm breaks with 'a tragic greatness that is rare in Surrey'. Forster's comedy deliberately brushes against tragedy. As Mr Beebe says, 'We shan't have rain, but we shall have darkness ... The darkness last night was appalling.' Which brings us to Miss Bartlett and Mr Beebe.

These two characters illustrate a distinction Forster made, with faux naïveté, between 'flat' and 'round' characters, in *Aspects of the Novel*. Flat characters, he says, are very useful – they can be pushed about like tokens; they never surprise us. Miss Bartlett is unquestionably the finest of all Forster's creations in this mode. She is the English spinster personified, the Platonic summation of all its parts. At the same time she's vividly individual, partly because she was based on Forster's own unfortunate Aunt Emily.[12] According to Forster, Aunt Emily was 'a ghastly bore, and a treacherous sneak', always forcing herself onto fishing expeditions, 'unsuitably dressed and at no one's invitation, to see the fun', just as Miss Bartlett, overdressed, tactless and incompetent, insists on helping Mrs Honeychurch tie up the storm-battered dahlias. Miss Bartlett is hardly changed between *Old Lucy* and *A Room with a View* – until the very end, when she suddenly spins into a 'round' character, and surprises us. She is the invisible agent who secretly brings about George and Lucy's reunion. Forster delays this revelation till his very last page, and we have to backtrack to realize exactly how and when Miss Bartlett engineered Lucy's decisive meeting with Mr Emerson.

The Merchant Ivory film of the novel brings out into the open what Forster intentionally hides. The film first shows Miss Bartlett perceptibly shaken by George's appeal for understanding (quoted above). Later it invents a scene where she tells Mr Emerson that Lucy has rejected Cecil, and will be travelling to Greece with the Miss Alans, but not with her ex-fiancé.

Her deliberate revelation allows Mr Emerson to bring about George and Lucy's reunion. In Forster's novel, the revelation is inadvertent, and accidentally let slip by Mr Beebe.

Thus Miss Bartlett turns from a Pluto figure of interdiction, to a maternal Ceres surreptitiously rescuing the lovers from their underworld. Such is Aunt Emily's happier immortality in art – a fulfilment clearly expressed by Maggie Smith's Miss Bartlett, last seen settling back in her single bed with softened features and a welcome contentment new to us.

Mr Beebe is Miss Bartlett's mirror opposite. Throughout the novel he seems a rounder character than Miss Bartlett – an image partly prompted, perhaps, by plump Simon Callow's perfect impersonation. Mr Beebe is roundish because he habitually resists standard Sawston-style responses in the novel – we can rely on his clerical anti-type, Mr Eager, for those. He seems humane, generous, insightful, tactfully dragging Miss Bartlett and the discontented Minnie off to the local inn when tensions at Windy Corner are high. He listens to Miss Bartlett's fretful spinsterish anxieties with amused indulgence. He seems to be a model of open-mindedness. It comes as a complete shock when he, of all people, responds with cold indifference to Mr Emerson's revelation that George and Lucy have loved each other all along. Where Miss Bartlett's unexpected *volte face* turns her into a positive life force, Mr Beebe is transformed into a monument of negation.

...his white face, with its ruddy whiskers, seemed suddenly inhuman. A long black column, he stood...

When Emerson demands, what's wrong with my George, then? Beebe replies, contemptuously, 'Nothing, Mr Emerson, except that he no longer interests me. Marry George, Miss Honeychurch. He will do admirably' – and walks out. The whole of this chilling reversal is omitted from the film, where Beebe's character remains unsullied.

Forster takes pains to prepare Beebe's motivation in the preceding chapter. He explains that Beebe has a 'belief in celibacy' which is 'very subtle and quite undogmatic', and 'alone explains his action subsequently'. Beebe agrees to help Miss Bartlett win Mrs Honeychurch's approval of Lucy's flight abroad, in order to 'place her out of danger until she could confirm her resolution of virginity'. He wishes to help 'not only Lucy, but religion also'. This awkward and barely credible explanation is only momentarily convincing when Forster mentions that Beebe 'never heard that an engagement was broken off but with a slight feeling of pleasure'. This, rather than the doctrinaire excuses, tallies with a trail Forster has already set up, and which culminates naturally in Beebe's telling dismissal of George. 'He no longer interests me.'

Beebe's sexual orientation is lightly implied from the start. 'Mr Beebe was, from rather profound reasons, somewhat chilly in his attitude towards the other sex ...' According to Freddy, Beebe says that 'Mr Vyse is an ideal bachelor ... he's like me – better detached.' When Miss Bartlett passes off Lucy's intended flight to Greece as a feminine need for change, Beebe is half-convinced, saying 'I have no sisters or – and I don't understand these things.' Or – what? *New Lucy* provides a direct corroboration of what is unspoken here. In an extended, later rejected fragment, Mr Beebe finds George, the 'irresistible', 'mysterious and romantic', sleeping out in the woods. They talk together in companionable darkness. Although Beebe is ostensibly attempting to dissuade George from breaking up Lucy's engagement, there is an unmistakable personal interest stirring Beebe as the treetops stir above him.[13] In the novel, the impulse surfaces – transformed, open and exultant – in the delectable woodland scene where Freddy, George, and Beebe bathe naked, and race each other in the sun. Then the ladies inadvertently intrude, the parasols go up, and Cecil hastily ushers the women away. This innocent all-male romp, excellently recreated in the film, is the comic counterpart to George and Lucy's first kiss. The rivulets and cataracts of violets, irrigating the Florentine hillside with blue, collect in the flooded hollows of Summer Street's Sacred Lake. It is sad that in the end Beebe turns his back on this baptismal scene, and retreats into the lying dark.

INTRODUCTION

The Outsider Inside

In 1939, Forster compared the anti-Semitism increasingly apparent in England to the taboos of his prep-school days. At his first school, sisters were a disgrace. Forster got through all right, because his conscience was clear. (He was an only child.) The second school was worse; here mothers were shameful. Their visits were dreaded. Since nearly every little boy had a mother tucked away in a cupboard somewhere, there were scandalous revelations. Heroes of the playing field could just about carry it off. Cowards diverted suspicion from themselves by foisting mothers on weaker boys. From the vantage point of the frightened present, Forster recognizes his old enemy:

Having been a Gentile at my first school and a Jew at my second, I know what I am talking about. I know how the poison works, and I know too that if the average man is anyone in particular, he is a public school boy.[14]

Forster's quiet essay sums up his lifelong battle against conventional social propriety by identifying it in its newest and grossest form. The dangers of infantile Sawston are clear in fully-grown Nazism. Fascism, communism, totalitarianism are, most obviously, 'the vast armies of the benighted, who ... march to their destiny by catchwords'. Forster knew the power of mass orthodoxy, alias political correctness, only too well.

For, willy-nilly, Forster wanted very much to be, as it were, a Gentile. He is frequently torn between the social conventions he mocks and the values he inherits and instinctively espouses, even while rejecting them. The upper-class Lytton Strachey, enviably at ease with his own sexuality, wrote Forster a clear-headed criticism of *Maurice*, pointing out that Forster inadvertently expresses the conventional taboos his novel tries to combat. 'For instance ... à propos of Maurice tossing himself off (you call it a "malpractice"), you say – "He knew what the price would be – a creeping apathy towards all things." How did Maurice know that? And how do you? Surely the truth is that as often as not the effects are simply nil.'[15] In *Howards End*, Forster voices social snobbery about the working-class Basts while making Leonard Bast his hero. The narrative voice may

xxvii

E. M. FORSTER

be ironical, but the presentation of Jacky is unabashedly grotesque. The narrative viewpoint is unstable. In *A Room with a
View*, George's dismissal of Cecil as not marriageable tallies
with Forster's portrait. Cecil is portrayed as a snob and a male
chauvinist prig. Far from falling in love, Forster tells us, 'he
had passed, if not to passion, at least to a profound uneasiness'.
Poor, bloodless Cecil! George's measured denunciation is
invested with Forster's authority. Yet when Lucy repeats the
same criticisms of Cecil in the lying chapters, she isn't only
deceiving herself: they are no longer true of Cecil. They are,
and then they are not, true.

Cecil's memorable dignity in rejection is one thing that
wrong-foots her, and is a fine example of Forster's flexibly
redemptive imagination. In Lucy, he's also creating precisely
the double-think Strachey pinpointed in Forster himself. He
has every good writer's instinctive impulse to immerse himself
in the mind-set of his characters and their time. When Lucy
voices a coarser version of George's reasons for rupture, the
bewildered Cecil acutely observes, 'This evening you seem a
new person: new thoughts – even a new voice ... a new person
seems speaking through you.' Later, Mrs Honeychurch identi-
fies the same thing:

> Lucy screwed up her mouth and said: 'Perhaps I spoke hastily.'
> 'Oh goodness!' her mother flashed. 'How you do remind me of
> Charlotte Bartlett!'

Lucy's problem is that she has degenerated into an inadvertent,
indiscriminate mimic. Her words and her actions are dis-
coloured by what other people think. Forster was sufficiently
self-aware to admit to his own fluctuating vision, defending
it as being true to life, and consequently more than merely
admissible:

> A novelist can shift his viewpoint if it comes off ... Indeed this power
> to expand and contract perception ... this right to intermittent know-
> ledge: – I find it one of the great advantages of the novel form, and it
> has a parallel in our perception of life. We are stupider at some times
> than others; we can enter other people's minds occasionally but not
> always, because our own minds get tired; and this intermittence lends
> in the long run variety and colour to the experiences we receive.[16]

INTRODUCTION

It is ironic that Forster was unaware of the closeness of his semi-conscious, semi-apologetic practice, to James Joyce's deliberate immersion in the minds of his characters. Forster disliked *Ulysses*. Nevertheless, he was very aware of how malleably fallible language and perception can be. For affronted Lucy, George's kiss is no kiss but an 'insult'; he 'forgot himself'. Poor Cecil, on the other hand, can only think of kissing her as a 'scheme' that erroneously appears 'practical'. Which it isn't, because his specs get in the way. The very language of Forster's apparently objective narrative is inflected by oblique echoes of his characters' thoughts. Their unspoken words betray them. And Forster's irony stings.

For Forster was, according to his own metaphor, a Jew as well as a Gentile. An outsider inside, he attacked orthodoxy of every kind from within the pale. Even while providing his readers with the requisite heterosexual romance, he fretted against 'that idiotic use of marriage as a finale', that 'swish of the skirts and the non-sexual embraces' that irritated him on rereading *Howards End*.[17] *A Room with a View* is consistently anti-clerical. Mr Beebe is so nice, Lucy exclaims, with unconscious irony: 'He seems to see good in everyone. No one would take him for a clergyman.' Courageously mild, Forster attacked sacred cows past and present. Mr Emerson dismisses Giotto for lacking truth. Gino quotes Dante with conventional respect, but Forster 'cannot like' him.[18] 'The interpretations of Freud miss the values of art as infallibly as do those of Marx,' he observes. Proust's sentences are too long; his understanding of human nature is defective. Can Woolf create character? 'What wraiths, apart from their context, are the wind-sextet of *The Waves*!'[19]

In the titles of his short stories one significant word recurs. 'The Other Side of the Hedge', 'Other Kingdom', 'The Other Boat'. 'Other' is his prophetic term for the natural life *out* there, *out*lawed by social norms, the alternative life in the Arcadian greenwood of *Maurice*'s unique happy ending. It is most ironical of all that, in spite of the mockery of his schooldays, Forster defied the English taboo against having a mother, and even loving her. A quaint laughing-stock, he doggedly lived with her, in spite of many irritations, till she died at ninety, and he was sixty-six. Shortly after, he retreated to the lap of his *alma mater*, Cambridge. His apparently asexual spinsterishness is routinely denigrated by his contemporaries. 'E. M. Forster never gets any further than warming the teapot,' Katherine Mansfield scoffed. The pot is beautifully warm, but there is no tea. Helen Schlegel's baby is the product of a union with Leonard Bast's forgotten umbrella. 'He sucks his dummy,' said Lawrence; ' – you know, those child's comforters – long after his age.' Adding, in a moment of supreme, Lawrentian incomprehension, 'Why can't he act? Why can't he take a woman and fight clear to his own basic, primal being?'[20]

Well, Forster did fight clear to his own primal being. An outsider himself, he defended the Others – the Italian and the Indian, the working man and the homosexual, the Jew and the Muslim, the illegitimate son and the unmarried mother. Like Mrs Honeychurch, he disliked the militant feminist (all 'short skirts and latch-keys'; 'And call it Duty – when it means that you can't stand your own home!'). And yet he attacked sexist double standards, as does Margaret Schlegel. His leading women fight feminine subservience with the pained uncertainty Forster knew from inside. For Lawrence, the crippled Clifford Chatterley is a despised emblem of an emasculated modern world. For Forster, the crippled Rickie is not an emblem but an individual. Rickie, like Forster, feels himself to be the guiltless victim of an incurable congenital disability. Yet Forster fought clear of self-pity. In his own life, among his many friendships, his love and loyalty were for his world's unmentionables: his mother, an Indian, an Egyptian, an English policeman.

Ann Pasternak Slater

NOTES

1 Furbank, 124; *The Lucy Novels*, 8. For publication details of texts cited in these notes, see Bibliography.
2 Furbank, 135; *Maurice*, 136, 139.
3 See Furbank, 36–7 for more details.
4 *My books and I*, cited by Heine and Adair, 362. Unpublished in Forster's lifetime.
5 *Uncle Willie*, Heine and Adair, 356–9. Unpublished in Forster's lifetime.
6 *Where Angels Fear to Tread*, ed. Stallybrass, viii.
7 *The Tale of Beatrix Potter*, 63, 68.
8 *An Essay on Criticism*, l.625.
9 Furbank, 189.
10 *A Room with a View*, ed. Stallybrass, viii, xiii, xiv.
11 *Aspects of the Novel*, 27, 55.
12 'She loved society and pension life – which is why I have re-modelled her as Miss Bartlett in *A Room with a View*, hoping to give her a happier immortality in art.' *Uncle Willie*, 356–7.
13 *The Lucy Novels*, 106–112.
14 'Jew-consciousness', *Two Cheers for Democracy*, 24.
15 *Critical Heritage*, 430–31.
16 *Aspects of the Novel*, 78.
17 *Aspects*, 38; Furbank, 190.
18 *Forster Chronology*, 28.
19 'George Crabbe and Peter Grimes', 'Virginia Woolf'', *Two Cheers for Democracy*, 187, 256–7.
20 *Critical Heritage*, 162, 181–2.

ANN PASTERNAK SLATER is a Senior Research Fellow at St Anne's College, Oxford. She has edited and introduced *The Complete Works of George Herbert*, *The Complete Short Stories of Evelyn Waugh* and Evelyn Waugh's *Black Mischief, Scoop, The Loved One*, and *The Ordeal of Gilbert Pinfold*, for Everyman's Library. She translated and edited Tolstoy's *The Death of Ivan Ilyich* and *Master and Man* for The Modern Library, and the memoirs of Alexander Pasternak (*A Vanished Present*) for Oxford University Press. She is the author of *Shakespeare the Director*.

SELECT BIBLIOGRAPHY

PRIMARY TEXTS
The Lucy Novels, ed. O. Stallybrass. The Abinger Edition of E. M. Forster, vol. 3a, Edwin Arnold, London, 1977.
Where Angels Fear to Tread, ed. O. Stallybrass. The Abinger Edition, vol. 1, Edwin Arnold, London, 1975.
A Room with a View, ed. O. Stallybrass. The Abinger edition, vol. 3, Edwin Arnold, London, 1977.
My Books and I and *Uncle Willie,* reproduced in *Appendix B: Memoirs* in *The Longest Journey,* ed. E. Heine and G. Adair, Penguin Classics, 2006, Penguin Group USA, 360–66 and 353–60.
'The Story of a Panic', 'The Other Side of the Hedge', 'Other Kingdom', in *E. M. Forster: Collected Short Stories*, Penguin Classics, 2002, Penguin Putnam Inc., New York.
'The Other Boat' in *The Life to Come and Other Stories*, Penguin, 1975.
Maurice, Penguin Books Inc., Maryland, 1975.
Two Cheers for Democracy, Penguin reprint, 1965; Harcourt, Brace & Co., New York, 1951.
Aspects of the Novel, Edwin Arnold, London, 1961.

SECONDARY TEXTS
P. N. FURBANK, *E. M. Forster: A Life*, Oxford University Press, Oxford and New York, 1979.
P. GARDNER, ed., *E. M. Forster: The Critical Heritage*, Routledge & Kegan Paul, London and Boston, 1973.
J. H. STAPE, *An E. M. Forster Chronology*, Macmillan, London, 1993.
M. LANE, *The Tale of Beatrix Potter*, Warne, London and New York, 1946.

FILMS
A Room With a View, UK 1985, directed by James Ivory, starring Maggie Smith, Denholm Elliot, Judi Dench, Simon Callow, Helena Bonham Carter, Julian Sands, Daniel Day-Lewis.
Where Angels Fear to Tread, UK 1991, directed by Charles Sturridge, starring Helena Bonham Carter, Judy Davis, Helen Mirren, Rupert Graves.

CHRONOLOGY

———

DATE	AUTHOR'S LIFE	LITERARY CONTEXT
1879	Born, on 1 January.	
1880	Forster's father, Edward, dies.	
1881		James: *The Portrait of a Lady.*
1883	He and his mother go to live at 'Rooksnest' in Stevenage.	
1887	His great-aunt Marianne Thornton dies, leaving him £8,000.	
1893	Goes to Tonbridge School as day boy.	
1895		Hardy: *Jude the Obscure.*
1897	Goes to King's College, Cambridge, to study classics and history.	Housman: *A Shropshire Lad.* James: *What Maisie Knew.*
1898		
1899		
1900	Writes light articles for King's College magazine, *Basileona.* Becomes friendly with Lytton Strachey and E. J. Dent.	Conrad: *Lord Jim.*
1901	Is elected to the 'Apostles'. In October goes to Italy, including Sicily, with his mother.	Mann: *Buddenbrooks.* Kipling: *Kim.*
1902	Writes first story, 'The Story of a Panic' (published 1904). In September returns to England. Begins to hold Latin classes at the Working Men's College.	James: *The Wings of the Dove.*
1903	Goes with mother to Italy, and alone to Greece and Turkey. May: attends performance of *Lucia di Lammemoor* in Florence.	Moore: *Principia Ethica.* James: *The Ambassadors.*
1904	He and mother move to Weybridge, their home for twenty years.	James: *The Golden Bowl.* Conrad: *Nostromo.*
1905	Goes to Germany as tutor in household of 'Elizabeth' (von Arnim), for five months.	Wharton: *House of Mirth.*

First Zulu War.
Liberals win majority in general election; Gladstone Prime Minister
(to 1885). First Boer War (to 1881).

Queen Victoria's Golden Jubilee. 'Bloody Sunday': prohibited rally of
radicals and Irish militants in Trafalgar Square broken up by police and
troops.
Independent Labour Party formed under Keir Hardy. Second Irish Home
Rule Bill defeated.
Wilde's trial and imprisonment. Salisbury forms Unionist ministry (to 1902).
Jameson Raid on the Transvaal. Freud's *Studien über Hysterie* inaugurates
psychoanalysis.
Queen Victoria's Diamond Jubilee. After a century of expansion the British
Empire covers one fifth of the globe, home to one quarter of the world's
population.
First German Navy Law; arms race with Britain begins.
Second Boer War (to 1902).
First Labour MPs in British Parliament.

Death of Queen Victoria.

Coronation of Edward VII and Queen Alexandra. First celebration of
Empire Day in Britain (24 May). Balfour succeeds Salisbury as Prime
Minister.

Emmeline Pankhurst founds Women's Social and Political Union.

Entente Cordiale between Britain and France. Russo-Japanese War
(to 1905).

First Russian Revolution. Balfour's government splits over tariff reform.
Einstein's Theory of Special Relativity.

DATE	AUTHOR'S LIFE	LITERARY CONTEXT
1905 *cont.*	Publishes *Where Angels Fear to Tread* and 'The Other Side of the Hedge' (story).	
1906	Gets to know Syed Ross Masood.	
1907	Publishes *The Longest Journey.*	Conrad: *The Secret Agent.*
1908	Publishes *A Room With a View.*	Bennett: *The Old Wives' Tale.*
1909	'Other Kingdom' (story) published.	Death of George Meredith 'closes the Victorian era' (says Forster).
1910	Publishes *Howards End. (Circa* 1910, gets to know Virginia Woolf.)	
1911	Publishes *The Celestial Omnibus* (short stories).	Forrest Reid: *The Bracknels.* Lawrence: *The White Peacock.* Conrad: *Under Western Eyes.*
1912	Goes to India for six months.	Mann: *Death in Venice.*
1913	Visits Edward Carpenter. Writes *Maurice* (published posthumously).	Conrad: *Chance.* Lawrence: *Sons and Lovers.* Proust: *A la recherche du temps perdu* (to 1927).
1914		Joyce: *Dubliners.* Lawrence: *The Prussian Officer and Other Stories.*
1915	Visits D. H. Lawrence and Frieda Lawrence. Goes to Alexandria as 'hospital searcher'.	Ford: *The Good Soldier.* Conrad: *Victory.* Woolf: *The Voyage Out.* Lawrence: *The Rainbow.*
1916	Becomes friendly with Cavafy. Writes articles for local Egyptian journals.	Joyce: *A Portrait of the Artist as a Young Man.*
1917		Eliot: *Prufrock and Other Observations.*
1918		Strachey: *Eminent Victorians.* Conrad: *The Shadow Line.* Sassoon: *Counterattack and Other Poems.*
1919	Returns from Egypt. Visits Max Gate (home of Thomas Hardy).	Woolf: *Night and Day.*
1920		Eliot: *Poems.* Lawrence: *Women in Love.* Wells: *Outline of History.*

CHRONOLOGY

Landslide Liberal victory in election; Campbell-Bannerman's cabinet embarks on sweeping social reforms. Launch of HMS *Dreadnought*, first modern battleship.
Russia joins the Entente Cordiale to form the Triple Entente.
Asquith's Liberal ministry (to 1916). Hans Richter conducts first peformance of Wagner's complete *Ring* in English at Covent Garden.
Lloyd George introduces People's Budget.

Death of Edward VII. Suffragette riots at Westminster. First Post-Impressionist exhibition in London.

Delhi Durbar: coronation of George V and Queen Mary as Emperor and Empress of India. Agadir crisis. Industrial unrest in Britain. Parliament Act reduces power of House of Lords. Italo-Turkish War (to 1912).
Captain's Scott's Antarctic expedition ends in tragedy. The *Titanic* sinks.
First Balkan War.
Second Balkan War.

Outbreak of World War I.

First Zeppelin air raid on London. Gallipoli landings.

Battle of the Somme. Easter Rising in Ireland. General conscription introduced in Britain. Asquith resigns; Lloyd George becomes Prime Minister (to 1922), splitting the Liberal Party.
February and October Revolutions in Russia. US joins war. Balfour Declaration promises Palestine to the Jews.
World War I ends. Collapse of Habsburg empire. Abdication of Kaiser Wilhelm II; Weimar Republic established in Germany. Russian Civil War; Nicholas II and family assassinated. Women over 30 obtain the vote in Britain.
Treaty of Versailles: punitive financial and territorial measures imposed on Germany. Short-lived Soviet republics in Hungary and Bavaria. Amritsar massacre in India. Nancy Astor first woman MP.
League of Nations founded (US does not join). Threat of general strike forces Lloyd George to abandon military intervention in Russia. Prohibition in US (to 1933).

DATE	AUTHOR'S LIFE	LITERARY CONTEXT
1921	Goes to India (March), as private secretary of Maharaja of Dewas.	Huxley: *Crome Yellow*.
1922	Returns (in January) from India via Egypt. Gets to know J. R. Ackerley. Publishes *Alexandria: a History and a Guide*.	Joyce: *Ulysses*. Woolf: *Jacob's Room*. Eliot: *The Waste Land*.
1923	Publishes *Pharos and Pharillon*.	
1924	His Aunt Laura dies, leaving him 'West Hackhurst' in Abinger, Surrey. Gets to know T. E. Lawrence. Publishes *A Passage to India*. Moves with mother to 'West Hackhurst'.	Mann: *The Magic Mountain*. Ford: *Parade's End* (to 1928).
1925	Takes flat in Brunswick Square, in Bloomsbury, for weekday use.	Fitzgerald: *The Great Gatsby*. Kafka: *The Trial*. Gide: *Les Faux-Monnayeurs*.
1926	Gives Clark Lectures in Cambridge, published as *Aspects of the Novel*.	Hemingway: *The Sun Also Rises*. T. E. Lawrence: *The Seven Pillars of Wisdom*.
1927		Woolf: *To the Lighthouse*.
1928	Gives radio talk, the first of many. Publishes *The Eternal Moment* (short stories).	Lawrence: *Lady Chatterley's Lover*. Waugh: *Decline and Fall*. Woolf: *Orlando*. Sassoon: *The Sherston Trilogy* (to 1937).
1929	Visits South Africa for four months.	Hemingway: *A Farewell to Arms*. Faulkner: *The Sound and the Fury*.
1930		Death of D. H. Lawrence.
1931	Visits Romania.	Woolf: *The Waves*.
1932	Becomes friendly with Christopher Isherwood.	Huxley: *Brave New World*. J. R. Ackerley: *Hindoo Holiday*.
1933		

CHRONOLOGY

Mussolini's march on Rome; forms Fascist government. Stalin becomes Secretary of the Communist Party Central Committee. Russia becomes USSR. Irish Free State established; Irish Civil War (to 1923).

Baldwin forms Conservative ministry. Women gain legal equality in divorce suits. German hyperinflation. When Germans default on war reparations, French occupy Ruhr Valley (to 1925). Turkish Republic established under Mustafa Kemal.
First Labour (minority) government in Britain, with Ramsay MacDonald as Prime Minister (Jan). Conservatives resume power under Baldwin (Oct). Death of Lenin. Failure of Hitler's Munich *putsch*. Dawes Plan (to 1929) eases reparations crisis.

Locarno Pact guarantees existing Franco-German frontier. Hitler: *Mein Kampf* (vol. 1).

Miners' strike (May–Nov). General Strike (4–12 May). Germany admitted to League of Nations. Television demonstrated by J. L. Baird.

Trotsky expelled from the Communist Party. BBC founded. *The Jazz Singer* – first 'talkie'.
Kellogg-Briand Pact, outlawing war and providing for peaceful settlement of disputes. Suffrage in Britain extended to women over 21. First Five Year Plan in USSR; Stalin *de facto* dictator and object of nationwide cult.

Wall Street Crash: beginning of worldwide Depression. Second minority Labour government under MacDonald.
Allies evacuate Rhineland. Gandhi's civil disobedience campaign in India. First Round Table Conference between Britain and India.
MacDonald forms National Government to balance budget (to 1935). Britain abandons the Gold Standard.
UK unemployment peaks at over 2,900,000, around 23% of the workforce. Clashes between Hunger Marchers and police in London. Oswald Mosley founds British Union of Fascists. Nazis largest party in German Reichstag. Geneva conference on disarmament (to 1934). Roosevelt elected US President. Cockcroft and Walton split the atom.
Hitler becomes German Chancellor. Germany and Japan leave League of Nations. Dollfuss right-wing dictator in Austria. US President Roosevelt announces 'New Deal' for economic recovery.

DATE	AUTHOR'S LIFE	LITERARY CONTEXT
1934	Becomes first President of the National Council for Civil Liberties. Publishes *Goldsworthy Lowes Dickinson* (biography).	Waugh: *A Handful of Dust.*
1935	Addresses International Congress of Writers, in Paris.	
1936	Publishes *Abinger Harvest.*	Death of Kipling.
1937		
1938		Sartre: *La Nausée.*
1939		Joyce: *Finnegans Wake.* Auden and Isherwood: *Journey to a War.*
1940	Begins regular talks on the BBC's Indian Service.	Greene: *The Power and the Glory.* Hemingway: *For Whom the Bell Tolls.* Death of Fitzgerald.
1941		Woolf: *Between the Acts.* Death of Virginia Woolf.
1942		Camus: *The Outsider.*
1943		
1944		
1945	Forster's mother dies. He goes to India for conference of All-Indian PEN.	Waugh: *Brideshead Revisited.* Eliot: *Four Quarters.*
1946	Is appointed Honorary Fellow of King's College, Cambridge, and takes up residence in Cambridge.	Death of H. G. Wells.
1947	Pays first visit to USA.	

CHRONOLOGY

Hitler becomes German Führer. Churchill warns against German rearmament. Riots in Paris; Doumergue forms National Union ministry to avert civil war. Dollfuss murdered in attempted Nazi coup.

Nuremberg Laws in Germany debar Jews from public life. Italy invades Abyssinia. Baldwin Prime Minister again.
Popular Front win election in Spain, prompting Fascist military coup and Spanish Civil War (to 1939). Léon Blum becomes first Socialist Prime Minister in France. Hitler marches into demilitarized Rhineland. Rome–Berlin Axis signed. Death of George V and accession of Edward VIII; abdication crisis; George VI becomes king. Jarrow March. Moscow show trials begin.
Japanese invade China. Baldwin retires; Neville Chamberlain becomes Prime Minister.
Germany invades Austria. Munich Agreement. Nazis occupy Sudetenland (part of Czecholslovakia). 'Kristallnacht': Nazis terrorize Jewish community in Germany.
Hitler occupies the rest of Czechoslovakia. Nationalists under Franco win Spanish Civil War. Alliances between Germany and Italy, and Germany and USSR. Germans invade Poland. France and Britain declare war on Germany (September 3).
Germany invades Norway and Denmark. Churchill becomes Prime Minister. Dunkirk evacuation. Italy declares war on Britain and France. Fall of France. Battle of Britain. The Blitz.

Germany invades USSR. Japanese attack Pearl Harbor; US joins war.

Fall of Singapore. Germans reach Stalingrad. North African campaign; Allies victorious at Battle of El Alamein.
German army retreats in Russia and Africa. Allies invade Italy.
Allied landings in Normandy; liberation of Paris. Butler's Education Act.
Mussolini killed by Italian partisans. Battle of Berlin; suicide of Hitler; unconditional surrender of Germany. Atomic bombs dropped on Hiroshima and Nagasaki. End of World War II. Attlee's Labour Party win landslide victory in general election. Death of Roosevelt; Truman becomes US President. United Nations founded.
Nuremberg trials. 'Iron Curtain' speech by Churchill. Attlee government begins programme of nationalization of basic industries and public utilities.Violent clashes between Hindus and Moslems in India as negotiations for independence proceed. Italy becomes a republic.
The Marshall Plan to aid postwar Europe. Beginning of Cold War. Indian Independence Act: India partitioned into two dominions, India (Hindu) and Pakistan (Moslem).

DATE	AUTHOR'S LIFE	LITERARY CONTEXT
1948		Greene: *The Heart of the Matter.* Sassoon: *Biography of G. Meredith.*
1949	Begins work (with Eric Crozier) on libretto of Benjamin Britten's *Billy Budd* (first performance 1951).	Greene: *The Third Man.* A. Miller: *Death of a Salesman.*
1950		
1951	Publishes *Two Cheers for Democracy.* Made a Companion of Honour.	Death of Gide.
1952		
1953	Publishes *The Hill of Devi.*	
1954		
1955		Lampedusa: *The Leopard.*
1956		J. R. Ackerley: *My Dog Tulip.*
1957	Publishes *Marianne Thornton* (biography of his great-aunt). Begins writing 'The Other Boat' (story).	Pasternak: *Doctor Zhivago.*
1959		
1960	Is witness at *Lady Chatterley* trial.	J. R. Ackerley: *We Think the World of You.* Deaths of Camus and Pasternak.
1961		
1967		
1969	Awarded the Order of Merit.	
1970	Dies on 7 January, at home of his friends Robert and May Buckingham, in Coventry.	
1971	*Maurice* published.	
2001	'The Feminine Note in Literature' published.	
2003	*Arctic Summer* (written, but unfinished, 1912–13) published.	

CHRONOLOGY

A ROOM
WITH A VIEW

E. M. Forster dedicated
A Room with a View
to
H. O. M.

CONTENTS

PART ONE

CHAPTER I

The Bertolini

'THE SIGNORA HAD no business to do it,' said Miss Bartlett, 'no business at all. She promised us south rooms with a view, close together, instead of which here are north rooms, here are north rooms, looking into a courtyard, and a long way apart. Oh, Lucy!'

'And a Cockney, besides!' said Lucy, who had been further saddened by the Signora's unexpected accent. 'It might be London.' She looked at the two rows of English people who were sitting at the table; at the row of white bottles of water and red bottles of wine that ran between the English people; at the portraits of the late Queen and the late Poet Laureate that hung behind the English people, heavily framed; at the notice of the English church (Rev. Cuthbert Eager, M.A. Oxon.), that was the only other decoration of the wall. 'Charlotte, don't you feel, too, that we might be in London? I can hardly believe that all kinds of other things are just outside. I suppose it is one's being so tired.'

'This meat has surely been used for soup,' said Miss Bartlett, laying down her fork.

'I wanted so to see the Arno. The rooms the Signora promised us in her letter would have looked over the Arno. The Signora had no business to do it at all. Oh, it is a shame!'

'Any nook does for me,' Miss Bartlett continued; 'but it does seem hard that you shouldn't have a view.'

Lucy felt that she had been selfish. 'Charlotte, you mustn't spoil me: of course, you must look over the Arno, too. I meant that. The first vacant room in the front –'

'You must have it,' said Miss Bartlett, part of whose travelling

expenses were paid by Lucy's mother – a piece of generosity to
which she made many a tactful allusion.

'No, no. You must have it.'

'I insist on it. Your mother would never forgive me, Lucy.'

'She would never forgive *me*.'

The ladies' voices grew animated, and – if the sad truth be
owned – a little peevish. They were tired, and under the guise of
unselfishness they wrangled. Some of their neighbours inter-
changed glances, and one of them – one of the ill-bred people
whom one does meet abroad – leant forward over the table and
actually intruded into their argument. He said:

'I have a view, I have a view.'

Miss Bartlett was startled. Generally at a pension people
looked them over for a day or two before speaking, and often
did not find out that they would 'do' till they had gone. She knew
that the intruder was ill-bred, even before she glanced at him.
He was an old man, of heavy build, with a fair, shaven face and
large eyes. There was something childish in those eyes, though
it was not the childishness of senility. What exactly it was Miss
Bartlett did not stop to consider, for her glance passed on to his
clothes. These did not attract her. He was probably trying to
become acquainted with them before they got into the swim.
So she assumed a dazed expression when he spoke to her, and
then said: 'A view? Oh, a view! How delightful a view is!'

'This is my son,' said the old man; 'his name's George. He has
a view, too.'

'Ah,' said Miss Bartlett, repressing Lucy, who was about to
speak.

'What I mean,' he continued, 'is that you can have our rooms,
and we'll have yours. We'll change.'

The better class of tourist was shocked at this, and sympathized with the newcomers. Miss Bartlett, in reply, opened her
mouth as little as possible, and said:

'Thank you very much indeed; that is out of the question.'

'Why?' said the old man, with both fists on the table.

'Because it is quite out of the question, thank you.'

'You see, we don't like to take –' began Lucy.

Her cousin again repressed her.

'But why?' he persisted. 'Women like looking at a view; men don't.' And he thumped with his fists like a naughty child, and turned to his son, saying, 'George, persuade them!'

'It's so obvious they should have the rooms,' said the son. 'There's nothing else to say.'

He did not look at the ladies as he spoke, but his voice was perplexed and sorrowful. Lucy, too, was perplexed; but she saw that they were in for what is known as 'quite a scene', and she had an odd feeling that whenever these ill-bred tourists spoke the contest widened and deepened till it dealt, not with rooms and views, but with – well, with something quite different, whose existence she had not realized before. Now the old man attacked Miss Bartlett almost violently: Why should she not change? What possible objection had she? They would clear out in half an hour.

Miss Bartlett, though skilled in the delicacies of conversation, was powerless in the presence of brutality. It was impossible to snub anyone so gross. Her face reddened with displeasure. She looked around as much as to say, 'Are you all like this?' And two little old ladies, who were sitting further up the table, with shawls hanging over the backs of the chairs, looked back, clearly indicating, 'We are not; we are genteel.'

'Eat your dinner, dear,' she said to Lucy, and began to toy again with the meat that she had once censured.

Lucy mumbled that those seemed very odd people opposite.

'Eat your dinner, dear. This pension is a failure. Tomorrow we will make a change.'

Hardly had she announced this fell decision when she reversed it. The curtains at the end of the room parted, and revealed a clergyman, stout but attractive, who hurried forward to take his place at the table, cheerfully apologizing for his lateness. Lucy, who had not yet acquired decency, at once rose to her feet, exclaiming: 'Oh, oh! Why, it's Mr Beebe! Oh, how perfectly lovely! Oh, Charlotte, we must stop now, however bad the rooms are. Oh!'

Miss Bartlett said, with more restraint:

'How do you do, Mr Beebe? I expect that you have forgotten us: Miss Bartlett and Miss Honeychurch, who were at Tunbridge Wells when you helped the vicar of St Peter's that very cold Easter.'

The clergyman, who had the air of one on a holiday, did not remember the ladies quite as clearly as they remembered him. But he came forward pleasantly enough and accepted the chair into which he was beckoned by Lucy.

'I *am* so glad to see you,' said the girl, who was in a state of spiritual starvation, and would have been glad to see the waiter if her cousin had permitted it. 'Just fancy how small the world is. Summer Street, too, makes it so specially funny.'

'Miss Honeychurch lives in the parish of Summer Street,' said Miss Bartlett, filling up the gap, 'and she happened to tell me in the course of conversation that you have just accepted the living –'

'Yes, I heard from mother so last week. She didn't know that I knew you at Tunbridge Wells; but I wrote back at once, and I said: "Mr Beebe is –" '

'Quite right,' said the clergyman. 'I move into the rectory at Summer Street next June. I am lucky to be appointed to such a charming neighbourhood.'

'Oh, how glad I am! The name of our house is Windy Corner.'

Mr Beebe bowed.

'There is mother and me generally, and my brother, though it's not often we get him to ch – the church is rather far off, I mean.'

'Lucy dearest, let Mr Beebe eat his dinner.'

'I am eating it, thank you, and enjoying it.'

He preferred to talk to Lucy, whose playing he remembered, rather than to Miss Bartlett, who probably remembered his sermons. He asked the girl whether she knew Florence well, and was informed at some length that she had never been there before. It is delightful to advise a newcomer, and he was first in the field.

'Don't neglect the country round,' his advice concluded. 'The first fine afternoon drive up to Fiesole, and round by Settignano, or something of that sort.'

'No!' cried a voice from the top of the table. 'Mr Beebe, you are wrong. The first fine afternoon your ladies must go to Prato.'

'That lady looks so clever,' whispered Miss Bartlett to her cousin. 'We are in luck.'

And, indeed, a perfect torrent of information burst on them. People told them what to see, when to see it, how to stop the electric trams, how to get rid of the beggars, how much to give for a vellum blotter, how much the place would grow upon them. The Pension Bertolini had decided, almost enthusias-tically, that they would do. Whichever way they looked, kind ladies smiled and shouted at them. And above all rose the voice of the clever lady, crying: 'Prato! They must go to Prato. That place is too sweetly squalid for words. I love it; I revel in shaking off the trammels of respectability, as you know.'

The young man named George glanced at the clever lady, and then returned moodily to his plate. Obviously he and his father did not do. Lucy, in the midst of her success, found time to wish they did. It gave her no extra pleasure that anyone should be left in the cold; and when she rose to go she turned back and gave the two outsiders a nervous little bow.

The father did not see it; the son acknowledged it, not by another bow, but by raising his eyebrows and smiling; he seemed to be smiling across something.

She hastened after her cousin, who had already disappeared through the curtains – curtains which smote one in the face, and seemed heavy with more than cloth. Beyond them stood the unreliable Signora, bowing good-evening to her guests, and supported by 'Enery, her little boy, and Victorier, her daughter.

It made a curious little scene, this attempt of the Cockney to convey the grace and geniality of the South. And even more curious was the drawing-room, which attempted to rival the solid comfort of a Bloomsbury boarding-house. Was this really Italy?

Miss Bartlett was already seated on a tightly stuffed armchair, which had the colour and the contours of a tomato. She was talking to Mr Beebe, and as she spoke her long narrow head drove backwards and forwards, slowly, regularly, as though she were demolishing some invisible obstacle. 'We are most grateful to you,' she was saying. 'The first evening means so much. When you arrived we were in for a peculiarly *mauvais quart d'heure.*'

He expressed his regret.

'Do you, by any chance, know the name of an old man who sat opposite us at dinner?'

'Emerson.'

'Is he a friend of yours?'

'We are friendly – as one is in pensions.'

'Then I will say no more.'

He pressed her very slightly, and she said more.

'I am, as it were,' she concluded, 'the chaperon of my young cousin, Lucy, and it would be a serious thing if I put her under an obligation to people of whom we knew nothing. His manner was somewhat unfortunate. I hope I acted for the best.'

'You acted very naturally,' said he. He seemed thoughtful, and after a few moments added: 'All the same, I don't think much harm would have come of accepting.'

'No *harm*, of course. But we could not be under an obligation.'

'He is rather a peculiar man.' Again he hesitated, and then said gently: 'I think he would not take advantage of your acceptance, nor expect you to show gratitude. He has the merit – if it is one – of saying exactly what he means. He has rooms he does not value, and he thinks you would value them. He no more thought of putting you under an obligation than he thought of being polite. It is so difficult – at least, I find it difficult – to understand people who speak the truth.'

Lucy was pleased, and said: 'I was hoping that he was nice; I do so always hope that people will be nice.'

'I think he is; nice and tiresome. I differ from him on almost every point of any importance, and so, I expect – I may say I hope – you will differ. But his is a type one disagrees with rather than deplores. When he first came here he not unnaturally put people's backs up. He has no tact and no manners – I don't mean by that that he has bad manners – and he will not keep his opinions to himself. We nearly complained about him to our depressing Signora, but I am glad to say we thought better of it.'

'Am I to conclude,' said Miss Bartlett, 'that he is a Socialist?'

Mr Beebe accepted the convenient word, not without a slight twitching of the lips.

'And presumably he has brought up his son to be a Socialist, too?'

'I hardly know George, for he hasn't learned to talk yet. He seems a nice creature, and I think he has brains. Of course, he has all his father's mannerisms, and it is quite possible that he, too, may be a Socialist.'

'Oh, you relieve me,' said Miss Bartlett. 'So you think I ought to have accepted their offer? You feel I have been narrow-minded and suspicious?'

'Not at all,' he answered; 'I never suggested that.'

'But ought I not to apologize, at all events, for my apparent rudeness?'

He replied, with some irritation, that it would be quite unnecessary, and got up from his seat to go to the smoking-room.

'Was I a bore?' said Miss Bartlett, as soon as he had disappeared. 'Why didn't you talk, Lucy? He prefers young people, I'm sure. I do hope I haven't monopolized him. I hoped you would have him all the evening, as well as all dinner-time.'

'He is nice,' exclaimed Lucy. 'Just what I remember. He seems to see good in everyone. No one would take him for a clergyman.'

'My dear Lucia –'

'Well, you know what I mean. And you know how clergymen generally laugh; Mr Beebe laughs just like an ordinary man.'

'Funny girl! How you do remind me of your mother. I wonder if she will approve of Mr Beebe.'

'I'm sure she will; and so will Freddy.'

'I think everyone at Windy Corner will approve; it is the fashionable world. I am used to Tunbridge Wells, where we are all hopelessly behind the times.'

'Yes,' said Lucy despondently.

There was a haze of disapproval in the air, but whether the disapproval was of herself, or of Mr Beebe, or of the fashionable world at Windy Corner, or of the narrow world at Tunbridge Wells, she could not determine. She tried to locate it, but as usual she blundered. Miss Bartlett sedulously denied disapproving of anyone, and added: 'I am afraid you are finding me a very depressing companion.'

And the girl again thought: 'I must have been selfish or unkind; I must be more careful. It is so dreadful for Charlotte, being poor.'

Fortunately one of the little old ladies, who for some time had been smiling very benignly, now approached and asked if she might be allowed to sit where Mr Beebe had sat. Permission granted, she began to chatter gently about Italy, the plunge it had been to come there, the gratifying success of the plunge, the improvement in her sister's health, the necessity of closing the bedroom windows at night, and of thoroughly emptying the water-bottles in the morning. She handled her subjects agreeably, and they were, perhaps, more worthy of attention than the high discourse upon Guelfs and Ghibellines which was proceeding tempestuously at the other end of the room. It was a real catastrophe, not a mere episode, that evening of hers at Venice, when she had found in her bedroom something that is one worse than a flea, though one better than something else.

'But here you are as safe as in England; Signora Bertolini is so English.'

'Yet our rooms smell,' said poor Lucy. 'We dread going to bed.'

'Ah, then you look into the court.' She sighed. 'If only Mr Emerson was more tactful! We were so sorry for you at dinner.'

'I think he was meaning to be kind.'

'Undoubtedly he was,' said Miss Bartlett. 'Mr Beebe has just been scolding me for my suspicious nature. Of course, I was holding back on my cousin's account.'

'Of course,' said the little old lady; and they murmured that one could not be too careful with a young girl.

Lucy tried to look demure, but could not help feeling a great fool. No one was careful with her at home; or, at all events, she had not noticed it.

'About old Mr Emerson – I hardly know. No, he is not tactful; yet, have you ever noticed that there are people who do things which are most indelicate, and yet at the same time – beautiful?'

'Beautiful?' said Miss Bartlett, puzzled at the word. 'Are not beauty and delicacy the same?'

'So one would have thought,' said the other helplessly. 'But things are so difficult, I sometimes think.'

She proceeded no further into things, for Mr Beebe re-appeared, looking extremely pleasant.

'Miss Bartlett,' he cried, 'it's all right about the rooms. I'm so glad. Mr Emerson was talking about it in the smoking-room, and, knowing what I did, I encouraged him to make the offer again. He has let me come and ask you. He would be so pleased.'

'Oh, Charlotte,' cried Lucy to her cousin, 'we must have the rooms now. The old man is just as nice and kind as he can be.'

Miss Bartlett was silent.

'I fear,' said Mr Beebe, after a pause, 'that I have been officious. I must apologize for my interference.'

Gravely displeased, he turned to go. Not till then did Miss Bartlett reply: 'My own wishes, dearest Lucy, are unimportant in comparison with yours. It would be hard indeed if I stopped you doing as you liked at Florence, when I am only here through your kindness. If you wish me to turn these gentlemen out of their rooms, I will do it. Would you then, Mr Beebe, kindly tell Mr Emerson that I accept his kind offer, and then conduct him to me, in order that I may thank him personally?'

She raised her voice as she spoke; it was heard all over the drawing-room, and silenced the Guelfs and the Ghibellines. The clergyman, inwardly cursing the female sex, bowed and departed with her message.

'Remember, Lucy, I alone am implicated in this. I do not wish the acceptance to come from you. Grant me that, at all events.'

Mr Beebe was back, saying rather nervously:

'Mr Emerson is engaged, but here is his son instead.'

The young man gazed down on the three ladies, who felt seated on the floor, so low were their chairs.

'My father,' he said, 'is in his bath, so you cannot thank him personally. But any message given by you to me will be given by me to him as soon as he comes out.'

Miss Bartlett was unequal to the bath. All her barbed civilities came forth wrong end first. Young Mr Emerson scored a notable triumph, to the delight of Mr Beebe and to the secret delight of Lucy.

'Poor young man!' said Miss Bartlett, as soon as he had gone. 'How angry he is with his father about the rooms! It is all he can do to keep polite.'

'In half an hour or so your rooms will be ready,' said Mr Beebe. Then, looking rather thoughtfully at the two cousins, he retired to his own room, to write up his philosophic diary.

'Oh dear!' breathed the little old lady, and shuddered as if all the winds of heaven had entered the apartment. 'Gentlemen sometimes do not realize –' Her voice faded away, but Miss Bartlett seemed to understand, and a conversation developed, in which gentlemen who did not thoroughly realize played a principal part. Lucy, not realizing either, was reduced to literature. Taking up Baedeker's *Handbook to Northern Italy*, she committed to memory the most important dates of Florentine history. For she was determined to enjoy herself on the morrow. Thus the half-hour crept profitably away, and at last Miss Bartlett rose with a sigh, and said:

'I think one might venture now. No, Lucy, do not stir. I will superintend the move.'

'How you do do everything,' said Lucy.

'Naturally, dear. It is my affair.'

'But I would like to help you.'

'No, dear.'

Charlotte's energy! And her unselfishness! She had been thus all her life, but really, on this Italian tour, she was surpassing herself. So Lucy felt, or strove to feel. And yet – there was a rebellious spirit in her which wondered whether the acceptance might not have been less delicate and more beautiful. At all events, she entered her own room without any feeling of joy.

'I want to explain,' said Miss Bartlett, 'why it is that I have taken the largest room. Naturally, of course, I should have given it to you; but I happen to know that it belongs to the young man, and I was sure your mother would not like it.'

Lucy was bewildered.

'If you are to accept a favour, it is more suitable you should be under an obligation to his father than to him. I am a woman of the world, in my small way, and I know where things lead to. However, Mr Beebe is a guarantee of a sort that they will not presume on this.'

'Mother wouldn't mind, I'm sure,' said Lucy, but again had the sense of larger and unsuspected issues.

Miss Bartlett only sighed, and enveloped her in a protecting embrace as she wished her goodnight. It gave Lucy the sensation of a fog, and when she reached her own room she opened the window and breathed the clean night air, thinking of the kind old man who had enabled her to see the lights dancing in the Arno, and the cypresses of San Miniato, and the foothills of the Apennines, black against the rising moon.

Miss Bartlett, in her room, fastened the window-shutters and locked the door, and then made a tour of the apartment to see where the cupboards led, and whether there were any oubliettes or secret entrances. It was then that she saw, pinned up over the washstand, a sheet of paper on which was scrawled an enormous note of interrogation. Nothing more.

'What does it mean?' she thought, and she examined it carefully by the light of a candle. Meaningless at first, it gradually became menacing, obnoxious, portentous with evil. She was seized with an impulse to destroy it, but fortunately remembered that she had no right to do so, since it must be the property of young Mr Emerson. So she unpinned it carefully, and put it between two pieces of blotting-paper to keep it clean for him. Then she completed her inspection of the room, sighed heavily according to her habit, and went to bed.

CHAPTER II

In Santa Croce with no Baedeker

IT WAS PLEASANT to wake up in Florence, to open the eyes upon a bright bare room, with a floor of red tiles which look clean though they are not; with a painted ceiling whereon pink griffins and blue amorini sport in a forest of yellow violins and bassoons. It was pleasant, too, to fling wide the windows, pinching the fingers in unfamiliar fastenings, to lean out into sunshine with beautiful hills and trees and marble churches opposite, and, close below, the Arno, gurgling against the embankment of the road.

Over the river men were at work with spades and sieves on the sandy foreshore, and on the river was a boat, also diligently employed for some mysterious end. An electric tram came rushing underneath the window. No one was inside it, except one tourist; but its platforms were overflowing with Italians, who preferred to stand. Children tried to hang on behind, and the conductor, with no malice, spat in their faces to make them let go. Then soldiers appeared – good-looking, undersized men – wearing each a knapsack covered with mangy fur, and a greatcoat which had been cut for some larger soldier. Beside them walked officers, looking foolish and fierce, and before them went little boys, turning somersaults in time with the band. The tram-car became entangled in their ranks, and moved on painfully, like a caterpillar in a swarm of ants. One of the little boys fell down, and some white bullocks came out of an archway. Indeed, if it had not been for the good advice of an old man who was selling buttonhooks, the road might never have got clear.

Over such trivialities as these many a valuable hour may slip away, and the traveller who has gone to Italy to study the tactile values of Giotto, or the corruption of the Papacy, may return remembering nothing but the blue sky and the men and women who live under it. So it was as well that Miss Bartlett should tap and come in, and having commented on Lucy's leaving the door unlocked, and on her leaning out of the window before she was fully dressed, should urge her to hasten herself, or the best of the day would be gone. By the time Lucy was ready her cousin had done her breakfast, and was listening to the clever lady among the crumbs.

A conversation then ensued, on not unfamiliar lines. Miss Bartlett was, after all, a wee bit tired, and thought they had better spend the morning settling in; unless Lucy would at all like to go out? Lucy would rather like to go out, as it was her first day in Florence, but, of course, she could go alone. Miss Bartlett could not allow this. Of course she would accompany Lucy everywhere. Oh, certainly not; Lucy would stop with her cousin. Oh no! That would never do! Oh yes!

At this point the clever lady broke in.

'If it is Mrs Grundy who is troubling you, I do assure you that you can neglect the good person. Being English, Miss Honey-church will be perfectly safe. Italians understand. A dear friend of mine, Contessa Baroncelli, has two daughters, and when she cannot send a maid to school with them she lets them go in sailor-hats instead. Everyone takes them for English, you see, especially if their hair is strained tightly behind.'

Miss Bartlett was unconvinced by the safety of Contessa Baroncelli's daughters. She was determined to take Lucy herself, her head not being so very bad. The clever lady then said that she was going to spend a long morning in Santa Croce, and if Lucy would come too she would be delighted.

'I will take you by a dear dirty back way, Miss Honeychurch, and if you bring me luck we shall have an adventure.'

Lucy said that this was most kind, and at once opened the Baedeker, to see where Santa Croce was.

'Tut, tut! Miss Lucy! I hope we shall soon emancipate you from Baedeker. He does but touch the surface of things. As to the true Italy – he does not even dream of it. The true Italy is only to be found by patient observation.'

This sounded very interesting, and Lucy hurried over her breakfast, and started with her new friend in high spirits. Italy was coming at last. The Cockney Signora and her works had vanished like a bad dream.

Miss Lavish – for that was the clever lady's name – turned to the right along the sunny Lungarno. How delightfully warm! But a wind down the side-streets that cut like a knife, didn't it? Ponte alle Grazie – particularly interesting, mentioned by Dante. San Miniato – beautiful as well as interesting; the crucifix that kissed a murderer – Miss Honeychurch would remember the story. The men on the river were fishing. (Untrue; but then so is most information.) Then Miss Lavish darted under the archway of the white bullocks, and she stopped, and she cried:

'A smell! A true Florentine smell! Every city, let me teach you, has its own smell.'

'Is it a very nice smell?' said Lucy, who had inherited from her mother a distaste to dirt.

'One doesn't come to Italy for niceness,' was the retort; 'one comes for life. Buon giorno! Buon giorno!' bowing right and left. 'Look at that adorable wine-cart! How the driver stares at us, dear, simple soul!'

So Miss Lavish proceeded through the streets of the city of Florence, short, fidgety, and playful as a kitten, though without a kitten's grace. It was a treat for the girl to be with anyone so clever and so cheerful; and a blue military cloak, such as an Italian officer wears, only increased the sense of festivity.

'Buon giorno! Take the word of an old woman, Miss Lucy: you will never repent of a little civility to your inferiors. *That* is the true democracy. Though I am a real Radical as well. There, now you're shocked.'

'Indeed, I'm not!' exclaimed Lucy. 'We are Radicals, too, out and out. My father always voted for Mr Gladstone, until he was so dreadful about Ireland.'

'I see, I see. And now you have gone over to the enemy.'

'Oh, please –! If my father was alive, I am sure he would vote Radical again now that Ireland is all right. And as it is, the glass over our front door was broken last election, and Freddy is sure it was the Tories; but mother says nonsense, a tramp.'

'Shameful! A manufacturing district, I suppose?'

'No – in the Surrey hills. About five miles from Dorking, looking over the Weald.'

Miss Lavish seemed interested, and slackened her trot.

'What a delightful part; I know it so well. It is full of the very nicest people. Do you know Sir Harry Otway – a Radical if ever there was?'

'Very well indeed.'

'And old Mrs Butterworth the philanthropist?'

'Why, she rents a field of us! How funny!'

Miss Lavish looked at the narrow ribbon of sky, and murmured:

'Oh, you have property in Surrey?'

'Hardly any,' said Lucy, fearful of being thought a snob. 'Only thirty acres – just the garden, all downhill, and some fields.'

Miss Lavish was not disgusted, and said it was just the size of her aunt's Suffolk estate. Italy receded. They tried to remember the last name of Lady Louisa someone, who had taken a house near Summer Street the other year, but she had not liked it, which was odd of her. And just as Miss Lavish had got the name she broke off and exclaimed:

'Bless us! Bless us and save us! We've lost the way.'

Certainly they had seemed a long time in reaching Santa Croce, the tower of which had been plainly visible from the landing window. But Miss Lavish had said so much about knowing her Florence by heart, that Lucy had followed her with no misgivings.

'Lost! Lost! My dear Miss Lucy, during our political diatribes we have taken a wrong turning. How those horrid Conservatives would jeer at us! What are we to do? Two lone females in an unknown town. Now, this is what *I* call an adventure.'

Lucy, who wanted to see Santa Croce, suggested, as a possible solution, that they should ask the way there.

'Oh, but that is the word of a craven! And no, you are not, not, *not* to look at your Baedeker. Give it to me; I shan't let you carry it. We will simply drift.'

Accordingly they drifted through a series of those grey-brown streets, neither commodious nor picturesque, in which the eastern quarter of the city abounds. Lucy soon lost interest in the discontent of Lady Louisa, and became discontented herself. For one ravishing moment Italy appeared. She stood in the Square of the Annunziata and saw in the living terracotta those divine babies whom no cheap reproduction can ever stale. There they stood, with their shining limbs bursting from the garments of charity, and their strong white arms extended against circlets of heaven. Lucy thought she had never seen anything more beautiful; but Miss Lavish, with a shriek of dismay, dragged her forward, declaring that they were out of their path now by at least a mile.

The hour was approaching at which the continental breakfast begins, or rather ceases, to tell, and the ladies bought some hot chestnut paste out of a little shop, because it looked so typical. It tasted partly of the paper in which it was wrapped, partly of hair-oil, partly of the great unknown. But it gave them strength to drift into another piazza, large and dusty, on the further side of which rose a black-and-white façade of surpassing ugliness. Miss Lavish spoke to it dramatically. It was Santa Croce. The adventure was over.

'Stop a minute; let those two people go on, or I shall have to speak to them. I do detest conventional intercourse. Nasty! They are going into the church, too. Oh, the Britisher abroad!'

'We sat opposite them at dinner last night. They have given us their rooms. They were so very kind.'

'Look at their figures!' laughed Miss Lavish. 'They walk

through my Italy like a pair of cows. It's very naughty of me, but I would like to set an examination paper at Dover, and turn back every tourist who couldn't pass it.'

'What would you ask us?'

Miss Lavish laid her hand pleasantly on Lucy's arm, as if to suggest that she, at all events, would get full marks. In this exalted mood they reached the steps of the great church, and were about to enter it when Miss Lavish stopped, squeaked, flung up her arms, and cried:

'There goes my local-colour box! I must have a word with him!'

And in a moment she was away over the Piazza, her military cloak flapping in the wind; nor did she slacken speed till she caught up an old man with white whiskers, and nipped him playfully upon the arm.

Lucy waited for nearly ten minutes. Then she began to get tired. The beggars worried her, the dust blew in her eyes, and she remembered that a young girl ought not to loiter in public places. She descended slowly into the Piazza with the intention of rejoining Miss Lavish, who was really almost too original. But at that moment Miss Lavish and her local-colour box moved also, and disappeared down a side-street, both gesticulating largely.

Tears of indignation came to Lucy's eyes – partly because Miss Lavish had jilted her, partly because she had taken her Baedeker. How could she find her way home? How could she find her way about in Santa Croce? Her first morning was ruined, and she might never be in Florence again. A few minutes ago she had been all high spirits, talking as a woman of culture, and half-persuading herself that she was full of originality. Now she entered the church depressed and humiliated, not even able to remember whether it was built by the Franciscans or the Dominicans.

Of course, it must be a wonderful building. But how like a barn! And how very cold! Of course, it contained frescoes by Giotto, in the presence of whose tactile values she was capable of feeling what was proper. But who was to tell her which they were? She walked about disdainfully, unwilling to be enthusiastic over monuments of uncertain authorship or date. There was no one even to tell her which, of all the sepulchral slabs that paved the nave and transepts, was the one that was really beautiful, the one that had been most praised by Mr Ruskin.

Then the pernicious charm of Italy worked on her, and, instead of acquiring information, she began to be happy. She puzzled out the Italian notices – the notice that forbade people to introduce dogs into the church – the notice that prayed people, in the interests of health and out of respect to the sacred edifice in which they found themselves, not to spit. She watched the tourists: their noses were as red as their Baedekers, so cold was Santa Croce. She beheld the horrible fate that overtook three Papists – two he-babies and a she-baby – who began their career by sousing each other with the Holy Water, and then proceeded to the Machiavelli memorial, dripping, but hallowed. Advancing towards it very slowly and from immense distances, they touched the stone with their fingers, with their handkerchiefs, with their heads, and then retreated. What could this mean? They did it again and again. Then Lucy realized that they had mistaken Machiavelli for some saint, and by continual contact with his shrine were hoping to acquire virtue. Punishment followed quickly. The smallest he-baby stumbled over one of the sepul-chral slabs so much admired by Mr Ruskin, and entangled his feet in the features of a recumbent bishop. Protestant as she was, Lucy darted forward. She was too late. He fell heavily upon the prelate's upturned toes.

'Hateful bishop!' exclaimed the voice of old Mr Emerson, who had darted forward also. 'Hard in life, hard in death. Go out into the sunshine, little boy, and kiss your hand to the sun, for that is where you ought to be. Intolerable bishop!'

The child screamed frantically at these words, and at these dreadful people who picked him up, dusted him, rubbed his bruises, and told him not to be superstitious.

'Look at him!' said Mr Emerson to Lucy. 'Here's a mess: a baby hurt, cold and frightened! But what else can you expect from a church?'

The child's legs had become as melting wax. Each time that old Mr Emerson and Lucy set it erect it collapsed with a roar. Fortunately an Italian lady, who ought to have been saying her prayers, came to the rescue. By some mysterious virtue, which mothers alone possess, she stiffened the little boy's backbone and imparted strength to his knees. He stood. Still gibbering with agitation, he walked away.

'You are a clever woman,' said Mr Emerson. 'You have done more than all the relics in the world. I am not of your creed, but I do believe in those who make their fellow creatures happy. There is no scheme of the universe –'

He paused for a phrase.

'Niente,' said the Italian lady, and returned to her prayers.

'I'm not sure she understands English,' suggested Lucy.

In her chastened mood she no longer despised the Emersons. She was determined to be gracious to them, beautiful rather than delicate, and, if possible, to erase Miss Bartlett's civility by some gracious reference to the pleasant rooms.

'That woman understands everything,' was Mr Emerson's reply. 'But what are you doing here? Are you doing the church? Are you through with the church?'

'No,' cried Lucy, remembering her grievance. 'I came here with Miss Lavish, who was to explain everything; and just by the door – it is too bad! – she simply ran away, and after waiting quite a time I had to come in by myself.'

'Why shouldn't you?' said Mr Emerson.

'Yes, why shouldn't you come by yourself?' said the son, addressing the young lady for the first time.

'But Miss Lavish has even taken away Baedeker.'

'Baedeker?' said Mr Emerson. 'I'm glad it's *that* that you minded. It's worth minding, the loss of a Baedeker. *That's* worth minding.'

Lucy was puzzled. She was again conscious of some new idea, and was not sure whither it would lead her.

'If you've no Baedeker,' said the son, 'you'd better join us.'

Was this where the idea would lead? She took refuge in her dignity.

'Thank you very much, but I could not think of that. I hope you do not suppose that I came to join on to you. I really came to help with the child, and to thank you for so kindly giving us your rooms last night. I hope that you have not been put to any great inconvenience.'

'My dear,' said the old man gently, 'I think that you are repeating what you have heard older people say. You are pretending to be touchy; but you are not really. Stop being so tiresome, and tell me instead what part of the church you want to see. To take you to it will be a real pleasure.'

Now, this was abominably impertinent, and she ought to have been furious. But it is sometimes as difficult to lose one's temper as it is difficult at other times to keep it. Lucy could not get cross. Mr Emerson was an old man, and surely a girl might humour him. On the other hand, his son was a young man, and she felt that a girl ought to be offended with him, or at all events be offended before him. It was at him that she gazed before replying.

'I am not touchy, I hope. It is the Giottos that I want to see, if you will kindly tell me which they are.'

The son nodded. With a look of sombre satisfaction, he led the way to the Peruzzi Chapel. There was a hint of the teacher about him. She felt like a child in school who had answered a question rightly.

The chapel was already filled with an earnest congregation, and out of them rose the voice of a lecturer, directing them how to worship Giotto, not by tactile valuations, but by the standards of the spirit.

'Remember,' he was saying, 'the facts about this church of Santa Croce; how it was built by faith in the full fervour of medievalism, before any taint of the Renaissance had appeared.

Observe how Giotto in these frescoes – now, unhappily, ruined by restoration – is untroubled by the snares of anatomy and perspective. Could anything be more majestic, more pathetic, beautiful, true? How little, we feel, avails knowledge and technical cleverness against a man who truly feels!'

'No!' exclaimed Mr Emerson, in much too loud a voice for church. 'Remember nothing of the sort! Built by faith indeed! That simply means the workmen weren't paid properly. And as for the frescoes, I see no truth in them. Look at that fat man in blue! He must weigh as much as I do, and he is shooting into the sky like an air-balloon.'

He was referring to the fresco of the Ascension of St John. Inside, the lecturer's voice faltered, as well it might. The audience shifted uneasily, and so did Lucy. She was sure that she ought not to be with these men; but they had cast a spell over her. They were so serious and so strange that she could not remember how to behave.

'Now, did this happen, or didn't it? Yes or no?'

George replied:

'It happened like this, if it happened at all. I would rather go up to heaven by myself than be pushed by cherubs; and if I got there I should like my friends to lean out of it, just as they do here.'

'You will never go up,' said his father. 'You and I, dear boy, will lie at peace in the earth that bore us, and our names will disappear as surely as our work survives.'

'Some of the people can only see the empty grave, not the saint, whoever he is, going up. It did happen like that, if it happened at all.'

'Pardon me,' said a frigid voice. 'The chapel is somewhat small for two parties. We will incommode you no longer.'

The lecturer was a clergyman, and his audience must be also his flock, for they held prayerbooks as well as guidebooks in their hands. They filed out of the chapel in silence. Amongst them were the two little old ladies of the Pension Bertolini – Miss Teresa and Miss Catharine Alan.

'Stop!' cried Mr Emerson. 'There's plenty of room for us all. Stop!'

The procession disappeared without a word. Soon the lecturer could be heard in the next chapel, describing the life of St Francis.

'George, I do believe that clergyman is the Brixton curate.'

George went into the next chapel and returned, saying: 'Perhaps he is. I don't remember.'

'Then I had better speak to him and remind him who I am. It's that Mr Eager. Why did he go? Did we talk too loud? How vexatious! I shall go and say we are sorry. Hadn't I better? Then perhaps he will come back.'

'He will not come back,' said George.

But Mr Emerson, contrite and unhappy, hurried away to apologize to the Rev. Cuthbert Eager. Lucy, apparently absorbed in a lunette, could hear the lecture again interrupted, the anxious, aggressive voice of the old man, the curt, injured replies of his opponent. The son, who took every little contretemps as if it were a tragedy, was listening also.

'My father has that effect on nearly everyone,' he informed her. 'He will try to be kind.'

'I hope we all try,' said she, smiling nervously.

'Because we think it improves our characters. But he is kind to people because he loves them; and they find him out, and are offended, or frightened.'

'How silly of them!' said Lucy, though in her heart she sympathized; 'I think that a kind action done tactfully –'

'Tact!'

He threw up his head in disdain. Apparently she had given the wrong answer. She watched the singular creature pace up and down the chapel. For a young man his face was rugged, and – until the shadows fell upon it – hard. Enshadowed, it sprang into tenderness. She saw him once again at Rome, on the ceiling of the Sistine Chapel, carrying a burden of acorns. Healthy and muscular, he yet gave her the feeling of greyness, of tragedy that might only find solution in the night. The feeling soon passed;

it was unlike her to have entertained anything so subtle. Born of silence and of unknown emotion, it passed when Mr Emerson returned, and she could re-enter the world of rapid talk, which was alone familiar to her.

'Were you snubbed?' asked his son tranquilly.

'But we have spoilt the pleasure of I don't know how many people. They won't come back.'

'... full of innate sympathy ... quickness to perceive good in others ... vision of the brotherhood of man ...' Scraps of the lecture on St Francis came floating round the partition wall.

'Don't let us spoil yours,' he continued to Lucy. 'Have you looked at those saints?'

'Yes,' said Lucy. 'They are lovely. Do you know which is the tombstone that is praised in Ruskin?'

He did not know, and suggested that they should try to guess it. George, rather to her relief, refused to move, and she and the old man wandered not unpleasantly about Santa Croce, which, though it is like a barn, has harvested many beautiful things inside its walls. There were also beggars to avoid, and guides to dodge round the pillars, and an old lady with her dog, and here and there was a priest modestly edging to his Mass through the groups of tourists. But Mr Emerson was only half-interested. He watched the lecturer, whose success he believed that he had impaired, and then he anxiously watched his son.

'Why will he look at that fresco?' he said uneasily. 'I saw nothing in it.'

'I like Giotto,' she replied. 'It is so wonderful what they say about his tactile values. Though I like things like the Della Robbia babies better.'

'So you ought. A baby is worth a dozen saints. And my baby's worth the whole of Paradise, and as far as I can see he lives in Hell.'

Lucy again felt that this did not do.

'In Hell,' he repeated. 'He's unhappy.'

'Oh dear!' said Lucy.

'How can he be unhappy when he is strong and alive? What more is one to give him? And think how he has been brought up – free from all the superstition and ignorance that lead men to hate one another in the name of God. With such an education as that, I thought he was bound to grow up happy.'

She was no theologian, but she felt that here was a very foolish old man, as well as a very irreligious one. She also felt that her mother might not like her talking to that kind of person, and that Charlotte would object most strongly.

'What are we to do with him?' he asked. 'He comes out for his holiday to Italy, and behaves – like that; like the little child who ought to have been playing, and who hurt himself upon the tombstone. Eh? What did you say?'

Lucy had made no suggestion. Suddenly he said:

'Now, don't be stupid over this. I don't require you to fall in love with my boy, but I do think you might try and understand him. You are nearer his age, and if you let yourself go I am sure you are sensible. You might help me. He has known so few women, and you have the time. You stop here several weeks, I suppose? But let yourself go. You are inclined to get muddled, if I may judge from last night. Let yourself go. Pull out from the depths those thoughts that you do not understand, and spread them out in the sunlight and know the meaning of them. By understanding George you may learn to understand yourself. It will be good for both of you.'

To this extraordinary speech Lucy found no answer.

'I only know what it is that's wrong with him; not why it is.'

'And what is it?' asked Lucy fearfully, expecting some harrowing tale.

'The old trouble: things won't fit.'

'What things?'

'The things of the universe. It is quite true. They don't.'

'Oh, Mr Emerson, what ever do you mean?'

In his ordinary voice, so that she scarcely realized he was quoting poetry, he said:

'From far, from eve and morning
And yon twelve-winded sky,
The stuff of life to knit me
Blew hither: here am I.

George and I both know this, but why does it distress him? We
know that we come from the winds, and that we shall return to
them; that all life is perhaps a knot, a tangle, a blemish in the
eternal smoothness. But why should this make us unhappy? Let
us rather love one another, and work and rejoice. I don't believe
in this world-sorrow.'

Miss Honeychurch assented.

'Then make my boy think like us. Make him realize that by
the side of the everlasting Why there is a Yes – a transitory Yes
if you like, but a Yes.'

Suddenly she laughed; surely one ought to laugh. A young
man melancholy because the universe wouldn't fit, because life
was a tangle or a wind, or a Yes, or something!

'I'm very sorry,' she cried. 'You'll think me unfeeling, but –
but –' Then she became matronly. 'Oh, but your son wants
employment. Has he no particular hobby? Why, I myself have
worries, but I can generally forget them at the piano; and collecting stamps did no end of good for my brother. Perhaps Italy
bores him; you ought to try the Alps or the Lakes.'

The old man's face saddened, and he touched her gently with
his hand. This did not alarm her; she thought that her advice
had impressed him, and that he was thanking her for it. Indeed,
he no longer alarmed her at all; she regarded him as a kind thing,
but quite silly. Her feelings were as inflated spiritually as they
had been an hour ago aesthetically, before she lost Baedeker. The
dear George, now striding towards them over the tombstones,
seemed both pitiable and absurd. He approached, his face in the
shadow. He said:

'Miss Bartlett.'

'Oh, good gracious me!' said Lucy, suddenly collapsing and

again seeing the whole of life in a new perspective. 'Where? Where?'

'In the nave.'

'I see. Those gossiping little old Miss Alans must have –' She checked herself.

'Poor girl!' exploded old Mr Emerson. 'Poor girl!'

She could not let this pass, for it was just what she was feeling herself.

'Poor girl? I fail to understand the point of that remark. I think myself a very fortunate girl, I assure you. I'm thoroughly happy, and having a splendid time. Pray don't waste time mourning over *me*. There's enough sorrow in the world, isn't there, without trying to invent it. Goodbye. Thank you both so much for all your kindness. Ah yes! There does come my cousin. A delightful morning! Santa Croce is a wonderful church.'

She rejoined her cousin.

CHAPTER III

Music, Violets and the Letter S

IT SO HAPPENED that Lucy, who found daily life rather chaotic, entered a more solid world when she opened the piano. She was then no longer either deferential or patronizing; no longer either a rebel or a slave. The kingdom of music is not the kingdom of this world; it will accept those whom breeding and intellect and culture have alike rejected. The commonplace person begins to play, and shoots into the empyrean without effort, whilst we look up, marvelling how he has escaped us, and thinking how we could worship him and love him, would he but translate his visions into human words, and his experiences into human actions. Perhaps he cannot; certainly he does not, or does so very seldom. Lucy had done so never.

She was no dazzling *exécutante*; her runs were not at all like strings of pearls, and she struck no more right notes than was suitable for one of her age and situation. Nor was she the passionate young lady, who performs so tragically on a summer's evening with the window open. Passion was there, but it could not be easily labelled; it slipped between love and hatred and jealousy, and all the furniture of the pictorial style. And she was tragical only in the sense that she was great, for she loved to play on the side of Victory. Victory of what and over what – that is more than the words of daily life can tell us. But that some sonatas of Beethoven are written tragic no one can gainsay; yet they can triumph or despair as the player decides, and Lucy had decided that they should triumph.

A very wet afternoon at the Bertolini permitted her to do the thing she really liked, and after lunch she opened the little draped piano. A few people lingered round and praised her

playing, but, finding that she made no reply, dispersed to their
rooms to write up their diaries or to sleep. She took no notice of
Mr Emerson looking for his son, nor of Miss Bartlett looking
for Miss Lavish, nor of Miss Lavish looking for her cigarette-
case. Like every true performer, she was intoxicated by the mere
feel of the notes: they were fingers caressing her own; and by
touch, not by sound alone, did she come to her desire.

Mr Beebe, sitting unnoticed in the window, pondered over
this illogical element in Miss Honeychurch, and recalled the
occasion at Tunbridge Wells when he had discovered it. It was
at one of those entertainments where the upper classes entertain
the lower. The seats were filled with a respectful audience, and
the ladies and gentlemen of the parish, under the auspices of
their vicar, sang, or recited, or imitated the drawing of a cham-
pagne-cork. Among the promised items was 'Miss Honeychurch. Piano. Beethoven', and Mr Beebe was wondering
whether it would be *Adelaide* or the march of *The Ruins of
Athens*, when his composure was disturbed by the opening bars
of Opus III. He was in suspense all through the introduction, for
not until the pace quickens does one know what the performer
intends. With the roar of the opening theme he knew that things
were going extraordinarily; in the chords that herald the conclusion he heard the hammer-strokes of victory. He was glad that
she only played the first movement, for he could have paid no
attention to the winding intricacies of the measure of nine-six-
teen. The audience clapped, no less respectful. It was Mr Beebe
who started the stamping; it was all that one could do.

'Who is she?' he asked the vicar afterwards.

'Cousin of one of my parishioners. I do not consider her
choice of a piece happy. Beethoven is usually so simple and direct
in his appeal that it is sheer perversity to choose a thing like that,
which, if anything, disturbs.'

'Introduce me.'

'She will be delighted. She and Miss Bartlett are full of the
praises of your sermon.'

'My sermon?' cried Mr Beebe. 'Why ever did she listen to it?'

When he was introduced he understood why, for Miss Honeychurch, disjoined from her music-stool, was only a young lady with a quantity of dark hair and a very pretty, pale, undeveloped face. She loved going to concerts, she loved stopping with her cousin, she loved iced coffee and meringues. He did not doubt that she loved his sermon also. But before he left Tunbridge Wells he made a remark to the vicar, which he now made to Lucy herself when she closed the little piano and moved dreamily towards him.

'If Miss Honeychurch ever takes to live as she plays, it will be very exciting – both for us and for her.'

Lucy at once re-entered daily life.

'Oh, what a funny thing! Someone said just the same to mother, and she said she trusted I should never live a duet.'

'Doesn't Mrs Honeychurch like music?'

'She doesn't mind it. But she doesn't like one to get excited over anything; she thinks I am silly about it. She thinks – I can't make out. Once, you know, I said that I liked my own playing better than anyone's. She has never got over it. Of course, I didn't mean that I played well; I only meant –'

'Of course,' said he, wondering why she bothered to explain.

'Music –' said Lucy, as if attempting some generality. She could not complete it, and looked out absently upon Italy in the wet. The whole life of the South was disorganized, and the most graceful nation in Europe had turned into formless lumps of clothes. The street and the river were dirty yellow, the bridge was dirty grey, and the hills were dirty purple. Somewhere in their folds were concealed Miss Lavish and Miss Bartlett, who had chosen this afternoon to visit the Torre del Gallo.

'What about music?' said Mr Beebe.

'Poor Charlotte will be sopped,' was Lucy's reply.

The expedition was typical of Miss Bartlett, who would return cold, tired, hungry and angelic, with a ruined skirt, a pulpy Baedeker, and a tickling cough in her throat. On another day, when the whole world was singing and the air ran into the mouth like wine, she would refuse to stir from the drawing-room, saying that she was an old thing, and no fit companion for a hearty girl.

'Miss Lavish has led your cousin astray. She hopes to find the true Italy in the wet, I believe.'

'Miss Lavish is so original,' murmured Lucy. This was the stock remark, the supreme achievement of the Pension Bertolini in the way of definition. Miss Lavish was so original. Mr Beebe had his doubts, but they would have been put down to clerical narrowness. For that and for other reasons, he held his peace.

'Is it true,' continued Lucy in awestruck tones, 'that Miss Lavish is writing a book?'

'They do say so.'

'What is it about?'

'It will be a novel,' replied Mr Beebe, 'dealing with modern Italy. Let me refer you for an account to Miss Catharine Alan, who uses words herself more admirably than anyone I know.'

'I wish Miss Lavish would tell me herself. We started such friends. But I don't think she ought to have run away with Bae-deker that morning in Santa Croce. Charlotte was most annoyed at finding me practically alone, and so I couldn't help being a little annoyed with Miss Lavish.'

'The two ladies, at all events, have made it up.'

He was interested in the sudden friendship between women so apparently dissimilar as Miss Bartlett and Miss Lavish. They were always in each other's company, with Lucy a slighted third. Miss Lavish he believed he understood, but Miss Bartlett might reveal unknown depths of strangeness, though not, perhaps, of meaning. Was Italy deflecting her from the path of prim chap-eron, which he had assigned to her at Tunbridge Wells? All his life he had loved to study maiden ladies; they were his speciality, and his profession had provided him with ample opportunities for the work. Girls like Lucy were charming to look at, but Mr Beebe was, from rather profound reasons, somewhat chilly in his attitude towards the other sex, and preferred to be interested rather than enthralled.

Lucy, for the third time, said that poor Charlotte would be sopped. The Arno was rising in flood, washing away the traces of the little carts upon the foreshore. But in the southwest there had appeared a dull haze of yellow, which might mean better weather if it did not mean worse. She opened the window to inspect, and a cold blast entered the room, drawing a plaintive cry from Miss Catharine Alan, who entered at the same moment by the door.

'Oh, dear Miss Honeychurch, you will catch a chill! And Mr Beebe here besides. Who would suppose this is Italy? There is my sister actually nursing the hot-water can; no comforts or proper provisions.'

She sidled towards them and sat down, self-conscious as she always was on entering a room which contained one man, or a man and one woman.

'I could hear your beautiful playing, Miss Honeychurch, though I was in my room with the door shut. Doors shut; indeed, most necessary. No one has the least idea of privacy in this country. And one person catches it from another.'

Lucy answered suitably. Mr Beebe was not able to tell the ladies of his adventure at Modena, where the chambermaid burst in upon him in his bath, exclaiming cheerfully, 'Fa niente, sono vecchia.' He contented himself with saying: 'I quite agree with you, Miss Alan. The Italians are a most unpleasant people. They pry everywhere, they see everything, and they know what we want before we know it ourselves. We are at their mercy. They read our thoughts, they foretell our desires. From the cab-driver down to – to Giotto, they turn us inside out, and I resent it. Yet in their heart of hearts they are – how superficial! They have no conception of the intellectual life. How right is Signora Bertolini, who exclaimed to me the other day: "Ho, Mr Beebe, if you knew what I suffer over the children's edjucaishion! *Hi* won't 'ave my little Victorier taught by a hignorant Italian what can't explain nothink!"'

Miss Alan did not follow, but gathered that she was being mocked in an agreeable way. Her sister was a little disappointed in Mr Beebe, having expected better things from a clergyman whose head was bald and who wore a pair of russet whiskers. Indeed, who would have supposed that tolerance, sympathy and a sense of humour would inhabit that militant form?

In the midst of her satisfaction she continued to sidle, and at last the cause was disclosed. From the chair beneath her she extracted a gun-metal cigarette-case, on which were powdered in turquoise the initials E. L.

'That belongs to Lavish,' said the clergyman. 'A good fellow, Lavish, but I wish she'd start a pipe.'

'Oh, Mr Beebe,' said Miss Alan, divided between awe and mirth. 'Indeed, though it is dreadful of her to smoke, it is not quite as dreadful as you suppose. She took to it, practically in despair, after her life's work was carried away in a landslip. Surely that makes it more excusable.'

'What was that?' asked Lucy.

Mr Beebe sat back complacently, and Miss Alan began as follows:

'It was a novel – and I am afraid, from what I can gather, not a very nice novel. It is so sad when people who have abilities misuse them, and I must say they nearly always do. Anyhow, she left it almost finished in the Grotto of the Calvary at the Cappuccini Hotel at Amalfi while she went for a little ink. She said: "Can I have a little ink, please?" But you know what Italians are, and meanwhile the Grotto fell roaring onto the beach, and the saddest thing of all is that she cannot remember what she has written. The poor thing was very ill after it, and so got tempted into cigarettes. It is a great secret, but I am glad to say that she is writing another novel. She told Teresa and Miss Pole the other day that she had got up all the local colour – this novel is to be about modern Italy; the other was historical – but that she could not start till she had an idea. First she tried Perugia for an inspiration, then she came here – this must on no account get round. And so cheerful through it all! I cannot help thinking that there is something to admire in everyone, even if you do not approve of them.'

Miss Alan was always thus being charitable against her better judgement. A delicate pathos perfumed her disconnected remarks, giving them unexpected beauty, just as in the decaying autumn woods there sometimes rise odours reminiscent of spring. She felt she had made almost too many allowances, and apologized hurriedly for her toleration.

'All the same, she is a little too – I hardly like to say unwomanly, but she behaved most strangely when the Emersons arrived.'

Mr Beebe smiled as Miss Alan plunged into an anecdote which he knew she would be unable to finish in the presence of a gentleman.

'I don't know, Miss Honeychurch, if you have noticed that Miss Pole, the lady who has so much rather yellow hair, takes lemonade. That old Mr Emerson, who puts things very strangely –'

Her jaw dropped. She was silent. Mr Beebe, whose social resources were endless, went out to order some tea, and she continued to Lucy in a hasty whisper:

'Stomach. He warned Miss Pole of her stomach – acidity, he called it – and he may have meant to be kind. I must say I forgot myself and laughed; it was so sudden. As Teresa truly said, it was no laughing-matter. But the point is that Miss Lavish was positively *attracted* by his mentioning S., and said that she liked plain speaking, and meeting different grades of thought. She thought they were commercial travellers – "drummers" was the word she used – and all through dinner she tried to prove that England, our great and beloved country, rests on nothing but commerce. Teresa was very much annoyed and left the table before the cheese, saying as she did so: "There, Miss Lavish, is one who can confute you better than I," and pointed to that beautiful picture of Lord Tennyson. Then Miss Lavish said: "Tut! The early Victorians." Just imagine! "Tut! The early Victorians." My sister had gone, and I felt bound to speak. I said: "Miss Lavish, *I* am an early Victorian; at least, that is to say, I will hear no breath of censure against our dear Queen." It was horrible speaking. I reminded her how the Queen had been to Ireland when she did not want to go, and I must say she was dumbfoundered, and made no reply. But, unluckily, Mr Emerson overheard this part, and called in his deep voice: "Quite so, quite so! I honour the woman for her Irish visit." The woman! I tell things so badly; but you see what a tangle we were in by this time, all on account of S. having been mentioned in the first place. But that was not all. After dinner Miss Lavish actually came up and said: "Miss Alan, I am going into the smoking-room to talk to those two nice men. Come too." Needless to say, I refused such an unsuitable invitation, and she had the impertinence to tell me that it would broaden my ideas, and said that she had four brothers, all university men, except one who was in the Army, who always made a point of talking to commercial travellers.'

'Let me finish the story,' said Mr Beebe, who had returned. 'Miss Lavish tried Miss Pole, myself, everyone, and finally said: "I shall go alone." She went. At the end of five minutes she returned unobtrusively with a green baize board, and began playing patience.'

'What ever happened?' cried Lucy.

'No one knows. No one will ever know. Miss Lavish will never dare to tell, and Mr Emerson does not think it worth telling.'

'Mr Beebe – old Mr Emerson, is he nice or not nice? I do so want to know.'

Mr Beebe laughed and suggested that she should settle the question for herself.

'No; but it is so difficult. Sometimes he is so silly, and then I do not mind him. Miss Alan, what do you think? Is he nice?'

The little old lady shook her head, and sighed disapprovingly. Mr Beebe, whom the conversation amused, stirred her up by saying:

'I consider that you are bound to class him as nice, Miss Alan, after that business of the violets.'

'Violets? Oh dear! Who told you about the violets? How do things get round? A pension is a sad place for gossips. No, I cannot forget how they behaved at Mr Eager's lecture at Santa Croce. Oh, poor Miss Honeychurch! It really was too bad! No, I have quite changed. I do *not* like the Emersons. They are *not* nice.'

Mr Beebe smiled nonchalantly. He had made a gentle effort to introduce the Emersons into Bertolini society, and the effort had failed. He was almost the only person who remained friendly to them. Miss Lavish, who represented intellect, was avowedly hostile, and now the Miss Alans, who stood for good breeding, were following her. Miss Bartlett, smarting under an obligation, would scarcely be civil. The case of Lucy was different. She had given him a hazy account of her adventures in Santa Croce, and he gathered that the two men had made a curious and possibly concerted attempt to annex her, to show her the world from their own strange standpoint, to interest her in their private sorrows and joys. This was impertinent; he did not wish their cause to be championed by a young girl; he would rather it should fail. After all, he knew nothing about them, and pension joys, pension sorrows, are flimsy things; whereas Lucy would be his parishioner.

Lucy, with one eye upon the weather, finally said that she thought the Emersons were nice; not that she saw anything of them now. Even their seats at dinner had been moved.

'But aren't they always waylaying you to go out with them, dear?' said the little lady inquisitively.

'Only once. Charlotte didn't like it, and said something – quite politely, of course.'

'Most right of her. They don't understand our ways. They must find their level.'

Mr Beebe rather felt that they had gone under. They had given up their attempt – if it was one – to conquer society, and now the father was almost as silent as the son. He wondered whether he would not plan a pleasant day for these folk before they left – some expedition, perhaps, with Lucy well chaperoned to be nice to them. It was one of Mr Beebe's chief pleasures to provide people with happy memories.

Evening approached while they chatted; the air became brighter; the colours on the trees and hills were purified, and the Arno lost its muddy solidity and began to twinkle. There were a few streaks of bluish-green among the clouds, a few patches of watery light upon the earth, and then the dripping façade of San Miniato shone brilliantly in the declining sun.

'Too late to go out,' said Miss Alan in a voice of relief. 'All the galleries are shut.'

'I think I shall go out,' said Lucy. 'I want to go round the town in the circular tram – on the platform by the driver.'

Her two companions looked grave. Mr Beebe, who felt responsible for her in the absence of Miss Bartlett, ventured to say:

'I wish we could. Unluckily I have letters. If you do want to go out alone, won't you be better on your feet?'

'Italians, dear, you know,' said Miss Alan.

'Perhaps I shall meet someone who reads me through and through!'

But they still looked disapproval, and she so far conceded to Mr Beebe as to say that she would only go for a little walk, and keep to the streets frequented by tourists.

'She oughtn't really to go at all,' said Mr Beebe, as they watched her from the window, 'and she knows it. I put it down to too much Beethoven.'

CHAPTER IV

Fourth Chapter

MR BEEBE WAS RIGHT. Lucy never knew her desires so clearly as after music. She had not really appreciated the clergyman's wit, nor the suggestive twitterings of Miss Alan. Conversation was tedious; she wanted something big, and she believed that it would have come to her on the windswept platform of an electric tram.

This she might not attempt. It was unladylike. Why? Why were most big things unladylike? Charlotte had once explained to her why. It was not that ladies were inferior to men; it was that they were different. Their mission was to inspire others to achievement rather than to achieve themselves. Indirectly, by means of tact and a spotless name, a lady could accomplish much. But if she rushed into the fray herself she would be first censured, then despised, and finally ignored. Poems had been written to illustrate this point.

There is much that is immortal in this medieval lady. The dragons have gone, and so have the knights, but still she lingers in our midst. She reigned in many an early Victorian castle, and was queen of much early Victorian song. It is sweet to protect her in the intervals of business, sweet to pay her honour when she has cooked our dinner well. But alas! the creature grows degenerate. In her heart also there are springing up strange desires. She too is enamoured of heavy winds, and vast panoramas, and green expanses of the sea. She has marked the kingdom of this world, how full it is of wealth, and beauty, and war – a radiant crust, built around the central fires, spinning towards the receding heavens. Men, declaring that she inspires them to it, move joyfully over the surface, having the most delightful meetings with other men, happy, not because they are masculine, but because they are alive. Before the show breaks up she would like to drop the august title of the Eternal Woman, and go there as her transitory self.

Lucy does not stand for the medieval lady, who was rather an ideal to which she was bidden to lift her eyes when feeling serious. Nor has she any system of revolt. Here and there a restriction annoyed her particularly, and she would transgress it, and perhaps be sorry that she had done so. This afternoon she was peculiarly restive. She would really like to do something of which her well-wishers disapproved. As she might not go on the electric tram, she went to Alinari's shop.

There she bought a photograph of Botticelli's *Birth of Venus*. Venus, being a pity, spoiled the picture, otherwise so charming, and Miss Bartlett had persuaded her to do without it. (A pity in art of course signified the nude.) Giorgione's *Tempesta*, the *Idolino*, some of the Sistine frescoes and the Apoxyomenos were added to it. She felt a little calmer then, and bought Fra Angelico's *Coronation*, Giotto's *Ascension of St John*, some Della Robbia babies, and some Guido Reni Madonnas. For her taste was catholic, and she extended uncritical approval to every well-known name.

But though she spent nearly seven lire the gates of liberty seemed still unopened. She was conscious of her discontent; it was new to her to be conscious of it. 'The world,' she thought, 'is certainly full of beautiful things, if only I could come across them.' It was not surprising that Mrs Honeychurch disapproved of music, declaring that it always left her daughter peevish, unpractical and touchy.

'Nothing ever happens to me,' she reflected, as she entered the Piazza Signoria and looked nonchalantly at its marvels, now fairly familiar to her. The great square was in shadow; the sunshine had come too late to strike it. Neptune was already unsubstantial in the twilight, half god, half ghost, and his fountain plashed dreamily to the men and satyrs who idled together on its marge. The Loggia showed as the triple entrance of a cave, wherein dwelt many a deity, shadowy but immortal, looking forth upon the arrivals and departures of mankind. It was the hour of unreality – the hour, that is, when unfamiliar things are real. An older person at such an hour and in such a place might think that sufficient was happening to him, and rest content. Lucy desired more.

She fixed her eyes wistfully on the tower of the palace, which rose out of the lower darkness like a pillar of roughened gold. It seemed no longer a tower, no longer supported by earth, but some unattainable treasure throbbing in the tranquil sky. Its brightness mesmerized her, still dancing before her eyes when she bent them to the ground and started towards home.

Then something did happen.

Two Italians by the Loggia had been bickering about a debt. 'Cinque lire,' they had cried, 'cinque lire!' They sparred at each other, and one of them was hit lightly upon the chest. He frowned; he bent towards Lucy with a look of interest, as if he had an important message for her. He opened his lips to deliver it, and a stream of red came out between them and trickled down his unshaven chin.

That was all. A crowd rose out of the dusk. It hid this extraordinary man from her, and bore him away to the fountain. Mr George Emerson happened to be a few paces away, looking at her across the spot where the man had been. How very odd! Across something. Even as she caught sight of him he grew dim; the palace itself grew dim, swayed above her, fell onto her softly, slowly, noiselessly, and the sky fell with it.

She thought: 'Oh, what have I done?'

'Oh, what have I done?' she murmured, and opened her eyes.

George Emerson still looked at her, but not across anything. She had complained of dullness, and lo! one man was stabbed, and another held her in his arms.

They were sitting on some steps in the Uffizi Arcade. He must have carried her. He rose when she spoke, and began to dust his knees. She repeated:

'Oh, what have I done?'

'You fainted.'

'I – I am very sorry.'

'How are you now?'

'Perfectly well – absolutely well.' And she began to nod and smile.

'Then let us come home. There's no point in our stopping.'

He held out his hand to pull her up. She pretended not to see it. The cries from the fountain – they had never ceased – rang emptily. The whole world seemed pale and void of its original meaning.

'How very kind you have been! I might have hurt myself falling. But now I am well. I can go alone, thank you.'

His hand was still extended.

'Oh, my photographs!' she exclaimed suddenly.

'What photographs?'

'I bought some photographs at Alinari's. I must have dropped them out there in the square.' She looked at him cautiously. 'Would you add to your kindness by fetching them?'

He added to his kindness. As soon as he had turned his back, Lucy arose with the cunning of a maniac and stole down the arcade towards the Arno.

'Miss Honeychurch!'

She stopped with her hand on her heart.

'You sit still; you aren't fit to go home alone.'

'Yes, I am, thank you so very much.'

'No, you aren't. You'd go openly if you were.'

'But I had rather –'

'Then I don't fetch your photographs.'

'I had rather be alone.'

He said imperiously: 'The man is dead – the man is probably dead; sit down till you are rested.' She was bewildered, and obeyed him. 'And don't move till I come back.'

In the distance she saw creatures with black hoods, such as appear in dreams. The palace tower had lost the reflection of the

declining day, and joined itself to earth. How should she talk
to Mr Emerson when he returned from the shadowy square?
Again the thought occurred to her, 'Oh, what have I done?' –
the thought that she, as well as the dying man, had crossed some
spiritual boundary.

He returned, and she talked of the murder. Oddly enough, it
was an easy topic. She spoke of the Italian character; she became
almost garrulous over the incident that had made her faint five
minutes before. Being strong physically, she soon overcame the
horror of blood. She rose without his assistance, and though
wings seemed to flutter inside her she walked firmly enough
towards the Arno. There a cabman signalled to them; they
refused him.

'And the murderer tried to kiss him, you say – how very odd
Italians are! – and gave himself up to the police! Mr Beebe was
saying that Italians know everything, but I think they are rather
childish. When my cousin and I were at the Pitti yesterday –
what was that?'

He had thrown something into the stream.

'What did you throw in?'

'Things I didn't want,' he said crossly.

'Mr Emerson!'

'Well?'

'Where are the photographs?'

He was silent.

'I believe it was my photographs that you threw away.'

'I didn't know what to do with them,' he cried, and his voice
was that of an anxious boy. Her heart warmed towards him for
the first time. 'They were covered with blood. There! I'm glad
I've told you; and all the time we were making conversation I was
wondering what to do with them.' He pointed downstream.
'They've gone.' The river swirled under the bridge. 'I did mind
them so, and one is so foolish, it seemed better that they should
go out to the sea – I don't know; I may just mean that they frightened me.' Then the boy verged into a man! 'For something

tremendous has happened; I must face it without getting muddled. It isn't exactly that a man has died.'

Something warned Lucy that she must stop him.

'It has happened,' he repeated, 'and I mean to find out what it is.'

'Mr Emerson –'

He turned towards her frowning, as if she had disturbed him in some abstract quest.

'I want to ask you something before we go in.'

They were close to their pension. She stopped and leant her elbows against the parapet of the embankment. He did likewise. There is at times a magic in identity of position; it is one of the things that have suggested to us eternal comradeship. She moved her elbows before saying:

'I have behaved ridiculously.'

He was following his own thoughts.

'I was never so much ashamed of myself in my life; I cannot think what came over me.'

'I nearly fainted myself,' he said; but she felt that her attitude repelled him.

'Well, I owe you a thousand apologies.'

"Oh, all right.'

'And – this is the real point – you know how silly people are gossiping – ladies especially, I am afraid – you understand what I mean?'

'I'm afraid I don't.'

'I mean, would you not mention it to anyone, my foolish behaviour?'

'Your behaviour? Oh yes, all right – all right.'

'Thank you so much. And would you –'

She could not carry her request any further. The river was gushing below them, almost black in the advancing night. He had thrown her photographs into it, and then he had told her the reason. It struck her that it was hopeless to look for chivalry in such a man. He would do her no harm by idle gossip; he was trustworthy, intelligent, and even kind; he might even have a high opinion of her. But he lacked chivalry; his thoughts, like his behaviour, would not be modified by awe. It was useless to say to him, 'And would you –' and hope that he would complete the sentence for himself, averting his eyes from her nakedness like the knight in that beautiful picture. She had been in his arms, and he remembered it, just as he remembered the blood on the photographs that she had bought in Alinari's shop. It was not exactly that a man had died; something had happened to the living: they had come to a situation where character tells, and where Childhood enters upon the branching paths of Youth.

'Well, thank you so much,' she repeated. 'How quickly these accidents do happen, and then one returns to the old life!'

'I don't.'

Anxiety moved her to question him.

His answer was puzzling: 'I shall probably want to live.'

'But why, Mr Emerson? What do you mean?'

'I shall want to live, I say.'

Leaning her elbows on the parapet, she contemplated the River Arno, whose roar was suggesting some unexpected melody to her ears.

CHAPTER V

Possibilities of a Pleasant Outing

IT WAS A FAMILY saying that 'you never knew which way Charlotte Bartlett would turn'. She was perfectly pleasant and sensible over Lucy's adventure, found the abridged account of it quite adequate, and paid suitable tribute to the courtesy of Mr George Emerson. She and Miss Lavish had had an adventure also. They had been stopped at the *dazio* coming back, and the young officials there, who seemed impudent and *désœuvré*, had tried to search their reticules for provisions. It might have been most unpleasant. Fortunately, Miss Lavish was a match for anyone.

For good or for evil, Lucy was left to face her problem alone. None of her friends had seen her, either in the Piazza or, later on, by the embankment. Mr Beebe, indeed, noticing her startled eyes at dinner-time, had again passed to himself the remark of 'Too much Beethoven'. But he only supposed that she was ready for an adventure, not that she had encountered it. This solitude oppressed her; she was accustomed to have her thoughts confirmed by others or, at all events, contradicted; it was too dreadful not to know whether she was thinking right or wrong.

At breakfast next morning she took decisive action. There were two plans between which she had to choose. Mr Beebe was walking up to the Torre del Gallo with the Emersons and some American ladies. Would Miss Bartlett and Miss Honeychurch join the party? Charlotte declined for herself; she had been there in the rain the previous afternoon. But she thought it an admirable idea for Lucy, who hated shopping, changing money, fetching letters, and other irksome duties – all of which Miss Bartlett must accomplish this morning, and could easily accomplish alone.

'No, Charlotte!' cried the girl, with real warmth. 'It's very kind of Mr Beebe, but I am certainly coming with you. I had much rather.'

'Very well, dear,' said Miss Bartlett, with a faint flush of pleasure that called forth a deep flush of shame on the cheeks of Lucy. How abominably she behaved to Charlotte, now as always! But now she should alter. All the morning she would be really nice to her.

She slipped her arm into her cousin's, and they started off along the Lungarno. The river was a lion that morning in strength, voice and colour. Miss Bartlett insisted on leaning over the parapet to look at it. She then made her usual remark, which was:

'How I do wish Freddy and your mother could see this, too!'

Lucy fidgeted; it was tiresome of Charlotte to have stopped exactly where she did.

'Look, Lucia! Oh, you are watching for the Torre del Gallo party. I feared you would repent you of your choice.'

Serious as the choice had been, Lucy did not repent. Yesterday had been a muddle – queer and odd, the kind of thing one could not write down easily on paper – but she had a feeling that Charlotte and her shopping were preferable to George Emerson and the summit of the Torre del Gallo. Since she could not unravel the tangle, she must take care not to re-enter it. She could protest sincerely against Miss Bartlett's insinuations.

But, though she had avoided the chief actor, the scenery unfortunately remained. Charlotte, with the complacency of fate, led her from the river to the Piazza Signoria. She could not have believed that stones, a loggia, a fountain, a palace tower, would have such significance. For a moment she understood the nature of ghosts.

The exact site of the murder was occupied, not by a ghost, but by Miss Lavish, who had the morning newspaper in her hand. She hailed them briskly. The dreadful catastrophe of the previous day had given her an idea which she thought would work up into a book.

'Oh, let me congratulate you!' said Miss Bartlett. 'After your despair of yesterday! What a fortunate thing!'

'Aha! Miss Honeychurch, come you here! I am in luck. Now, you are to tell me absolutely everything that you saw from the beginning.'

Lucy poked at the ground with her parasol.

'But perhaps you would rather not?'

'I'm sorry – if you could manage without it, I think I would rather not.'

The elder ladies exchanged glances, not of disapproval; it is suitable that a girl should feel deeply.

'It is I who am sorry,' said Miss Lavish. 'We literary hacks are shameless creatures. I believe there's no secret of the human heart into which we wouldn't pry.'

She marched cheerfully to the fountain and back, and did a few calculations in realism. Then she said that she had been in the Piazza since eight o'clock collecting material. A good deal of it was unsuitable, but of course one always had to adapt. The two men had quarrelled over a five-franc note. For the five-franc note she should substitute a young lady, which would raise the tone of the tragedy, and at the same time furnish an excellent plot.

'What is the heroine's name?' asked Miss Bartlett.

'Leonora,' said Miss Lavish; her own name was Eleanor.

'I do hope she's nice.'

That desideratum would not be omitted.

'And what is the plot?'

Love, murder, abduction, revenge, was the plot. Out it all came while the fountain plashed to the satyrs in the morning sun.

'I hope you will excuse me for boring on like this,' Miss Lavish concluded. 'It is so tempting to talk to really sympathetic people. Of course, this is the barest outline. There will be a deal of local colouring, descriptions of Florence and the neighbourhood, and I shall also introduce some humorous characters. And let me give you all fair warning: I intend to be unmerciful to the British tourist.'

'Oh, you wicked woman!' cried Miss Bartlett. 'I am sure you are thinking of the Emersons.'

Miss Lavish gave a Machiavellian smile.

'I confess that in Italy my sympathies are not with my own countrymen. It is the neglected Italians who attract me, and whose lives I am going to paint so far as I can. For I repeat and I insist, and I have always held most strongly, that a tragedy such as yesterday's is not the less tragic because it happened in humble life.'

There was a fitting silence when Miss Lavish had concluded. Then the cousins wished success to her labours, and walked slowly away across the square.

'She is my idea of a really clever woman,' said Miss Bartlett. 'That last remark struck me as so particularly true. It should be a most pathetic novel.'

Lucy assented. At present her great aim was not to get put into it. Her perceptions this morning were curiously keen, and she believed that Miss Lavish had her on trial for an *ingénue*.

'She is emancipated, but only in the very best sense of the word,' continued Miss Bartlett slowly. 'None but the superficial would be shocked at her. We had a long talk yesterday. She believes in justice and truth and human interest. She told me also that she has a high opinion of the destiny of woman – Mr Eager! Why, how nice! What a pleasant surprise!'

'Ah, not for me,' said the chaplain blandly, 'for I have been watching you and Miss Honeychurch for quite a little time.'

'We were chatting to Miss Lavish.'

His brow contracted.

'So I saw. Were you indeed? Andate via! Sono occupato!' The last remark was made to a vendor of panoramic photographs who was approaching with a courteous smile. 'I am about to venture a suggestion. Would you and Miss Honeychurch be disposed to join me in a drive some day this week – a drive in the hills? We might go up by Fiesole and back by Settignano. There is a point on that road where we could get down and have an hour's ramble

on the hillside. The view thence of Florence is most beautiful –
far better than the hackneyed view from Fiesole. It is the view that
Alessio Baldovinetti is fond of introducing into his pictures. That
man had a decided feeling for landscape. Decidedly. But who
looks at it today? Ah, the world is too much with us.'

Miss Bartlett had not heard of Alessio Baldovinetti, but she
knew that Mr Eager was no commonplace chaplain. He was a
member of the residential colony who had made Florence their
home. He knew the people who never walked about with Baedekers, who had learned to take a siesta after lunch, who took
drives the pension tourists had never heard of, and saw by private
influence galleries which were closed to them. Living in delicate
seclusion, some in furnished flats, others in Renaissance villas on
Fiesole's slope, they read, wrote, studied and exchanged ideas,
thus attaining to that intimate knowledge, or rather perception,
of Florence which is denied to all who carry in their pockets the
coupons of Cook.

Therefore an invitation from the chaplain was something to
be proud of. Between the two sections of his flock he was often
the only link, and it was his avowed custom to select those of his
migratory sheep who seemed worthy, and give them a few hours
in the pastures of the permanent. Tea at a Renaissance villa?
Nothing had been said about it yet. But if it did come to that –
how Lucy would enjoy it!

A few days ago and Lucy would have felt the same. But the
joys of life were grouping themselves anew. A drive in the hills
with Mr Eager and Miss Bartlett – even if culminating in a residential tea-party – was no longer the greatest of them. She echoed the raptures of Charlotte somewhat faintly. Only when she
heard that Mr Beebe was also coming did her thanks become
more sincere.

'So we shall be a *partie carrée*,' said the chaplain. 'In these days
of toil and tumult one has great need of the country and its message of purity. Andate via! Andate presto, presto! Ah, the town!
Beautiful as it is, it is the town.'

They assented.

'This very square – so I am told – witnessed yesterday the most sordid of tragedies. To one who loves the Florence of Dante and Savonarola there is something portentous in such desecration – portentous and humiliating.'

'Humiliating indeed,' said Miss Bartlett. 'Miss Honeychurch happened to be passing through as it happened. She can hardly bear to speak of it.' She glanced at Lucy proudly.

'And how came we to have you here?' asked the chaplain paternally.

Miss Bartlett's recent liberalism oozed away at the question.

'Do not blame her, please, Mr Eager. The fault is mine: I left her unchaperoned.'

'So you were here alone, Miss Honeychurch?' His voice suggested sympathetic reproof, but at the same time indicated that a few harrowing details would not be unacceptable. His dark, handsome face drooped mournfully towards her to catch her reply.

'Practically.'

'One of our pension acquaintances kindly brought her home,' said Miss Bartlett, adroitly concealing the sex of the preserver.

'For her also it must have been a terrible experience. I trust that neither of you were at all – that it was not in your immediate proximity.'

Of the many things Lucy was noticing today, not the least remarkable was this: the ghoulish fashion in which respectable people will nibble after blood. George Emerson had kept the subject strangely pure.

'He died by the fountain, I believe,' was her reply.

'And you and your friend –'

'Were over at the Loggia.'

'That must have saved you much. You have not, of course, seen the disgraceful illustrations which the gutter press – This man is a public nuisance; he knows that I am a resident perfectly well, and yet he goes on worrying me to buy his vulgar views.'

Surely the vendor of photographs was in league with Lucy – in the eternal league of Italy with youth. He had suddenly extended his book before Miss Bartlett and Mr Eager, binding their hands together by a long glossy ribbon of churches, pictures, and views.

'This is too much!' cried the chaplain, striking petulantly at one of Fra Angelico's angels. She tore. A shrill cry arose from the vendor. The book, it seemed, was more valuable than one would have supposed.

'Willingly would I purchase –' began Miss Bartlett.

'Ignore him,' said Mr Eager sharply, and they all walked rapidly away from the square.

But an Italian can never be ignored, least of all when he has a grievance. His mysterious persecution of Mr Eager became relentless; the air rang with his threats and lamentations. He appealed to Lucy; would not she intercede? He was poor – he sheltered a family – the tax on bread. He waited, he gibbered, he was recompensed, he was dissatisfied, he did not leave them until he had swept their minds clean of all thoughts, whether pleasant or unpleasant.

Shopping was the topic that now ensued. Under the chaplain's guidance they selected many hideous presents and mementoes – florid little picture-frames that seemed fashioned in gilded pastry; other little frames, more severe, that stood on little easels, and were carven out of oak; a blotting book of vellum; a Dante of the same material; cheap mosaic brooches, which the maids, next Christmas, would never tell from real; pins, pots, heraldic saucers, brown art-photographs; Eros and Psyche in alabaster; St Peter to match – all of which would have cost less in London.

This successful morning left no pleasant impressions on Lucy. She had been a little frightened, both by Miss Lavish and by Mr Eager, she knew not why. And as they frightened her she had, strangely enough, ceased to respect them. She doubted that Miss Lavish was a great artist. She doubted that Mr Eager was as full of spirituality and culture as she had been led to suppose. They were tried by some new test, and they were found wanting. As for Charlotte – as for Charlotte, she was exactly the same. It might be possible to be nice to her; it was impossible to love her.

'The son of a labourer; I happen to know it for a fact. A mechanic of some sort himself when he was young; then he took to writing for the Socialistic press. I came across him at Brixton.'

They were talking about the Emersons.

'How wonderfully people rise in these days!' sighed Miss Bartlett, fingering a model of the leaning Tower of Pisa.

'Generally,' replied Mr Eager, 'one has only sympathy with their success. The desire for education and for social advance – in these things there is something not wholly vile. There are some working men whom one would be very willing to see out here in Florence – little as they would make of it.'

'Is he a journalist now?' Miss Bartlett asked.

'He is not; he made an advantageous marriage.'

He uttered this remark with a voice full of meaning, and ended it with a sigh.

'Oh, so he has a wife.'

'Dead, Miss Bartlett, dead. I wonder – yes, I wonder how he has the effrontery to look me in the face, to dare to claim acquaintance with me. He was in my London parish long ago. The other day in Santa Croce, when he was with Miss Honeychurch, I snubbed him. Let him beware that he does not get more than a snub.'

'What?' cried Lucy, flushing.

'Exposure!' hissed Mr Eager.

He tried to change the subject; but in scoring a dramatic point he had interested his audience more than he had intended. Miss Bartlett was full of very natural curiosity. Lucy, though she wished never to see the Emersons again, was not disposed to condemn them on a single word.

'Do you mean,' she asked, 'that he is an irreligious man? We know that already.'

'Lucy dear –' said Miss Bartlett, gently reproving her cousin's penetration.

'I should be astonished if you knew all. The boy – an innocent child at the time – I will exclude. God knows what his education and his inherited qualities may have made him.'

'Perhaps,' said Miss Bartlett, 'it is something that we had better not hear.'

'To speak plainly,' said Mr Eager, 'it is. I will say no more.'

For the first time Lucy's rebellious thoughts swept out in words – for the first time in her life.

'You have said very little.'

'It was my intention to say very little,' was his frigid reply.

He gazed indignantly at the girl, who met him with equal indignation. She turned towards him from the shop counter; her breast heaved quickly. He observed her brow, and the sudden strength of her lips. It was intolerable that she should disbelieve him.

'Murder, if you want to know,' he cried angrily. 'That man murdered his wife!'

'How?' she retorted.

'To all intents and purposes he murdered her. That day in Santa Croce – did they say anything against me?'

'Not a word, Mr Eager – not a single word.'

'Oh, I thought they had been libelling me to you. But I suppose it is only their personal charms that makes you defend them.'

'I'm not defending them,' said Lucy, losing her courage, and relapsing into the old chaotic methods. 'They're nothing to me.'

'How could you think she was defending them?' said Miss Bartlett, much discomfited by the unpleasant scene. The shopman was possibly listening.

'She will find it difficult. For that man has murdered his wife in the sight of God.'

The addition of God was striking. But the chaplain was really trying to qualify a rash remark. A silence followed which might have been impressive, but was merely awkward. Then Miss Bart-lett hastily purchased the Leaning Tower, and led the way into the street.

'I must be going,' said he, shutting his eyes and taking out his watch.

Miss Bartlett thanked him for his kindness, and spoke with enthusiasm of the approaching drive.

'Drive? Oh, is our drive to come off?'

Lucy was recalled to her manners, and after a little exertion the complacency of Mr Eager was restored.

'Bother the drive!' exclaimed the girl, as soon as he had departed. 'It is just the drive we had arranged with Mr Beebe without any fuss at all. Why should he invite us in that absurd manner? We might as well invite him. We are each paying for ourselves.'

Miss Bartlett, who had intended to lament over the Emersons, was launched by this remark into unexpected thoughts.

'If that is so, dear – if the drive we and Mr Beebe are going with Mr Eager is really the same as the one we were going with Mr Beebe, then I foresee a sad kettle of fish.'

'How?'

'Because Mr Beebe has asked Eleanor Lavish to come, too.'

'That will mean another carriage.'

'Far worse. Mr Eager does not like Eleanor. She knows it herself. The truth must be told: she is too unconventional for him.'

They were now in the newspaper-room at the English bank. Lucy stood by the central table, heedless of *Punch* and the *Graphic*, trying to answer, or at all events to formulate, the questions rioting in her brain. The well-known world had broken up, and there emerged Florence, a magic city where people thought and did the most extraordinary things. Murder, accusations of murder, a lady clinging to one man and being rude to another – were these the daily incidents of her streets? Was there more in her frank beauty than met the eye – the power, perhaps,

to evoke passions, good and bad, and to bring them speedily to
a fulfilment?

Happy Charlotte, who, though greatly troubled over things
that did not matter, seemed oblivious to things that did; who
could conjecture with admirable delicacy 'where things might
lead to', but apparently lost sight of the goal as she approached
it! Now she was crouching in the corner trying to extract a circular note from a kind of linen nosebag which hung in chaste con-
cealment round her neck. She had been told that this was the
only safe way to carry money in Italy; it must only be broached
within the walls of the English bank. As she groped she murmured: 'Whether it is Mr Beebe who forgot to tell Mr Eager, or
Mr Eager who forgot when he told us, or whether they have
decided to leave Eleanor out altogether – which they could
scarcely do – but in any case we must be prepared. It is you they
really want; I am only asked for appearances. You shall go with
the two gentlemen, and I and Eleanor will follow behind. A one-
horse carriage would do for us. Yet how difficult it is!'

'It is indeed,' replied the girl, with a gravity that sounded
sympathetic.

'What do you think about it?' asked Miss Bartlett, flushed
from the struggle, and buttoning up her dress.

'I don't know what I think, nor what I want.'

'Oh dear, Lucy! I do hope Florence isn't boring you. Speak the
word, and, as you know, I would take you to the ends of the
earth tomorrow.'

'Thank you, Charlotte,' said Lucy, and pondered over the
offer.

There were letters for her at the bureau – one from her
brother, full of athletics and biology; one from her mother,
delightful as only her mother's letters could be. She read in it of
the crocuses which had been bought for yellow and were coming
up puce, of the new parlour-maid, who had watered the ferns
with essence of lemonade, of the semi-detached cottages which
were ruining Summer Street, and breaking the heart of Sir Harry

Otway. She recalled the free, pleasant life of her home, where she was allowed to do everything, and where nothing ever happened to her. The road up through the pine-woods, the clean drawing-room, the view over the Sussex Weald – all hung before her bright and distinct, but pathetic as the pictures in a gallery to which, after much experience, a traveller returns.

'And the news?' asked Miss Bartlett.

'Mrs Vyse and her son have gone to Rome,' said Lucy, giving the news that interested her least. 'Do you know the Vyses?'

'Oh, not that way back. We can never have too much of the dear Piazza Signoria.'

'They're nice people, the Vyses. So clever – my idea of what's really clever. Don't you long to be in Rome?'

'I die for it!'

The Piazza Signoria is too stony to be brilliant. It has no grass, no flowers, no frescoes, no glittering walls of marble or comforting patches of ruddy brick. By an odd chance – unless we believe in a presiding genius of place – the statues that relieve its severity suggest, not the innocence of childhood nor the glorious bewilderment of youth, but the conscious achievements of maturity. Perseus and Judith, Hercules and Thusnelda, they have done or suffered something, and, though they are immortal, immortality has come to them after experience, not before. Here, not only in the solitude of Nature, might a hero meet a goddess, or a heroine a god.

'Charlotte!' cried the girl suddenly. 'Here's an idea. What if we popped off to Rome tomorrow – straight – to the Vyses' hotel? For I do know what I want. I'm sick of Florence. Now, you said you'd go to the ends of the earth! Do! Do!'

Miss Bartlett, with equal vivacity, replied:

'Oh, you droll person! Pray, what would become of your drive in the hills?'

They passed together through the gaunt beauty of the square, laughing over the unpractical suggestion.

CHAPTER VI

The Reverend Arthur Beebe, the Reverend Cuthbert Eager,
Mr Emerson, Mr George Emerson, Miss Eleanor Lavish,
Miss Charlotte Bartlett and Miss Lucy Honeychurch Drive
out in Carriages to See a View; Italians Drive them

IT WAS PHAETHON who drove them to Fiesole that memorable day, a youth all irresponsibility and fire, recklessly urging his master's horses up the stony hill. Mr Beebe recognized him at once. Neither the Ages of Faith nor the Age of Doubt had touched him; he was Phaethon in Tuscany driving a cab. And it was Persephone whom he asked leave to pick up on the way, saying that she was his sister – Persephone, tall and slender and pale, returning with the spring to her mother's cottage, and still shading her eyes from the unaccustomed light. To her Mr Eager objected, saying that here was the thin edge of the wedge, and one must guard against imposition. But the ladies interceded, and, when it had been made clear that it was a very great favour, the goddess was allowed to mount beside the god.

Phaethon at once slipped the left rein over her head, thus enabling himself to drive with his arm round her waist. She did not mind. Mr Eager, who sat with his back to the horses, saw nothing of the indecorous proceeding, and continued his conversation with Lucy. The other two occupants of the carriage were old Mr Emerson and Miss Lavish. For a dreadful thing had happened: Mr Beebe, without consulting Mr Eager, had doubled the size of the party. And, though Miss Bartlett and Miss Lavish had planned all the morning how people were to sit, at the critical moment when the carriages came round they lost their heads, and Miss Lavish got in with Lucy, while Miss Bartlett, with George Emerson and Mr Beebe, followed on behind.

It was hard on the poor chaplain to have his *partie carrée* thus transformed. Tea at a Renaissance villa, if he had ever meditated it, was now impossible. Lucy and Miss Bartlett had a certain style about them, and Mr Beebe, though unreliable, was a man of parts. But a shoddy lady writer and a journalist who had murdered his wife in the sight of God – they should enter no villa at his introduction.

Lucy, elegantly dressed in white, sat erect and nervous amid these explosive ingredients, attentive to Mr Eager, repressive towards Miss Lavish, watchful of old Mr Emerson – hitherto fortunately asleep, thanks to a heavy lunch and the drowsy atmosphere of spring. She looked on the expedition as the work of Fate. But for it she would have avoided George Emerson successfully. In an open manner he had shown that he wished to continue their intimacy. She had refused, not because she disliked him, but because she did not know what had happened, and suspected that he did know. And this frightened her.

For the real event – whatever it was – had taken place, not in the Loggia, but by the river. To behave wildly at the sight of death is pardonable. But to discuss it afterwards, to pass from discussion into silence, and through silence into sympathy, that is an error, not of a startled emotion, but of the whole fabric. There was really something blameworthy (she thought) in their joint contemplation of the shadowy stream, in the common impulse which had turned them to the house without the passing of a look or word. This sense of wickedness had been slight at first. She had nearly joined the party to the Torre del Gallo. But each time that she avoided George it became more imperative that she should avoid him again. And now celestial irony, working through her cousin and two clergymen, did not suffer her to leave Florence till she had made this expedition with him through the hills.

Meanwhile Mr Eager held her in civil converse; their little tiff was over.

'So, Miss Honeychurch, you are travelling? As a student of art?'

'Oh, dear me, no – oh no!'

'Perhaps as a student of human nature,' interposed Miss Lavish, 'like myself?'

'Oh no. I am here as a tourist.'

'Oh, indeed,' said Mr Eager. 'Are you indeed? If you will not think me rude, we residents sometimes pity you poor tourists not a little – handed about like a parcel of goods from Venice to Florence, from Florence to Rome, living herded together in pensions or hotels, quite unconscious of anything that is outside Baedeker, their one anxiety to get "done" or "through" and go on somewhere else. The result is, they mix up towns, rivers, palaces in one inextricable whirl. You know the American girl in *Punch* who says: "Say, poppa, what did we see at Rome?" And the father replies: "Why, guess Rome was the place where we saw the yaller dog." There's travelling for you. Ha! ha! ha!'

'I quite agree,' said Miss Lavish, who had several times tried to interrupt his mordant wit. 'The narrowness and superficiality of the Anglo-Saxon tourist is nothing less than a menace.'

'Quite so. Now, the English colony at Florence, Miss Honey-church – and it is of considerable size, though, of course, not all equally – a few are here for trade, for example. But the greater part are students. Lady Helen Laverstock is at present busy over Fra Angelico. I mention her name because we are passing her villa on the left. No, you can only see it if you stand – no, do not stand; you will fall. She is very proud of that thick hedge. Inside, perfect seclusion. One might have gone back six hundred years. Some critics believe that her garden was the scene of *The Decameron*, which lends it an additional interest, does it not?'

'It does indeed!' cried Miss Lavish. 'Tell me, where do they place the scene of that wonderful seventh day?'

But Mr Eager proceeded to tell Miss Honeychurch that on the right lived Mr Someone Something, an American of the best type – so rare! – and that the Somebody Elses were further down the hill. 'Doubtless you know her monographs in the series of "Mediaeval Byways"? He is working at "Gemistus Pletho". Sometimes as I take tea in their beautiful grounds I hear, over the wall, the electric tram squealing up the new road with its load of hot, dusty, unintelligent tourists who are going to "do" Fiesole in an hour in order that they may say they have been there, and I think – I think – I think how little they think what lies so near them.'

During this speech the two figures on the box were sporting with each other disgracefully. Lucy had a spasm of envy. Granted that they wished to misbehave, it was pleasant for them to be able to do so. They were probably the only people enjoying the expedition. The carriage swept with agonizing jolts up through the Piazza of Fiesole and into the Settignano road.

'Piano! Piano!' said Mr Eager, elegantly waving his hand over his head.

'Va bene, signore, va bene, va bene,' crooned the driver, and whipped his horses up again.

Now Mr Eager and Miss Lavish began to talk against each other on the subject of Alessio Baldovinetti. Was he a cause of the Renaissance, or was he one of its manifestations? The other carriage was left behind. As the pace increased to a gallop the large, slumbering form of Mr Emerson was thrown against the chaplain with the regularity of a machine.

'Piano! Piano!' said he, with a martyred look at Lucy.

An extra lurch made him turn angrily in his seat. Phaethon, who for some time had been endeavouring to kiss Persephone, had just succeeded.

A little scene ensued, which, as Miss Bartlett said afterwards, was most unpleasant. The horses were stopped, the lovers were ordered to disentangle themselves, the boy was to lose his *pourboire*, the girl was immediately to get down.

'She is my sister,' said he, turning round on them with piteous eyes.

Mr Eager took the trouble to tell him that he was a liar. Phaethon hung down his head, not at the matter of the accusation, but at its manner. At this point Mr Emerson, whom the shock of stopping had awoken, declared that the lovers must on no account be separated, and patted them on the back to signify his approval. And Miss Lavish, though unwilling to ally with him, felt bound to support the cause of bohemianism.

'Most certainly I would let them be,' she cried. 'But I dare say I shall receive scant support. I have always flown in the face of the conventions all my life. This is what *I* call an adventure.'

'We must not submit,' said Mr Eager. 'I knew he was trying it on. He is treating us as if we were a party of Cook's tourists.'

'Surely no!' said Miss Lavish, her ardour visibly decreasing.

The other carriage had drawn up behind, and sensible Mr Beebe called out that after this warning the couple would be sure to behave themselves properly.

'Leave them alone,' Mr Emerson begged the chaplain, of whom he stood in no awe. 'Do we find happiness so often that we should turn it off the box when it happens to sit there? To be driven by lovers – a king might envy us, and if we part them it's more like sacrilege than anything I know.'

Here the voice of Miss Bartlett was heard saying that a crowd had begun to collect.

Mr Eager, who suffered from an over-fluent tongue rather than a resolute will, was determined to make himself heard. He addressed the driver again. Italian in the mouth of Italians is a deep-voiced stream, with unexpected cataracts and boulders to preserve it from monotony. In Mr Eager's mouth it resembled nothing so much as an acid whistling fountain which played ever higher and higher, and quicker and quicker, and more and more shrilly, till abruptly it was turned off with a click.

'Signorina!' said the man to Lucy, when the display had ceased. Why should he appeal to Lucy?

'Signorina!' echoed Persephone in her glorious contralto. She pointed at the other carriage. Why?

For a moment the two girls looked at each other. Then Persephone got down from the box.

'Victory at last!' said Mr Eager, smiting his hands together as the carriages started again.

'It is not victory,' said Mr Emerson. 'It is defeat. You have parted two people who were happy.'

Mr Eager shut his eyes. He was obliged to sit next to Mr Emerson, but he would not speak to him. The old man was refreshed by sleep, and took up the matter warmly. He commanded Lucy to agree with him; he shouted for support to his son.

'We have tried to buy what cannot be bought with money. He has bargained to drive us, and he is doing it. We have no rights over his soul.'

Miss Lavish frowned. It is hard when a person you have classed as typically British speaks out of his character.

'He was not driving us well,' she said. 'He jolted us.'

'That I deny. It was as restful as sleeping. Aha! He is jolting us now. Can you wonder? He would like to throw us out, and most certainly he is justified. And if I were superstitious I'd be frightened of the girl, too. It doesn't do to injure young people. Have you ever heard of Lorenzo de' Medici?'

Miss Lavish bristled.

'Most certainly I have. Do you refer to Lorenzo il Magnifico, or to Lorenzo, Duke of Urbino, or to Lorenzo surnamed Lorenzino on account of his diminutive stature?'

'The Lord knows. Possibly he does know, for I refer to Lorenzo the poet. He wrote a line – so I heard yesterday – which runs like this: "Don't go fighting against the spring." '

Mr Eager could not resist the opportunity for erudition.

'Non fate guerra al Maggio,' he murmured. ' "War not with the May" would render a correct meaning.'

'The point is, we have warred with it. Look.' He pointed to the Val d'Arno, which was visible far below them, through the budding trees. 'Fifty miles of spring, and we've come up to admire them. Do you suppose there's any difference between spring in nature and spring in man? But there we go, praising the one and condemning the other as improper, ashamed that the same laws work eternally through both.'

No one encouraged him to talk. Presently Mr Eager gave a

signal for the carriages to stop, and marshalled the party for their
ramble on the hill. A hollow like a great amphitheatre, full of
terraced steps and misty olives, now lay between them and the
heights of Fiesole, and the road, still following its curve, was
about to sweep on to a promontory which stood out into the
plain. It was this promontory, uncultivated, wet, covered with
bushes and occasional trees, which had caught the fancy of
Alessio Baldovinetti nearly five hundred years before. He had
ascended it, that diligent and rather obscure master, possibly
with an eye to business, possibly for the joy of ascending. Standing there, he had seen that view of the Val d'Arno and distant
Florence, which he afterwards had introduced not very effec-
tively into his work. But where exactly had he stood? That was
the question which Mr Eager hoped to solve now. And Miss
Lavish, whose nature was attracted by anything problematical,
had become equally enthusiastic.

But it is not easy to carry the pictures of Alessio Baldovinetti in
your head, even if you have remembered to look at them before
starting. And the haze in the valley increased the difficulty of the
quest. The party sprang about from tuft to tuft of grass, their
anxiety to keep together being only equalled by their desire to
go in different directions. Finally they split into groups. Lucy
clung to Miss Bartlett and Miss Lavish; the Emersons returned
to hold laborious converse with the drivers; while the two clergymen, who were expected to have topics in common, were left to
each other.

The two elder ladies soon threw off the mask. In the audible
whisper that was now so familiar to Lucy they began to discuss,
not Alessio Baldovinetti, but the drive. Miss Bartlett had asked
Mr George Emerson what his profession was, and he had
answered 'the railway'. She was very sorry that she had asked
him. She had no idea that it would be such a dreadful answer,
or she would not have asked him. Mr Beebe had turned the conversation so cleverly, and she hoped that the young man was not
very much hurt at her asking him.

'The railway!' gasped Miss Lavish. 'Oh, but I shall die! Of course it was the railway!' She could not control her mirth. 'He is the image of a porter – on, on the South-Eastern.'

'Eleanor, be quiet,' plucking at her vivacious companion. 'Hush! They'll hear – the Emersons –'

'I can't stop. Let me go my wicked way. A porter –'

'Eleanor!'

'I'm sure it's all right,' put in Lucy. 'The Emersons won't hear, and they wouldn't mind if they did.'

Miss Lavish did not seem pleased at this.

'Miss Honeychurch listening!' she said rather crossly. 'Pouf! Wouf! You naughty girl! Go away!'

'Oh, Lucy, you ought to be with Mr Eager, I'm sure.'

'I can't find them now, and I don't want to either.'

'Mr Eager will be offended. It is your party.'

'Please, I'd rather stop here with you.'

'No, I agree,' said Miss Lavish. 'It's like a school feast; the boys have got separated from the girls. Miss Lucy, you are to go. We wish to converse on high topics unsuited for your ear.'

The girl was stubborn. As her time at Florence drew to its close she was only at ease amongst those to whom she felt indifferent. Such a one was Miss Lavish, and such for the moment was Charlotte. She wished she had not called attention to herself; they were both annoyed at her remark and seemed determined to get rid of her.

'How tired one gets,' said Miss Bartlett. 'Oh, I do wish Freddy and your mother could be here.'

Unselfishness with Miss Bartlett had entirely usurped the functions of enthusiasm. Lucy did not look at the view either. She would not enjoy anything till she was safe at Rome.

'Then sit you down,' said Miss Lavish. 'Observe my foresight.'

With many a smile she produced two of those mackintosh squares that protect the frame of the tourist from damp grass or cold marble steps. She sat on one; who was to sit on the other?

'Lucy; without a moment's doubt, Lucy. The ground will do

for me. Really I have not had rheumatism for years. If I do feel it coming on I shall stand. Imagine your mother's feelings if I let you sit in the wet in your white linen.' She sat down heavily where the ground looked particularly moist. 'Here we are, all settled delightfully. Even if my dress is thinner it will not show so much, being brown. Sit down, dear; you are too unselfish; you don't assert yourself enough.' She cleared her throat. 'Now don't be alarmed; this isn't a cold. It's the tiniest cough, and I have had it three days. It's nothing to do with sitting here at all.'

There was only one way of treating the situation. At the end of five minutes Lucy departed in search of Mr Beebe and Mr Eager, vanquished by the mackintosh square.

She addressed herself to the drivers, who were sprawling in the carriages, perfuming the cushions with cigars. The miscreant, a bony young man scorched black by the sun, rose to greet her with the courtesy of a host and the assurance of a relative.

'*Dove?*' said Lucy, after much anxious thought.

His face lit up. Of course he knew where. Not so far either. His arm swept three-fourths of the horizon. He should just think he did know where. He pressed his finger-tips to his forehead and then pushed them towards her, as if oozing with visible extract of knowledge.

More seemed necessary. What was the Italian for 'clergymen'?

'Dove buoni uomini?' said she at last.

Good? Scarcely the adjective for those noble beings! He showed her his cigar.

'Uno – piu – piccolo,' was her next remark, implying 'Has the cigar been given to you by Mr Beebe, the smaller of the two good men?'

She was correct as usual. He tied the horse to a tree, kicked it to make it stay quiet, dusted the carriage, arranged his hair, remoulded his hat, encouraged his moustache, and in rather less than a quarter of a minute was ready to conduct her. Italians are born knowing the way. It would seem that the whole earth lay before them, not as a map, but as a chessboard, whereon they continually behold the changing pieces as well as the squares. Anyone can find places, but the finding of people is a gift from God.

He only stopped once, to pick her some great blue violets. She thanked him with real pleasure. In the company of this common man the world was beautiful and direct. For the first time she felt the influence of spring. His arm swept the horizon gracefully; violets, like other things, existed in great profusion there; would she like to see them?

'Ma buoni uomini.'

He bowed. Certainly. Good men first, violets afterwards. They proceeded briskly through the undergrowth, which became thicker and thicker. They were nearing the edge of the promontory, and the view was stealing round them, but the brown network of the bushes shattered it into countless pieces. He was occupied in his cigar, and in holding back the pliant boughs. She was rejoicing in her escape from dullness. Not a step, not a twig, was unimportant to her.

'What is that?'

There was a voice in the wood, in the distance behind them. The voice of Mr Eager? He shrugged his shoulders. An Italian's ignorance is sometimes more remarkable than his knowledge. She could not make him understand that perhaps they had missed the clergymen. The view was forming at last; she could discern the river, the golden plain, other hills.

'Eccolo!' he exclaimed.

At the same moment the ground gave way, and with a cry she fell out of the wood. Light and beauty enveloped her. She had fallen onto a little open terrace, which was covered with violets from end to end.

'Courage!' cried her companion, now standing some six feet above. 'Courage and love.'

She did not answer. From her feet the ground sloped sharply into the view, and violets ran down in rivulets and streams and cataracts, irrigating the hillside with blue, eddying round the tree stems, collecting into pools in the hollows, covering the grass with spots of azure foam. But never again were they in such profusion; this terrace was the well-head, the primal source whence beauty gushed out to water the earth.

Standing at its brink, like a swimmer who prepares, was the good man. But he was not the good man that she had expected, and he was alone.

George had turned at the sound of her arrival. For a moment he contemplated her, as one who had fallen out of heaven. He saw radiant joy in her face, he saw the flowers beat against her dress in blue waves. The bushes above them closed. He stepped quickly forward and kissed her.

Before she could speak, almost before she could feel, a voice called, 'Lucy! Lucy! Lucy!' The silence of life had been broken by Miss Bartlett, who stood brown against the view.

CHAPTER VII

They Return

SOME COMPLICATED GAME had been playing up and down the hillside all the afternoon. What it was and exactly how the players had sided, Lucy was slow to discover. Mr Eager had met them with a questioning eye. Charlotte had repulsed him with much small-talk. Mr Emerson, seeking his son, was told whereabouts to find him. Mr Beebc, who wore the heated aspect of a neutral, was bidden to collect the factions for the return home. There was a general sense of groping and bewilderment. Pan had been amongst them – not the great god Pan, who has been buried these two thousand years, but the little god Pan, who presides over social contretemps and unsuccessful picnics. Mr Beebe had lost everyone, and had consumed in solitude the tea-basket which he had brought up as a pleasant surprise. Miss Lavish had lost Miss Bartlett. Lucy had lost Mr Eager. Mr Emerson had lost George. Miss Bartlett had lost a mackintosh square. Phaethon had lost the game.

That last fact was undeniable. He climbed onto the box shivering, with his collar up, prophesying the swift approach of bad weather.

'Let us go immediately,' he told them. 'The signorino will walk.'

'All the way? He will be hours,' said Mr Beebe.

'Apparently. I told him it was unwise.' He would look no one in the face; perhaps defeat was particularly mortifying for him. He alone had played skilfully, using the whole of his instinct, while the others had used scraps of their intelligence. He alone had divined what things were, and what he wished them to be. He alone had interpreted the message that Lucy had received five days before from the lips of a dying man. Persephone, who spends half her life in the grave – she could interpret it also. Not so these English. They gain knowledge slowly, and perhaps too late.

The thoughts of a cab-driver, however just, seldom affect the lives of his employers. He was the most competent of Miss Bartlett's opponents, but infinitely the least dangerous. Once back in the town, he and his insight and his knowledge would trouble English ladies no more. Of course, it was most unpleasant; she had seen his black head in the bushes; he might make a tavern story out of it. But, after all, what have we to do with taverns? Real menace belongs to the drawing-room. It was of drawing-room people that Miss Bartlett thought as she journeyed downwards towards the fading sun. Lucy sat beside her; Mr Eager sat opposite, trying to catch her eye; he was vaguely suspicious. They spoke of Alessio Baldovinetti.

Rain and darkness came on together. The two ladies huddled together under an inadequate parasol. There was a lightning flash, and Miss Lavish, who was nervous, screamed from the carriage in front. At the next flash, Lucy screamed also. Mr Eager addressed her professionally.

'Courage, Miss Honeychurch, courage and faith. If I might say so, there is something almost blasphemous in this horror of the elements. Are we seriously to suppose that all these clouds, all this immense electrical display, is simply called into existence to extinguish you or me?'

'No – of course –'

'Even from the scientific standpoint the chances against our being struck are enormous. The steel knives, the only articles which might attract the current, are in the other carriage. And, in any case, we are infinitely safer than if we were walking. Courage – courage and faith.'

Under the rug, Lucy felt the kindly pressure of her cousin's hand. At times our need for a sympathetic gesture is so great that we care not what exactly it signifies or how much we may have to pay for it afterwards. Miss Bartlett, by this timely exercise of her muscles, gained more than she would have got in hours of preaching or cross-examination.

She renewed it when the two carriages stopped, half into Florence.

'Mr Eager!' called Mr Beebe. 'We want your assistance. Will you interpret for us?'

'George!' cried Mr Emerson. 'Ask your driver which way George went. The boy may lose his way. He may be killed.'

'Go, Mr Eager,' said Miss Bartlett. 'No, don't ask our driver; our driver is no help. Go and support poor Mr Beebe; he is nearly demented.'

'He may be killed!' cried the old man. 'He may be killed!'

'Typical behaviour,' said the chaplain, as he quitted the carriage. 'In the presence of reality that kind of person invariably breaks down.'

'What does he know?' whispered Lucy as soon as they were alone. 'Charlotte, how much does Mr Eager know?'

'Nothing, dearest; he knows nothing. But' – she pointed at the driver – '*he* knows everything. Dearest, had we better? Shall I?' She took out her purse. 'It is dreadful to be entangled with low-class people. He saw it all.' Tapping Phaethon's back with her guidebook, she said, 'Silenzio!' and offered him a franc.

'Va bene,' he replied, and accepted it. As well this ending to his day as any. But Lucy, a mortal maid, was disappointed in him.

There was an explosion up the road. The storm had struck the overhead wire of the tramline, and one of the great supports had fallen. If they had not stopped perhaps they might have been hurt. They chose to regard it as a miraculous preservation, and the floods of love and sincerity, which might fructify every hour of life, burst forth in tumult. They descended from the carriages; they embraced each other. It was as joyful to be forgiven past unworthinesses as to forgive them. For a moment they realized vast possibilities of good.

The older people recovered quickly. In the very height of their emotion they knew it to be unmanly or unladylike. Miss Lavish calculated that, even if they had continued, they would not have been caught in the accident. Mr Eager mumbled a temperate prayer. But the drivers, through miles of dark squalid road, poured out their souls to the dryads and the saints, and Lucy poured out hers to her cousin.

'Charlotte, dear Charlotte, kiss me. Kiss me again. Only you can understand me. You warned me to be careful. And I – I thought I was developing.'

'Do not cry, dearest. Take your time.'

'I have been obstinate and silly – worse than you know, far worse. Once by the river – oh, but he isn't killed – he wouldn't be killed, would he?'

The thought disturbed her repentance. As a matter of fact, the storm was worst along the road; but she had been near danger, and so she thought it must be near to everyone.

'I trust not. One would always pray against that.'

'He is really – I think he was taken by surprise, just as I was before. But this time I'm not to blame; I do want you to believe that. I simply slipped into those violets. No, I want to be really truthful. I am a little to blame. I had silly thoughts. The sky, you know, was gold, and the ground all blue, and for a moment he looked like someone in a book.'

'In a book?'

'Heroes – gods – the nonsense of schoolgirls.'

'And then?'

'But, Charlotte, you know what happened then.'

Miss Bartlett was silent. Indeed, she had little more to learn. With a certain amount of insight she drew her young cousin affectionately to her. All the way back Lucy's body was shaken by deep sighs, which nothing could repress.

'I want to be truthful,' she whispered. 'It is so hard to be absolutely truthful.'

'Don't be troubled, dearest. Wait till you are calmer. We will talk it over before bed-time in my room.'

So they re-entered the city with hands clasped. It was a shock to the girl to find how far emotion had ebbed in others. The storm had ceased, and Mr Emerson was easier about his son. Mr Beebe had regained good humour, and Mr Eager was already snubbing Miss Lavish. Charlotte alone she was sure of – Charlotte, whose exterior concealed so much insight and love.

The luxury of self-exposure kept her almost happy through the long evening. She thought not so much of what had happened as of how she should describe it. All her sensations, her spasms of courage, her moments of unreasonable joy, her mysterious discontent, should be carefully laid before her cousin. And together in divine confidence they would disentangle and interpret them all.

'At last,' thought she, 'I shall understand myself. I shan't again be troubled by things that come out of nothing, and mean I don't know what.'

Miss Alan asked her to play. She refused vehemently. Music seemed to her the employment of a child. She sat close to her cousin, who, with commendable patience, was listening to a long story about lost luggage. When it was over she capped it by a story of her own. Lucy became rather hysterical with the delay. In vain she tried to check, or at all events to accelerate, the tale. It was not till a late hour that Miss Bartlett had recovered her luggage and could say in her usual tone of gentle reproach: 'Well, dear, I at all events am ready for Bedfordshire. Come into my room, and I will give a good brush to your hair.'

With some solemnity the door was shut, and a cane chair placed for the girl. Then Miss Bartlett said:

'So what is to be done?'

She was unprepared for the question. It had not occurred to her that she would have to do anything. A detailed exhibition of her emotions was all that she had counted upon.

'What is to be done? A point, dearest, which you alone can settle.'

The rain was streaming down the black windows, and the great room felt damp and chilly. One candle burned trembling on the chest of drawers close to Miss Bartlett's toque, which cast monstrous and fantastic shadows on the bolted door. A tram roared by in the dark, and Lucy felt unaccountably sad, though she had long since dried her eyes. She lifted them to the ceiling, where the griffins and bassoons were colourless and vague, the very ghosts of joy.

'It has been raining for nearly four hours,' she said at last.

Miss Bartlett ignored the remark.

'How do you propose to silence him?'

'The driver?'

'My dear girl, no; Mr George Emerson.'

Lucy began to pace up and down the room.

'I don't understand,' she said at last.

She understood very well, but she no longer wished to be absolutely truthful.

'How are you going to stop him talking about it?'

'I have a feeling that talk is a thing he will never do.'

'I, too, intend to judge him charitably. But unfortunately I have met the type before. They seldom keep their exploits to themselves.'

'Exploits?' cried Lucy, wincing under the horrible plural.

'My poor dear, did you suppose that this was his first? Come here and listen to me. I am only gathering it from his own remarks. Do you remember that day at lunch when he argued with Miss Alan that liking one person is an extra reason for liking another?'

'Yes,' said Lucy, whom at the time the argument had pleased.

'Well, I am no prude. There is no need to call him a wicked young man, but obviously he is thoroughly unrefined. Let us put it down to his deplorable antecedents and education, if you wish. But we are no further on with our question. What do you propose to do?'

An idea rushed across Lucy's brain, which, had she thought of it sooner and made it part of her, might have proved victorious.

'I propose to speak to him,' said she.

Miss Bartlett uttered a cry of genuine alarm.

'You see, Charlotte, your kindness – I shall never forget it. But – as you said – it is my affair. Mine and his.'

'And you are going to *implore* him, to *beg* him to keep silence?'

'Certainly not. There would be no difficulty. Whatever you ask him he answers, yes or no; then it is over. I have been frightened of him. But now I am not one little bit.'

'But we fear him for you, dear. You are so young and inexperienced, you have lived among such nice people, that you cannot realize what men can be – how they can take a brutal pleasure in insulting a woman whom her sex does not protect and rally round. This afternoon, for example, if I had not arrived, what would have happened?'

'I can't think,' said Lucy gravely.

Something in her voice made Miss Bartlett repeat her question, intoning it more vigorously.

'What would have happened if I hadn't arrived?'

'I can't think,' said Lucy again.

'When he insulted you, how would you have replied?'

'I hadn't time to think. You came.'

'Yes, but won't you tell me now what you would have done?'

'I should have –' She checked herself, and broke the sentence off. She went up to the dripping window and strained her eyes into the darkness. She could not think what she would have done.

'Come away from the window, dear,' said Miss Bartlett. 'You will be seen from the road.'

Lucy obeyed. She was in her cousin's power. She could not modulate out of the key of self-abasement in which she had started. Neither of them referred again to her suggestion that she should speak to George and settle the matter, whatever it was, with him.

Miss Bartlett became plaintive.

'O for a real man! We are only two women, you and I. Mr Beebe is hopeless. There is Mr Eager, but you do not trust him.

O for your brother! He is young, but I know that his sister's insult would rouse in him a very lion. Thank God, chivalry is not yet dead. There are still left some men who can reverence woman.'

As she spoke, she pulled off her rings, of which she wore several, and ranged them upon the pin-cushion. Then she blew into her gloves and said:

'It will be a push to catch the morning train, but we must try.'

'What train?'

'The train to Rome.' She looked at her gloves critically.

The girl received the announcement as easily as it had been given.

'When does the train to Rome go?'

'At eight.'

'Signora Bertolini would be upset.'

'We must face that,' said Miss Bartlett, not liking to say that she had given notice already.

'She will make us pay for a whole week's pension.'

'I expect she will. However, we shall be much more comfortable at the Vyses' hotel. Isn't afternoon tea given there for nothing?'

'Yes, but they pay extra for wine.'

After this remark she remained motionless and silent. To her tired eyes Charlotte throbbed and swelled like a ghostly figure in a dream.

They began to sort their clothes for packing, for there was no time to lose, if they were to catch the train to Rome. Lucy, when admonished, began to move to and fro between the rooms, more conscious of the discomforts of packing by candlelight than of a subtler ill. Charlotte, who was practical without ability, knelt by the side of an empty trunk, vainly endeavouring to pave it with books of varying thickness and size. She gave two or three sighs, for the stooping posture hurt her back, and, for all her diplomacy, she felt that she was growing old. The girl heard her as she entered the room, and was seized with one of those emotional impulses to which she could never attribute a cause.

She only felt that the candle would burn better, the packing go easier, the world be happier, if she could give and receive some human love. The impulse had come before today, but never so strongly. She knelt down by her cousin's side and took her in her arms.

Miss Bartlett returned the embrace with tenderness and warmth. But she was not a stupid woman, and she knew perfectly well that Lucy did not love her, but needed her to love. For it was in ominous tones that she said, after a long pause:

'Dearest Lucy, how will you ever forgive me?'

Lucy was on her guard at once, knowing by bitter experience what forgiving Miss Bartlett meant. Her emotion relaxed; she modified her embrace a little, and she said:

'Charlotte dear, what do you mean? As if I have anything to forgive!'

'You have a great deal, and I have a very great deal to forgive myself, too. I know well how much I vex you at every turn.'

'But no –'

Miss Bartlett assumed her favourite role, that of the prematurely aged martyr.

'Ah, but yes! I feel that our tour together is hardly the success I had hoped. I might have known it would not do. You want someone younger and stronger and more in sympathy with you. I am too uninteresting and old-fashioned – only fit to pack and unpack your things.'

'Please –'

'My only consolation was that you found people more to your taste, and were often able to leave me at home. I had my own poor ideas of what a lady ought to do, but I hope I did not inflict them on you more than was necessary. You had your own way about these rooms, at all events.'

'You mustn't say these things,' said Lucy softly.

She still clung to the hope that she and Charlotte loved each other, heart and soul. They continued to pack in silence.

'I have been a failure,' said Miss Bartlett, as she struggled with the straps of Lucy's trunk instead of strapping her own. 'Failed to make you happy; failed in my duty to your mother. She has been so generous to me; I shall never face her again after this disaster.'

'But mother will understand. It is not your fault, this trouble, and it isn't a disaster either.'

'It is my fault, it is a disaster. She will never forgive me, and rightly. For instance, what right had I to make friends with Miss Lavish?'

'Every right.'

'When I was here for your sake? If I have vexed you it is equally true that I have neglected you. Your mother will see this as clearly as I do, when you tell her.'

Lucy, from a cowardly wish to improve the situation, said: 'Why need mother hear of it?'

'But you tell her everything?'

'I suppose I do generally.'

'I dare not break your confidence. There is something sacred in it. Unless you feel that it is a thing you could not tell her.'

The girl would not be degraded to this.

'Naturally I should have told her. But in case she should blame you in any way, I promise I will not. I am very willing not to. I will never speak of it either to her or to anyone.'

Her promise brought the long-drawn interview to a sudden close. Miss Bartlett pecked her smartly on both cheeks, wished her goodnight, and sent her to her own room.

For a moment the original trouble was in the background. George would seem to have behaved like a cad throughout; perhaps that was the view which one would take eventually. At present she neither acquitted nor condemned him; she did not pass judgement. At the moment when she was about to judge him her cousin's voice had intervened, and, ever since, it was Miss Bartlett who had dominated; Miss Bartlett who, even now, could be heard sighing into a crack in the partition wall; Miss Bartlett who had really been neither pliable nor humble nor inconsistent. She had worked like a great artist; for a time – indeed, for years – she had been meaningless, but at the end there was presented to the girl the complete picture of a cheerless, loveless world in which the young rush to destruction until they learn better – a shamefaced world of precautions and barriers which may avert evil, but which do not seem to bring good, if we may judge from those who have used them most.

Lucy was suffering from the most grievous wrong which this world has yet discovered: diplomatic advantage had been taken of her sincerity, of her craving for sympathy and love. Such a wrong is not easily forgotten. Never again did she expose herself without due consideration and precaution against rebuff. And such a wrong may react disastrously upon the soul.

The doorbell rang, and she started to the shutters. Before she reached them she hesitated, turned, and blew out the candle. Thus it was that, though she saw someone standing in the wet below, he, though he looked up, did not see her.

To reach his room he had to go by hers. She was still dressed. It struck her that she might slip into the passage and just say that she would be gone before he was up, and that their extraordinary intercourse was over.

Whether she would have dared to do this was never proved. At the critical moment Miss Bartlett opened her own door, and her voice said:

'I wish one word with you in the drawing-room, Mr Emerson, please.'

Soon their footsteps returned, and Miss Bartlett said: 'Goodnight, Mr Emerson.'

His heavy, tired breathing was the only reply; the chaperon had done her work.

Lucy cried aloud: 'It isn't true. It can't all be true. I want not to be muddled. I want to grow older quickly.'

Miss Bartlett tapped on the wall.

'Go to bed at once, dear. You need all the rest you can get.'

In the morning they left for Rome.

PART TWO

CHAPTER VIII

Medieval

THE DRAWING-ROOM curtains at Windy Corner had been pulled to meet, for the carpet was new and deserved protection from the August sun. They were heavy curtains, reaching almost to the ground, and the light that filtered through them was subdued and varied. A poet – none was present – might have quoted, 'Life like a dome of many-coloured glass', or might have compared the curtains to sluice-gates, lowered against the intolerable tides of heaven. Without was poured a sea of radiance; within, the glory, though visible, was tempered to the capacities of man.

Two pleasant people sat in the room. One – a boy of nineteen – was studying a small manual of anatomy, and peering occasionally at a bone which lay upon the piano. From time to time he bounced in his chair and puffed and groaned, for the day was hot and the print small, and the human frame fearfully made; and his mother, who was writing a letter, did continually read out to him what she had written. And continually did she rise from her seat and part the curtains so that a rivulet of light fell across the carpet, and make the remark that they were still there.

'Where aren't they?' said the boy, who was Freddy, Lucy's brother. 'I tell you I'm getting fairly sick.'

'For goodness' sake go out of my drawing-room, then!' cried Mrs Honeychurch, who hoped to cure her children of slang by taking it literally.

Freddy did not move or reply.

'I think things are coming to a head,' she observed, rather wanting her son's opinion on the situation if she could obtain it without undue supplication.

'Time they did.'

'I am glad that Cecil is asking her this once more.'

'It's his third go, isn't it?'

'Freddy, I do call the way you talk unkind.'

'I didn't mean to be unkind.' Then he added: 'But I do think Lucy might have got this off her chest in Italy. I don't know how girls manage things, but she can't have said "No" properly before, or she wouldn't have to say it again now. Over the whole thing – I can't explain – I do feel so uncomfortable.'

'Do you indeed, dear? How interesting!'

'I feel – never mind.'

He returned to his work.

'Just listen to what I have written to Mrs Vyse. I said: "Dear Mrs Vyse –" '

'Yes, mother, you told me. A jolly good letter.'

'I said: "Dear Mrs Vyse, Cecil has just asked my permission about it, and I should be delighted, if Lucy wishes it. But –" ' She stopped reading. 'I was rather amused at Cecil asking my permission at all. He has always gone in for unconventionality, and parents nowhere, and so forth. When it comes to the point, he can't get on without me.'

'Nor me.'

'You?'

Freddy nodded.

'What do you mean?'

'He asked me for my permission also.'

She exclaimed: 'How very odd of him!'

'Why so?' asked the son and heir. 'Why shouldn't my permission be asked?'

'What do you know about Lucy or girls or anything? What ever did you say?'

'I said to Cecil, "Take her or leave her; it's no business of mine!" '

'What a helpful answer!' But her own answer, though more normal in its wording, had been to the same effect.

'The bother is this,' began Freddy.

Then he took up his work again, too shy to say what the bother was. Mrs Honeychurch went back to the window.

'Freddy, you must come. There they still are!'

'I don't see you ought to go peeping like that.'

'Peeping like that! Can't I look out of my own window?'

But she returned to the writing-table, observing, as she passed her son, 'Still page 322?' Freddy snorted, and turned over two leaves. For a brief space they were silent. Close by, beyond the curtains, the gentle murmur of a long conversation had never ceased.

'The bother is this: I have put my foot in it with Cecil most awfully.' He gave a nervous gulp. 'Not content with "permission", which I did give – that is to say, I said, "I don't mind" – well, not content with that, he wanted to know whether I wasn't off my head with joy. He practically put it like this: Wasn't it a splendid thing for Lucy and for Windy Corner generally if he married her? And he would have an answer – he said it would strengthen his hand.'

'I hope you gave a careful answer, dear.'

'I answered "No",' said the boy, grinding his teeth. 'There! Fly into a stew! I can't help it – I had to say it. I had to say no. He ought never to have asked me.'

'Ridiculous child!' cried his mother. 'You think you're so holy and truthful, but really it's only abominable conceit. Do you suppose that a man like Cecil would take the slightest notice of anything you say? I hope he boxed your ears. How dare you say no?'

'Oh, do keep quiet, mother! I had to say no when I couldn't say yes. I tried to laugh as if I didn't mean what I said, and, as Cecil laughed too, and went away, it may be all right. But I feel my foot's in it. Oh, do keep quiet, though, and let a man do some work.'

'No,' said Mrs Honeychurch, with the air of one who had considered the subject, 'I shall not keep quiet. You know all that has passed between them in Rome; you know why he is down here, and yet you deliberately insult him, and try to turn him out of my house.'

'Not a bit!' he pleaded. 'I only let out I didn't like him. I don't hate him, but I don't like him. What I mind is that he'll tell Lucy.'

He glanced at the curtains dismally.

'Well, *I* like him,' said Mrs Honeychurch. 'I know his mother; he's good, he's clever, he's rich, he's well connected – oh, you needn't kick the piano! He's well connected – I'll say it again if you like: he's well connected.' She paused, as if rehearsing her eulogy, but her face remained dissatisfied. She added: 'And he has beautiful manners.'

'I liked him till just now. I suppose it's having him spoiling Lucy's first week at home; and it's also something that Mr Beebe said, not knowing.'

'Mr Beebe?' said his mother, trying to conceal her interest. 'I don't see how Mr Beebe comes in.'

'You know Mr Beebe's funny way, when you never quite know what he means. He said: "Mr Vyse is an ideal bachelor." I was very cute. I asked him what he meant. He said: "Oh, he's like me – better detached." I couldn't make him say any more, but it set me thinking. Since Cecil has come after Lucy he hasn't been so pleasant, at least – I can't explain.'

'You never can, dear. But I can. You are jealous of Cecil because he may stop Lucy knitting you silk ties.'

The explanation seemed plausible, and Freddy tried to accept it. But at the back of his brain there lurked a dim mistrust. Cecil praised one too much for being athletic. Was that it? Cecil made one talk in his way, instead of letting one talk in one's own way. This tired one. Was that it? And Cecil was the kind of fellow who would never wear another fellow's cap. Unaware of his own profundity, Freddy checked himself. He must be jealous, or he would not dislike a man for such foolish reasons.

'Will this do?' called his mother. ' "Dear Mrs Vyse, Cecil has just asked my permission about it, and I should be delighted if Lucy wishes it." Then I put in at the top, "and I have told Lucy so." I must write the letter out again – "and I have told Lucy so. But Lucy seems very uncertain, and in these days young people must decide for themselves." I said that because I didn't want Mrs Vyse to think us old-fashioned. She goes in for lectures and improving her mind, and all the time a thick layer of flue under the beds, and the maids' dirty thumb-marks where you turn on the electric light. She keeps that flat abominably –'

'Suppose Lucy marries Cecil, would she live in a flat, or in the country?'

'Don't interrupt so foolishly. Where was I? Oh yes – "Young people must decide for themselves. I know that Lucy likes your son, because she tells me everything, and she wrote to me from Rome when he asked her first." No, I'll cross that last bit out – it looks patronizing. I'll stop at "because she tells me everything". Or shall I cross that out, too?'

'Cross it out, too,' said Freddy.

Mrs Honeychurch left it in.

'Then the whole thing runs: "Dear Mrs Vyse, Cecil has just asked my permission about it, and I should be delighted if Lucy wishes it, and I have told Lucy so. But Lucy seems very uncertain, and in these days young people must decide for themselves. I know that Lucy likes your son, because she tells me everything. But I do not know –"'

'Look out!' cried Freddy.

The curtains parted.

Cecil's first movement was one of irritation. He couldn't bear the Honeychurch habit of sitting in the dark to save the furniture. Instinctively he gave the curtains a twitch, and sent them swinging down their poles. Light entered. There was revealed a terrace, such as is owned by many villas, with trees each side of it, and on it a little rustic seat, and two flower-beds. But it was transfigured by the view beyond, for Windy Corner was built on the range that overlooks the Sussex Weald. Lucy, who was in the little seat, seemed on the edge of a green magic carpet which hovered in the air above the tremulous world.

Cecil entered.

Appearing thus late in the story, Cecil must be at once described. He was medieval. Like a Gothic statue. Tall and refined, with shoulders that seemed braced square by an effort of the will, and a head that was tilted a little higher than the usual level of vision, he resembled those fastidious saints who guard the portals of a French cathedral. Well educated, well endowed, and not deficient physically, he remained in the grip of a certain devil whom the modern world knows as self-consciousness, and whom the medieval, with dimmer vision, worshipped as asceticism. A Gothic statue implies celibacy, just as a Greek statue implies fruition, and perhaps this was what Mr Beebe meant. And Freddy, who ignored history and art, perhaps meant the same when he failed to imagine Cecil wearing another fellow's cap.

Mrs Honeychurch left her letter on the writing-table and moved towards her young acquaintance.

'Oh, Cecil!' she exclaimed – 'oh, Cecil, do tell me!'

'I promessi sposi,' said he.

They stared at him anxiously.

'She has accepted me,' he said, and the sound of the thing in English made him flush and smile with pleasure, and look more human.

'I am so glad,' said Mrs Honeychurch, while Freddy proffered a hand that was yellow with chemicals. They wished that they also knew Italian, for our phrases of approval and of amazement are so connected with little occasions that we fear to use them on great ones. We are obliged to become vaguely poetic, or to take refuge in Scriptural reminiscence.

'Welcome as one of the family!' said Mrs Honeychurch, waving her hand at the furniture. 'This is indeed a joyous day! I feel sure that you will make dear Lucy happy.'

'I hope so,' replied the young man, shifting his eyes to the ceiling.

'We mothers –' simpered Mrs Honeychurch, and then

realized that she was affected, sentimental, bombastic – all the things she hated most. Why could she not be as Freddy, who stood stiff in the middle of the room, looking very cross and almost handsome?

'I say, Lucy!' called Cecil, for conversation seemed to flag.

Lucy rose from the seat. She moved across the lawn and smiled in at them, just as if she was going to ask them to play tennis. Then she saw her brother's face. Her lips parted, and she took him in her arms. He said, 'Steady on!'

'Not a kiss for me?' asked her mother.

Lucy kissed her also.

'Would you take them into the garden and tell Mrs Honeychurch all about it?' Cecil suggested. 'And I'd stop here and tell my mother.'

'We go with Lucy?' said Freddy, as if taking orders.

'Yes, you go with Lucy.'

They passed into the sunlight. Cecil watched them cross the terrace, and descend out of sight by the steps. They would descend – he knew their ways – past the shrubbery, and past the tennis lawn and the dahlia-bed, until they reached the kitchen-garden, and there, in the presence of the potatoes and the peas, the great event would be discussed.

Smiling indulgently, he lit a cigarette, and rehearsed the events that had led to such a happy conclusion.

He had known Lucy for several years, but only as a common-place girl who happened to be musical. He could still remember his depression that afternoon at Rome, when she and her terrible cousin fell on him out of the blue, and demanded to be taken to St Peter's. That day she had seemed a typical tourist – shrill, crude, and gaunt with travel. But Italy worked some marvel in her. It gave her light, and – which he held more precious – it gave her shadow. Soon he detected in her a wonderful reticence. She was like a woman of Leonardo da Vinci's, whom we love not so much for herself as for the things that she will not tell us. The things are assuredly not of this life; no woman of Leonardo's could have anything so vulgar as a 'story'. She did develop most wonderfully day by day.

So it happened that from patronizing civility he had slowly passed, if not to passion, at least to a profound uneasiness. Already at Rome he had hinted to her that they might be suitable for each other. It had touched him greatly that she had not broken away at the suggestion. Her refusal had been clear and gentle; after it – as the horrid phrase went – she had been exactly the same to him as before. Three months later, on the margin of Italy, among the flower-clad Alps, he had asked her again in bald, traditional language. She reminded him of a Leonardo more than ever; her sunburnt features were shadowed by fantastic rocks; at his words she had turned and stood between him and the light with immeasurable plains behind her. He walked home with her unashamed, feeling not at all like a rejected suitor. The things that really mattered were unshaken.

So now he had asked her once more, and, clear and gentle as ever, she had accepted him, giving no coy reasons for her delay, but simply saying that she loved him and would do her best to make him happy. His mother, too, would be pleased; she had counselled the step; he must write her a long account.

Glancing at his hand, in case any of Freddy's chemicals had come off on it, he moved to the writing-table. There he saw 'Dear Mrs Vyse', followed by many erasures. He recoiled without reading any more, and after a little hesitation sat down elsewhere, and pencilled a note on his knee.

Then he lit another cigarette, which did not seem quite as divine as the first, and considered what might be done to make the Windy Corner drawing-room more distinctive. With that outlook it should have been a successful room, but the trail of Tottenham Court Road was upon it; he could almost visualize the motor-vans of Messrs Shoolbred and Messrs Maple arriving at the door and depositing this chair, those varnished book-cases, that writing-table. The table recalled Mrs Honeychurch's letter. He did not want to read that letter – his temptations never lay in that direction; but he worried about it none the less. It was his own fault that she was discussing him with his mother; he had wanted her support in his third attempt to win Lucy; he wanted to feel that others, no matter who they were, agreed with him, and so he had asked their permission. Mrs Honeychurch had been civil, but obtuse in essentials, while as for Freddy –

'He is only a boy,' he reflected. 'I represent all that he despises. Why should he want me for a brother-in-law?'

The Honeychurches were a worthy family, but he began to realize that Lucy was of another clay; and perhaps – he did not put it very definitely – he ought to introduce her into more congenial circles as soon as possible.

'Mr Beebe!' said the maid, and the new rector of Summer Street was shown in; he had at once started on friendly relations, owing to Lucy's praise of him in her letters from Florence.

Cecil greeted him rather critically.

'I've come for tea, Mr Vyse. Do you suppose that I shall get it?'

'I should say so. Food is the thing one does get here – don't sit in that chair; young Honeychurch has left a bone in it.'

'Pfui!'

'I know,' said Cecil, 'I know. I can't think why Mrs Honeychurch allows it.'

For Cecil considered the bone and the Maple's furniture separately; he did not realize that, taken together, they kindled the room into the life that he desired.

'I've come for tea and for gossip. Isn't this news?'

'News? I don't understand you,' said Cecil. 'News?'

Mr Beebe, whose news was of a very different nature, prattled forward.

'I met Sir Harry Otway as I came up; I have every reason to hope that I am first in the field. He has bought Cissie and Albert from Mr Flack!'

'Has he indeed?' said Cecil, trying to recover himself. Into what a grotesque mistake had he fallen! Was it likely that a clergyman and a gentleman would refer to his engagement in a manner so flippant? But his stiffness remained, and, though he asked who Cissie and Albert might be, he still thought Mr Beebe rather a bounder.

'Unpardonable question! To have stopped a week at Windy Corner and not to have met Cissie and Albert, the semi-detached villas that have been run up opposite the church! I'll set Mrs Honeychurch after you.'

'I'm shockingly stupid over local affairs,' said the young man languidly. 'I can't even remember the difference between a Parish Council and a Local Government Board. Perhaps there is no difference, or perhaps those aren't the right names. I only go into the country to see my friends and to enjoy the scenery. It is very remiss of me. Italy and London are the only places where I don't feel to exist on sufferance.'

Mr Beebe, distressed at this heavy reception of Cissie and Albert, determined to shift the subject.

'Let me see, Mr Vyse – I forget – what is your profession?'

'I have no profession,' said Cecil. 'It is another example of my decadence. My attitude – quite an indefensible one – is that so long as I am no trouble to anyone I have a right to do as I like. I know I ought to be getting money out of people, or devoting myself to things I don't care a straw about, but somehow I've not been able to begin.'

'You are very fortunate,' said Mr Beebe. 'It is a wonderful opportunity, the possession of leisure.'

His voice was rather parochial, but he did not quite see his way to answering naturally. He felt, as all who have regular occupation must feel, that others should have it also.

'I am glad that you approve. I daren't face the healthy person – for example, Freddy Honeychurch.'

'Oh, Freddy's a good sort, isn't he?'

'Admirable. The sort who has made England what she is.'

Cecil wondered at himself. Why, on this day of all others, was he so hopelessly contrary? He tried to get right by inquiring effusively after Mr Beebe's mother, an old lady for whom he had no particular regard. Then he flattered the clergyman, praised his liberal-mindedness, his enlightened attitude towards philosophy and science.

'Where are the others?' said Mr Beebe at last. 'I insist on extracting tea before evening service.'

'I suppose Anne never told them you were here. In this house one is so coached in the servants the day one arrives. The fault of Anne is that she begs your pardon when she hears you perfectly, and kicks the chair-legs with her feet. The faults of Mary – I forget the faults of Mary, but they are very grave. Shall we look in the garden?'

'I know the faults of Mary. She leaves the dustpans standing on the stairs.'

'The fault of Euphemia is that she will not, simply will not, chop the suet sufficiently small.'

They both laughed, and things began to go better.

'The faults of Freddy –' Cecil continued.

'Ah, he has too many. No one but his mother can remember the faults of Freddy. Try the faults of Miss Honeychurch; they are not innumerable.'

'She has none,' said the young man, with grave sincerity.

'I quite agree. At present she has none.'

'At present?'

'I'm not cynical. I'm only thinking of my pet theory about Miss Honeychurch. Does it seem reasonable that she should play so wonderfully, and live so quietly? I suspect that one day she will be wonderful in both. The watertight compartments in her will break down, and music and life will mingle. Then we shall have her heroically good, heroically bad – too heroic, perhaps, to be good or bad.'

Cecil found his companion interesting.

'And at present you think her not wonderful as far as life goes?'

'Well, I must say I've only seen her at Tunbridge Wells, where she was not wonderful, and at Florence. Since I came to Summer Street she has been away. You saw her, didn't you, at Rome and in the Alps. Oh, I forgot; of course, you knew her before. No, she wasn't wonderful in Florence either, but I kept on expecting that she would be.'

'In what way?'

Conversation had become agreeable to them, and they were pacing up and down the terrace.

'I could as easily tell you what tune she'll play next. There was simply the sense that she had found wings, and meant to use them. I can show you a beautiful picture in my Italian diary: Miss Honeychurch as a kite, Miss Bartlett holding the string. Picture number two: the string breaks.'

The sketch was in his diary, but it had been made afterwards, when he viewed things artistically. At the time he had given surreptitious tugs to the string himself.

'But the string never broke?'

'No. I mightn't have seen Miss Honeychurch rise, but I should certainly have heard Miss Bartlett fall.'

'It has broken now,' said the young man in low, vibrating tones.

Immediately he realized that of all the conceited, ludicrous, contemptible ways of announcing an engagement this was the worst. He cursed his love of metaphor; had he suggested that he was a star and that Lucy was soaring up to reach him?

'Broken? What do you mean?'

'I meant,' said Cecil stiffly, 'that she is going to marry me.'

The clergyman was conscious of some bitter disappointment which he could not keep out of his voice.

'I am sorry; I must apologize. I had no idea you were intimate with her, or I should never have talked in this flippant, superficial way. Mr Vyse, you ought to have stopped me.' And down the garden he saw Lucy herself; yes, he was disappointed.

Cecil, who naturally preferred congratulations to apologies, drew down his mouth at the corners. Was this the reception his action would get from the world? Of course, he despised the world as a whole; every thoughtful man should; it is almost a test of refinement. But he was sensitive to the successive particles of it which he encountered.

Occasionally he could be quite crude.

'I am sorry I have given you a shock,' he said dryly. 'I fear that Lucy's choice does not meet with your approval.'

'Not that. But you ought to have stopped me. I know Miss Honeychurch only a little as time goes. Perhaps I oughtn't to have discussed her so freely with anyone; certainly not with you.'

'You are conscious of having said something indiscreet?'

Mr Beebe pulled himself together. Really, Mr Vyse had the art of placing one in the most tiresome positions. He was driven to use the prerogatives of his profession.

'No, I have said nothing indiscreet. I foresaw at Florence that her quiet, uneventful childhood must end, and it has ended. I realized dimly enough that she might take some momentous step. She has taken it. She has learned – you will let me talk freely, as I have begun freely – she has learned what it is to love: the greatest lesson, some people will tell you, that our earthly life provides.' It was now time for him to wave his hat at the approaching trio. He did not omit to do so. 'She has learned through you,' and if his voice was still clerical it was now also sincere; 'let it be your care that her knowledge is profitable to her.'

'Grazie tante!' said Cecil, who did not like parsons.

'Have you heard?' shouted Mrs Honeychurch as she toiled up the sloping garden. 'Oh, Mr Beebe, have you heard the news?'

Freddy, now full of geniality, whistled the wedding march. Youth seldom criticizes the accomplished fact.

'Indeed I have!' he cried. He looked at Lucy. In her presence he could not act the parson any longer – at all events not without apology. 'Mrs Honeychurch, I'm going to do what I am always supposed to do, but generally I'm too shy. I want to invoke every kind of blessing on them, grave and gay, great and small. I want them all their lives to be supremely good and supremely happy as husband and wife, as father and mother. And now I want my tea.'

'You only asked for it just in time,' the lady retorted. 'How dare you be serious at Windy Corner?'

He took his tone from her. There was no more heavy beneficence, no more attempts to dignify the situation with poetry or the Scriptures. None of them dared or was able to be serious any more.

An engagement is so potent a thing that sooner or later it reduces all who speak of it to this state of cheerful awe. Away from it, in the solitude of their rooms, Mr Beebe, and even Freddy, might again be critical. But in its presence and in the presence of each other they were sincerely hilarious. It has a strange power, for it compels not only the lips, but the very heart. The chief parallel – to compare one great thing with another – is the power over us of a temple of some alien creed. Standing outside, we deride or oppose it, or at the most feel sentimental. Inside, though the saints and gods are not ours, we become true believers, in case any true believer should be present.

So it was that after the gropings and the misgivings of the afternoon they pulled themselves together and settled down to a very pleasant tea-party. If they were hypocrites they did not know it, and their hypocrisy had every chance of setting and of becoming true. Anne, putting down each plate as if it were a wedding present, stimulated them greatly. They could not lag behind that smile of hers which she gave them ere she kicked the drawing-room door. Mr Beebe chirruped. Freddy was at his wittiest, referring to Cecil as the 'Fiasco' – family-honoured pun on fiancé. Mrs Honeychurch, amusing and portly, promised well as a mother-in-law. As for Lucy and Cecil, for whom the temple had been built, they also joined in the merry ritual, but waited, as earnest worshippers should, for the disclosure of some holier shrine of joy.

CHAPTER IX

Lucy as a Work of Art

A FEW DAYS after the engagement was announced Mrs Honey-church made Lucy and her Fiasco come to a little garden party in the neighbourhood, for naturally she wanted to show people that her daughter was marrying a presentable man.

Cecil was more than presentable; he looked distinguished, and it was very pleasant to see his slim figure keeping step with Lucy, and his long, fair face responding when Lucy spoke to him. People congratulated Mrs Honeychurch, which is, I believe, a social blunder, but it pleased her, and she introduced Cecil rather indiscriminately to some stuffy dowagers.

At tea a misfortune took place: a cup of coffee was upset over Lucy's figured silk, and though Lucy feigned indifference her mother feigned nothing of the sort, but dragged her indoors to have the frock treated by a sympathetic maid. They were gone some time, and Cecil was left with the dowagers. When they returned he was not as pleasant as he had been.

'Do you go to much of this sort of thing?' he asked when they were driving home.

'Oh, now and then,' said Lucy, who had rather enjoyed herself.

'Is it typical of county society?'

'I suppose so. Mother, would it be?'

'Plenty of society,' said Mrs Honeychurch, who was trying to remember the hang of one of the dresses.

Seeing that her thoughts were elsewhere, Cecil bent towards Lucy and said:

'To me it seemed perfectly appalling, disastrous, portentous.'

'I am so sorry that you were stranded.'

'Not that, but the congratulations. It is so disgusting, the way an engagement is regarded as public property – a kind of waste place where every outsider may shoot his vulgar sentiment. All those old women smirking!'

'One has to go through it, I suppose. They won't notice us so much next time.'

'But my point is that their whole attitude is wrong. An engagement – horrid word in the first place – is a private matter, and should be treated as such.'

Yet the smirking old women, however wrong individually, were racially correct. The spirit of the generations had smirked through them, rejoicing in the engagement of Cecil and Lucy because it promised the continuance of life on earth. To Cecil and Lucy it promised something quite different – personal love. Hence Cecil's irritation and Lucy's belief that his irritation was just.

'How tiresome!' she said. 'Couldn't you have escaped to tennis?'

'I don't play tennis – at least, not in public. The neighbourhood is deprived of the romance of me being athletic. Such romance as I have is that of the Inglese Italianato.'

'Inglese Italianato?'

'È un diavolo incarnato! You know the proverb?'

She did not. Nor did it seem applicable to a young man who had spent a quiet winter in Rome with his mother. But Cecil, since his engagement, had taken to affect a cosmopolitan naughtiness which he was far from possessing.

'Well,' said he, 'I cannot help it if they do disapprove of me. There are certain irremovable barriers between myself and them, and I must accept them.'

'We all have our limitations, I suppose,' said wise Lucy.

'Sometimes they are forced on us, though,' said Cecil, who saw from her remark that she did not quite understand his position.

'How?'

'It makes a difference, doesn't it, whether we fence ourselves in, or whether we are fenced out by the barriers of others?'

She thought a moment, and agreed that it did make a difference.

'Difference?' cried Mrs Honeychurch, suddenly alert. 'I don't see any difference. Fences are fences, especially when they are in the same place.'

'We were speaking of motives,' said Cecil, on whom the interruption jarred.

'My dear Cecil, look here.' She spread out her knees and perched her card-case on her lap. 'This is me. That's Windy Corner. The rest of the pattern is the other people. Motives are all very well, but the fence comes here.'

'We weren't talking of real fences,' said Lucy, laughing.

'Oh, I see, dear – poetry.'

She leant placidly back. Cecil wondered why Lucy had been amused.

'I tell you who has no "fences", as you call them,' she said, 'and that's Mr Beebe.'

'A parson fenceless would mean a parson defenceless.'

Lucy was slow to follow what people said, but quick enough to detect what they meant. She missed Cecil's epigram, but grasped the feeling that prompted it.

'Don't you like Mr Beebe?' she asked thoughtfully.

'I never said so!' he cried. 'I consider him far above the average. I only denied –' And he swept off on the subject of fences again, and was brilliant.

'Now, a clergyman that I do hate,' said she, wanting to say something sympathetic, 'a clergyman that does have fences, and the most dreadful ones, is Mr Eager, the English chaplain at Florence. He was truly insincere – not merely the manner unfortunate. He was a snob, and so conceited, and he did say such unkind things.'

'What sort of things?'

'There was an old man at the Bertolini whom he said had murdered his wife.'

'Perhaps he had.'

'Why, no.'

'Why "no"?'

'He was such a nice old man, I'm sure.'

Cecil laughed at her feminine inconsequence.

'Well, I did try to sift the thing. Mr Eager would never come to the point. He prefers it vague – said the old man had "practically" murdered his wife – had murdered her in the sight of God.'

'Hush, dear!' said Mrs Honeychurch absently.

'But isn't it intolerable that a person whom we're told to imitate should go round spreading slander? It was, I believe, chiefly owing to him that the old man was dropped. People pretended he was vulgar, but he certainly wasn't that.'

'Poor old man! What was his name?'

'Harris,' said Lucy glibly.

'Let's hope that Mrs Harris there warn't no sich person,' said her mother.

Cecil nodded intelligently.

'Isn't Mr Eager a parson of the cultured type?' he asked.

'I don't know. I hate him. I've heard him lecture on Giotto. I hate him. Nothing can hide a petty nature. I *hate* him!'

'My goodness gracious me, child!' said Mrs Honeychurch. 'You'll blow my head off! What ever is there to shout over? I forbid you and Cecil to hate any more clergymen.'

He smiled. There was indeed something rather incongruous in Lucy's moral outburst over Mr Eager. It was as if one should see the Leonardo on the ceiling of the Sistine. He longed to hint to her that not here lay her vocation; that a woman's power and charm reside in mystery, not in muscular rant. But possibly rant is a sign of vitality: it mars the beautiful creature, but shows that she is alive. After a moment, he contemplated her flushed face and excited gestures with a certain approval. He forbore to repress the sources of youth.

Nature – simplest of topics, he thought – lay around them.
He praised the pine-woods, the deep lakes of bracken, the
crimson leaves that spotted the hurt-bushes, the serviceable
beauty of the turnpike road. The outdoor world was not very
familiar to him, and occasionally he went wrong in a question
of fact. Mrs Honeychurch's mouth twitched when he spoke of
the perpetual green of the larch.

'I count myself a lucky person,' he concluded. 'When I'm
in London I feel I could never live out of it. When I'm in the
country I feel the same about the country. After all, I do believe
that birds and trees and the sky are the most wonderful things
in life, and that the people who live amongst them must be the
best. It's true that in nine cases out of ten they don't seem to
notice anything. The country gentleman and the country
labourer are each in their way the most depressing of companions. Yet they may have a tacit sympathy with the workings of
Nature which is denied to us of the town. Do you feel that, Mrs
Honeychurch?'

Mrs Honeychurch started and smiled. She had not been
attending. Cecil, who was rather crushed on the front seat of
the victoria, felt irritable, and determined not to say anything
interesting again.

Lucy had not attended either. Her brow was wrinkled, and
she still looked furiously cross – the result, he concluded, of too
much moral gymnastics. It was sad to see her thus blind to the
beauties of an August wood.

' "Come down, O maid, from yonder mountain height," ' he
quoted, and touched her knee with his own.

She flushed again and said: 'What height?'

'Come down, O maid, from yonder mountain height:
What pleasure lives in height (the shepherd sang),
In height and in the splendour of the hills?

Let us take Mrs Honeychurch's advice and hate clergymen no
more. What's this place?'

'Summer Street, of course,' said Lucy, and roused herself.

The woods had opened to leave space for a sloping triangular meadow. Pretty cottages lined it on two sides, and the upper and third side was occupied by a new stone church, expensively simple, with a charming shingled spire. Mr Beebe's house was near the church. In height it scarcely exceeded the cottages. Some great mansions were at hand, but they were hidden in the trees. The scene suggested a Swiss alp rather than the shrine and centre of a leisured world, and was only marred by two ugly little villas – the villas that had competed with Cecil's engagement, having been acquired by Sir Harry Otway the very afternoon that Lucy had been acquired by him.

'Cissie' was the name of one of these villas, 'Albert' of the other. These titles were not only picked out in shaded Gothic on the garden gates, but appeared a second time on the porches, where they followed the semicircular curve of the entrance arch in block capitals. Albert was inhabited. His tortured garden was bright with geraniums and lobelias and polished shells. His little windows were chastely swathed in Nottingham lace. Cissie was to let. Three noticeboards, belonging to Dorking agents, lolled on her fence and announced the not surprising fact. Her paths were already weedy; her pocket-handkerchief of a lawn was yellow with dandelions.

'The place is ruined!' said the ladies mechanically. 'Summer Street will never be the same again.'

As the carriage passed, Cissie's door opened, and a gentleman came out of her.

'Stop!' cried Mrs Honeychurch, touching the coachman with her parasol. 'Here's Sir Harry. Now we shall know. Sir Harry, pull those things down at once!'

Sir Harry Otway – who need not be described – came to the carriage and said:

'Mrs Honeychurch, I meant to. I can't, I really can't turn out Miss Flack.'

'Am I not always right? She ought to have gone before the

contract was signed. Does she still live rent-free, as she did in her nephew's time?'

'But what can I do?' He lowered his voice. 'An old lady, so very vulgar, and almost bedridden.'

'Turn her out,' said Cecil bravely.

Sir Harry sighed, and looked at the villas mournfully. He had had full warning of Mr Flack's intentions, and might have bought the plot before building commenced; but he was apathetic and dilatory. He had known Summer Street for so many years that he could not imagine it being spoilt. Not till Mrs Flack had laid the foundation stone, and the apparition of red and cream brick began to rise, did he take alarm. He called on Mr Flack, the local builder – a most reasonable and respectful man – who agreed that tiles would have made a more artistic roof, but pointed out that slates were cheaper. He ventured to differ, however, about the Corinthian columns which were to cling like leeches to the frames of the bow-windows, saying that, for his part, he liked to relieve the façade by a bit of decoration. Sir Harry hinted that a column, if possible, should be structural as well as decorative. Mr Flack replied that all the columns had been ordered, adding, 'and all the capitals different – one with dragons in the foliage, another approaching to the Ionian style, another introducing Mrs Flack's initials – every one different.' For he had read his Ruskin. He built his villas according to his desire; and not till he had inserted an immovable aunt into one of them did Sir Harry buy.

This futile and unprofitable transaction filled the knight with sadness as he leant on Mrs Honeychurch's carriage. He had failed in his duties to the countryside, and the countryside was laughing at him as well. He had spent money, and yet Summer Street was spoilt as much as ever. All he could do now was to find a desirable tenant for Cissie – someone really desirable.

'The rent is absurdly low,' he told them, 'and perhaps I am an easy landlord. But it is such an awkward size. It is too large for the peasant class, and too small for anyone the least like ourselves.'

Cecil had been hesitating whether he should despise the villas or despise Sir Harry for despising them. The latter impulse seemed the more fruitful.

'You ought to find a tenant at once,' he said maliciously. 'It would be a perfect paradise for a bank-clerk.'

'Exactly!' said Sir Harry excitedly. 'That is exactly what I fear, Mr Vyse. It will attract the wrong type of people. The train service has improved – a fatal improvement, to my mind. And what are five miles from a station in these days of bicycles?'

'Rather a strenuous clerk it would be,' said Lucy.

Cecil, who had his full share of medieval mischievousness, replied that the physique of the lower middle classes was improving at a most appalling rate. She saw that he was laughing at their harmless neighbour, and roused herself to stop him.

'Sir Harry!' she exclaimed, 'I have an idea. How would you like spinsters?'

'My dear Lucy, it would be splendid. Do you know any such?'

'Yes; I met them abroad.'

'Gentlewomen?' he asked tentatively.

'Yes, indeed, and at the present moment homeless. I heard from them last week. Miss Teresa and Miss Catharine Alan. I'm really not joking. They are quite the right people. Mr Beebe knows them, too. May I tell them to write to you?'

'Indeed you may!' he cried. 'Here we are with the difficulty solved already. How delightful it is! Extra facilities – please tell them they shall have extra facilities, for I shall have no agents' fees. Oh, the agents! The appalling people they have sent me! One woman, when I wrote – a tactful letter, you know – asking her to explain her social position to me, replied that she would pay the rent in advance. As if one cares about that! And several references I took up were most unsatisfactory – people swindlers, or not respectable. And oh, the deceit! I have seen a good deal of the seamy side this last week. The deceit of the most promising people! My dear Lucy, the deceit!'

She nodded.

'My advice,' put in Mrs Honeychurch, 'is to have nothing to do with Lucy and her decayed gentlewomen at all. I know the type. Preserve me from people who have seen better days, and bring heirlooms with them that make the house smell stuffy. It's a sad thing, but I'd far rather let to someone who is going up in the world than to someone who has come down.'

'I think I follow you,' said Sir Harry; 'but it is, as you say, a very sad thing.'

'The Miss Alans aren't that!' cried Lucy.

'Yes, they are!' said Cecil. 'I haven't met them, but I should say they were a highly unsuitable addition to the neighbourhood.'

'Don't listen to him, Sir Harry – he's tiresome.'

'It's I who am tiresome,' he replied. 'I oughtn't to come with my troubles to young people. But really I am so worried, and Lady Otway will only say that I cannot be too careful, which is quite true, but no real help.'

'Then may I write to my Miss Alans?'

'Please!' he cried.

But his eye wavered when Mrs Honeychurch exclaimed:

'Beware! They are certain to have canaries. Sir Harry, beware of canaries: they spit the seed out through the bars of the cages, and then the mice come. Beware of women altogether. Only let to a man.'

'Really –' he murmured gallantly, though he saw the wisdom of her remark.

'Men don't gossip over teacups. If they get drunk, there's an end of them – they lie down comfortably, and sleep it off. If they're vulgar, they somehow keep it to themselves. It doesn't spread so. Give me a man – of course, provided he's clean.'

Sir Harry blushed. Neither he nor Cecil enjoyed these open compliments to their sex. Even the exclusion of the dirty did not leave them much distinction. He suggested that Mrs Honeychurch, if she had time, should descend from the carriage and inspect Cissie for herself. She was delighted. Nature had intended her to be poor and to live in such a house. Domestic arrangements always attracted her, especially when they were on a small scale.

Cecil pulled Lucy back as she followed her mother.

'Mrs Honeychurch,' he said, 'what if we two walk home and leave you?'

'Certainly!' was her cordial reply.

Sir Harry likewise seemed almost too glad to get rid of them. He beamed at them knowingly, said, 'Aha! Young people, young people, young people!' and then hastened to unlock the house.

'Hopeless vulgarian!' exclaimed Cecil, almost before they were out of earshot.

'Oh, Cecil!'

'I can't help it. It would be wrong not to loathe that man.'

'He isn't clever, but really he is nice.'

'No, Lucy; he stands for all that is bad in country life. In London he would keep his place. He would belong to a brainless club, and his wife would give brainless dinner-parties. But down here he acts the little god with his gentility, and his patronage, and his sham aesthetics, and everyone – even your mother – is taken in.'

'All that you say is quite true,' said Lucy, though she felt discouraged. 'I wonder whether – whether it matters so very much.'

'It matters supremely. Sir Harry is the essence of that garden party. Oh, goodness, how cross I feel! How I do hope he'll get some vulgar tenant in that villa – some woman so really vulgar that he'll notice it. *Gentlefolks*! Ugh! With his bald head and retreating chin! But let's forget him.'

This Lucy was glad enough to do. If Cecil disliked Sir Harry Otway and Mr Beebe, what guarantee was there that the people who really mattered to her would escape? For instance, Freddy. Freddy was neither clever nor subtle nor beautiful, and what prevented Cecil from saying, any minute, 'It would be wrong not to loathe Freddy'? And what would she reply? Further than Freddy she did not go, but he gave her anxiety enough. She could only assure herself that Cecil had known Freddy some time, and that they had always got on pleasantly, except, perhaps, during the last few days, which was an accident, perhaps.

'Which way shall we go?' she asked him.

Nature – simplest of topics, she thought – was around them. Summer Street lay deep in the woods, and she had stopped where a footpath diverged from the highroad.

'Are there two ways?'

'Perhaps the road is more sensible, as we're got up smart.'

'I'd rather go through the wood,' said Cecil, with that subdued irritation that she had noticed in him all the afternoon. 'Why is it, Lucy, that you always say the road? Do you know that you have never once been with me in the fields or the wood since we were engaged?'

'Haven't I? The wood, then,' said Lucy, startled at his queerness, but pretty sure that he would explain later; it was not his habit to leave her in doubt as to his meaning.

She led the way into the whispering pines, and sure enough he did explain before they had gone a dozen yards.

'I had got an idea – I dare say wrongly – that you feel more at home with me in a room.'

'A room?' she echoed, hopelessly bewildered.

'Yes. Or, at the most, in a garden, or on a road. Never in the real country like this.'

'Oh, Cecil, what ever do you mean? I have never felt anything of the sort. You talk as if I was a kind of poetess sort of person.'

'I don't know that you aren't. I connect you with a view – a certain type of view. Why shouldn't you connect me with a room?'

She reflected a moment, and then said, laughing:

'Do you know that you're right? I do. I must be a poetess after all. When I think of you it's always as in a room. How funny!'

To her surprise, he seemed annoyed.

'A drawing-room, pray? With no view?'

'Yes, with no view, I fancy. Why not?'

'I'd rather,' he said reproachfully, 'that you connected me with the open air.'

She said again, 'Oh, Cecil, what ever do you mean?'

As no explanation was forthcoming, she shook off the subject as too difficult for a girl, and led him further into the wood, pausing every now and then at some particularly beautiful or familiar combination of the trees. She had known the wood between Summer Street and Windy Corner ever since she could walk alone; she had played at losing Freddy in it, when Freddy was a purple-faced baby; and though she had now been to Italy it had lost none of its charm.

Presently they came to a little clearing among the pines – another tiny green alp, solitary this time, and holding in its bosom a shallow pool.

She exclaimed, 'The Sacred Lake!'

'Why do you call it that?'

'I can't remember why. I suppose it comes out of some book. It's only a puddle now, but you see that stream going through it? Well, a good deal of water comes down after heavy rains, and can't get away at once, and the pool becomes quite large and beautiful. Then Freddy used to bathe there. He is very fond of it.'

'And you?'

He meant, 'Are you fond of it?' But she answered dreamily: 'I bathed here, too, till I was found out. Then there was a row.'

At another time he might have been shocked, for he had depths of prudishness within him. But now, with his momentary cult of the fresh air, he was delighted at her admirable simplicity. He looked at her as she stood by the pool's edge. She was got up smart, as she phrased it, and she reminded him of some brilliant flower that has no leaves of its own, but blooms abruptly out of a world of green.

'Who found you out?'

'Charlotte,' she murmured. 'She was stopping with us. Charlotte – Charlotte.'

'Poor girl!'

She smiled gravely. A certain scheme, from which hitherto he had shrunk, now appeared practical.

'Lucy!'

'Yes, I suppose we ought to be going,' was her reply.

'Lucy, I want to ask something of you that I have never asked before.'

At the serious note in his voice she stepped frankly and kindly towards him.

'What, Cecil?'

'Hitherto never – not even that day on the lawn when you agreed to marry me –'

He became self-conscious and kept glancing round·to see if they were observed. His courage had gone.

'Yes?'

'Up to now I have never kissed you.'

She was as scarlet as if he had put the thing most indelicately.

'No – more you have,' she stammered.

'Then I ask you – may I now?'

'Of course you may, Cecil. You might before. I can't run at you, you know.'

At that supreme moment he was conscious of nothing but absurdities. Her reply was inadequate. She gave such a business-like lift to her veil. As he approached her he found time to wish that he could recoil. As he touched her, his gold pince-nez became dislodged and was flattened between them.

Such was the embrace. He considered, with truth, that it had been a failure. Passion should believe itself irresistible. It should forget civility and consideration and all the other curses of a refined nature. Above all, it should never ask for leave where there is a right of way. Why could he not do as any labourer or navvy – nay, as any young man behind the counter would have done? He recast the scene. Lucy was standing flower-like by the water; he rushed up and took her in his arms; she rebuked him, permitted him, and revered him ever after for his manliness. For he believed that women revere men for their manliness.

They left the pool in silence, after this one salutation. He waited for her to make some remark which should show him her inmost thoughts. At last she spoke, and with fitting gravity.

'Emerson the name was, not Harris.'

'What name?'

'The old man's.'

'What old man?'

'That old man I told you about. The one Mr Eager was so unkind to.'

He could not know that this was the most intimate conversation they had ever had.

CHAPTER X

Cecil as a Humorist

THE SOCIETY OUT of which Cecil proposed to rescue Lucy was perhaps no very splendid affair, yet it was more splendid than her antecedents entitled her to. Her father, a prosperous local solicitor, had built Windy Corner as a speculation at the time the district was opening up, and, falling in love with his own creation, had ended by living there himself. Soon after his marriage, the social atmosphere began to alter. Other houses were built on the brow of that steep southern slope, and others, again, among the pine trees behind, and northward on the chalk barrier of the downs. Most of these houses were larger than Windy Corner, and were filled by people who came, not from the district, but from London, and who mistook the Honeychurches for the remnants of an indigenous aristocracy. He was inclined to be frightened, but his wife accepted the situation without either pride or humility. 'I cannot think what people are doing,' she would say, 'but it is extremely fortunate for the children.' She called everywhere; her calls were returned with enthusiasm, and by the time people found out that she was not exactly of their milieu they liked her, and it did not seem to matter. When Mr Honeychurch died, he had the satisfaction – which few honest solicitors despise – of leaving his family rooted in the best society obtainable.

The best obtainable. Certainly many of the immigrants were rather dull, and Lucy realized this more vividly since her return from Italy. Hitherto she had accepted their ideals without questioning – their kindly affluence, their inexplosive religion, their dislike of paper bags, orange-peel and broken bottles. A Radical out and out, she learned to speak with horror of Suburbia. Life, so far as she troubled to conceive it, was a circle of rich, pleasant people, with identical interests and identical foes. In this circle one thought, married, and died. Outside it were poverty and vulgarity, for ever trying to enter, just as the London fog tries to enter the pine-woods, pouring through the gaps in the northern hills. But in Italy, where anyone who chooses may warm himself in equality, as in the sun, this conception of life vanished. Her senses expanded; she felt that there was no one whom she might not get to like, that social barriers were irremovable, doubtless, but not particularly high. You jump over them just as you jump into a peasant's olive-yard in the Apennines, and he is glad to see you. She returned with new eyes.

So did Cecil; but Italy had quickened Cecil, not to tolerance, but to irritation. He saw that the local society was narrow, but instead of saying, 'Does this very much matter?' he rebelled, and tried to substitute for it the society he called broad. He did not realize that Lucy had consecrated her environment by the thousand little civilities that create a tenderness in time, and that though her eyes saw its defects her heart refused to despise it entirely. Nor did he realize a more important point – that if she was too great for this society she was too great for all society, and had reached the stage where personal intercourse would alone satisfy her. A rebel she was, but not of the kind he understood – a rebel who desired, not a wider dwelling-room, but equality beside the man she loved. For Italy was offering her the most priceless of all possessions – her own soul.

Playing bumble-puppy with Minnie Beebe, niece to the rector, and aged thirteen – an ancient and most honourable game, which consists in striking tennis-balls high into the air, so that they fall over the net and immoderately bounce; some hit Mrs Honeychurch; others are lost. The sentence is confused, but the better illustrates Lucy's state of mind, for she was trying to talk to Mr Beebe at the same time.

'Oh, it has been such a nuisance – first he, then they – no one knowing what they wanted, and everyone so tiresome.'

'But they really are coming now,' said Mr Beebe. 'I wrote to Miss Teresa a few days ago – she was wondering how often the butcher called, and my reply of once a month must have impressed her favourably. They are coming. I heard from them this morning.'

'I shall hate those Miss Alans!' Mrs Honeychurch cried. 'Just because they're old and silly one's expected to say, "How sweet!" I hate their "if"-ing and "but"-ing and "and"-ing. And poor Lucy – serve her right – worn to a shadow.'

Mr Beebe watched the shadow springing and shouting over the tennis court. Cecil was absent – one did not play bumble-puppy when he was there.

'Well, if they are coming – no, Minnie, not Saturn.' Saturn was a tennis-ball whose skin was partially unsewn. When in motion his orb was encircled by a ring. 'If they are coming, Sir Harry will let them move in before the twenty-ninth, and he will cross out the clause about whitewashing the ceilings, because it made them nervous, and put in the fair-wear-and-tear one. – That doesn't count. I told you not Saturn.'

'Saturn's all right for bumble-puppy,' cried Freddy, joining them. 'Minnie, don't you listen to her.'

'Saturn doesn't bounce.'

'Saturn bounces enough.'

'No, he doesn't.'

'Well, he bounces better than the Beautiful White Devil.'

'Hush, dear,' said Mrs Honeychurch.

'But look at Lucy – complaining of Saturn, and all the time's got the Beautiful White Devil in her hand, ready to plug it in. That's right, Minnie, go for her – get her over the shins with the racquet – get her over the shins!'

Lucy fell; the Beautiful White Devil rolled from her hand.

Mr Beebe picked it up, and said: 'The name of this ball is Vittoria Corombona, please.' But his correction passed unheeded.

Freddy possessed to a high degree the power of lashing little girls to fury, and in half a minute he had transformed Minnie from a well-mannered child into a howling wilderness. Up in the house Cecil heard them, and, though he was full of entertaining news, he did not come down to impart it, in case he got hurt. He was not a coward, and bore necessary pain as well as any man. But he hated the physical violence of the young. How right he was! Sure enough it ended in a cry.

'I wish the Miss Alans could see this,' observed Mr Beebe, just as Lucy, who was nursing the injured Minnie, was in turn lifted off her feet by her brother.

'Who are the Miss Alans?' Freddy panted.

'They have taken Cissie Villa.'

'That wasn't the name –'

Here his foot slipped, and they all fell most agreeably onto the grass. An interval elapses.

'Wasn't what name?' asked Lucy, with her brother's head in her lap.

'Alan wasn't. The name of the people Sir Harry's let to.'

'Nonsense, Freddy! You know nothing about it.'

'Nonsense yourself! I've this minute seen him. He said to me: "Ahem! Honeychurch" ' – Freddy was an indifferent mimic – ' "Ahem! Ahem! I have at last procured really dee-sire-rebel tenants." I said, "Hooray, old boy!" and slapped him on the back.'

'Exactly. The Miss Alans?'

'Rather not. More like Anderson.'

'Oh, good gracious, there isn't going to be another muddle!' Mrs Honeychurch exclaimed. 'Do you notice, Lucy, I'm always right? I *said* don't interfere with Cissie Villa. I'm always right. I'm quite uneasy at being always right so often.'

'It's only another muddle of Freddy's. Freddy doesn't even know the name of the people he pretends have taken it instead.'

'Yes, I do. I've got it. Emerson.'

'What name?'

'Emerson. I'll bet you anything you like.'

'What a weathercock Sir Harry is,' said Lucy quietly. 'I wish I had never bothered over it at all.'

Then she lay on her back and gazed at the cloudless sky. Mr Beebe, whose opinion of her rose daily, whispered to his niece that *that* was the proper way to behave if any little thing went wrong.

Meanwhile the name of the new tenants had diverted Mrs Honeychurch from the contemplation of her own abilities.

'Emerson, Freddy? Do you know what Emersons they are?'

'I don't know whether they're any Emersons,' retorted Freddy, who was democratic. Like his sister, and like most young people, he was naturally attracted by the idea of equality, and the undeniable fact that there are different kinds of Emersons annoyed him beyond due measure.

'I trust they are the right sort of person. All right, Lucy' – she was sitting up again – 'I see you looking down your nose and thinking your mother's a snob. But there *is* a right sort and a wrong sort, and it's affectation to pretend there isn't.'

'Emerson's a common enough name,' Lucy remarked.

She was gazing sideways. Seated on a promontory herself, she could see the pine-clad promontories descending one beyond another into the Weald. The further one descended the garden, the more glorious was this lateral view.

'I was merely going to remark, Freddy, that I trusted they were no relations of Emerson the philosopher, a most trying man. Pray, does that satisfy you?'

'Oh yes,' he grumbled. 'And you will be satisfied, too, for they're friends of Cecil; so' – with elaborate irony – 'you and the other county families will be able to call in perfect safety.'

'*Cecil*?' exclaimed Lucy.

'Don't be rude, dear,' said his mother placidly. 'Lucy, don't screech. It's a new bad habit you're getting into.'

'But has Cecil –'

'Friends of Cecil's,' he repeated, ' "and so really dee-sire-rebel. Ahem! Honeychurch, I have just telegraphed to them." '

She got up from the grass.

It was hard on Lucy. Mr Beebe sympathized with her very much. While she believed that her snub about the Miss Alans came from Sir Harry Otway, she had borne it like a good girl. She might well 'screech' when she heard that it came partly from her lover. Mr Vyse was a tease – something worse than a tease: he took a malicious pleasure in thwarting people. The clergyman, knowing this, looked at Miss Honeychurch with more than his usual kindness.

When she exclaimed, 'But Cecil's Emersons – they can't possibly be the same ones – there is that –' he did not consider that the exclamation was strange, but saw in it an opportunity of diverting the conversation while she recovered her composure. He diverted it as follows:

'The Emersons who were at Florence, do you mean? No, I don't suppose it will prove to be them. It is probably a long cry from them to friends of Mr Vyse's. Oh, Mrs Honeychurch, the oddest people! The queerest people! For our part we liked them, didn't we?' He appealed to Lucy. 'There was a great scene over some violets. They picked violets and filled all the vases in the room of these very Miss Alans who have failed to come to Cissie Villa. Poor little ladies! So shocked and so pleased. It used to be one of Miss Catharine's great stories. "My dear sister loves flowers," it began. They found the whole room a mass of blue – vases and jugs – and the story ends with "So ungentlemanly and yet so beautiful. It is all very difficult." Yes, I always connect those Florentine Emersons with violets.'

'Fiasco's done you this time,' remarked Freddy, not seeing that his sister's face was very red. She could not recover herself. Mr Beebe saw it, and continued to divert the conversation.

'These particular Emersons consisted of a father and a son – the son a goodly, if not a good young man; not a fool, I fancy, but very immature – pessimism, *et cetera*. Our special joy was the father – such a sentimental darling, and people declared he had murdered his wife.'

In his normal state Mr Beebe would never have repeated such gossip, but he was trying to shelter Lucy in her little trouble. He repeated any rubbish that came into his head.

'Murdered his wife?' said Mrs Honeychurch. 'Lucy, don't desert us – go on playing bumble-puppy. Really, the Pension Bertolini must have been the oddest place. That's the second murderer I've heard of as being there. What ever was Charlotte doing to stop? By the by, we really must ask Charlotte here some time.'

Mr Beebe could recall no second murderer. He suggested that his hostess was mistaken. At the hint of opposition she warmed. She was perfectly sure that there had been a second tourist of whom the same story had been told. The name escaped her. What was the name? Oh, what was the name? She clasped her knees for the name. Something in Thackeray. She struck her matronly forehead.

Lucy asked her brother whether Cecil was in.

'Oh, don't go!' he cried, and tried to catch her by the ankles.

'I must go,' she said gravely. 'Don't be silly. You always overdo it when you play.'

As she left them her mother's shout of 'Harris!' shivered the tranquil air, and reminded her that she had told a lie and had never put it right. Such a senseless lie, too, yet it shattered her nerves, and made her connect these Emersons, friends of Cecil's, with a pair of nondescript tourists. Hitherto truth had come to her naturally. She saw that for the future she must be more vigilant, and be – absolutely truthful? Well, at all events, she must not tell lies. She hurried up the garden, still flushed with shame. A word from Cecil would soothe her, she was sure.

'Cecil!'

'Hullo!' he called, and leant out of the smoking-room window. He seemed in high spirits. 'I was hoping you'd come. I heard you all bear-gardening, but there's better fun up here. I, even I, have won a great victory for the Comic Muse. George Meredith's right – the cause of Comedy and the cause of Truth are really the same; and I, even I, have found tenants for the distressful Cissie Villa. Don't be angry! Don't be angry! You'll forgive me when you hear it all.'

He looked very attractive when his face was bright, and he dispelled her ridiculous forebodings at once.

'I have heard,' she said. 'Freddy has told us. Naughty Cecil! I suppose I must forgive you. Just think of all the trouble I took for nothing! Certainly the Miss Alans are a little tiresome, and I'd rather have nice friends of yours. But you oughtn't to tease one so.'

'Friends of mine?' he laughed. 'But, Lucy, the whole joke is to come! Come here.' But she remained standing where she was. 'Do you know where I met these desirable tenants? In the National Gallery, when I was up to see my mother last week.'

'What an odd place to meet people!' she said nervously. 'I don't quite understand.'

'In the Umbrian Room. Absolute strangers. They were admiring Luca Signorelli – of course, quite stupidly. However, we got talking, and they refreshed me not a little. They had been to Italy.'

'But, Cecil –'

He proceeded hilariously.

'In the course of conversation they said that they wanted a country cottage – the father to live there, the son to run down for week-ends. I thought, "What a chance of scoring off Sir Harry!" and I took their address and a London reference, found they weren't actual blackguards – it was great sport – and wrote to him, making out –'

'Cecil! No, it's not fair. I've probably met them before –'

He bore her down.

'Perfectly fair. Anything is fair that punishes a snob. That old man will do the neighbourhood a world of good. Sir Harry is too disgusting with his "decayed gentlewomen". I meant to read him a lesson some time. No, Lucy, the classes ought to mix, and before long you'll agree with me. There ought to be inter-marriage – all sorts of things. I believe in democracy –'

'No, you don't,' she snapped. 'You don't know what the word means.'

He stared at her, and felt again that she had failed to be Leonardesque. 'No, you don't!' Her face was inartistic – that of a peevish virago.

'It isn't fair, Cecil. I blame you – I blame you very much indeed. You had no business to undo my work about the Miss Alans, and make me look ridiculous. You call it scoring off Sir Harry, but do you realize that it is all at my expense? I consider it most disloyal of you.'

She left him.

'Temper!' he thought, raising his eyebrows.

No, it was worse than temper – snobbishness. As long as Lucy thought that his own smart friends were supplanting the Miss Alans, she had not minded. He perceived that these new tenants might be of value educationally. He would tolerate the father and draw out the son, who was silent. In the interests of the Comic Muse and of Truth, he would bring them to Windy Corner.

CHAPTER XI

In Mrs Vyse's Well-Appointed Flat

THE COMIC MUSE, though able to look after her own interests, did not disdain the assistance of Mr Vyse. His idea of bringing the Emersons to Windy Corner struck her as decidedly good, and she carried through the negotiations without a hitch. Sir Harry Otway signed the agreement, met Mr Emerson, and was duly disillusioned. The Miss Alans were duly offended, and wrote a dignified letter to Lucy, whom they held responsible for the failure. Mr Beebe planned pleasant moments for the newcomers, and told Mrs Honeychurch that Freddy must call on them as soon as they arrived. Indeed, so ample was the Muse's equipment that she permitted Mr Harris, never a very robust criminal, to droop his head, to be forgotten, and to die.

Lucy – to descend from bright heaven to earth, whereon there are shadows because there are hills – Lucy was at first plunged into despair, but settled after a little thought that it did not matter in the very least. Now that she was engaged, the Emersons would scarcely insult her, and were welcome to come into the neighbourhood. And Cecil was welcome to bring whom he would into the neighbourhood. Therefore Cecil was welcome to bring the Emersons into the neighbourhood. But, as I say, this took a little thinking, and – so illogical are girls – the event remained rather greater and rather more dreadful than it should have done. She was glad that a visit to Mrs Vyse now fell due; the tenants moved into Cissie Villa while she was safe in the London flat.

'Cecil – Cecil darling,' she whispered the evening she arrived, and crept into his arms.

Cecil, too, became demonstrative. He saw that the needful

fire had been kindled in Lucy. At last she longed for attention, as a woman should, and looked up to him because he was a man.

'So you do love me, little thing?' he murmured.

'Oh, Cecil, I do, I do! I don't know what I should do without you.'

Several days passed. Then she had a letter from Miss Bartlett. A coolness had sprung up between the two cousins, and they had not corresponded since they parted in August. The coolness dated from what Charlotte would call 'the flight to Rome', and in Rome it had increased amazingly. For the companion who is merely uncongenial in the medieval world becomes exasperating in the classical. Charlotte, unselfish in the Forum, would have tried a sweeter temper than Lucy's, and once, in the Baths of Caracalla, they had doubted whether they could continue their tour. Lucy had said she would join the Vyses – Mrs Vyse was an acquaintance of her mother, so there was no impropriety in the plan – and Miss Bartlett had replied that she was quite used to being abandoned suddenly. Finally nothing happened; but the coolness remained, and, for Lucy, was even increased when she opened the letter and read as follows. It had been forwarded from Windy Corner.

> *Tunbridge Wells,*
> *September.*

Dearest Lucia,

   I have news of you at last! Miss Lavish has been bicycling in your parts, but was not sure whether a call would be welcome. Puncturing her tyre near Summer Street, and it being mended while she sat very woebegone in that pretty churchyard, she saw, to her astonishment, a door open opposite and the younger Emerson man come out. He said his father had just taken the house. He said *he did not know that you lived in the neighbourhood (?). He never suggested giving Eleanor a cup of tea. Dear Lucy, I am much worried, and I advise you to make a clean breast of his past behaviour to your mother, Freddy and Mr Vyse, who will forbid*

him to enter the house, etc. That was a great misfortune, and I
dare say you have told them already. Mr Vyse is so sensitive.
I remember how I used to get on his nerves at Rome. I am very
sorry about it all, and should not feel easy unless I warned you.
                                    Believe me,
                          Your anxious and loving cousin,
                                            Charlotte.

Lucy was much annoyed, and replied as follows:

                              Beauchamp Mansions, S.W.
Dear Charlotte,
    Many thanks for your warning. When Mr Emerson forgot
himself on the mountain, you made me promise not to tell mother,
because you said she would blame you for not being always with
me. I have kept that promise, and cannot possibly tell her now.
I have said both to her and to Cecil that I met the Emersons at
Florence, and that they are respectable people – which I do
think – and the reason that he offered Miss Lavish no tea was
probably that he had none himself. She should have tried at the
Rectory. I cannot begin making a fuss at this stage. You must see
that it would be too absurd. If the Emersons heard I had com-
plained of them, they would think themselves of importance,
which is exactly what they are not. I like the old father, and look
forward to seeing him again. As for the son, I am sorry for him
when we meet, rather than for myself. They are known to Cecil,
who is very well, and spoke of you the other day. We expect to be
married in January.
    Miss Lavish cannot have told you much about me, for I am
not at Windy Corner at all, but here. Please do not put 'Private'
outside your envelope again. No one opens my letters.
                                  Yours affectionately,
                                  L. M. Honeychurch.

Secrecy has this disadvantage: we lose the sense of proportion;
we cannot tell whether our secret is important or not. Were Lucy

and her cousin closeted with a great thing which would destroy Cecil's life if he discovered it, or with a little thing which he would laugh at? Miss Bartlett suggested the former. Perhaps she was right. It had become a great thing now. Left to herself, Lucy would have told her mother and her lover ingenuously, and it would have remained a little thing. 'Emerson, not Harris': it was only that a few weeks ago. She tried to tell Cecil even now when they were laughing about some beautiful lady who had smitten his heart at school. But her body behaved so ridiculously that she stopped.

She and her secret stayed ten days longer in the deserted metropolis visiting the scenes they were to know so well later on. It did her no harm, Cecil thought, to learn the framework of society, while society itself was absent on the golf-links or the moors. The weather was cool, and it did her no harm. In spite of the season, Mrs Vyse managed to scrape together a dinner-party consisting entirely of the grandchildren of famous people. The food was poor, but the talk had a witty weariness that impressed the girl. One was tired of everything, it seemed. One launched into enthusiasms only to collapse gracefully, and pick oneself up amid sympathetic laughter. In this atmosphere the Pension Bertolini and Windy Corner appeared equally crude, and Lucy saw that her London career would estrange her a little from all that she had loved in the past.

The grandchildren asked her to play the piano. She played Schumann. 'Now some Beethoven,' called Cecil, when the querulous beauty of the music had died. She shook her head and played Schumann again. The melody rose, unprofitably magical. It broke; it was resumed broken, not marching once from the cradle to the grave. The sadness of the incomplete – the sadness that is often Life, but should never be Art – throbbed in its dis- jected phrases, and made the nerves of the audience throb. Not thus had she played on the little draped piano at the Bertolini, and 'Too much Schumann' was not the remark that Mr Beebe had passed to himself when she returned.

When the guests were gone, and Lucy had gone to bed, Mrs Vyse paced up and down the drawing-room, discussing her little party with her son. Mrs Vyse was a nice woman, but her personality, like many another's, had been swamped by London, for it needs a strong head to live among many people. The too vast orb of her fate had crushed her; she had seen too many seasons, too many cities, too many men for her abilities, and even with Cecil she was mechanical, and behaved as if he was not one son, but, so to speak, a filial crowd.

'Make Lucy one of us,' she said, looking round intelligently at the end of each sentence, and straining her lips apart until she spoke again. 'Lucy is becoming wonderful – wonderful.'

'Her music always was wonderful.'

'Yes, but she is purging off the Honeychurch taint – most excellent Honeychurches, but you know what I mean. She is not always quoting servants, or asking one how the pudding is made.'

'Italy has done it.'

'Perhaps,' she murmured, thinking of the museum that represented Italy to her. 'It is just possible. Cecil, mind you marry her next January. She is one of us already.'

'But her music!' he exclaimed. 'The style of her! How she kept to Schumann when, like an idiot, I wanted Beethoven. Schumann was right for this evening. Schumann was the thing. Do you know, mother, I shall have our children educated just like Lucy. Bring them up among honest country folk for freshness, send them to Italy for subtlety, and then – not till then – let them come to London. I don't believe in these London educations –' He broke off, remembering that he had had one himself, and concluded, 'At all events, not for women.'

'Make her one of us,' repeated Mrs Vyse, and processed to bed.

As she was dozing off, a cry – the cry of nightmare – rang from Lucy's room. Lucy could ring for the maid if she liked, but Mrs Vyse thought it kind to go herself. She found the girl sitting upright with her hand on her cheek.

'I am so sorry, Mrs Vyse – it is these dreams.'

'Bad dreams?'

'Just dreams.'

The elder lady smiled and kissed her, saying very distinctly: 'You should have heard us talking about you, dear. He admires you more than ever. Dream of that.'

Lucy returned the kiss, still covering one cheek with her hand. Mrs Vyse recessed to bed. Cecil, whom the cry had not awoke, snored. Darkness enveloped the flat.

CHAPTER XII

Twelfth Chapter

IT WAS A Saturday afternoon, gay and brilliant after abundant rains, and the spirit of youth dwelt in it, though the season was now autumn. All that was gracious triumphed. As the motor-cars passed through Summer Street they raised only a little dust, and their stench was soon dispersed by the wind and replaced by the scent of the wet birches or of the pines. Mr Beebe, at leisure for life's amenities, leant over his rectory gate. Freddy leant by him, smoking a pendant pipe.

'Suppose we go and hinder those new people opposite for a little.'

'M'm.'

'They might amuse you.'

Freddy, whom his fellow creatures never amused, suggested that the new people might be feeling a bit busy, and so on, since they had only just moved in.

'I suggested we should hinder them,' said Mr Beebe. 'They are worth it.' Unlatching the gate, he sauntered over the tri-angular green to Cissie Villa. 'Hullo!' he called, shouting in at the open door, through which much squalor was visible.

A grave voice replied, 'Hullo!'

'I've brought someone to see you.'

'I'll be down in a minute.'

The passage was blocked by a wardrobe, which the removal men had failed to carry up the stairs. Mr Beebe edged round it with difficulty. The sitting-room itself was blocked with books.

'Are these people great readers?' Freddy whispered. 'Are they that sort?'

'I fancy they know how to read – a rare accomplishment.

What have they got? Byron. Exactly. *A Shropshire Lad*. Never heard of it. *The Way of All Flesh*. Never heard of it. Gibbon. Hullo! Dear George reads German. Um – um – Schopenhauer, Nietzsche, and so we go on. Well, I suppose your generation knows its own business, Honeychurch.'

'Mr Beebe, look at that,' said Freddy in awestruck tones.

On the cornice of the wardrobe the hand of an amateur had painted this inscription: 'Mistrust all enterprises that require new clothes.'

'I know. Isn't it jolly? I like that. I'm certain that's the old man's doing.'

'How very odd of him!'

'Surely you agree?'

But Freddy was his mother's son and felt that one ought not to go spoiling the furniture.

'Pictures!' the clergyman continued, scrambling about the room. 'Giotto – they got that at Florence, I'll be bound.'

'The same as Lucy's got.'

'Oh, by the by, did Miss Honeychurch enjoy London?'

'She came back yesterday.'

'I suppose she had a good time?'

'Yes, very,' said Freddy, taking up a book. 'She and Cecil are thicker than ever.'

'That's good hearing.'

'I wish I wasn't such a fool, Mr Beebe.'

Mr Beebe ignored the remark.

'Lucy used to be nearly as stupid as I am, but it'll be very different now, mother thinks. She will read all kinds of books.'

'So will you.'

'Only medical books. Not books that you can talk about afterwards. Cecil is teaching Lucy Italian, and he says her playing is wonderful. There are all kinds of things in it that we have never noticed. Cecil says –'

'What on earth are those people doing upstairs? Emerson – we think we'll come another time.'

George ran downstairs and pushed them into the room without speaking.

'Let me introduce Mr Honeychurch, a neighbour.'

Then Freddy hurled one of the thunderbolts of youth. Perhaps he was shy, perhaps he was friendly, or perhaps he thought that George's face wanted washing. At all events, he greeted him with: 'How d'ye do? Come and have a bathe.'

'Oh, all right,' said George, impassive.

Mr Beebe was highly entertained.

' "How d'ye do? How d'ye do? Come and have a bathe," ' he chuckled. 'That's the best conversational opening I've ever heard. But I'm afraid it will only act between men. Can you picture a lady who has been introduced to another lady by a third lady opening civilities with "How do you do? Come and have a bathe"? And yet you will tell me that the sexes are equal.'

'I tell you that they shall be,' said Mr Emerson, who had been slowly descending the stairs. 'Good afternoon, Mr Beebe. I tell you they shall be comrades, and George thinks the same.'

'We are to raise ladies to our level?' the clergyman inquired.

'The Garden of Eden,' pursued Mr Emerson, still descending, 'which you place in the past, is really yet to come. We shall enter it when we no longer despise our bodies.'

Mr Beebe disclaimed placing the Garden of Eden anywhere.

'In this – not in other things – we men are ahead. We despise the body less than women do. But not until we are comrades shall we enter the Garden.'

'I say, what about this bathe?' murmured Freddy, appalled at the mass of philosophy that was approaching him.

'I believed in a return to Nature once. But how can we return to Nature when we have never been with her? Today, I believe that we must discover Nature. After many conquests we shall attain simplicity. It is our heritage.'

'Let me introduce Mr Honeychurch, whose sister you will remember at Florence.'

'How do you do? Very glad to see you, and that you are taking George for a bathe. Very glad to hear that your sister is going to marry. Marriage is a duty. I am sure that she will be happy, for we know Mr Vyse, too. He has been most kind. He met us by chance in the National Gallery, and arranged everything about this delightful house. Though I hope I have not vexed Sir Harry Otway. I have met so few Liberal landowners, and I was anxious to compare his attitude towards the game laws with the Conservative attitude. Ah, this wind! You do well to bathe. Yours is a glorious country, Honeychurch!'

'Not a bit!' mumbled Freddy. 'I must – that is to say, I have to – have the pleasure of calling on you later on, my mother says, I hope.'

'*Call*, my lad? Who taught us that drawing-room twaddle? Call on your grandmother! Listen to the wind among the pines! Yours is a glorious country.'

Mr Beebe came to the rescue.

'Mr Emerson, he will call, I shall call; you or your son will return our calls before ten days have elapsed. I trust that you have realized about the ten days' interval. It does not count that I helped you with the stair-eyes yesterday. It does not count that they are going to bathe this afternoon.'

'Yes, go and bathe, George. Why do you dawdle talking? Bring them back to tea. Bring back some milk, cakes, honey. The change will do you good. George has been working very hard at his office. I can't believe he's well.'

George bowed his head, dusty and sombre, exhaling the peculiar smell of one who has handled furniture.

'Do you really want this bathe?' Freddy asked him. 'It is only a pond, don't you know. I dare say you are used to something much better.'

'Yes – I have said "Yes" already.'

Mr Beebe felt bound to assist his young friend, and led the way out of the house and into the pine-woods. How glorious it was! For a little time the voice of old Mr Emerson pursued them, dispensing good wishes and philosophy. It ceased, and they only heard the fair wind blowing the bracken and the trees.

Mr Beebe, who could be silent, but who could not bear silence, was compelled to chatter, since the expedition looked like a failure, and neither of his companions would utter a word. He spoke of Florence. George attended gravely, assenting or dissenting with slight but determined gestures that were as inexplicable as the motions of the treetops above their heads.

'And what a coincidence that you should meet Mr Vyse! Did you realize that you would find all the Pension Bertolini down here?'

'I did not. Miss Lavish told me.'

'When I was a young man I always meant to write a "History of Coincidence".'

No enthusiasm.

'Though, as a matter of fact, coincidences are much rarer than we suppose. For example, it isn't pure coincidentality that you are here now, when one comes to reflect.'

To his relief, George began to talk.

'It is. I have reflected. It is Fate. Everything is Fate. We are flung together by Fate, drawn apart by Fate – flung together, drawn apart. The twelve winds blow us – we settle nothing –'

'You have not reflected at all,' rapped the clergyman. 'Let me give you a useful tip, Emerson: attribute nothing to Fate. Don't say, "I didn't do this," for you did it, ten to one. Now I'll cross-question you. Where did you first meet Miss Honeychurch and myself?'

'Italy.'

'And where did you meet Mr Vyse, who is going to marry Miss Honeychurch?'

'National Gallery.'

'Looking at Italian art. There you are, and yet you talk of coincidence and Fate! You naturally seek out things Italian, and so do we and our friends. This narrows the field immeasurably, and we meet again in it.'

'It is Fate that I am here,' persisted George. 'But you can call it Italy if it makes you less unhappy.'

Mr Beebe slid away from such heavy treatment of the subject. But he was infinitely tolerant of the young, and had no desire to snub George.

'And so for this and for other reasons my "History of Coincidence" is still to write.'

Silence.

Wishing to round off the episode, he added:

'We are all so glad that you have come.'

Silence.

'Here we are!' called Freddy.

'Oh, good!' exclaimed Mr Beebe, mopping his brow.

'In there's the pond. I wish it was bigger,' he added apologetically.

They climbed down a slippery bank of pine-needles. There lay the pond, set in its little alp of green – only a pond, but large enough to contain the human body, and pure enough to reflect the sky. On account of the rains, the waters had flooded the surrounding grass, which showed like a beautiful emerald path, tempting the feet towards the central pool.

'It's distinctly successful, as ponds go,' said Mr Beebe. 'No apologies are necessary for the pond.'

George sat down where the ground was dry, and drearily unlaced his boots.

'Aren't those masses of willow-herb splendid? I love willow-herb in seed. What's the name of this aromatic plant?'

No one knew or seemed to care.

'These abrupt changes of vegetation – this little spongeous tract of water-plants, and on either side of it all the growths are tough or brittle – heather, bracken, hurts, pines. Very charming, very charming.'

'Mr Beebe, aren't you bathing?' called Freddy, as he stripped himself.

Mr Beebe thought he was not.

'Water's wonderful!' cried Freddy, prancing in.

'Water's water,' murmured George. Wetting his hair first – a sure sign of apathy – he followed Freddy into the divine, as indifferent as if he were a statue and the pond a pail of soapsuds. It was necessary to use his muscles. It was necessary to keep clean. Mr Beebe watched them, and watched the seeds of the willow-herb dance chorically above their heads.

'Apooshoo, apooshoo, apooshoo,' went Freddy, swimming for two strokes in either direction, and then becoming involved in reeds or mud.

'Is it worth it?' asked the other, Michelangelesque on the flooded margin.

The bank broke away, and he fell into the pool before he had weighed the question properly.

'Hee – poof – I've swallowed a polly-wog. Mr Beebe, water's wonderful, water's simply ripping.'

'Water's not so bad,' said George, reappearing from his plunge, and sputtering at the sun.

'Water's wonderful. Mr Beebe, do.'

'Apooshoo, kouf.'

Mr Beebe, who was hot, and who always acquiesced where possible, looked around him. He could detect no parishioners except the pine trees, rising up steeply on all sides, and gesturing to each other against the blue. How glorious it was! The world of motor-cars and Rural Deans receded illimitably. Water, sky, evergreens, a wind – these things not even the seasons can touch, and surely they lie beyond the intrusion of man?

'I may as well wash too'; and soon his garments made a third little pile on the sward, and he too asserted the wonder of the water.

It was ordinary water, nor was there very much of it, and, as Freddy said, it reminded one of swimming in a salad. The three gentlemen rotated in the pool breast high, after the fashion of the nymphs in *Götterdämmerung*. But either because the rains had given a freshness, or because the sun was shedding a most glorious heat, or because two of the gentlemen were young in years and the third young in the spirit – for some reason or other a change came over them, and they forgot Italy and Botany and Fate. They began to play. Mr Beebe and Freddy splashed each other. A little deferentially, they splashed George. He was quiet; they feared they had offended him. Then all the forces of youth burst out. He smiled, flung himself at them, splashed them, ducked them, kicked them, muddied them, and drove them out of the pool.

'Race you round it, then,' cried Freddy, and they raced in the sunshine, and George took a short cut and dirtied his shins, and had to bathe a second time. Then Mr Beebe consented to run – a memorable sight.

They ran to get dry, they bathed to get cool, they played at being Indians in the willow-herbs and in the bracken, they bathed to get clean. And all the time three little bundles lay discreetly on the sward, proclaiming:

'No. We are what matters. Without us shall no enterprise begin. To us shall all flesh turn in the end.'

'A try! A try!' yelled Freddy, snatching up George's bundle and placing it beside an imaginary goalpost.

'Soccer rules,' George retorted, scattering Freddy's bundle with a kick.

'Goal!'

'Goal!'

'Pass!'

'Take care my watch!' cried Mr Beebe.

Clothes flew in all directions.

'Take care my hat! No, that's enough, Freddy. Dress now. No, I say!'

But the two young men were delirious. Away they twinkled into the trees, Freddy with a clerical waistcoat under his arm, George with a wide-awake hat on his dripping hair.

'That'll do!' shouted Mr Beebe, remembering that after all he was in his own parish. Then his voice changed as if every pine tree was a Rural Dean. 'Hi! Steady on! I see people coming, you fellows!'

Yells, and widening circles over the dappled earth.

'Hi! Hi! *Ladies*!'

Neither George nor Freddy was truly refined. Still, they did not hear Mr Beebe's last warning, or they would have avoided Mrs Honeychurch, Cecil and Lucy, who were walking down to call on old Mrs Butterworth. Freddy dropped the waistcoat at their feet, and dashed into some bracken. George whooped in their faces, turned, and scudded away down the path to the pond, still clad in Mr Beebe's hat.

'Gracious alive!' cried Mrs Honeychurch. 'Who ever were those unfortunate people? Oh, dears, look away! And poor Mr Beebe, too! What ever has happened?'

'Come this way immediately,' commanded Cecil, who always felt that he must lead women, though he knew not whither, and protect them, though he knew not against what. He led them now towards the bracken where Freddy sat concealed.

'Oh, poor Mr Beebe! Was that his waistcoat we left in the path? Cecil, Mr Beebe's waistcoat –'

'No business of ours,' said Cecil, glancing at Lucy, who was all parasol and evidently 'minded'.

'I fancy Mr Beebe jumped back into the pond.'

'This way, please, Mrs Honeychurch, this way.'

They followed him up the bank, attempting the tense yet nonchalant expression that is suitable for ladies on such occasions.

'Well, *I* can't help it,' said a voice close ahead, and Freddy reared a freckled face and a pair of snowy shoulders out of the fronds. 'I can't be trodden on, can I?'

'Good gracious me, dear; so it's you! What miserable management! Why not have a comfortable bath at home, with hot and cold laid on?'

'Look here, mother: a fellow must wash, and a fellow's got to dry, and if another fellow –'

'Dear, no doubt you're right as usual, but you are in no position to argue. Come, Lucy.' They turned. 'Oh, look – don't look! Oh, poor Mr Beebe! How unfortunate again –'

For Mr Beebe was just crawling out of the pond, on whose surface garments of an intimate nature did float; while George, the world-weary George, shouted to Freddy that he had hooked a fish.

'And me, I've swallowed one,' answered he of the bracken. 'I've swallowed a polly-wog. It wriggleth in my tummy. I shall die – Emerson, you beast, you've got on my bags.'

'Hush, dears,' said Mrs Honeychurch, who found it impossible to remain shocked. 'And do be sure you dry yourselves thoroughly first. All these colds come of not drying thoroughly.'

'Mother, do come away,' said Lucy. 'Oh, for goodness' sake, do come.'

'Hullo!' cried George, so that again the ladies stopped.

He regarded himself as dressed. Barefoot, bare-chested, radiant and personable against the shadowy woods, he called:

'Hullo, Miss Honeychurch! Hullo!'

'Bow, Lucy; better bow. Who ever is it? I shall bow.'

Miss Honeychurch bowed.

That evening and all that night the water ran away. On the morrow the pool had shrunk to its old size and lost its glory. It had been a call to the blood and to the relaxed will, a passing benediction whose influence did not pass, a holiness, a spell, a momentary chalice for youth.

CHAPTER XIII

How Miss Bartlett's Boiler was so Tiresome

HOW OFTEN HAD Lucy rehearsed this bow, this interview! But she had always rehearsed them indoors, and with certain accessories, which surely we have a right to assume. Who could foretell that she and George would meet in the rout of a civilization, amidst an army of coats and collars and boots that lay wounded over the sunlit earth? She had imagined a young Mr Emerson, who might be shy or morbid or indifferent or furtively impudent. She was prepared for all of these. But she had never imagined one who would be happy and greet her with the shout of the morning star.

Indoors herself, partaking of tea with old Mrs Butterworth, she reflected that it is impossible to foretell the future with any degree of accuracy, that it is impossible to rehearse life. A fault in the scenery, a face in the audience, an irruption of the audience onto the stage, and all our carefully planned gestures mean nothing, or mean too much. 'I will bow,' she had thought. 'I will not shake hands with him. That will be just the proper thing.' She had bowed – but to whom? To gods, to heroes, to the nonsense of schoolgirls! She had bowed across the rubbish that cumbers the world.

So ran her thoughts, while her faculties were busy with Cecil. It was another of those dreadful engagement calls. Mrs Butterworth had wanted to see him, and he did not want to be seen. He did not want to hear about hydrangeas, why they change their colour at the seaside. He did not want to join the C.O.S. When cross he was always elaborate, and made long, clever answers where 'Yes' or 'No' would have done. Lucy soothed him and tinkered at the conversation in a way that promised well for their married peace. No one is perfect, and surely it is wiser to discover the imperfections before wedlock. Miss Bartlett, in deed, though not in word, had taught the girl that this our life contains nothing satisfactory. Lucy, though she disliked the teacher, regarded the teaching as profound, and applied it to her lover.

'Lucy,' said her mother, when they got home, 'is anything the matter with Cecil?'

The question was ominous: up till now Mrs Honeychurch had behaved with charity and restraint.

'No, I don't think so, mother; Cecil's all right.'

'Perhaps he's tired.'

Lucy compromised: perhaps Cecil was a little tired.

'Because otherwise' – she pulled out her bonnet-pins with gathering displeasure – 'because otherwise I cannot account for him.'

'I do think Mrs Butterworth is rather tiresome, if you mean that.'

'Cecil has told you to think so. You were devoted to her as a little girl, and nothing will describe her goodness to you through the typhoid fever. No – it is just the same thing everywhere.'

'Let me just put your bonnet away, may I?'

'Surely he could answer her civilly for one half-hour?'

'Cecil has a very high standard for people,' faltered Lucy, seeing trouble ahead. 'It's part of his ideals – it is really that that makes him sometimes seem –'

'Oh, rubbish! If high ideals make a young man rude, the sooner he gets rid of them the better,' said Mrs Honeychurch, handing her the bonnet.

'Now mother! I've seen you cross with Mrs Butterworth yourself!'

'Not in that way. At times I could wring her neck. But not in that way. No. It is the same with Cecil all over.'

'By the by – I never told you. I had a letter from Charlotte while I was away in London.'

This attempt to divert the conversation was too puerile, and Mrs Honeychurch resented it.

'Since Cecil came back from London, nothing appears to please him. Whenever I speak he winces – I see him, Lucy; it is useless to contradict me. No doubt I am neither artistic nor literary nor intellectual nor musical, but I cannot help the drawing-room furniture: your father bought it and we must put up with it, will Cecil kindly remember.'

'I – I see what you mean, and certainly Cecil oughtn't to. But he does not mean to be uncivil – he once explained – it is the *things* that upset him – he is easily upset by ugly things – he is not uncivil to *people*.'

'Is it a thing or a person when Freddy sings?'

'You can't expect a really musical person to enjoy comic songs as we do.'

'Then why didn't he leave the room? Why sit wriggling and sneering and spoiling everyone's pleasure?'

'We mustn't be unjust to people,' faltered Lucy. Something had enfeebled her, and the case for Cecil, which she had mastered so perfectly in London, would not come forth in an effective form. The two civilizations had clashed – Cecil had hinted that they might – and she was dazzled and bewildered, as though the radiance that lies behind all civilization had blinded her eyes. Good taste and bad taste were only catchwords, garments of diverse cut; and music itself dissolved to a whisper through pine trees, where the song is not distinguishable from the comic song.

She remained in much embarrassment, while Mrs Honey-church changed her frock for dinner; and every now and then she said a word, and made things no better. There was no concealing the fact – Cecil had meant to be supercilious, and he had succeeded. And Lucy – she knew not why – wished that the trouble could have come at any other time.

'Go and dress, dear; you'll be late.'

'All right, mother –'

'Don't say "All right" and stop. Go.'

She obeyed, but loitered disconsolately at the landing window. It faced north, so there was little view, and no view of the sky. Now, as in the winter, the pine trees hung close to her eyes. One connected the landing window with depression. No definite problem menaced her, but she sighed to herself, 'Oh dear, what shall I do, what shall I do?' It seemed to her that everyone else was behaving very badly. And she ought not to have mentioned Miss Bartlett's letter. She must be more careful: her mother was rather inquisitive, and might have asked what it was about. Oh dear, what should she do? – and then Freddy came bounding upstairs, and joined the ranks of the ill-behaved.

'I say, those are topping people.'

'My dear baby, how tiresome you've been! You had no business to take them bathing in the Sacred Lake; it's much too public. It was all right for you, but most awkward for everyone else. Do be more careful. You forget the place is growing half suburban.'

'I say, is anything on tomorrow week?'

'Not that I know of.'

'Then I want to ask the Emersons up to Sunday tennis.'

'Oh, I wouldn't do that, Freddy, I wouldn't do that with all this muddle.'

'What's wrong with the court? They won't mind a bump or two, and I've ordered new balls.'

'I meant *it's* better not. I really mean it.'

He seized her by the elbows and humorously danced her up and down the passage. She pretended not to mind, but she could have screamed with temper. Cecil glanced at them as he proceeded to his toilet and they impeded Mary with her brood of hot-water cans. Then Mrs Honeychurch opened her door and said: 'Lucy, what a noise you're making! I have something to say to you. Did you say you had had a letter from Charlotte?' and Freddy ran away.

'Yes. I really can't stop. I must dress too.'

'How's Charlotte?'

'All right.'

'Lucy!'

The unfortunate girl returned.

'You've a bad habit of hurrying away in the middle of one's sentences. Did Charlotte mention her boiler?'

'Her *what*?'

'Don't you remember that her boiler was to be had out in October, and her bath cistern cleaned out, and all kinds of terrible to-doing?'

'I can't remember all Charlotte's worries,' said Lucy bitterly. 'I shall have enough of my own, now that you are not pleased with Cecil.'

Mrs Honeychurch might have flamed out. She did not. She said: 'Come here, old lady – thank you for putting away my bonnet – kiss me.' And, though nothing is perfect, Lucy felt for the moment that her mother and Windy Corner and the Weald in the declining sun were perfect.

So the grittiness went out of life. It generally did at Windy Corner. At the last minute, when the social machine was clogged hopelessly, one member or other of the family poured in a drop of oil. Cecil despised their methods – perhaps rightly. At all events, they were not his own.

Dinner was at half past seven. Freddy gabbled a grace, and they drew up their heavy chairs and fell to. Fortunately, the men were hungry. Nothing untoward occurred until the pudding. Then Freddy said:

'Lucy, what's Emerson like?'

'I saw him in Florence,' said Lucy, hoping that this would pass for a reply.

'Is he the clever sort, or is he a decent chap?'

'Ask Cecil; it is Cecil who brought him here.'

'He is the clever sort, like myself,' said Cecil.

Freddy looked at him doubtfully.

'How well did you know them at the Bertolini?' asked Mrs Honeychurch.

'Oh, very slightly. I mean, Charlotte knew them even less than I did.'

'Oh, that reminds me – you never told me what Charlotte said in her letter.'

'One thing and another,' said Lucy, wondering whether she would get through the meal without a lie. 'Among other things, that an awful friend of hers had been bicycling through Summer Street, wondered if she'd come up and see us, and mercifully didn't.'

'Lucy, I do call the way you talk unkind.'

'She was a novelist,' said Lucy craftily. The remark was a happy one, for nothing roused Mrs Honeychurch so much as literature in the hands of females. She would abandon every topic to inveigh against those women who (instead of minding their houses and their children) seek notoriety by print. Her attitude was: 'If books must be written, let them be written by men'; and she developed it at great length, while Cecil yawned and Freddy played at 'This year, next year, now, never' with his plumstones, and Lucy artfully fed the flames of her mother's wrath. But soon the conflagration died down, and the ghosts began to gather in the darkness. There were too many ghosts about. The original ghost – that touch of lips on her cheek – had surely been laid long ago; it could be nothing to her that a man had kissed her on a mountain once. But it had begotten a spectral family – Mr Harris, Miss Bartlett's letter, Mr Beebe's memories of violets – and one or other of these was bound to haunt her before Cecil's very eyes. It was Miss Bartlett who returned now, and with appalling vividness.

'I have been thinking, Lucy, of that letter of Charlotte's. How is she?'

'I tore the thing up.'

'Didn't she say how she was? How does she sound? Cheerful?'

'Oh yes, I suppose so – no – not very cheerful, I suppose.'

'Then, depend upon it, it *is* the boiler. I know myself how water preys upon one's mind. I would rather anything else – even a misfortune with the Meat.'

Cecil laid his hand over his eyes.

'So would I,' asserted Freddy, backing his mother up – backing up the spirit of her remark rather than its substance.

'And I have been thinking,' she added rather nervously, 'surely we could squeeze Charlotte in here next week, and give her a nice holiday while the plumbers at Tunbridge Wells finish. I have not seen poor Charlotte for so long.'

It was more than her nerves could stand. And yet she could not protest violently after her mother's goodness to her upstairs.

'Mother, no!' she pleaded. 'It's impossible. We can't have Charlotte on the top of the other things; we're squeezed to death as it is. Freddy's got a friend coming Tuesday, there's Cecil, and you've promised to take in Minnie Beebe because of the diphtheria scare. It simply can't be done.'

'Nonsense! It can.'

'If Minnie sleeps in the bath. Not otherwise.'

'Minnie can sleep with you.'

'I won't have her.'

'Then, if you're so selfish, Mr Floyd must share a room with Freddy.'

'Miss Bartlett, Miss Bartlett, Miss Bartlett,' moaned Cecil, again laying his hand over his eyes.

'It's impossible,' repeated Lucy. 'I don't want to make difficulties, but it really isn't fair on the maids to fill up the house so.'

Alas!

'The truth is, dear, you don't like Charlotte.'

'No, I don't. And no more does Cecil. She gets on our nerves. You haven't seen her lately, and don't realize how tiresome she can be, though so good. So please, mother, don't worry us this last summer; but spoil us by not asking her to come.'

'Hear, hear!' said Cecil.

Mrs Honeychurch, with more gravity than usual, and with more feeling than she usually permitted herself, replied: 'This isn't very kind of you two. You have each other and all these woods to walk in, so full of beautiful things; and poor Charlotte has only the water turned off and plumbers. You are young, dears, and however clever young people are, and however many books they read, they will never guess what it feels like to grow old.'

Cecil crumbled his bread.

'I must say Cousin Charlotte was very kind to me that year I called on my bike,' put in Freddy. 'She thanked me for coming till I felt like such a fool, and fussed round no end to get an egg boiled for my tea just right.'

'I know, dear. She is kind to everyone, and yet Lucy makes this difficulty when we try to give her some little return.'

But Lucy hardened her heart. It was no good being kind to Miss Bartlett. She had tried herself too often and too recently. One might lay up treasure in heaven by the attempt, but one enriched neither Miss Bartlett nor anyone else upon earth. She was reduced to saying: 'I can't help it, mother. I don't like Charlotte. I admit it's horrid of me.'

'From your own account, you told her as much.'

'Well, she would leave Florence so stupidly. She flurried –'

The ghosts were returning; they filled Italy, they were even usurping the places she had known as a child. The Sacred Lake would never be the same again, and, on Sunday week, something would even happen to Windy Corner. How would she fight against ghosts? For a moment the visible world faded away, and memories and emotions alone seemed real.

'I suppose Miss Bartlett must come, since she boils eggs so well,' said Cecil, who was in rather a happier frame of mind, thanks to the admirable cooking.

'I didn't mean the egg was *well* boiled,' corrected Freddy, 'because in point of fact she forgot to take it off, and as a matter of fact I don't care for eggs. I only meant how jolly kind she seemed.'

Cecil frowned again. Oh, these Honeychurches! Eggs, boilers, hydrangeas, maids – of such were their lives compact. 'May me and Lucy get down from our chairs?' he asked, with scarcely veiled insolence. 'We don't want no dessert.'

CHAPTER XIV

How Lucy Faced the External Situation Bravely

OF COURSE MISS Bartlett accepted. And, equally of course, she felt sure that she would prove a nuisance, and begged to be given an inferior spare room – something with no view, anything. Her love to Lucy. And, equally of course, George Emerson could come to tennis on the Sunday week.

Lucy faced the situation bravely, though, like most of us, she only faced the situation that encompassed her. She never gazed inwards. If at times strange images rose from the depths, she put them down to nerves. When Cecil brought the Emersons to Summer Street, it had upset her nerves. Charlotte would burnish up past foolishness, and this might upset her nerves. She was nervous at night. When she talked to George – they met again almost immediately at the rectory – his voice moved her deeply, and she wished to remain near him. How dreadful if she really wished to remain near him! Of course, the wish was due to nerves, which love to play such perverse tricks upon us. Once she had suffered from 'things that came out of nothing and meant she didn't know what'. Now Cecil had explained psychology to her one wet afternoon, and all the troubles of youth in an unknown world could be dismissed.

It is obvious enough for the reader to conclude, 'She loves young Emerson.' A reader in Lucy's place would not find it obvious. Life is easy to chronicle, but bewildering to practise, and we welcome 'nerves' or any other shibboleth that will cloak our personal desire. She loved Cecil; George made her nervous; will the reader explain to her that the phrases should have been reversed?

But the external situation – she will face that bravely.

The meeting at the rectory had passed off well enough. Standing between Mr Beebe and Cecil, she had made a few temperate allusions to Italy, and George had replied. She was anxious to show that she was not shy, and was glad that he did not seem shy either.

'A nice fellow,' said Mr Beebe afterwards. 'He will work off his crudities in time. I rather mistrust young men who slip into life gracefully.'

Lucy said: 'He seems in better spirits. He laughs more.'

'Yes,' replied the clergyman. 'He is waking up.'

That was all. But, as the week wore on, more of her defences fell, and she entertained an image that had physical beauty.

In spite of the clearest directions, Miss Bartlett contrived to bungle her arrival. She was due at the South-Eastern station at Dorking, whither Mrs Honeychurch drove to meet her. She arrived at the London and Brighton station, and had to hire a cab up. No one was at home except Freddy and his friend, who had to stop their tennis and to entertain her for a solid hour. Cecil and Lucy turned up at four o'clock, and these, with little Minnie Beebe, made a somewhat lugubrious sextet upon the upper lawn for tea.

'I shall never forgive myself,' said Miss Bartlett, who kept on rising from her seat, and had to be begged by the united company to remain. 'I have upset everything. Bursting in on young people! But I insist on paying for my cab up. Grant me that, at any rate.'

'Our visitors never do such a dreadful thing,' said Lucy, while her brother, in whose memory the boiled egg had already grown unsubstantial, exclaimed in irritable tones: 'Just what I've been trying to convince Cousin Charlotte of, Lucy, for the last half-hour.'

'I do not feel myself an ordinary visitor,' said Miss Bartlett, and looked at her frayed gloves.

'All right, if you'd really rather. Five shillings, and I gave a bob to the driver.'

Miss Bartlett looked in her purse. Only sovereigns and pennies. Could anyone give her change? Freddy had half a quid and his friend had four half-crowns. Miss Bartlett accepted their moneys and then said: 'But who am I to give the sovereign to?'

'Let's leave it all till mother comes back,' suggested Lucy.

'No, dear; your mother may take quite a long drive now that she is not hampered with me. We all have our little foibles, and mine is the promptly settling of accounts.'

Here Freddy's friend, Mr Floyd, made the one remark of his that need be quoted: he offered to toss Freddy for Miss Bartlett's quid. A solution seemed in sight, and even Cecil, who had been ostentatiously drinking his tea at the view, felt the eternal attraction of Chance, and turned round.

But this did not do, either.

'Please – please – I know I am a sad spoil-sport, but it would make me wretched. I should practically be robbing the one who lost.'

'Freddy owes me fifteen shillings,' interposed Cecil. 'So it will work out right if you give the pound to me.'

'Fifteen shillings,' said Miss Bartlett dubiously. 'How is that, Mr Vyse?'

'Because, don't you see, Freddy paid your cab. Give me the pound, and we shall avoid this deplorable gambling.'

Miss Bartlett, who was poor at figures, became bewildered and rendered up the sovereign, amidst the suppressed gurgles of the other youths. For a moment Cecil was happy. He was playing at nonsense among his peers. Then he glanced at Lucy, in whose face petty anxieties had marred the smiles. In January he would rescue his Leonardo from this stupefying twaddle.

'But I don't see that!' exclaimed Minnie Beebe, who had narrowly watched the iniquitous transaction. 'I don't see why Mr Vyse is to have the quid.'

'Because of the fifteen shillings and the five,' they said solemnly. 'Fifteen shillings and five shillings make one pound, you see.'

'But I don't see –'

They tried to stifle her with cake.

'No, thank you. I'm done. I don't see why – Freddy, don't poke me. Miss Honeychurch, your brother's hurting me. Ow! What about Mr Floyd's ten shillings? Ow! No, I don't see and I never shall see why Miss What's-her-name shouldn't pay that bob for the driver.'

'I had forgotten the driver,' said Miss Bartlett, reddening. 'Thank you, dear, for reminding me. A shilling, was it? Can anyone give me change for half a crown?'

'I'll get it,' said the young hostess, rising with decision. 'Cecil, give me that sovereign. No – give me up that sovereign. I'll get Euphemia to change it, and we'll start the whole thing again from the beginning.'

'Lucy – Lucy – what a nuisance I am!' protested Miss Bartlett, and followed her across the lawn. Lucy tripped ahead, simulating hilarity. When they were out of earshot, Miss Bartlett stopped her wails and said quite briskly: 'Have you told him about him yet?'

'No, I haven't,' replied Lucy, and then could have bitten her tongue for understanding so quickly what her cousin meant. 'Let me see – a sovereign's worth of silver.'

She escaped into the kitchen. Miss Bartlett's sudden transitions were too uncanny. It sometimes seemed as if she planned every word she spoke or caused to be spoken; as if all this worry about cabs and change had been a ruse to surprise the soul.

'No, I haven't told Cecil or anyone,' she remarked, when she returned. 'I promised you I shouldn't. Here is your money – all shillings, except two half-crowns. Would you count it? You can settle your debt nicely now.'

Miss Bartlett was in the drawing-room, gazing at the photograph of St John ascending, who had been framed.

'How dreadful!' she murmured, 'how more than dreadful, if Mr Vyse should come to hear of it from some other source.'

'Oh no, Charlotte,' said the girl, entering the battle, 'George Emerson is all right, and what other source is there?'

Miss Bartlett considered. 'For instance, the driver. I saw him

looking through the bushes at you. I remember he had a violet
between his teeth.'

Lucy shuddered a little. 'We shall get the silly affair on our
nerves if we aren't careful. How could a Florentine cab-driver
ever get hold of Cecil?'

'We must think of every possibility.'

'Oh, it's all right.'

'Or perhaps old Mr Emerson knows. In fact, he is certain to
know.'

'I don't care if he does. I was grateful to you for your letter,
but even if the news does get round, I think I can trust Cecil to
laugh at it.'

'To contradict it?'

'No, to laugh at it.' But she knew in her heart that she could
not trust him, for he desired her untouched.

'Very well, dear, you know best. Perhaps gentlemen are different to what they were when I was young. Ladies are certainly
different.'

'Now, Charlotte!' She struck at her playfully. 'You kind,
anxious thing! What *would* you have me do? First you say, "Don't
tell"; and then you say, "Tell." Which is it to be? Quick!'

Miss Bartlett sighed. 'I am no match for you in conversation,
dearest. I blush when I think how I interfered at Florence, and
you so well able to look after yourself, and so much cleverer in
all ways than I am. You will never forgive me.'

'Shall we go out, then? They will smash all the china if we
don't.'

For the air rang with the shrieks of Minnie, who was being
scalped with a teaspoon.

'Dear, one moment – we may not have this chance for a chat
again. Have you seen the young one yet?'

'Yes, I have.'

'What happened?'

'We met at the rectory.'

'What line is he taking up?'

'No line. He talked about Italy, like any other person. It is really all right. What advantage would he get from being a cad, to put it bluntly? I do wish I could make you see it my way. He really won't be any nuisance, Charlotte.'

'Once a cad, always a cad. That is my poor opinion.'

Lucy paused. 'Cecil said one day – and I thought it so profound – that there are two kinds of cads – the conscious and the subconscious.' She paused again, to be sure of doing justice to Cecil's profundity. Through the window she saw Cecil himself, turning over the pages of a novel. It was a new one from Smith's library. Her mother must have returned from the station.

'Once a cad, always a cad,' droned Miss Bartlett.

'What I mean by subconscious is that Mr Emerson lost his head. I fell into all those violets, and he was silly and surprised. I don't think we ought to blame him very much. It makes such a difference when you see a person with beautiful things behind him unexpectedly. It really does; it makes an enormous difference, and he lost his head; he doesn't admire me, or any of that nonsense, one straw. Freddy rather likes him, and has asked him up here on Sunday, so you can judge for yourself. He has improved: he doesn't always look as if he is going to burst into tears. He is a clerk in the General Manager's office at one of the big railways – not a porter! – and runs down to his father for week-ends. Papa was to do with journalism, but is rheumatic and has retired. There! Now for the garden.' She took hold of her guest by the arm. 'Suppose we don't talk about this silly Italian business any more. We want you to have a nice restful visit at Windy Corner, with no worriting.'

Lucy thought this rather a good speech. The reader may have detected an unfortunate slip in it. Whether Miss Bartlett detected the slip one cannot say, for it is impossible to penetrate into the minds of elderly people. She might have spoken further, but they were interrupted by the entrance of her hostess. Explanations took place, and in the midst of them Lucy escaped, the images throbbing a little more vividly in her brain.

CHAPTER XV

The Disaster Within

THE SUNDAY AFTER Miss Bartlett's arrival was a glorious day, like most of the days of that year. In the Weald, autumn approached, breaking up the green monotony of summer, touching the parks with the grey bloom of mist, the beech trees with russet, the oak trees with gold. Up on the heights, battalions of black pines witnessed the change, themselves unchangeable. Either country was spanned by a cloudless sky, and in either arose the tinkle of church bells.

The garden of Windy Corner was deserted except for a red book, which lay sunning itself upon the gravel path. From the house came incoherent sounds, as of females preparing for worship. 'The men say they won't go' – 'Well, I don't blame them' – 'Minnie says, need she go?' – 'Tell her, no nonsense' – 'Anne! Mary! Hook me behind!' – 'Dearest Lucia, may I trespass upon you for a pin?' For Miss Bartlett had announced that she at all events was one for church.

The sun rose higher on its journey, guided, not by Phaethon, but by Apollo, competent, unswerving, divine. Its rays fell on the ladies whenever they advanced towards the bedroom windows; on Mr Beebe down at Summer Street as he smiled over a letter from Miss Catharine Alan; on George Emerson cleaning his father's boots; and lastly, to complete the catalogue of memorable things, on the red book mentioned above. The ladies move, Mr Beebe moves, George moves, and movement may engender shadow. But this book lies motionless, to be caressed all the morning by the sun and to raise its covers slightly, as though acknowledging the caress.

Presently Lucy steps out of the drawing-room window. Her

new cerise dress has been a failure, and makes her look tawdry
and wan. At her throat is a garnet brooch, on her finger a ring
set with rubies – an engagement-ring. Her eyes are bent to the
Weald. She frowns a little – not in anger, but as a brave child
frowns when he is trying not to cry. In all that expanse no human
eye is looking at her, and she may frown unrebuked and measure
the spaces that yet survive between Apollo and the western hills.

'Lucy! Lucy! What's that book? Who's been taking a book out
of the shelf and leaving it about to spoil?'

'It's only the library book that Cecil's been reading.'

'But pick it up, and don't stand idling there like a flamingo.'

Lucy picked up the book and glanced at the title listlessly:
Under a Loggia. She no longer read novels herself, devoting all
her spare time to solid literature in the hope of catching Cecil
up. It was dreadful how little she knew, and even when she
thought she knew a thing, like the Italian painters, she found she
had forgotten it. Only this morning she had confused Francesco
Francia with Piero della Francesca, and Cecil had said, 'What!
You aren't forgetting your Italy already?' And this too had lent
anxiety to her eyes when she saluted the dear view and the dear
garden in the foreground, and above them, scarce conceivable
elsewhere, the dear sun.

'Lucy – have you a sixpence for Minnie and a shilling for
yourself?'

She hastened in to her mother, who was rapidly working
herself into a Sunday fluster.

'It's a special collection – I forget what for. I do beg, no vulgar
clinking in the plate with halfpennies; see that Minnie has a nice
bright sixpence. Where is the child? Minnie! That book's all
warped. (Gracious, how plain you look!) Put it under the atlas
to press. Minnie!'

'Oh, Mrs Honeychurch –' from the upper regions.

'Minnie, don't be late. Here comes the horse' – it was always
the horse, never the carriage. 'Where's Charlotte? Run up and
hurry her. Why is she so long? She had nothing to do. She never

brings anything but blouses. Poor Charlotte – how I do detest blouses! Minnie!'

Paganism is infectious – more infectious than diphtheria or piety – and the Rector's niece was taken to church protesting. As usual, she didn't see why. Why shouldn't she sit in the sun with the young men? The young men, who had now appeared, mocked her with ungenerous words. Mrs Honeychurch defended orthodoxy, and in the midst of the confusion Miss Bartlett, dressed in the very height of the fashion, came strolling down the stairs.

'Dear Marian, I am very sorry, but I have no small change – nothing but sovereigns and half-crowns. Could anyone give me –'

'Yes, easily. Jump in. Gracious me, how smart you look. What a lovely frock! You put us all to shame.'

'If I did not wear my best rags and tatters now, when should I wear them?' said Miss Bartlett reproachfully. She got into the victoria and placed herself with her back to the horse. The necessary uproar ensued, and then they drove off.

'Goodbye! Be good!' called out Cecil.

Lucy bit her lip, for the tone was sneering. On the subject of 'church and so on' they had had rather an unsatisfactory conversation. He had said that people ought to overhaul themselves, and she did not want to overhaul herself; she did not know how it was done. Honest orthodoxy Cecil respected, but he always assumed that honesty is the result of a spiritual crisis; he could not imagine it as a natural birthright, that might grow heavenward like the flowers. All that he said on this subject pained her, though he exuded tolerance from every pore; somehow the Emersons were different.

She saw the Emersons after church. There was a line of carriages down the road, and the Honeychurch vehicle happened to be opposite Cissie Villa. To save time, they walked over the green to it, and found father and son smoking in the garden.

'Introduce me,' said her mother. 'Unless the young man considers that he knows me already.'

He probably did; but Lucy ignored the Sacred Lake and

introduced them formally. Old Mr Emerson claimed her with much warmth, and said how glad he was that she was going to be married. She said yes, she was glad too; and then, as Miss Bartlett and Minnie were lingering behind with Mr Beebe, she turned the conversation to a less disturbing topic, and asked him how he liked his new house.

'Very much,' he replied, but there was a note of offence in his voice; she had never known him offended before. He added: 'We find, though, that the Miss Alans were coming, and that we have turned them out. Women mind such a thing. I am very much upset about it.'

'I believe that there was some misunderstanding,' said Mrs Honeychurch uneasily.

'Our landlord was told that we should be a different type of person,' said George, who seemed disposed to carry the matter further. 'He thought we should be artistic. He is disappointed.'

'And I wonder whether we ought to write to the Miss Alans and offer to give it up. What do you think?' He appealed to Lucy.

'Oh, stop now you have come,' said Lucy lightly. She must avoid censuring Cecil. For it was on Cecil that the little episode turned, though his name was never mentioned.

'So George says. He says that the Miss Alans must go to the wall. Yet it does seem so unkind.'

'There is only a certain amount of kindness in the world,' said George, watching the sunlight flash on the panels of the passing carriages.

'Yes!' exclaimed Mrs Honeychurch. 'That's exactly what I say. Why all this twiddling and twaddling over two Miss Alans?'

'There is a certain amount of kindness, just as there is a certain amount of light,' he continued in measured tones. 'We cast a shadow on something wherever we stand, and it is no good moving from place to place to save things; because the shadow always follows. Choose a place where you won't do harm – yes, choose a place where you won't do very much harm, and stand in it for all you are worth, facing the sunshine.'

'Oh, Mr Emerson, I see you're clever!'

'Eh –?'

'I see you're going to be clever. I hope you didn't go behaving like that to poor Freddy.'

George's eyes laughed, and Lucy suspected that he and her mother would get on rather well.

'No, I didn't,' he said. 'He behaved that way to me. It is his philosophy. Only he starts life with it; and I have tried the Note of Interrogation first.'

'What *do* you mean? No, never mind what you mean. Don't explain. He looks forward to seeing you this afternoon. Do you play tennis? Do you mind tennis on Sunday –?'

'George mind tennis on Sunday! George, after his education, distinguish between Sunday –'

'Very well, George doesn't mind tennis on Sunday. No more do I. That's settled. Mr Emerson, if you could come with your son we should be so pleased.'

He thanked her, but the walk sounded rather far: he could only potter about in these days.

She turned to George: 'And then he wants to give up his house to the Miss Alans.'

'I know,' said George, and put his arm round his father's neck. The kindness that Mr Beebe and Lucy had always known to exist in him came out suddenly, like sunlight touching a vast land-scape – a touch of the morning sun? She remembered that in all his perversities he had never spoken against affection.

Miss Bartlett approached.

'You know our cousin, Miss Bartlett,' said Mrs Honeychurch pleasantly. 'You met her with my daughter in Florence.'

'Yes, indeed!' said the old man, and made as if he would come out of the garden to greet the lady. Miss Bartlett promptly got into the victoria. Thus entrenched, she emitted a formal bow. It was the Pension Bertolini again, the dining-table with the decanters of water and wine. It was the old, old battle of the room with the view.

George did not respond to the bow. Like any boy, he blushed and was ashamed; he knew that the chaperon remembered. He said: 'I – I'll come up to tennis if I can manage it,' and went into the house. Perhaps anything that he did would have pleased Lucy, but his awkwardness went straight to her heart: men were not gods after all, but as human and as clumsy as girls; even men might suffer from unexplained desires, and need help. To one of her upbringing, and of her destination, the weakness of men was a truth unfamiliar, but she had surmised it at Florence, when George threw her photographs into the river Arno.

'George, don't go,' cried his father, who thought it a great treat for people if his son would talk to them. 'George has been in such good spirits today, and I am sure he will end by coming up this afternoon.'

Lucy caught her cousin's eye. Something in its mute appeal made her reckless. 'Yes,' she said, raising her voice, 'I do hope he will.' Then she went to the carriage and murmured, 'The old man hasn't been told; I knew it was all right.' Mrs Honeychurch followed her, and they drove away.

Satisfactory that Mr Emerson had not been told of the Florence escapade; yet Lucy's spirits should not have leapt up as if she had sighted the ramparts of heaven. Satisfactory; yet surely she greeted it with disproportionate joy. All the way home the horses' hoofs sang a tune to her: 'He has not told, he has not told.' Her brain expanded the melody: 'He has not told his father – to whom he tells all things. It was not an exploit. He did not laugh at me when I had gone.' She raised her hand to her cheek. 'He does not love me. No. How terrible if he did! But he has not told. He will not tell.'

She longed to shout the words: 'It is all right. It's a secret between us two for ever. Cecil will never hear.' She was even glad that Miss Bartlett had made her promise secrecy, that last dark evening at Florence, when they had knelt packing in his room. The secret, big or little, was guarded. Only three English people knew of it in the world.

Thus she interpreted her joy. She greeted Cecil with unusual radiance, because she felt so safe. As he helped her out of the carriage, she said:

'The Emersons have been so nice. George Emerson has improved enormously.'

'Oh, how are my protégés?' asked Cecil, who took no real interest in them, and had long since forgotten his resolution to bring them to Windy Corner for educational purposes.

'Protégés!' she exclaimed with some warmth.

For the only relationship which Cecil conceived was feudal: that of protector and protected. He had no glimpse of the comradeship after which the girl's soul yearned.

'You shall see for yourself how your protégés are. George Emerson is coming up this afternoon. He is a most interesting man to talk to. Only don't –' She nearly said, 'Don't protect him.' But the bell was ringing for lunch, and, as often happened, Cecil had paid no great attention to her remarks. Charm, not argument, was to be her forte.

Lunch was a cheerful meal. Generally Lucy was depressed at meals. Someone had to be soothed – either Cecil or Miss Bartlett or a Being not visible to the mortal eye – a Being who whispered to her soul: 'It will not last, this cheerfulness. In January you must go to London to entertain the grandchildren of celebrated men.' But today she felt she had received a guarantee. Her mother would always sit there, her brother here. The sun, though it had moved a little since the morning, would never be hidden behind the western hills. After luncheon they asked her to play. She had seen Gluck's *Armide* that year, and played from memory the music of the enchanted garden – the music to which Renaud approaches, beneath the light of an eternal dawn, the music that never gains, never wanes, but ripples for ever like the tideless seas of fairyland. Such music is not for the piano, and her audience began to get restive, and Cecil, sharing the discontent, called out: 'Now play us the other garden – the one in *Parsifal*.'

She closed the instrument.

'Not very dutiful,' said her mother's voice.

Fearing that she had offended Cecil, she turned quickly round. There George was. He had crept in without interrupting her.

'Oh, I had no idea!' she exclaimed, getting very red; and then, without a word of greeting, she reopened the piano. Cecil should have the *Parsifal*, and anything else that he liked.

'Our performer has changed her mind,' said Miss Bartlett, perhaps implying, 'She will play the music to Mr Emerson.' Lucy did not know what to do, nor even what she wanted to do. She played a few bars of the Flower Maidens' song very badly, and then she stopped.

'I vote tennis,' said Freddy, disgusted at the scrappy entertainment.

'Yes, so do I.' Once more she closed the unfortunate piano. 'I vote you have a men's four.'

'All right.'

'Not for me, thank you,' said Cecil. 'I will not spoil the set.' He never realized that it may be an act of kindness in a bad player to make up a fourth.

'Oh, come along, Cecil. I'm bad, Floyd's rotten, and so I dare say's Emerson.'

George corrected him: 'I am not bad.'

One looked down one's nose at this. 'Then certainly I won't play,' said Cecil, while Miss Bartlett, under the impression that she was snubbing George, added: 'I agree with you, Mr Vyse. You had much better not play. Much better not.'

Minnie, rushing in where Cecil feared to tread, announced that she would play. 'I shall miss every ball anyway, so what does it matter?' But Sunday intervened and stamped heavily upon the kind suggestion.

'Then it will have to be Lucy,' said Mrs Honeychurch; 'you must fall back on Lucy. There is no other way out of it. Lucy, go and change your frock.'

Lucy's Sabbath was generally of this amphibious nature. She kept it without hypocrisy in the morning, and broke it without reluctance in the afternoon. As she changed her frock, she wondered whether Cecil was sneering at her; really she must overhaul herself and settle everything up before she married him.

Mr Floyd was her partner. She liked music, but how much better tennis seemed. How much better to run about in comfortable clothes than to sit at the piano and feel girt under the arms. Once more music appeared to her the employment of a child. George served, and surprised her by his anxiety to win. She remembered how he had sighed among the tombs at Santa Croce because things wouldn't fit; how after the death of that obscure Italian he had leant over the parapet by the Arno and said to her: 'I shall want to live, I tell you.' He wanted to live now, to win at tennis, to stand for all he was worth in the sun – in the sun which had begun to decline and was shining in her eyes; and he did win.

Ah, how beautiful the Weald looked! The hills stood out above its radiance, as Fiesole stands above the Tuscan plain, and the South Downs, if one chose, were the mountains of Carrara. She might be forgetting her Italy, but she was noticing more things in her England. One could play a new game with the view, and try to find in its innumerable folds some town or village that would do for Florence. Ah, how beautiful the Weald looked!

But now Cecil claimed her. He chanced to be in a lucid critical mood, and would not sympathize with exaltation. He had been rather a nuisance all through the tennis, for the novel that he was reading was so bad that he was obliged to read it aloud to others. He would stroll round the precincts of the court and call out: 'I say, listen to this, Lucy. Three split infinitives.' 'Dreadful!' said Lucy, and missed her stroke. When they had finished their set, he still went on reading; there was some murder scene, and really everyone must listen to it. Freddy and Mr Floyd were obliged to hunt for a lost ball in the laurels, but the other two acquiesced.

'The scene is laid in Florence.'

'What fun, Cecil! Read away. Come, Mr Emerson, sit down after all your energy.' She had 'forgiven' George, as she put it, and she made a point of being pleasant to him.

He jumped over the net and sat down at her feet, asking: 'You – and are you tired?'

'Of course I'm not!'

'Do you mind being beaten?'

She was going to answer 'No' when it struck her that she did mind, so she answered 'Yes'. She added merrily: 'I don't see *you're* such a splendid player, though. The light was behind you, and it was in my eyes.'

'I never said I was.'

'Why, you did!'

'You didn't attend.'

'You said – oh, don't go in for accuracy at this house. We all exaggerate, and we get very angry with people who don't.'

'The scene is laid in Florence,' repeated Cecil, with an upward note.

Lucy recollected herself.

' "Sunset. Leonora was speeding –" '

Lucy interrupted. 'Leonora? Is Leonora the heroine? Who's the book by?'

'Joseph Emery Prank. "Sunset. Leonora was speeding across the square. Pray the saints she might not arrive too late. Sunset – the sunset of Italy. Under Orcagna's Loggia – the Loggia de' Lanzi, as we sometimes call it now –" '

Lucy burst into laughter. ' "Joseph Emery Prank" indeed! Why, it's Miss Lavish! It's Miss Lavish's novel, and she's publishing it under somebody else's name.'

'Who may Miss Lavish be?'

'Oh, a dreadful person – Mr Emerson, you remember Miss Lavish?' Excited by her pleasant afternoon, she clapped her hands.

George looked up. 'Of course I do. I saw her the day I arrived at Summer Street. It was she who told me that you lived here.'

'Weren't you pleased?' She meant – 'to see Miss Lavish,' but when he bent down to the grass without replying it struck her that she could mean something else. She watched his head, which was almost resting against her knee, and she thought that the ears were reddening. 'No wonder the novel's bad,' she added. 'I never liked Miss Lavish. But I suppose one ought to read it as one's met her.'

'All modern books are bad,' said Cecil, who was annoyed at her inattention, and vented his annoyance on literature. 'Everyone writes for money in these days.'

'Oh, Cecil –!'

'It is so. I will inflict Joseph Emery Prank on you no longer.'

Cecil, this afternoon, seemed such a twittering sparrow. The ups and downs in his voice were noticeable, but they did not affect her. She had dwelt amongst melody and movement, and her nerves refused to answer to the clang of his. Leaving him to be annoyed, she gazed at the black head again. She did not want to stroke it, but she saw herself wanting to stroke it; the sensation was curious.

'How do you like this view of ours, Mr Emerson?'

'I never notice much difference in views.'

'What do you mean?'

'Because they are all alike. Because all that matters in them is distance and air.'

'H'm!' said Cecil, uncertain whether the remark was striking or not.

'My father' – he looked up at her (and he was a little flushed) – 'says that there is only one perfect view – the view of the sky straight over our heads, and that all these views on earth are but bungled copies of it.'

'I expect your father has been reading Dante,' said Cecil, fingering the novel, which alone permitted him to lead the conversation.

'He told us another day that views are really crowds – crowds of trees and houses and hills – and are bound to resemble each other, like human crowds – and that the power they have over us is something supernatural, for the same reason.'

Lucy's lips parted.

'For a crowd is more than the people who make it up. Something gets added to it – no one knows how – just as something has got added to those hills.'

He pointed with his racquet to the South Downs.

'What a splendid idea!' she murmured. 'I shall enjoy hearing your father talk again. I'm so sorry he's not so well.'

'No, he isn't well.'

'There's an absurd account of a view in this book,' said Cecil.

'Also that men fall into two classes – those who forget views and those who remember them, even in small rooms.'

'Mr Emerson, have you any brothers or sisters?'

'None. Why?'

'You spoke of "us".'

'My mother, I was meaning.'

Cecil closed the novel with a bang.

'Oh, Cecil – how you make me jump!'

'I will inflict Joseph Emery Prank on you no longer.'

'I can just remember us all three going into the country for the day and seeing as far as Hindhead. It is the first thing that I remember.'

Cecil got up: the man was ill-bred – he hadn't put on his coat after tennis – he didn't do. He would have strolled away if Lucy had not stopped him.

'Cecil, do read the thing about the view.'

'Not while Mr Emerson is here to entertain us.'

'No – read away. I think nothing's funnier than to hear silly things read out loud. If Mr Emerson thinks us frivolous, he can go.'

This struck Cecil as subtle, and pleased him. It put their visitor in the position of a prig. Somewhat mollified, he sat down again.

'Mr Emerson, go and find tennis balls.' She opened the book.

Cecil must have his reading and anything else that he liked. But her attention wandered to George's mother, who – according to Mr Eager – had been murdered in the sight of God and – according to her son – had seen as far as Hindhead.

'Am I really to go?' asked George.

'No, of course not really,' she answered.

'Chapter two,' said Cecil, yawning. 'Find me chapter two, if it isn't bothering you.'

Chapter two was found, and she glanced at its opening sentences.

She thought she had gone mad.

'Here – hand me the book.'

She heard her voice saying: 'It isn't worth reading – it's too silly to read – I never saw such rubbish – it oughtn't to be allowed to be printed.'

He took the book from her.

' "Leonora," ' he read, ' "sat pensive and alone. Before her lay the rich champaign of Tuscany, dotted over with many a smiling village. The season was spring." '

Miss Lavish knew, somehow, and had printed the past in draggled prose, for Cecil to read and for George to hear.

' "A golden haze," ' he read. He read: ' "Afar off the towers of Florence, while the bank on which she sat was carpeted with violets. All unobserved, Antonio stole up behind her –" '

Lest Cecil should see her face she turned to George, and she saw his face.

He read: ' "There came from his lips no wordy protestation such as formal lovers use. No eloquence was his, nor did he suffer from the lack of it. He simply enfolded her in his manly arms." '

There was a silence.

'This isn't the passage I wanted,' he informed them. 'There is another much funnier, further on.' He turned over the leaves.

'Should we go in to tea?' said Lucy, whose voice remained steady.

She led the way up the garden, Cecil following her, George

last. She thought a disaster was averted. But when they entered the shrubbery it came. The book, as if it had not worked mischief enough, had been forgotten, and Cecil must go back for it; and George, who loved passionately, must blunder against her in the narrow path.

'No –' she gasped, and, for the second time, was kissed by him.

As if no more was possible, he slipped back; Cecil rejoined her; they reached the upper lawn alone.

CHAPTER XVI

Lying to George

BUT LUCY HAD developed since the spring. That is to say, she was now better able to stifle the emotions of which the conventions and the world disapprove. Though the danger was greater, she was not shaken by deep sobs. She said to Cecil, 'I am not coming in to tea – tell mother – I must write some letters,' and went up to her room. There she prepared for action. Love felt and returned, love which our bodies exact and our hearts have transfigured, love which is the most real thing that we shall ever meet, reappeared now as the world's enemy, and she must stifle it.

She sent for Miss Bartlett.

The contest lay not between love and duty. Perhaps there never is such a contest. It lay between the real and the pretended, and Lucy's first aim was to defeat herself. As her brain clouded over, as the memory of the views grew dim and the words of the book died away, she returned to her old shibboleth of nerves. She 'conquered her breakdown'. Tampering with the truth, she forgot that the truth had ever been. Remembering that she was engaged to Cecil, she compelled herself to confused remembrances of George: he was nothing to her; he never had been anything; he had behaved abominably; she had never encouraged him. The armour of falsehood is subtly wrought out of darkness, and hides a man not only from others, but from his own soul. In a few moments Lucy was equipped for battle.

'Something too awful has happened,' she began, as soon as her cousin arrived. 'Do you know anything about Miss Lavish's novel?'

Miss Bartlett looked surprised, and said that she had not read the book, nor known that it was published; Eleanor was a reticent woman at heart.

'There is a scene in it. The hero and heroine make love. Do you know about that?'

'Dear –?'

'Do you know about it, please?' she repeated. 'They are on a hillside, and Florence is in the distance.'

'My good Lucia, I am all at sea. I know nothing about it whatever.'

'There are violets. I cannot believe it is a coincidence. Charlotte, Charlotte, how *could* you have told her? I have thought before speaking: it *must* be you.'

'Told her what?' she asked, with growing agitation.

'About that dreadful afternoon in February.'

Miss Bartlett was genuinely moved. 'Oh, Lucy, dearest girl – she hasn't put that in her book?'

Lucy nodded.

'Not so that one could recognize it?'

'Yes.'

'Then never – never – never more shall Eleanor Lavish be friend of mine.'

'So you did tell?'

'I did just happen – when I had tea with her at Rome – in the course of conversation –'

'But, Charlotte – what about the promise you gave me when we were packing? Why did you tell Miss Lavish, when you wouldn't even let me tell mother?'

'I will never forgive Eleanor. She has betrayed my confidence.'

'Why did you tell her, though? This is a most serious thing.'

Why does anyone tell anything? The question is eternal, and it was not surprising that Miss Bartlett should only sigh faintly in response. She had done wrong – she admitted it; she only hoped that she had not done harm; she had told Eleanor in the strictest confidence.

Lucy stamped with irritation.

'Cecil happened to read out the passage aloud to me and to Mr Emerson; it upset Mr Emerson, and he insulted me again.

Behind Cecil's back. Ugh! Is it possible that men are such brutes? Behind Cecil's back as we were walking up the garden.'

Miss Bartlett burst into self-accusations and regrets.

'What is to be done now? Can you tell me?'

'Oh, Lucy – I shall never forgive myself, never to my dying day. Fancy if your prospects –'

'I know,' said Lucy, wincing at the word. 'I see now why you wanted me to tell Cecil, and what you meant by "some other source". You knew that you had told Miss Lavish, and that she was not reliable.'

It was Miss Bartlett's turn to wince.

'However,' said the girl, despising her cousin's shiftiness, 'what's done's done. You have put me in a most awkward position. How am I to get out of it?'

Miss Bartlett could not think. The days of her energy were over. She was a visitor, not a chaperon, and a discredited visitor at that. She stood with clasped hands while the girl worked herself into the necessary rage.

'He must – that man must have such a setting down that he won't forget. And who's to give it him? I can't tell mother now – owing to you. Nor Cecil, Charlotte, owing to you. I am caught up every way. I think I shall go mad. I have no one to help me. That's why I've sent for you. What's wanted is a man with a whip.'

Miss Bartlett agreed: one wanted a man with a whip.

'Yes – but it's no good agreeing. What's to be *done*? We women go maundering on. What *does* a girl do when she comes across a cad?'

'I always said he was a cad, dear. Give me credit for that, at all events. From the very first moment – when he said his father was having a bath.'

'Oh, bother the credit and who's been right or wrong! We've both made a muddle of it. George Emerson is still down the garden there, and is he to be left unpunished, or isn't he? I want to know.'

Miss Bartlett was absolutely helpless. Her own exposure had

unnerved her, and thoughts were colliding painfully in her brain.
She moved feebly to the window, and tried to detect the cad's
white flannels among the laurels.

'You were ready enough at the Bertolini when you rushed me
off to Rome. Can't you speak again to him now?'

'Willingly would I move heaven and earth – '

'I want something more definite,' said Lucy contemptuously.
'Will you speak to him? It is the least you can do, surely, considering it all happened because you broke your word.'

'Never again shall Eleanor Lavish be friend of mine.'

Really, Charlotte was outdoing herself.

'Yes or no, please; yes or no.'

'It is the kind of thing that only a gentleman can settle.'

George Emerson was coming up the garden with a tennis-ball
in his hand.

'Very well,' said Lucy, with an angry gesture. 'No one will help
me. I will speak to him myself.' And immediately she realized
that this was what her cousin had intended all along.

'Hullo, Emerson!' called Freddy from below. 'Found the lost
ball? Good man! Want any tea?' And there was an irruption from
the house onto the terrace.

'Oh, Lucy, but that is brave of you! I admire you – '

They had gathered round George, who beckoned, she felt,
over the rubbish, the sloppy thoughts, the furtive yearnings that
were beginning to cumber her soul. Her anger faded at the sight
of him. Ah! The Emersons were fine people in their way. She
had to subdue a rush in her blood before saying:

'Freddy has taken him into the dining-room. The others are
going down the garden. Come. Let us get this over quickly.
Come. I want you in the room, of course.'

'Lucy, do you mind doing it?'

'How can you ask such a ridiculous question?'

'Poor Lucy – ' She stretched out her hand. 'I seem to bring
nothing but misfortune wherever I go.' Lucy nodded. She
remembered their last evening at Florence – the packing, the

candle, the shadow of Miss Bartlett's toque on the door. She was not to be trapped by pathos a second time. Eluding her cousin's caress, she led the way downstairs.

'Try the jam,' Freddy was saying. 'The jam's jolly good.'

George, looking big and dishevelled, was pacing up and down the dining-room. As she entered he stopped, and said:

'No – nothing to eat.'

'You go down to the others,' said Lucy; 'Charlotte and I will give Mr Emerson all he wants. Where's mother?'

'She's started on her Sunday writing. She's in the drawing-room.'

'That's all right. You go away.'

He went off singing.

Lucy sat down at the table. Miss Bartlett, who was thoroughly frightened, took up a book and pretended to read.

She would not be drawn into an elaborate speech. She just said: 'I can't have it, Mr Emerson. I cannot even talk to you. Go out of this house, and never come into it again as long as I live here' – flushing as she spoke, and pointing to the door. 'I hate a row. Go, please.'

'What –'

'No discussion.'

'But I can't –'

She shook her head. 'Go, please. I do not want to call in Mr Vyse.'

'You don't mean,' he said, absolutely ignoring Miss Bartlett – 'you don't mean that you are going to marry that man?'

The line was unexpected.

She shrugged her shoulders, as if his vulgarity wearied her. 'You are merely ridiculous,' she said quietly.

Then his words rose gravely over hers: 'You cannot live with Vyse. He's only for an acquaintance. He is for society and culti-vated talk. He should know no one intimately, least of all a woman.'

It was a new light on Cecil's character.

'Have you ever talked to Vyse without feeling tired?'

'I can scarcely discuss –'

'No, but have you ever? He is the sort who are all right so long as they keep to things – books, pictures – but kill when they come to people. That's why I'll speak out through all this muddle even now. It's shocking enough to lose you in any case, but generally a man must deny himself joy, and I would have held back if your Cecil had been a different person. I would never have let myself go. But I saw him first in the National Gallery, when he winced because my father mispronounced the names of great painters. Then he brings us here, and we find it is to play some silly trick on a kind neighbour. That is the man all over – playing tricks on people, on the most sacred form of life that he can find. Next, I meet you together, and find him protecting and teaching you and your mother to be shocked, when it was for *you* to settle whether you were shocked or no. Cecil all over again. He daren't let a woman decide. He's the type who's kept Europe back for a thousand years. Every moment of his life he's forming you, telling you what's charming or amusing or ladylike, telling you what a man thinks womanly; and you, you of all women, listen to his voice instead of to your own. So it was at the rectory, when I met you both again; so it has been the whole of this afternoon. Therefore – not "therefore I kissed you", because the book made me do that, and I wish to goodness I had more self-control. I'm not ashamed. I don't apologize. But it has frightened you, and you may not have noticed that I love you. Or would you have told me to go, and dealt with a tremendous thing so lightly? But therefore – therefore I settled to fight him.'

Lucy thought of a very good remark.

'You say Mr Vyse wants me to listen to him, Mr Emerson. Pardon me for suggesting that you have caught the habit.'

And he took the shoddy reproof and touched it into immortality. He said:

'Yes, I have,' and sank down as if suddenly weary. 'I'm the same kind of brute at bottom. This desire to govern a woman –

it lies very deep, and men and women must fight it together before they shall enter the Garden. But I do love you – surely in a better way than he does.' He thought. 'Yes – really in a better way. I want you to have your own thoughts even when I hold you in my arms.' He stretched them towards her. 'Lucy, be quick – there's no time for us to talk now – come to me as you came in the spring, and afterwards I will be gentle and explain. I have cared for you since that man died. I cannot live without you. "No good," I thought: "she is marrying someone else"; but I meet you again when all the world is glorious water and sun. As you came through the wood I saw that nothing else mattered. I called. I wanted to live and have my chance of joy.'

'And Mr Vyse?' said Lucy, who kept commendably calm. 'Does he not matter? That I love Cecil and shall be his wife shortly? A detail of no importance, I suppose?'

But he stretched his arms over the table towards her.

'May I ask what you intend to gain by this exhibition?'

He said: 'It is our last chance. I shall do all that I can.' And, as if he had done all else, he turned to Miss Bartlett, who sat like some portent against the skies of evening. 'You wouldn't stop us this second time if you understood,' he said. 'I have been into the dark, and I am going back into it, unless you will try to understand.'

Her long, narrow head drove backwards and forwards, as though demolishing some invisible obstacle. She did not answer.

'It is being young,' he said quietly, picking up his racquet from the floor and preparing to go. 'It is being certain that Lucy cares for me really. It is that love and youth matter intellectually.'

In silence the two women watched him. His last remark, they knew, was nonsense, but was he going after it or not? Would not he, the cad, the charlatan, attempt a more dramatic finish? No. He was apparently content. He left them, carefully closing the front door; and when they looked through the hall window they saw him go up the drive and begin to climb the slopes of withered fern behind the house. Their tongues were loosed, and they burst into stealthy rejoicings.

'Oh, Lucia – come back here – oh, what an awful man!'

Lucy had no reaction – at least, not yet. 'Well, he amuses me,' she said. 'Either I'm mad, or else he is, and I'm inclined to think it's the latter. One more fuss through with you, Charlotte. Many thanks. I think, though, that this is the last. My admirer will hardly trouble me again.'

And Miss Bartlett, too, essayed the roguish:

'Well, it isn't everyone who could boast such a conquest, dearest, is it? Oh, one oughtn't to laugh, really. It might have been very serious. But you were so sensible and brave – so unlike the girls of my day.'

'Let's go down to them.'

But, once in the open air, she paused. Some emotion – pity, terror, love, but the emotion was strong – seized her, and she was aware of autumn. Summer was ending, and the evening brought her odours of decay, the more pathetic because they were reminiscent of spring. That something or other mattered intellectually? A leaf, violently agitated, danced past her, while other leaves lay motionless. That the earth was hastening to re-enter darkness, and the shadows of those trees to creep over Windy Corner?

'Hullo, Lucy! There's still light enough for another set, if you two'll hurry.'

'Mr Emerson has had to go.'

'What a nuisance! That spoils the four. I say, Cecil, do play, do, there's a good chap. It's Floyd's last day. Do play tennis with us, just this once.'

Cecil's voice came: 'My dear Freddy, I am no athlete. As you well remarked this very morning, "There are some chaps who are no good for anything but books"; I plead guilty to being such a chap, and will not inflict myself on you.'

The scales fell from Lucy's eyes. How had she stood Cecil for a moment? He was absolutely intolerable, and the same evening she broke her engagement off.

CHAPTER XVII
Lying to Cecil

HE WAS BEWILDERED. He had nothing to say. He was not even angry, but stood, with a glass of whiskey between his hands, trying to think what had led her to such a conclusion.

She had chosen the moment before bed, when, in accordance with their bourgeois habit, she always dispensed drinks to the men. Freddy and Mr Floyd were sure to retire with their glasses, while Cecil invariably lingered, sipping at his while she locked up the sideboard.

'I am very sorry about it,' she said; 'I have carefully thought things over. We are too different. I must ask you to release me, and try to forget that there ever was such a foolish girl.'

It was a suitable speech, but she was more angry than sorry, and her voice showed it.

'Different – how – how –'

'I haven't had a really good education, for one thing,' she continued, still on her knees by the sideboard. 'My Italian trip came too late, and I am forgetting all that I learned there. I shall never be able to talk to your friends, or behave as a wife of yours should.'

'I don't understand you. You aren't like yourself. You're tired, Lucy.'

'Tired!' she retorted, kindling at once. 'That is exactly like you. You always think women don't mean what they say.'

'Well, you sound tired, as if something has worried you.'

'What if I do? It doesn't prevent me from realizing the truth. I can't marry you, and you will thank me for saying so some day.'

'You had that bad headache yesterday – all right' – for she had exclaimed indignantly – 'I see it's much more than headaches.

But give me a moment's time.' He closed his eyes. 'You must excuse me if I say stupid things, but my brain has gone to pieces. Part of it lives three minutes back, when I was sure that you loved me, and the other part – I find it difficult – I am likely to say the wrong thing.'

It struck her that he was not behaving so badly, and her irritation increased. She again desired a struggle, not a discussion. To bring on the crisis, she said:

'There are days when one sees clearly, and this is one of them. Things must come to a breaking-point some time, and it happens to be today. If you want to know, quite a little thing decided me to speak to you – when you wouldn't play tennis with Freddy.'

'I never do play tennis,' said Cecil, painfully bewildered; 'I never could play. I don't understand a word you say.'

'You can play well enough to make up a four. I thought it abominably selfish of you.'

'No, I can't – well, never mind the tennis. Why couldn't you – couldn't you have warned me if you felt anything wrong? You talked of our wedding at lunch – at least, you let me talk.'

'I knew you wouldn't understand,' said Lucy quite crossly. 'I might have known there would have been these dreadful explanations. Of course, it isn't the tennis – that was only the last straw to all I have been feeling for weeks. Surely it was better not to speak till I felt certain.' She developed this position. 'Often before, I have wondered if I was fitted for your wife – for instance, in London; and are you fitted to be my husband? I don't think so. You don't like Freddy, nor my mother. There was always a lot against our engagement, Cecil, but all our relations seemed pleased, and we met so often, and it was no good mentioning it until – well, until all things came to a point. They have today. I see clearly. I must speak. That's all.'

'I cannot think you were right,' said Cecil gently. 'I cannot tell why, but though all that you say sounds true, I feel that you are not treating me fairly. It's all too horrible.'

'What's the good of a scene?'

'No good. But surely I have a right to hear a little more.'

He put down his glass and opened the window. From where she knelt, jangling her keys, she could see a slit of darkness, and, peering into it, as if it would tell him that 'little more', his long, thoughtful face.

'Don't open the window; and you'd better draw the curtain, too; Freddy or anyone might be outside.' He obeyed. 'I really think we had better go to bed, if you don't mind. I shall only say things that will make me unhappy afterwards. As you say, it is all too horrible, and it is no good talking.'

But to Cecil, now that he was about to lose her, she seemed each moment more desirable. He looked at her, instead of through her, for the first time since they were engaged. From a Leonardo she had become a living woman, with mysteries and forces of her own, with qualities that even eluded art. His brain recovered from the shock, and, in a burst of genuine devotion, he cried: 'But I love you, and I did think you loved me!'

'I did not,' she said. 'I thought I did at first. I am sorry, and ought to have refused you this last time, too.'

He began to walk up and down the room, and she grew more and more vexed at his dignified behaviour. She had counted on his being petty. It would have made things easier for her. By a cruel irony she was drawing out all that was finest in his disposition.

'You don't love me, evidently. I dare say you are right not to. But it would hurt a little less if I knew why.'

'Because' – a phrase came to her, and she accepted it – 'you're the sort who can't know anyone intimately.'

A horrified look came into his eyes.

'I don't mean exactly that. But you will question me, though I beg you not to, and I must say something. It is that, more or less. When we were only acquaintances, you let me be myself, but now you're always protecting me.' Her voice swelled. 'I won't be protected. I will choose for myself what is ladylike and right.

To shield me is an insult. Can't I be trusted to face the truth but I must get it second-hand through you? A woman's place! You despise my mother – I know you do – because she's conventional and bothers over puddings; but, oh goodness!' – she rose to her feet – 'conventional, Cecil, you're that, for you may understand beautiful things, but you don't know how to use them; and you wrap yourself up in art and books and music, and would try to wrap up me. I won't be stifled, not by the most glorious music, for people are more glorious, and you hide them from me. That's why I break off my engagement. You were all right as long as you kept to things, but when you came to people –' She stopped.

There was a pause. Then Cecil said with great emotion: 'It is true.'

'True on the whole,' she corrected, full of some vague shame.

'True, every word. It is a revelation. It is – I.'

'Anyhow, those are my reasons for not being your wife.'

He repeated: ' "The sort that can know no one intimately." It is true. I fell to pieces the very first day we were engaged. I behaved like a cad to Beebe and to your brother. You are even greater than I thought.' She withdrew a step. 'I'm not going to worry you. You are far too good to me. I shall never forget your insight; and, dear, I only blame you for this: you might have warned me in the early stages, before you felt you wouldn't marry me, and so have given me a chance to improve. I have never known you till this evening. I have just used you as a peg for my silly notions of what a woman should be. But this evening you are a different person: new thoughts – even a new voice –'

'What do you mean by a new voice?' she asked, seized with incontrollable anger.

'I mean that a new person seems speaking through you,' said he.

Then she lost her balance. She cried: 'If you think I am in love with someone else, you are very much mistaken.'

'Of course I don't think that. You are not that kind, Lucy.'

'Oh yes, you do think it. It's your old idea, the idea that has kept Europe back – I mean the idea that women are always thinking of men. If a girl breaks off her engagement, everyone says: "Oh, she had someone else in her mind; she hopes to get someone else." It's disgusting, brutal! As if a girl can't break it off for the sake of freedom.'

He answered reverently: 'I may have said that in the past. I shall never say it again. You have taught me better.'

She began to redden, and pretended to examine the windows again.

'Of course, there is no question of "someone else" in this, no "jilting" or any such nauseous stupidity. I beg your pardon most humbly if my words suggested that there was. I only meant that there was a force in you that I hadn't known of up till now.'

'All right, Cecil, that will do. Don't apologize to me. It was my mistake.'

'It is a question between ideals, yours and mine – pure abstract ideals, and yours are the nobler. I was bound up in the old vicious notions, and all the time you were splendid and new.' His voice broke. 'I must actually thank you for what you have done – for showing me what I really am. Solemnly, I thank you for showing me a true woman. Will you shake hands?'

'Of course I will,' said Lucy, twisting up her other hand in the curtains. 'Goodnight, Cecil. Goodbye. That's all right. I'm sorry about it. Thank you very much for your gentleness.'

'Let me light your candle, shall I?'

They went into the hall.

'Thank you. Goodnight again. God bless you, Lucy!'

'Goodbye, Cecil.'

She watched him steal upstairs, while the shadows from the banisters passed over his face like the beat of wings. On the landing he paused, strong in his renunciation, and gave her a look of memorable beauty. For all his culture, Cecil was an ascetic at heart, and nothing in his love became him like the leaving of it.

She could never marry. In the tumult of her soul, that stood firm. Cecil believed in her; she must some day believe in herself.

She must be one of the women whom she had praised so elo-quently, who care for liberty and not for men; she must forget that George loved her, that George had been thinking through her and gained her this honourable release, that George had gone away into – what was it? – the darkness.

She put out the lamp.

It did not do to think, nor, for the matter of that, to feel. She gave up trying to understand herself, and joined the vast armies of the benighted, who follow neither the heart nor the brain, and march to their destiny by catchwords. The armies are full of pleasant and pious folk. But they have yielded to the only enemy that matters – the enemy within. They have sinned against passion and truth, and vain will be their strife after virtue. As the years pass, they are censured. Their pleasantry and their piety show cracks, their wit becomes cynicism, their unselfishness hypocrisy; they feel and produce discomfort wherever they go. They have sinned against Eros and against Pallas Athene, and not by any heavenly intervention, but by the ordinary course of nature, those allied deities will be avenged.

Lucy entered this army when she pretended to George that she did not love him, and pretended to Cecil that she loved no one. The night received her, as it had received Miss Bartlett thirty years before.

CHAPTER XVIII

Lying to Mr Beebe, Mrs Honeychurch, Freddy and the Servants

WINDY CORNER LAY, not on the summit of the ridge, but a few hundred feet down the southern slope, at the springing of one of the great buttresses that supported the hill. On either side of it was a shallow ravine, filled with ferns and pine trees, and down the ravine on the left ran the highway into the Weald.

Whenever Mr Beebe crossed the ridge and caught sight of these noble dispositions of the earth, and, poised in the middle of them, Windy Corner – he laughed. The situation was so glorious, the house so commonplace, not to say impertinent. The late Mr Honeychurch had affected the cube, because it gave him the most accommodation for his money, and the only addition made by his widow had been a small turret, shaped like a rhinoceros' horn, where she could sit in wet weather and watch the carts going up and down the road. So impertinent – and yet the house 'did', for it was the home of people who loved their surroundings honestly. Other houses in the neighbourhood had been built by expensive architects, over others their inmates had fidgeted sedulously, yet all these suggested the accidental, the temporary; while Windy Corner seemed as inevitable as an ugliness of Nature's own creation. One might laugh at the house, but one never shuddered.

Mr Beebe was bicycling over this Monday afternoon with a little piece of gossip. He had heard from the Miss Alans. These admirable ladies, since they could not go to Cissie Villa, had changed their plans. They were going to Greece instead.

'Since Florence did my poor sister so much good,' wrote Miss Catharine, 'we do not see why we should not try Athens this winter. Of course, Athens is a plunge, and the doctor has ordered her special digestive bread; but, after all, we can take that with us, and it is only getting first into a steamer and then into a train. But is there an English Church?' And the letter went on to say: 'I do not expect we shall go any further than Athens, but if you knew of a really comfortable pension at Constantinople, we should be so grateful.'

Lucy would enjoy this letter, and the smile with which Mr Beebe greeted Windy Corner was partly for her. She would see the fun of it, and some of its beauty, for she must see some beauty. Though she was hopeless about pictures, and though she dressed so unevenly – oh, that cerise frock yesterday at church! – she must see some beauty in life, or she could not play the piano as she did. He had a theory that musicians are incredibly complex, and know far less than other artists what they want and what they are; that they puzzle themselves as well as their friends; that their psychology is a modern development, and has not yet been understood. This theory, had he known it, had possibly just been illustrated by facts. Ignorant of the events of yesterday, he was only riding over to get some tea, to see his niece, and to observe whether Miss Honeychurch saw anything beautiful in the desire of two old ladies to visit Athens.

A carriage was drawn up outside Windy Corner, and just as he caught sight of the house it started, bowled up the drive, and stopped abruptly when it reached the main road. Therefore it must be the horse, who always expected people to walk up the hill in case they tired him. The door opened obediently, and two men emerged, whom Mr Beebe recognized as Cecil and Freddy. They were an odd couple to go driving; but he saw a trunk beside the coachman's legs. Cecil, who wore a bowler, must be going away, while Freddy – a cap – was seeing him to the station. They walked rapidly, taking the short cuts, and reached the summit while the carriage was still pursuing the windings of the road.

They shook hands with the clergyman, but did not speak.

'So you're off for a minute, Mr Vyse?' he asked.

Cecil said, 'Yes,' while Freddy edged away.

'I was coming to show you this delightful letter from those friends of Miss Honeychurch's.' He quoted from it. 'Isn't it wonderful? Isn't it Romance? Most certainly they will go to Constantinople. They are taken in a snare that cannot fail. They will end by going round the world.'

Cecil listened civilly, and said he was sure that Lucy would be amused and interested.

'Isn't Romance capricious! I never notice it in you young people; you do nothing but play lawn-tennis, and say that Romance is dead, while the Miss Alans are struggling with all the weapons of propriety against the terrible thing. "A really comfortable pension at Constantinople"! So they call it out of decency, but in their hearts they want a pension with magic windows opening on the foam of perilous seas in fairylands forlorn! No ordinary view will content the Miss Alans. They want the Pension Keats.'

'I'm awfully sorry to interrupt, Mr Beebe,' said Freddy, 'but have you any matches?'

'I have,' said Cecil, and it did not escape Mr Beebe's notice that he spoke to the boy more kindly.

'You have never met these Miss Alans, have you, Mr Vyse?'

'Never.'

'Then you don't see the wonder of this Greek visit. I haven't been to Greece myself, and don't mean to go, and I can't imagine any of my friends going. It is altogether too big for our little lot. Don't you think so? Italy is just about as much as we can manage. Italy is heroic, but Greece is godlike or devilish – I am not sure which, and in either case absolutely out of our suburban focus. All right, Freddy – I am not being clever, upon my word I am not – I took the idea from another fellow; and give me those matches when you've done with them.' He lit a cigarette, and went on talking to the two young men. 'I was saying, if our poor little Cockney lives must have a background, let it be Italian. Big enough in all conscience. The ceiling of the Sistine Chapel for me. There the contrast is just as much as I can realize. But not the Parthenon, not the frieze of Phidias at any price; and here comes the victoria.'

'You're quite right,' said Cecil. 'Greece is not for our little lot'; and he got in. Freddy followed, nodding to the clergyman, whom he trusted not to be pulling one's leg, really. And before they had gone a dozen yards he jumped out, and came running back for Vyse's matchbox, which had not been returned. As he took it, he said: 'I am so glad you only talked about books. Cecil's hard hit. Lucy won't marry him. If you'd gone on about her, as you did about them, he might have broken down.'

'But when –'

'Late last night. I must go.'

'Perhaps they won't want me down there.'

'No – go on. Goodbye.'

'Thank goodness!' exclaimed Mr Beebe to himself, and struck the saddle of his bicycle approvingly. 'It was the one foolish thing she ever did. Oh, what a glorious riddance!' And, after a little thought, he negotiated the slope into Windy Corner, light of heart. The house was again as it ought to be – cut off for ever from Cecil's pretentious world.

He would find Miss Minnie down the garden.

In the drawing-room Lucy was tinkling at a Mozart sonata. He hesitated a moment, but went down the garden as requested. There he found a mournful company. It was a blustering day, and the wind had taken and broken the dahlias. Mrs Honeychurch, who looked cross, was tying them up, while Miss Bartlett, unsuitably dressed, impeded her with offers of assistance. At a little distance stood Minnie and the 'garden child', a minute importation, each holding either end of a long piece of bass.

'Oh, how do you do, Mr Beebe? Gracious, what a mess everything is! Look at my scarlet pompoms, and the wind blowing your skirts about, and the ground so hard that not a prop will stick in, and then the carriage having to go out, when I had counted on having Powell, who – give everyone their due – does tie up dahlias properly.'

Evidently Mrs Honeychurch was shattered.

'How do you do?' said Miss Bartlett, with a meaning glance, as though conveying that more than dahlias had been broken off by the autumn gales.

'Here, Lennie, the bass,' cried Mrs Honeychurch. The garden child, who did not know what bass was, stood rooted to the path with horror. Minnie slipped to her uncle and whispered that everyone was very disagreeable today, and that it was not her fault if dahlia-strings would tear longways instead of across.

'Come for a walk with me,' he told her. 'You have worried them as much as they can stand. Mrs Honeychurch, I only called in aimlessly. I shall take her up to tea at the Beehive Tavern, if I may.'

'Oh, must you? Yes, do. – Not the scissors, thank you, Charlotte, when both my hands are full already – I'm perfectly certain that the orange cactus will go before I can get to it.'

Mr Beebe, who was an adept at relieving situations, invited Miss Bartlett to accompany them to this mild festivity.

'Yes, Charlotte, I don't want you – do go; there's nothing to stop about for, either in the house or out of it.'

Miss Bartlett said that her duty lay in the dahlia-bed, but, when she had exasperated everyone, except Minnie, by a refusal, she turned round and exasperated Minnie by an acceptance. As they walked up the garden, the orange cactus fell, and Mr Beebe's last vision was of the garden child clasping it like a lover, his dark head buried in a wealth of blossom.

'It is terrible, this havoc among the flowers,' he remarked.

'It is always terrible when the promise of months is destroyed in a moment,' enunciated Miss Bartlett.

'Perhaps we ought to send Miss Honeychurch down to her mother. Or will she come with us?'

'I think we had better leave Lucy to herself, and to her own pursuits.'

'They're angry with Miss Honeychurch, because she was late for breakfast,' whispered Minnie, 'and Mr Floyd has gone, and

Mr Vyse has gone, and Freddy won't play with me. In fact, Uncle Arthur, the house is not *at all* what it was yesterday.'

'Don't be a prig,' said her Uncle Arthur. 'Go and put on your boots.'

He stepped into the drawing-room, where Lucy was still attentively pursuing the sonatas of Mozart. She stopped when he entered.

'How do you do? Miss Bartlett and Minnie are coming with me to tea at the Beehive. Would you come too?'

'I don't think I will, thank you.'

'No, I didn't suppose you would care to much.'

Lucy turned to the piano and struck a few chords.

'How delicate those sonatas are!' said Mr Beebe, though, at the bottom of his heart, he thought them silly little things.

Lucy passed into Schumann.

'Miss Honeychurch!'

'Yes.'

'I met them on the hill. Your brother told me.'

'Oh, did he?' She sounded annoyed. Mr Beebe felt hurt, for he had thought that she would like him to be told.

'I needn't say that it will go no further.'

'Mother, Charlotte, Cecil, Freddy, you,' said Lucy, playing a note for each person who knew, and then playing a sixth note.

'If you'll let me say so, I am very glad, and I am certain that you have done the right thing.'

'So I hoped other people would think, but they don't seem to.'

'I could see that Miss Bartlett thought it unwise.'

'So does mother. Mother minds dreadfully.'

'I am very sorry for that,' said Mr Beebe with feeling.

Mrs Honeychurch, who hated all changes, did mind, but not nearly as much as her daughter pretended, and only for the minute. It was really a ruse of Lucy's to justify her despondency – a ruse of which she was not herself conscious, for she was marching in the armies of darkness.

'And Freddy minds.'

'Still, Freddy never hit it off with Vyse much, did he? I gathered that he disliked the engagement, and felt it might separate him from you.'

'Boys are so odd.'

Minnie could be heard arguing with Miss Bartlett through the floor. Tea at the Beehive apparently involved a complete change of apparel. Mr Beebe saw that Lucy – very properly – did not wish to discuss her action, so after a sincere expression of sympathy he said: 'I have had an absurd letter from Miss Alan. That was really what brought me over. I thought it might amuse you all.'

'How delightful!' said Lucy, in a dull voice.

For the sake of something to do, he began to read her the letter. After a few words her eyes grew alert, and soon she interrupted him with – 'Going abroad? When do they start?'

'Next week, I gather.'

'Did Freddy say whether he was driving straight back?'

'No, he didn't.'

'Because I do hope he won't go gossiping.'

So she did want to talk about her broken engagement. Always complaisant, he put the letter away. But she at once exclaimed in a high voice: 'Oh, do tell me more about the Miss Alans! How perfectly splendid of them to go abroad!'

'I want them to start from Venice, and go in a cargo steamer down the Illyrian coast!'

She laughed heartily. 'Oh, delightful! I wish they'd take me.'

'Has Italy filled you with the fever of travel? Perhaps George Emerson is right. He says that Italy is only an euphemism for Fate.'

'Oh, not Italy, but Constantinople. I have always longed to go to Constantinople. Constantinople is practically Asia, isn't it?'

Mr Beebe reminded her that Constantinople was still unlikely, and that the Miss Alans only aimed at Athens, 'with Delphi, perhaps, if the roads are safe'. But this made no difference to her enthusiasm. She had always longed to go to Greece even more, it seemed. He saw, to his surprise, that she was apparently serious.

'I didn't realize that you and the Miss Alans were still such friends, after Cissie Villa.'

'Oh, that's nothing; I assure you Cissie Villa's nothing to me; I would give anything to go with them.'

'Would your mother spare you again so soon? You have scarcely been home three months.'

'She *must* spare me!' cried Lucy, in growing excitement. 'I simply *must* go away. I have to.' She ran her fingers hysterically through her hair. 'Don't you see that I *have* to go away? I didn't realize at the time – and of course I want to see Constantinople so particularly.'

'You mean that since you have broken off your engagement you feel –'

'Yes, yes. I knew you would understand.'

Mr Beebe did not quite understand. Why could not Miss Honeychurch repose in the bosom of her family? Cecil had evidently taken up the dignified line, and was not going to annoy her. Then it struck him that her family itself might be annoying. He hinted this to her, and she accepted the hint eagerly.

'Yes, of course; to go to Constantinople until they are used to the idea and everything has calmed down.'

'I am afraid it has been a bothersome business,' he said gently.

'No, not at all. Cecil was very kind indeed; only – I had better tell you the whole truth, since you have heard a little – it was that he is so masterful. I found that he wouldn't let me go my own way. He would improve me in places where I can't be improved. Cecil won't let a woman decide for herself – in fact, he daren't. What nonsense I do talk! But that is the kind of thing.'

'It is what I gathered from my own observation of Mr Vyse; it is what I gather from all that I have known of you. I do sympathize and agree most profoundly. I agree so much that you must let me make one little criticism: is it worth while rushing off to Greece?'

'But I must go somewhere!' she cried. 'I have been worrying all the morning, and here comes the very thing.' She struck her knees with clenched fists, and repeated: 'I must! And the time I shall have with mother, and all the money she spent on me last spring. You all think much too highly of me. I wish you weren't so kind.' At this moment Miss Bartlett entered, and her nervousness increased. 'I must get away, ever so far. I must know my own mind and where I want to go.'

'Come along; tea, tea, tea,' said Mr Beebe, and hustled his guests out of the front door. He hustled them so quickly that he forgot his hat. When he returned for it he heard, to his relief and surprise, the tinkling of a Mozart sonata.

'She is playing again,' he said to Miss Bartlett.

'Lucy can always play,' was the acid reply.

'One is very thankful that she has such a resource. She is evidently much worried, as, of course, she ought to be. I know all about it. The marriage was so near that it must have been a hard struggle before she could wind herself up to speak.'

Miss Bartlett gave a kind of wriggle, and he prepared for a discussion. He had never fathomed Miss Bartlett. As he had put it to himself at Florence, 'she might yet reveal depths of strangeness, if not of meaning.' But she was so unsympathetic that she must be reliable. He assumed that much, and he had no hesitation in discussing Lucy with her. Minnie was fortunately collecting ferns.

She opened the discussion with: 'We had much better let the matter drop.'

'I wonder.'

'It is of the highest importance that there should be no gossip in Summer Street. It would be *death* to gossip about Mr Vyse's dismissal at the present moment.'

Mr Beebe raised his eyebrows. Death is a strong word – surely too strong. There was no question of tragedy. He said: 'Of course, Miss Honeychurch will make the fact public in her own way, and when she chooses. Freddy only told me because he knew she would not mind.'

'I know,' said Miss Bartlett civilly. 'Yet Freddy ought not to have told even you. One cannot be too careful.'

'Quite so.'

'I do implore absolute secrecy. A chance word to a chattering friend, and – '

'Exactly.' He was used to these nervous old maids and to the exaggerated importance that they attach to words. A rector lives in a web of petty secrets, and confidences, and warnings, and the wiser he is the less he will regard them. He will change the subject, as did Mr Beebe, saying cheerfully: 'Have you heard from any Bertolini people lately? I believe you keep up with Miss Lavish. It is odd how we of that pension, who seemed such a fortuitous collection, have been working into one another's lives. Two, three, four, six of us – no, eight; I had forgotten the Emersons – have kept more or less in touch. We must really give the Signora a testimonial.'

And, Miss Bartlett not favouring the scheme, they walked up the hill in a silence which was only broken by the rector naming some fern. On the summit they paused. The sky had grown wilder since he stood there last hour, giving to the land a tragic greatness that is rare in Surrey. Grey clouds were charging across tissues of white, which stretched and shredded and tore slowly, until through their final layers there gleamed a hint of the disappearing blue. Summer was retreating. The wind roared, the trees groaned, yet the noise seemed insufficient for those vast operations in heaven. The weather was breaking up, breaking, broken, and it is a sense of the fit rather than of the supernatural that equips such crises with the salvos of angelic artillery. Mr Beebe's eyes rested on Windy Corner, where Lucy sat, practising Mozart. No smile came to his lips, and, changing the subject again, he said: 'We shan't have rain, but we shall have darkness, so let us hurry on. The darkness last night was appalling.'

They reached the Beehive Tavern at about five o'clock. That amiable hostelry possesses a veranda, in which the young and the unwise do dearly love to sit, while guests of more mature years seek a pleasant sanded room, and have tea at a table comfortably. Mr Beebe saw that Miss Bartlett would be cold if she sat out, and that Minnie would be dull if she sat in, so he proposed a division of forces. They would hand the child her food through the window. Thus he was incidentally enabled to discuss the fortunes of Lucy.

'I have been thinking, Miss Bartlett,' he said, 'and, unless you very much object, I would like to reopen that discussion.' She bowed. 'Nothing about the past. I know little and care less about that; I am absolutely certain that it is to your cousin's credit. She has acted loftily and rightly, and it is like her gentle modesty to say that we think too highly of her. But the future. Seriously, what do you think of this Greek plan?' He pulled out the letter again. 'I don't know whether you overheard, but she wants to join the Miss Alans in their mad career. It's all – I can't explain – it's wrong.'

Miss Bartlett read the letter in silence, laid it down, seemed to hesitate, and then read it again.

'I can't see the point of it myself.'

To his astonishment, she replied: 'There I cannot agree with you. In it I spy Lucy's salvation.'

'Really. Now, why?'

'She wanted to leave Windy Corner.'

'I know – but it seems so odd, so unlike her, so – I was going to say – selfish.'

'It is natural, surely – after such painful scenes – that she should desire a change.'

Here, apparently, was one of those points that the male intellect misses. Mr Beebe exclaimed: 'So she says herself, and since another lady agrees with her, I must own that I am partially convinced. Perhaps she must have a change. I have no sisters or – and I don't understand these things. But why need she go as far as Greece?'

'You may well ask that,' replied Miss Bartlett, who was evidently interested, and had almost dropped her evasive manner. 'Why Greece? (What is it, Minnie dear – jam?) Why not Tunbridge Wells? Oh, Mr Beebe! I had a long and most unsatisfactory interview with dear Lucy this morning. I cannot help her. I will say no more. Perhaps I have already said too much. I am not to talk – a point on which she is almost bitter. I am not to talk. I wanted her to spend six months with me at Tunbridge Wells, and she refused.'

Mr Beebe poked at a crumb with his knife.

'But my feelings are of no importance. I know too well that I get on Lucy's nerves. Our tour was a failure. She wanted to leave Florence, and when we got to Rome she did not want to be in Rome, and all the time I felt that I was spending her mother's money –'

'Let us keep to the future, though,' interrupted Mr Beebe. 'I want your advice.'

'Very well,' said Charlotte, with a choky abruptness that was new to him, though familiar to Lucy. 'I for one will help her to go to Greece. Will you?'

Mr Beebe considered.

'It is absolutely necessary,' she continued, lowering her veil and whispering through it with a passion, an intensity, that surprised him. 'I know – I *know*.' The darkness was coming on, and he felt that this odd woman really did know. 'She must not stop here a moment, and we must keep quiet till she goes. I trust that the servants know nothing. Afterwards – but I may have said too much already. Only, Lucy and I are helpless against Mrs Honeychurch alone. If you help, we may succeed. Otherwise –'

'Otherwise –?'

'Otherwise,' she repeated, as if the word held finality.

'Yes, I will help her,' said the clergyman, setting his jaw firm. 'Come, let us go back now, and settle the whole thing up.'

Miss Bartlett burst into florid gratitude. The tavern sign – a beehive trimmed evenly with bees – creaked in the wind outside as she thanked him. Mr Beebe did not quite understand the situation; but then, he did not desire to understand it, nor to jump to the conclusion of 'another man' that would have attracted a grosser mind. He only felt that Miss Bartlett knew of some vague influence from which the girl desired to be delivered, and which might well be clothed in the fleshly form. Its very vagueness spurred him into knight-errantry. His belief in celibacy, so reticent, so carefully concealed beneath his tolerance and culture, now came to the surface and expanded like some delicate flower. 'They that marry do well, but they that refrain do better.' So ran his belief, and he never heard that an engagement was broken off but with a slight feeling of pleasure. In the case of Lucy, the feeling was intensified through dislike of Cecil; and he was willing to go further – to place her out of danger until she could confirm her resolution of virginity. The feeling was very subtle and quite undogmatic, and he never imparted it to any other of the characters in this entanglement. Yet it existed, and it alone explains his action subsequently, and his influence on the action of others. The compact that he made with Miss Bartlett in the tavern was to help not only Lucy, but religion also.

They hurried home through a world of black and grey. He conversed on indifferent topics: the Emersons' need of a house-keeper; servants; Italian servants; novels about Italy; novels with a purpose; could literature influence life? Windy Corner glimmered. In the garden, Mrs Honeychurch, now helped by Freddy, still wrestled with the lives of her flowers.

'It gets too dark,' she said hopelessly. 'This comes of putting off. We might have known the weather would break up soon; and now Lucy wants to go to Greece. I don't know what the world's coming to.'

'Mrs Honeychurch,' he said, 'go to Greece she must. Come up to the house and let's talk it over. Do you, in the first place, mind her breaking with Vyse?'

'Mr Beebe, I'm thankful – simply thankful.'

'So am I,' said Freddy.

'Good. Now come up to the house.'

They conferred in the dining-room for half an hour.

Lucy would never have carried the Greek scheme alone. It was expensive and dramatic – both qualities that her mother loathed. Nor would Charlotte have succeeded. The honours of the day rested with Mr Beebe. By his tact and common sense, and by his influence as a clergyman – for a clergyman who was not a fool influenced Mrs Honeychurch greatly – he bent her to their purpose.

'I don't see why Greece is necessary,' she said; 'but as you do, I suppose it is all right. It must be something I can't understand. Lucy! Let's tell her. Lucy!'

'She is playing the piano,' Mr Beebe said. He opened the door, and heard the words of a song:

'Look not thou on beauty's charming –'

'I didn't know that Miss Honeychurch sang, too.'

'Sit thou still when kings are arming,
Taste not when the wine-cup glistens –'

'It's a song that Cecil gave her. How odd girls are!'

'What's that?' called Lucy, stopping short.

'All right, dear,' said Mrs Honeychurch kindly. She went into the drawing-room, and Mr Beebe heard her kiss Lucy and say: 'I am sorry I was so cross about Greece, but it came on the top of the dahlias.'

Rather a hard voice said: 'Thank you, mother; that doesn't matter a bit.'

'And you are right, too – Greece will be all right; you can go if the Miss Alans will have you.'

'Oh, splendid! Oh, thank you!'

Mr Beebe followed. Lucy still sat at the piano with her hands over the keys. She was glad, but he had expected greater gladness.

Her mother bent over her. Freddy, to whom she had been singing, reclined on the floor with his head against her, and an unlit
pipe between his lips. Oddly enough, the group was beautiful.
Mr Beebe, who loved the art of the past, was reminded of a
favourite theme, the *Santa Conversazione*, in which people who
care for one another are painted chatting together about noble
things – a theme neither sensual nor sensational, and therefore
ignored by the art of today. Why should Lucy want either to
marry or to travel when she had such friends at home?

> 'Taste not when the wine-cup glistens,
> Speak not when the people listens,'

she continued.

'Here's Mr Beebe.'

'Mr Beebe knows my rude ways.'

'It's a beautiful song and a wise one,' said he. 'Go on.'

'It isn't very good,' she said listlessly. 'I forget why – harmony
or something.'

'I suspected it was unscholarly. It's so beautiful.'

'The tune's right enough,' said Freddy, 'but the words are
rotten. Why throw up the sponge?'

'How stupidly you talk!' said his sister. The *Santa Conversazione* was broken up. After all, there was no reason that Lucy
should talk about Greece or thank him for persuading her
mother, so he said goodbye.

Freddy lit his bicycle-lamp for him in the porch, and, with his
usual felicity of phrase, said: 'This has been a day and a half.'

> 'Stop thine ear against the singer –'

'Wait a minute; she is finishing.'

> 'From the red gold keep thy finger;
> Vacant heart, and hand, and eye,
> Easy live and quiet die.'

'I love weather like this,' said Freddy.

Mr Beebe passed into it.

The two main facts were clear. She had behaved splendidly, and he had helped her. He could not expect to master the details of so big a change in a girl's life. If here and there he was dissatisfied or puzzled, he must acquiesce; she was choosing the better part.

> 'Vacant heart, and hand, and eye –'

Perhaps the song stated 'the better part' rather too strongly. He half fancied that the soaring accompaniment – which he did not lose in the shout of the gale – really agreed with Freddy, and was gently criticizing the words that it adorned:

> 'Vacant heart, and hand, and eye,
> Easy live and quiet die.'

However. For the fourth time Windy Corner lay poised below him – now as a beacon in the roaring tides of darkness.

CHAPTER XIX

Lying to Mr Emerson

THE MISS ALANS were found in their beloved temperance hotel near Bloomsbury – a clean, airless establishment much patronized by provincial England. They always perched there before crossing the great seas, and for a week or two would fidget gently over clothes, guidebooks, mackintosh squares, digestive bread, and other continental necessaries. That there are shops abroad, even in Athens, never occurred to them, for they regarded travel as a species of warfare, only to be undertaken by those who have been fully armed at the Haymarket Stores. Miss Honeychurch, they trusted, would take care to equip herself duly. Quinine could now be obtained in tabloids; paper soap was a great help towards freshening up one's face in the train. Lucy promised, a little depressed.

'But, of course, you know all about these things, and you have Mr Vyse to help you. A gentleman is such a standby.'

Mrs Honeychurch, who had come up to town with her daughter, began to drum nervously upon her card-case.

'We think it so good of Mr Vyse to spare you,' Miss Catharine continued. 'It is not every young man who would be so unselfish. But perhaps he will come out and join you later on.'

'Or does his work keep him in London?' said Miss Teresa, the more acute and less kindly of the two sisters.

'However, we shall see him when he sees you off. I do so long to see him.'

'No one will see Lucy off,' interposed Mrs Honeychurch. 'She doesn't like it.'

'No, I hate seeings-off,' said Lucy.

'Really? How funny! I should have thought that in this case –'

'Oh, Mrs Honeychurch, you aren't going? It is such a pleasure to have met you!'

They escaped, and Lucy said with relief: 'That's all right. We just got through that time.'

But her mother was annoyed. 'I shall be told, dear, that I am unsympathetic. But I cannot see why you didn't tell your friends about Cecil and be done with it. There all the time we had to sit fencing, and almost telling lies, and be seen through, too, I dare say, which is most unpleasant.'

Lucy had plenty to say in reply. She described the Miss Alans' character: they were such gossips, and, if one told them, the news would be everywhere in no time.

'But why shouldn't it be everywhere in no time?'

'Because I settled with Cecil not to announce it until I left England. I shall tell them then. It's much pleasanter. How wet it is! Let's turn in here.'

'Here' was the British Museum. Mrs Honeychurch refused. If they must take shelter, let it be in a shop. Lucy felt contemptuous, for she was on the tack of caring for Greek sculpture, and had already borrowed a mythological dictionary from Mr Beebe to get up the names of the goddesses and gods.

'Oh, well, let it be a shop, then. Let's go to Mudie's. I'll buy a guidebook.'

'You know, Lucy, you and Charlotte and Mr Beebe all tell me I'm so stupid, so I suppose I am, but I shall never understand this hole-and-corner work. You've got rid of Cecil – well and good, and I'm thankful he's gone, though I did feel angry for the minute. But why not announce it? Why this hushing up and tiptoeing?'

'It's only for a few days.'

'But why at all?'

Lucy was silent. She was drifting away from her mother. It was quite easy to say, 'Because George Emerson has been bothering me, and if he hears I've given up Cecil may begin again' – quite easy, and it had the incidental advantage of being true. But she could not say it. She disliked confidences, for they might lead to self-knowledge and to that king of terrors – Light. Ever since that last evening at Florence she had deemed it unwise to reveal her soul.

Mrs Honeychurch, too, was silent. She was thinking: 'My daughter won't answer me; she would rather be with those inquisitive old maids than with Freddy and me. Any rag, tag and bobtail apparently does if she can leave her home.' And, as in her case thoughts never remained unspoken long, she burst out with: 'You're tired of Windy Corner.'

This was perfectly true. Lucy had hoped to return to Windy Corner when she escaped from Cecil, but she discovered that her home existed no longer. It might exist for Freddy, who still lived and thought straight, but not for one who had deliberately warped the brain. She did not acknowledge that her brain was warped, for the brain itself must assist in that acknowledgement, and she was disordering the very instruments of life. She only felt: 'I do not love George; I broke off my engagement because I did not love George; I must go to Greece because I do not love George; it is more important that I should look up gods in the dictionary than that I should help my mother; everyone else is behaving very badly.' She only felt irritable and petulant, and anxious to do what she was not expected to do, and in this spirit she proceeded with the conversation.

'Oh, mother, what rubbish you talk! Of course I'm not tired of Windy Corner.'

'Then why not say so at once, instead of considering half an hour first?'

She laughed faintly. 'Half a *minute* would be nearer.'

'Perhaps you would like to stay away from your home altogether?'

'Hush, mother! People will hear you'; for they had entered Mudie's. She bought Baedeker, and then continued: 'Of course I want to live at home; but as we are talking about it, I may as well say that I shall want to be away in the future more than I have been. You see, I come into my money next year.'

Tears came into her mother's eyes.

Driven by nameless bewilderment, by what is in older people termed 'eccentricity', Lucy determined to make this point clear. 'I've seen the world so little – I felt so out of things in Italy. I have seen so little of life; one ought to come up to London more – not a cheap ticket like today, but to stop. I might even share a flat for a little with some other girl.'

'And mess with typewriters and latchkeys,' exploded Mrs Honeychurch. 'And agitate and scream, and be carried off kicking by the police. And call it a Mission – when no one wants you! And call it Duty – when it means that you can't stand your own home! And call it Work – when thousands of men are starving with the competition as it is! And then to prepare yourself, find two doddering old ladies, and go abroad with them.'

'I want more independence,' said Lucy lamely; she knew that she wanted something, and independence is a useful cry; we can always say that we have not got it. She tried to remember her emotions in Florence: those had been sincere and passionate, and had suggested beauty rather than short skirts and latchkeys. But independence was certainly her cue.

'Very well. Take your independence and be gone. Rush up and down and round the world, and come back as thin as a lath with the bad food. Despise the house that your father built and the garden that he planted, and our dear view – and then share a flat with another girl.'

Lucy screwed up her mouth and said: 'Perhaps I spoke hastily.'

'Oh, goodness!' her mother flashed. 'How you do remind me of Charlotte Bartlett!'

'*Charlotte*?' flashed Lucy in her turn, pierced at last by a vivid pain.

'More every moment.'

'I don't know what you mean, mother; Charlotte and I are not the very least alike.'

'Well, I see the likeness. The same eternal worrying, the same taking back of words. You and Charlotte trying to divide two apples among three people last night might be sisters.'

'What rubbish! And if you dislike Charlotte so, it's rather a pity you asked her to stop. I warned you about her; I begged you, implored you not to, but of course I was not listened to.'

'There you go.'

'I beg your pardon?'

'Charlotte again, my dear; that's all; her very words.'

Lucy clenched her teeth. 'My point is that you oughtn't to have asked Charlotte to stop. I wish you would keep to the point.' And the conversation dies off into a wrangle.

She and her mother shopped in silence, spoke little in the train, little again in the carriage, which met them at Dorking station. It had poured all day, and as they ascended through the deep Surrey lanes showers of water fell from the overhanging beech trees and rattled on the hood. Lucy complained that the hood was stuffy. Leaning forward, she looked out into the steaming dusk, and watched the carriage-lamp pass like a searchlight over mud and leaves, and reveal nothing beautiful. 'The crush when Charlotte gets in will be abominable,' she remarked. For they were to pick up Miss Bartlett at Summer Street, where she had been dropped as the carriage went down, to pay a call on Mr Beebe's old mother. 'We shall have to sit three a side, because the trees drop, and yet it isn't raining. O for a little air!' Then she listened to the horse's hoofs – 'He has not told – he has not told.' That melody was blurred by the soft road. '*Can't* we have the hood down?' she demanded, and her mother, with sudden tenderness, said: 'Very well, old lady, stop the horse.' And the horse was stopped, and Lucy and Powell wrestled with the hood, and squirted water down Mrs Honeychurch's neck. But now that the hood was down she did see something that she would have missed – there were no lights in the windows of Cissie Villa, and round the garden gate she fancied she saw a padlock.

'Is that house to let again, Powell?' she called.

'Yes, miss,' he replied.

'Have they gone?'

'It is too far out of town for the young gentleman, and his father's rheumatism has come on, so he can't stop on alone, so they are trying to let furnished,' was the answer.

'They have gone, then?'

'Yes, miss, they have gone.'

Lucy sank back. The carriage stopped at the rectory. She got out to call for Miss Bartlett. So the Emersons had gone, and all this bother about Greece had been unnecessary. Waste! That word seemed to sum up the whole of life. Wasted plans, wasted money, wasted love, and she had wounded her mother. Was it possible that she had muddled things away? Quite possible. Other people had. When the maid opened the door, she was unable to speak, and stared stupidly into the hall.

Miss Bartlett at once came forward, and after a long preamble asked a great favour: might she go to church? Mr Beebe and his mother had already gone, but she had refused to start until she obtained her hostess's full sanction, for it would mean keeping the horse waiting a good ten minutes more.

'Certainly,' said the hostess wearily. 'I forgot it was Friday. Let's all go. Powell can go round to the stables.'

'Lucy dearest –'

'No church for me, thank you.'

A sigh, and they departed. The church was invisible, but up in the darkness to the left there was a hint of colour. This was a stained window, through which some feeble light was shining, and when the door opened Lucy heard Mr Beebe's voice running through the litany to a minute congregation. Even their church, built upon the slope of the hill so artfully, with its beautiful raised transept and its spire of silvery shingle – even their church had lost its charm; and the thing one never talked about – religion – was fading like all the other things.

She followed the maid into the rectory.

Would she object to sitting in Mr Beebe's study? There was only that one fire.

She would not object.

Someone was there already, for Lucy heard the words: 'A lady to wait, sir.'

Old Mr Emerson was sitting by the fire, with his foot upon a gout-stool.

'Oh, Miss Honeychurch, that you should come!' he quavered; and Lucy saw an alteration in him since last Sunday.

Not a word would come to her lips. George she had faced, and could have faced again, but she had forgotten how to treat his father.

'Miss Honeychurch, dear, we are so sorry! George is so sorry! He thought he had a right to try. I cannot blame my boy, and yet I wish he had told me first. He ought not to have tried. I knew nothing about it at all.'

If only she could remember how to behave!

He held up his hand. 'But you must not scold him.'

Lucy turned her back, and began to look at Mr Beebe's books.

'I taught him,' he quavered, 'to trust in love. I said: "When love comes, that is reality." I said: "Passion does not blind. No. Passion is sanity, and the woman you love, she is the only person you will ever really understand."' He sighed: 'True, everlastingly true, though my day is over, and though there is the result. Poor boy! He is so sorry! He said he knew it was madness when you brought your cousin in; that whatever you felt you did not mean. Yet' – his voice gathered strength; he spoke out to make certain – 'Miss Honeychurch, do you remember Italy?'

Lucy selected a book – a volume of Old Testament commentaries. Holding it up to her eyes, she said: 'I have no wish to discuss Italy or any subject connected with your son.'

'But you do remember it?'

'He has misbehaved himself from the first.'

'I only was told that he loved you last Sunday. I never could judge behaviour. I – I – suppose he has.'

Feeling a little steadier, she put the book back and turned round to him. His face was drooping and swollen, but his eyes, though they were sunken deep, gleamed with a child's courage.

'Why, he has behaved abominably,' she said. 'I am glad he is sorry. Do you know what he did?'

'Not "abominably",' was the gentle correction. 'He only tried when he should not have tried. You have all you want, Miss Honeychurch: you are going to marry the man you love. Do not go out of George's life saying he is abominable.'

'No, of course,' said Lucy, ashamed at the reference to Cecil. ' "Abominable" is much too strong. I am sorry I used it about your son. I think I will go to church, after all. My mother and my cousin have gone. I shall not be so very late –'

'Especially as he has gone under,' he said quietly.

'What was that?'

'Gone under naturally.' He beat his palms together in silence; his head fell on his chest.

'I don't understand.'

'As his mother did.'

'But, Mr Emerson – *Mr Emerson* – what are you talking about?'

'When I wouldn't have George baptized,' said he.

Lucy was frightened.

'And she agreed that baptism was nothing, but he caught that fever when he was twelve, and she turned round. She thought it a judgement.' He shuddered. 'Oh, horrible, when we had given up that sort of thing and broken away from her parents. Oh, horrible – worst of all – worse than death, when you have made a little clearing in the wilderness, planted your little garden, let in your sunlight, and then the weeds creep in again! A judgement! And our boy had typhoid because no clergyman had dropped water on him in church! Is it possible, Miss Honeychurch? Shall we slip back into the darkness for ever?'

'I don't know,' gasped Lucy. 'I don't understand this sort of thing. I was not meant to understand it.'

'But Mr Eager – he came when I was out, and acted according to his principles. I don't blame him or anyone . . . but by the time George was well she was ill. He made her think about sin, and she went under thinking about it.'

It was thus that Mr Emerson had murdered his wife in the sight of God.

'Oh, how terrible!' said Lucy, forgetting her own affairs at last.

'He was not baptized,' said the old man. 'I did hold firm.' And he looked with unwavering eyes at the rows of books, as if – at what cost! – he had won a victory over them. 'My boy shall go back to the earth untouched.'

She asked whether young Mr Emerson was ill.

'Oh – last Sunday.' He started into the present. 'George last Sunday – no, not ill; just gone under. He is never ill. But he is his mother's son. Her eyes were his, and she had that forehead that I think so beautiful, and he will not think it worth while to live. It was always touch and go. He will live; but he will not think it worth while to live. He will never think anything worth while. You remember that church at Florence?'

Lucy did remember, and how she had suggested that George should collect postage-stamps.

'After you left Florence – horrible. Then we take the house here, and he goes bathing with your brother, and became better. You saw him bathing?'

'I am so sorry, but it is no good discussing this affair. I am really deeply sorry about it.'

'Then there came something about a novel. I didn't follow it all; I had to hear so much, and he minded telling me; he finds me too old. Ah, well, one must have failures. George comes down tomorrow, and takes me up to his London rooms. He can't bear to be about here, and I must be where he is.'

'Mr Emerson,' cried the girl, 'don't leave – at least, not on my account. I am going to Greece. Don't leave your comfortable house.'

It was the first time her voice had been kind, and he smiled.

'How good everyone is! And look at Mr Beebe housing me – came over this morning and heard I was going! Here I am so comfortable with a fire.'

'Yes, but you won't go back to London. It's absurd.'

'I must be with George; I must make him care to live, and down here he can't. He says the thought of seeing you and of hearing about you – I am not justifying him; I am only saying what has happened.'

'Oh, Mr Emerson' – she took hold of his hand – 'you mustn't. I've been bother enough to the world by now. I can't have you moving out of your house when you like it, and perhaps losing money through it – all on my account. You must stop! I am just going to Greece.'

'All the way to Greece?'

Her manner altered.

'To Greece?'

'So you must stop. You won't talk about this business, I know. I can trust you both.'

'Certainly you can. We either have you in our lives, or leave you to the life that you have chosen.'

'I shouldn't want –'

'I suppose Mr Vyse is very angry with George? No, it was wrong of George to try. We have pushed our beliefs too far. I fancy that we deserve sorrow.'

She looked at the books again – black, brown, and that acrid, theological blue. They surrounded the visitors on every side; they were piled on the tables, they pressed against the very ceiling. To Lucy – who could not see that Mr Emerson was profoundly religious, and differed from Mr Beebe chiefly by his acknowledgement of passion – it seemed dreadful that the old man should crawl into such a sanctum, when he was unhappy, and be dependent on the bounty of a clergyman.

More certain than ever that she was tired, he offered her his chair.

'No, please sit still. I think I will sit in the carriage.'

'Miss Honeychurch, you do sound tired.'

'Not a bit,' said Lucy, with trembling lips.

'But you are, and there's a look of George about you. And what were you saying about going abroad?'

She was silent.

'Greece' – and she saw that he was thinking the word over – 'Greece; but you were to be married this year, I thought.'

'Not till January, it wasn't,' said Lucy, clasping her hands. Would she tell an actual lie when it came to the point?

'I suppose that Mr Vyse is going with you. I hope – it isn't because George spoke that you are both going?'

'No.'

'I hope that you will enjoy Greece with Mr Vyse.'

'Thank you.'

At that moment Mr Beebe came back from church. His cassock was covered with rain. 'That's all right,' he said kindly. 'I counted on you two keeping each other company. It's pouring again. The entire congregation, which consists of your cousin, your mother and my mother, stands waiting in the church till the carriage fetches it. Did Powell go round?'

'I think so; I'll see.'

'No – of course, I'll see. How are the Miss Alans?'

'Very well, thank you.'

'Did you tell Mr Emerson about Greece?'

'I – I did.'

'Don't you think it very plucky of her, Mr Emerson, to under-take the two Miss Alans? Now, Miss Honeychurch, go back – keep warm. I think three is such a courageous number to go travelling.' And he hurried off to the stables.

'He is not going,' she said hoarsely. 'I made a slip. Mr Vyse does stop behind in England.' Somehow it was impossible to cheat this old man. To George, to Cecil, she would have lied again; but he seemed so near the end of things, so dignified in his approach to the gulf, of which he gave one account, and the books that surrounded him another, so mild to the rough paths that he had traversed, that the true chivalry – not the worn-out chivalry of sex, but the true chivalry that all the young may show to all the old – awoke in her, and, at whatever risk, she told him that Cecil was not her companion to Greece. And she spoke so seriously that the risk became a certainty and he, lifting his eyes, said: 'You are leaving him? You are leaving the man you love?'

'I – I had to.'

'Why, Miss Honeychurch, why?'

Terror came over her, and she lied again. She made the long, convincing speech that she had made to Mr Beebe, and intended to make to the world when she announced that her engagement was no more. He heard her in silence, and then said: 'My dear, I am worried about you. It seems to me' – dreamily; she was not alarmed – 'that you are in a muddle.'

She shook her head.

'Take an old man's word: there's nothing worse than a muddle in all the world. It is easy to face Death and Fate, and the things that sound so dreadful. It is on my muddles that I look back with horror – on the things that I might have avoided. We can help one another but little. I used to think I could teach young people the whole of life, but I know better now, and all my teaching of George has come down to this: beware of muddle. Do you remember in that church, when you pretended to be annoyed with me and weren't? Do you remember before, when you refused the room with the view? Those were muddles – little, but ominous – and I am fearing that you are in one now.' She was silent. 'Do trust me, Miss Honeychurch. Though life is very glorious, it is difficult.' She was still silent. ' "Life," wrote a friend of mine, "is a public performance on the violin, in which you must learn the instrument as you go along." I think he puts it well. Man has to pick up the use of his functions as he goes along – especially the function of Love.' Then he burst out excitedly: 'That's it; that's what I mean. You love George!' And after his long preamble the three words burst against Lucy like waves from the open sea.

'But you do,' he went on, not waiting for contradiction. 'You love the boy body and soul, plainly, directly, as he loves you, and no other word expresses it. You won't marry the other man for his sake.'

'How dare you!' gasped Lucy, with the roaring of waters in her ears. 'Oh, how like a man! – I mean, to suppose that a woman is always thinking about a man.'

'But you are.'

She summoned physical disgust.

'You're shocked, but I mean to shock you. It's the only hope at times. I can reach you no other way. You must marry, or your life will be wasted. You have gone too far to retreat. I have no time for the tenderness, and the comradeship, and the poetry, and the things that really matter, and *for which* you marry. I know that, with George, you will find them, and that you love him. Then be his wife. He is already part of you. Though you fly to Greece, and never see him again, or forget his very name, George will work in your thoughts till you die. It isn't possible to love and to part. You will wish that it was. You can transmute love, ignore it, muddle it, but you can never pull it out of you. I know by experience that the poets are right: love is eternal.'

Lucy began to cry with anger, and, though her anger passed away soon, her tears remained.

'I only wish poets would say this, too: that love is of the body; not the body, but of the body. Ah! the misery that would be saved if we confessed that! Ah for a little directness to liberate the soul! Your soul, dear Lucy! I hate the word now, because of all the cant with which superstition has wrapped it round. But we have souls. I cannot say how they came nor whither they go, but we have them, and I see you ruining yours. I cannot bear it. It is again the darkness creeping in; it is hell.' Then he checked himself. 'What nonsense I have talked – how abstract and remote! And I have made you cry! Dear girl, forgive my prosiness; marry my boy. When I think what life is, and how seldom love is answered by love – marry him; it is one of the moments for which the world was made.'

She could not understand him; the words were indeed remote. Yet as he spoke the darkness was withdrawn, veil after veil, and she saw to the bottom of her soul.

'Then, Lucy –'

'You've frightened me,' she moaned. 'Cecil – Mr Beebe – the ticket's bought – everything.' She fell sobbing into the chair. 'I'm caught in the tangle. I must suffer and grow old away from him. I cannot break the whole of life for his sake. They trusted me.'

A carriage drew up at the front door.

'Give George my love – once only. Tell him, "Muddle." ' Then she arranged her veil, while the tears poured over her cheeks inside.

'Lucy –'

'No – they are in the hall – oh, please not, Mr Emerson – they trust me –'

'But why should they, when you have deceived them?'

Mr Beebe opened the door saying: 'Here's my mother.'

'You're not worthy of their trust.'

'What's that?' said Mr Beebe sharply.

'I was saying, why should you trust her when she deceived you?'

'One minute, mother.' He came in and shut the door.

'I don't follow you, Mr Emerson. To whom do you refer? Trust whom?'

'I mean, she has pretended to you that she did not love George. They have loved one another all along.'

Mr Beebe looked at the sobbing girl. He was very quiet, and his white face, with its ruddy whiskers, seemed suddenly in-human. A long black column, he stood and awaited her reply.

'I shall never marry him,' quavered Lucy.

A look of contempt came over him, and he said, 'Why not?'

'Mr Beebe – I have misled you – I have misled myself –'

'Oh, rubbish, Miss Honeychurch!'

'It is not rubbish!' said the old man hotly. 'It's the part of people that you don't understand.'

Mr Beebe laid his hand on his shoulder pleasantly.

'Lucy! Lucy!' called voices from the carriage.

'Mr Beebe, could you help me?'

He looked amazed at the request, and said in a low, stern voice: 'I am more grieved than I can possibly express. It is lamentable, lamentable – incredible.'

'What's wrong with the boy?' fired up the other again.

'Nothing, Mr Emerson, except that he no longer interests me. Marry George, Miss Honeychurch. He will do admirably.'

He walked out and left them. They heard him guiding his mother upstairs.

'Lucy!' the voices called.

She turned to Mr Emerson in despair. But his face revived her. It was the face of a saint who understood.

'Now it is all dark. Now Beauty and Passion seem never to have existed. I know. But remember the mountains over Florence and the view. Ah, dear, if I were George, and gave you one kiss, it would make you brave. You have to go cold into a battle that needs warmth, out into the muddle that you have made yourself; and your mother and all your friends will despise you, oh my darling, and rightly, if it is ever right to despise. George still dark, all the tussle and the misery without a word from him. Am I justified?' Into his own eyes tears came. 'Yes, for we fight for more than Love or Pleasure: there is Truth. Truth counts, Truth does count.'

'You kiss me,' said the girl. 'You kiss me. I will try.'

He gave her a sense of deities reconciled, a feeling that, in gaining the man she loved, she would gain something for the whole world. Throughout the squalor of her homeward drive – she spoke at once – his salutation remained. He had robbed the body of its taint, the world's taunts of their sting; he had shown her the holiness of direct desire. She 'never exactly understood,' she would say in after years, 'how he managed to strengthen her. It was as if he had made her see the whole of everything at once.'

CHAPTER XX

The End of the Middle Ages

THE MISS ALANS did go to Greece, but they went by themselves. They alone of this little company will double Malea and plough the waters of the Saronic gulf. They alone will visit Athens and Delphi, and either shrine of intellectual song – that upon the Acropolis, encircled by blue seas; that under Parnassus, where the eagles build and the bronze charioteer drives undismayed towards infinity. Trembling, anxious, cumbered with much digestive bread, they did proceed to Constantinople, they did go round the world. The rest of us must be contented with a fair, but a less arduous, goal. *Italiam petimus*: we return to the Pension Bertolini.

George said it was his old room.

'No, it isn't,' said Lucy; 'because it is the room I had, and I had your father's room. I forget why; Charlotte made me, for some reason.'

He knelt on the tiled floor, and laid his face in her lap.

'George, you baby, get up.'

'Why shouldn't I be a baby?' murmured George.

Unable to answer this question, she put down his sock, which she was trying to mend, and gazed out through the window. It was evening and again the spring.

'Oh, bother Charlotte,' she said thoughtfully. 'What can such people be made of?'

'Same stuff as parsons are made of.'

'Nonsense!'

'Quite right. It is nonsense.'

'Now you get up off the cold floor, or you'll be starting rheumatism next, and you stop laughing and being so silly.'

'Why shouldn't I laugh?' he asked, pinning her with his elbows, and advancing his face to hers. 'What's there to cry at? Kiss me here.' He indicated the spot where a kiss would be welcome.

He was a boy, after all. When it came to the point, it was she who remembered the past, she into whose soul the iron had entered, she who knew whose this room had been last year. It endeared him to her strangely that he should be sometimes wrong.

'Any letters?' he asked.

'Just a line from Freddy.'

'Now kiss me here; then here.'

Then, threatened again with rheumatism, he strolled to the window, opened it (as the English will), and leant out. There was the parapet, there the river, there to the left the beginnings of the hills. The cab-driver, who at once saluted him with the hiss of a serpent, might be that very Phaethon who had set this happiness in motion twelve months ago. A passion of gratitude – all feelings grow to passions in the South – came over the husband, and he blessed the people and the things who had taken so much trouble about a young fool. He had helped himself, it is true, but how stupidly! All the fighting that mattered had been done by others – by Italy, by his father, by his wife.

'Lucy, you come and look at the cypresses; and the church, whatever its name is, still shows.'

'San Miniato. I'll just finish your sock.'

'Signorino, domani faremo un giro,' called the cabman, with engaging certainty.

George told him that he was mistaken; they had no money to throw away on driving.

And the people who had not meant to help – the Miss Lavishes, the Cecils, the Miss Bartletts! Ever prone to magnify Fate, George counted up the forces that had swept him into this contentment.

'Anything good in Freddy's letter?'

'Not yet.'

His own content was absolute, but hers held bitterness: the Honeychurches had not forgiven them; they were disgusted at her past hypocrisy; she had alienated Windy Corner, perhaps for ever.

'What does he say?'

'Silly boy! He thinks he's being dignified. He knew we should go off in the spring – he has known it for six months – that if mother wouldn't give her consent we should take the thing into our own hands. They had fair warning, and now he calls it an elopement. Ridiculous boy –'

'Signorino, domani faremo un giro –'

'But it will all come right in the end. He has to build us both up from the beginning again. I wish, though, that Cecil had not turned so cynical about women. He has, for the second time, quite altered. Why will men have theories about women? I haven't any about men. I wish, too, that Mr Beebe –'

'You may well wish that.'

'He will never forgive us – I mean, he will never be interested in us again. I wish that he did not influence them so much at Windy Corner. I wish he hadn't – but if we act the truth, the people who really love us are sure to come back to us in the long run.'

'Perhaps.' Then he said more gently: 'Well, I acted the truth – the only thing I did do – and you came back to me. So possibly you know.' He turned back into the room. 'Nonsense with that sock.' He carried her to the window, so that she, too, saw all the view. They sank upon their knees invisible from the road, they hoped, and began to whisper one another's names. Ah! it was worth while; it was the great joy that they had expected, and countless little joys of which they had never dreamt. They were silent.

'Signorino, domani faremo –'

'Oh, bother that man!'

But Lucy remembered the vendor of photographs and said,

'No, don't be rude to him.' Then, with a catching of her breath, she murmured: 'Mr Eager and Charlotte, dreadful frozen Charlotte! How cruel she would be to a man like that!'

'Look at the lights going over the bridge.'

'But this room reminds me of Charlotte. How horrible to grow old in Charlotte's way! To think that evening at the rectory that she shouldn't have heard your father was in the house. For she would have stopped me going in, and he was the only person alive who could have made me see sense. You couldn't have made me. When I am very happy' – she kissed him – 'I remember on how little it all hangs. If Charlotte had only known, she would have stopped me going in, and I should have gone to silly Greece, and become different for ever.'

'But she did know,' said George; 'she did see my father, surely. He said so.'

'Oh no, she didn't see him. She was upstairs with old Mrs Beebe, don't you remember, and then went straight to the church. She said so.'

George was obstinate again. 'My father,' said he, 'saw her, and I prefer his word. He was dozing by the study fire, and he opened his eyes, and there was Miss Bartlett. A few minutes before you came in. She was turning to go as he woke up. He didn't speak to her.'

Then they spoke of other things – the desultory talk of those who have been fighting to reach one another, and whose reward is to rest quietly in each other's arms. It was long ere they returned to Miss Bartlett, but when they did her behaviour seemed more interesting. George, who disliked any darkness, said: 'It's clear that she knew. Then, why did she risk the meeting? She knew he was there, and yet she went to church.'

They tried to piece the thing together.

As they talked, an incredible solution came into Lucy's mind. She rejected it, and said: 'How like Charlotte to undo her work by a feeble muddle at the last moment.' But something in the dying evening, in the roar of the river, in their very embrace, warned them that her words fell short of life, and George whispered: 'Or did she mean it?'

'Mean what?'

'Signorino, domani faremo un giro –'

Lucy bent forward and said with gentleness: 'Lascia, prego, lascia. Siamo sposati.'

'Scusi tanto, signora,' he replied, in tones as gentle, and whipped up his horse.

'Buona sera – e grazie.'

'Niente.'

The cabman drove away singing.

'Mean what, George?'

He whispered: 'Is it this? Is this possible? I'll put a marvel to you. That your cousin has always hoped. That from the very first moment we met, she hoped, far down in her mind, that we should be like this – of course, very far down. That she fought us on the surface, and yet she hoped. I can't explain her any other way. Can you? Look how she kept me alive in you all the summer; how she gave you no peace; how month after month she became more eccentric and unreliable. The sight of us haunted her – or she couldn't have described us as she did to her friend. There are details – it burned. I read the book afterwards. She is not frozen, Lucy, she is not withered up all through. She tore us apart twice, but in the rectory that evening she was given one more chance to make us happy. We can never make friends with her or thank her. But I do believe that, far down in her heart, far below all speech and behaviour, she is glad.'

'It is impossible,' murmured Lucy, and then, remembering the experiences of her own heart, she said: 'No – it is just possible.'

Youth enwrapped them; the song of Phaethon announced passion requited, love attained. But they were conscious of a love more mysterious than this. The song died away; they heard the river, bearing down the snows of winter into the Mediterranean.

APPENDIX

A View without a Room

A Room with a View was published in 1908. Here we are in 1958 and it occurs to me to wonder what the characters have been doing during the interval. They were created even earlier than 1908. The Italian half of the novel was almost the first piece of fiction I attempted. I laid it aside to write and publish two other novels, and then returned to it and added the English half. It is not my preferred novel – *The Longest Journey* is that – but it may fairly be called the nicest. It contains a hero and heroine who are supposed to be good, good-looking and in love – and who are promised happiness. Have they achieved it?

Let me think.

Lucy (Mrs George Emerson) must now be in her late sixties, George in his early seventies – a ripe age, though not as ripe as my own. They are still a personable couple, and fond of each other and of their children and grandchildren. But where do they live? Ah, that is the difficulty, and that is why I have entitled this article 'A View without a Room'. I cannot think where George and Lucy live.

After their Florentine honeymoon they probably settled down in Hampstead. No – in Highgate. That is pretty clear, and the next six years were from the point of view of amenity the best they ever experienced. George cleared out of the railway and got a better-paid clerkship in a government office, Lucy brought a nice little dowry along with her, which they were too sensible not to enjoy, and Miss Bartlett left them what she termed her little all. (Who would have thought it of Cousin Charlotte? I should never have thought anything else.) They had a servant who slept in, and were becoming comfortable capitalists when World War I exploded – the war that was to end war – and spoiled everything.

George instantly became a conscientious objector. He accepted alternative service, so did not go to prison, but he lost his government job and was out of the running for Homes for Heroes when peace came. Mrs Honeychurch was terribly upset by her son-in-law's conduct.

Lucy now got on her high horse and declared herself a conscientious objector too, and ran a more immediate risk by continuing to play Beethoven. Hun music! She was overheard and reported, and the police called. Old Mr Emerson, who lived with the young couple, addressed the police at length. They told him he had better look out. Shortly afterwards he died, still looking out and confident that Love and Truth would see humanity through in the end.

They saw the family through, which is something. No government authorized or ever will authorize either Love or Truth, but they worked privately in this case and helped the squalid move from Highgate to Carshalton. The George Emersons now had two girls and a boy and were beginning to want a real home – somewhere in the country where they could take root and unobtrusively found a dynasty. But civilization was not moving that way. The characters in my other novels were experiencing similar troubles. *Howards End* is a hunt for a home. India is a Passage for Indians as well as English. No resting-place.

For a time Windy Corner dangled illusively. After Mrs Honeychurch's death there was a chance of moving into that much loved house. But Freddy, who had inherited it, was obliged to sell and realize the capital for the upbringing of his family. An unsuccessful yet prolific doctor, Freddy could not do other than sell. Windy Corner disappeared, its garden was built over, and the name of Honeychurch resounded in Surrey no more.

In due course World War II broke out – the one that was to end with a durable peace. George instantly enlisted. Being both intelligent and passionate, he could distinguish between a Germany that was not much worse than England and a Germany that was devilish. At the age of fifty he could recognize in Hitlerism an enemy of the heart as well as of the head and the arts. He discovered that he loved fighting and had been starved by its absence, and also discovered that away from his wife he did not remain chaste.

For Lucy the war was less varied. She gave some music lessons and broadcast some Beethoven, who was quite all right this time, but the little flat at Watford, where she was trying to keep things together against George's return, was bombed, the loss of her possessions and mementos was complete, and the same thing happened to their married daughter, away at Nuneaton.

At the front George rose to the rank of corporal, was wounded and taken prisoner in Africa, and imprisoned in Mussolini's Italy, where he found the Italians sometimes as sympathetic as they had been in his tourist days, and sometimes less sympathetic.

When Italy collapsed he moved northward through the chaos towards Florence. The beloved city had changed, but not unrecognizably. The Trinità Bridge had been destroyed, both ends of the Ponte Vecchio were in a mess, but the Piazza Signoria, where once a trifling murder had occurred, still survived. So did the district where the Pension Bertolini had once flourished – nothing damaged at all.

And George set out – as I did myself a few years later – to locate the particular building. He failed. For though nothing is damaged all is changed. The houses on that stretch of the Lungarno have been renumbered and remodelled and, as it were, remelted, some of the façades have been extended, others have shrunk, so that it is impossible to decide which room was romantic half a century ago. George had therefore to report to Lucy that the View was still there and that the Room must be there, too, but could not be found. She was glad of the news, although at that moment she was homeless. It was something to have retained a View, and, secure in it and in their love as long as they have one another to love, George and Lucy await World War III – the one that would end war and everything else, too.

Cecil Vyse must not be omitted from this prophetic retrospect. He moved out of the Emersons' circle but not altogether out of mine. With his integrity and intelligence he was destined for confidential work, and in 1914 he was seconded to Information or whatever the withholding of information was then entitled. I had an example of his propaganda, and a very welcome one, at Alexandria. A quiet little party was held on the outskirts of that city, and someone wanted a little Beethoven. The hostess demurred. Hun music might compromise us. But a young officer spoke up. 'No, it's all right,' he said, 'a chap who knows about those things from the inside told me Beethoven's definitely Belgian.'

The chap in question must have been Cecil. That mixture of mischief and culture is unmistakable. Our hostess was reassured, the ban was lifted, and the Moonlight Sonata shimmered into the desert.

WHERE ANGELS
FEAR TO TREAD

CHAPTER I

THEY WERE ALL at Charing Cross to see Lilia off – Philip, Harriet, Irma, Mrs Herriton herself. Even Mrs Theobald, squired by Mr Kingcroft, had braved the journey from Yorkshire to bid her only daughter goodbye. Miss Abbott was likewise attended by numerous relatives, and the sight of so many people talking at once and saying such different things caused Lilia to break into ungovernable peals of laughter.

'Quite an ovation,' she cried, sprawling out of her first-class carriage. 'They'll take us for royalty. Oh, Mr Kingcroft, get us foot-warmers.'

The good-natured young man hurried away, and Philip, taking his place, flooded her with a final stream of advice and injunctions – where to stop, how to learn Italian, when to use mosquito-nets, what pictures to look at. 'Remember,' he concluded, 'that it is only by going off the track that you get to know the country. See the little towns – Gubbio, Pienza, Cortona, San Gimignano, Monteriano. And don't, let me beg you, go with that awful tourist idea that Italy's only a museum of antiquities and art. Love and understand the Italians, for the people are more marvellous than the land.'

'How I wish you were coming, Philip,' she said, flattered at the unwonted notice her brother-in-law was giving her.

'I wish I were.' He could have managed it without great difficulty, for his career at the Bar was not so intense as to prevent occasional holidays. But his family disliked his continual visits to the Continent, and he himself often found pleasure in the idea that he was too busy to leave town.

'Goodbye, dear everyone. What a whirl!' She caught sight of her little daughter Irma, and felt that a touch of maternal solemnity was required. 'Goodbye, darling. Mind you're always good, and do what Granny tells you.'

She referred not to her own mother, but to her mother-in-law, Mrs Herriton, who hated the title of Granny.

Irma lifted a serious face to be kissed, and said cautiously, 'I'll do my best.'

'She is sure to be good,' said Mrs Herriton, who was standing pensively a little out of the hubbub. But Lilia was already calling to Miss Abbott, a tall, grave, rather nice-looking young lady who was conducting her adieus in a more decorous manner on the platform.

'Caroline, my Caroline! Jump in, or your chaperon will go off without you.'

And Philip, whom the idea of Italy always intoxicated, had started again, telling her of the supreme moments of her coming journey – the Campanile of Airolo, which would burst on her when she emerged from the St Gotthard tunnel, presaging the future; the view of the Ticino and Lago Maggiore as the train climbed the slopes of Monte Ceneri; the view of Lugano, the view of Como – Italy gathering thick around her now – the arrival at her first resting-place, when, after long driving through dark and dirty streets, she should at last behold, amid the roar of trams and the glare of arc lamps, the buttresses of the cathedral of Milan.

'Handkerchiefs and collars,' screamed Harriet, 'in my inlaid box! I've lent you my inlaid box!'

'Good old Harry!' She kissed everyone again, and there was a moment's silence. They all smiled steadily, excepting Philip, who was choking in the fog, and old Mrs Theobald, who had begun to cry. Miss Abbott got into the carriage. The guard himself shut the door, and told Lilia that she would be all right. Then the train moved, and they all moved with it a couple of steps, and waved their handkerchiefs, and uttered cheerful little cries. At that moment Mr Kingcroft reappeared, carrying a foot-warmer by both ends, as if it was a tea-tray. He was sorry that he was too late, and called out in a quavering voice: 'Goodbye, Mrs Charles. May you enjoy yourself, and may God bless you.'

Lilia smiled and nodded, and then the absurd position of the foot-warmer overcame her, and she began to laugh again.

'Oh, I am so sorry,' she cried back, 'but you do look so funny. Oh, you all look so funny waving! Oh, pray!' And laughing helplessly she was carried out into the fog.

'High spirits to begin so long a journey,' said Mrs Theobald, dabbing her eyes.

Mr Kingcroft solemnly moved his head in token of agreement. 'I wish,' said he, 'that Mrs Charles had gotten the foot-warmer. These London porters won't take heed to a country chap.'

'But you did your best,' said Mrs Herriton. 'And I think it simply noble of you to have brought Mrs Theobald all the way here on such a day as this.' Then, rather hastily, she shook hands, and left him to take Mrs Theobald all the way back.

Sawston, her own home, was within easy reach of London, and they were not late for tea. Tea was in the dining-room, with an egg for Irma, to keep up the child's spirits. The house seemed strangely quiet after a fortnight's bustle, and their conversation was spasmodic and subdued. They wondered whether the travellers had got to Folkestone, whether it would be at all rough, and if so what would happen to poor Miss Abbott.

'And, Granny, when will the old ship get to Italy?' asked Irma.

' "Grandmother", dear; not "Granny",' said Mrs Herriton, giving her a kiss. 'And we say "a boat" or "a steamer", not "a ship". Ships have sails. And mother won't go all the way by sea. You look at the map of Europe, and you'll see why. Harriet, take her. Go with Aunt Harriet, and she'll show you the map.'

'Right-o!' said the little girl, and dragged the reluctant Harriet into the library. Mrs Herriton and her son were left alone. There was immediately confidence between them.

'Here beginneth the New Life,' said Philip.

'Poor child, how vulgar!' murmured Mrs Herriton. 'It's

surprising that she isn't worse. But she has got a look of poor Charles about her.'

'And – alas, alas! – a look of old Mrs Theobald. What appalling apparition was that? I did think the lady was bedridden as well as imbecile. Why ever did she come?'

'Mr Kingcroft made her. I am certain of it. He wanted to see Lilia again, and this was the only way.'

'I hope he is satisfied. I did not think my sister-in-law distinguished herself in her farewells.'

Mrs Herriton shuddered. 'I mind nothing, so long as she has gone – and gone with Miss Abbott. It is mortifying to think that a widow of thirty-three requires a girl ten years younger to look after her.'

'I pity Miss Abbott. Fortunately one admirer is chained to England. Mr Kingcroft cannot leave the crops or the climate or something. I don't think, either, he improved his chances today. He, as well as Lilia, has the knack of being absurd in public.'

Mrs Herriton replied, 'When a man is neither well-bred, nor well-connected, nor handsome, nor clever, nor rich, even Lilia may discard him in time.'

'No. I believe she would take anyone. Right up to the last, when her boxes were packed, she was "playing" the chinless curate. Both the curates are chinless, but hers had the dampest hands. I came on them in the Park. They were speaking of the Pentateuch.'

'My dear boy! If possible, she has got worse and worse. It was your idea of Italian travel that saved us!'

Philip brightened at the little compliment. 'The odd part is that she was quite eager – always asking me for information; and of course I was very glad to give it. I admit she is a philistine, appallingly ignorant, and her taste in art is false. Still, to have any taste at all is something. And I do believe that Italy really purifies and ennobles all who visit her. She is the school as well as the playground of the world. It is really to Lilia's credit that she wants to go there.'

'She would go anywhere,' said his mother, who had heard

enough of the praises of Italy. 'I and Caroline Abbott had the greatest difficulty in dissuading her from the Riviera.'

'No, mother; no. She was really keen on Italy. This travel is quite a crisis for her.' He found the situation full of whimsical romance: there was something half attractive, half repellent in the thought of this vulgar woman journeying to places he loved and revered. Why should she not be transfigured? The same had happened to the Goths.

Mrs Herriton did not believe in romance, nor in transfiguration, nor in parallels from history, nor in anything else that may disturb domestic life. She adroitly changed the subject before Philip got excited. Soon Harriet returned, having given her lesson in geography. Irma went to bed early, and was tucked up by her grandmother. Then the two ladies worked and played cards. Philip read a book. And so they all settled down to their quiet profitable existence, and continued it without interruption through the winter.

It was now nearly ten years since Charles had fallen in love with Lilia Theobald because she was pretty, and during that time Mrs Herriton had hardly known a moment's rest. For six months she schemed to prevent the match, and when it had taken place she turned to another task – the supervision of her daughter-in-law. Lilia must be pushed through life without bringing discredit on the family into which she had married. She was aided by Charles, by her daughter Harriet, and, as soon as he was old enough, by the clever one of the family, Philip. The birth of Irma made things still more difficult. But fortunately old Mrs Theobald, who had attempted interference, began to break up. It was an effort to her to leave Whitby, and Mrs Herriton discouraged the effort as far as possible. That curious duel which is fought over every baby was fought and decided early. Irma belonged to her father's family, not to her mother's.

Charles died, and the struggle recommenced. Lilia tried to assert herself, and said that she should go to take care of Mrs Theobald. It required all Mrs Herriton's kindness to prevent her.

A house was finally taken for her at Sawston, and there for three years she lived with Irma, continually subject to the refining influences of her late husband's family.

During one of her rare Yorkshire visits trouble began again. Lilia confided to a friend that she liked a Mr Kingcroft extremely, but that she was not exactly engaged to him. The news came round to Mrs Herriton, who at once wrote, begging for information, and pointing out that Lilia must either be engaged or not, since no intermediate state existed. It was a good letter, and flurried Lilia extremely. She left Mr Kingcroft without even the pressure of a rescue-party. She cried a great deal on her return to Sawston, and said she was very sorry. Mrs Herriton took the opportunity of speaking more seriously about the duties of widowhood and motherhood than she had ever done before. But somehow things never went easily after. Lilia would not settle down in her place among Sawston matrons. She was a bad house-keeper, always in the throes of some domestic crisis, which Mrs Herriton, who kept her servants for years, had to step across and adjust. She let Irma stop away from school for insufficient reasons, and she allowed her to wear rings. She learned to bicycle, for the purpose of waking the place up, and coasted down the High Street one Sunday evening, falling off at the turn by the church. If she had not been a relative, it would have been enter-taining. But even Philip, who in theory loved outraging English conventions, rose to the occasion, and gave her a talking which she remembered to her dying day. It was just then, too, that they discovered that she still allowed Mr Kingcroft to write to her 'as a gentleman friend', and to send presents to Irma.

Philip thought of Italy, and the situation was saved. Caroline, charming sober Caroline Abbott, who lived two turnings away, was seeking a companion for a year's travel. Lilia gave up her house, sold half her furniture, left the other half and Irma with Mrs Herriton, and had now departed, amid universal approval, for a change of scene.

She wrote to them frequently during the winter – more

frequently than she wrote to her mother. Her letters were always prosperous. Florence she found perfectly sweet, Naples a dream, but very whiffy. In Rome one had simply to sit still and feel. Philip, however, declared that she was improving. He was particularly gratified when in the early spring she began to visit the smaller towns that he had recommended. 'In a place like this,' she wrote, 'one really does feel in the heart of things, and off the beaten track. Looking out of a Gothic window every morning, it seems impossible that the Middle Ages have passed away.' The letter was from Monteriano, and concluded with a not unsuccessful description of the wonderful little town.

'It is something that she is contented,' said Mrs Herriton. 'But no one could live three months with Caroline Abbott and not be the better for it.'

Just then Irma came in from school, and she read her mother's letter to her, carefully correcting any grammatical errors, for she was a loyal supporter of parental authority. Irma listened politely, but soon changed the subject to hockey, in which her whole being was absorbed. They were to vote for colours that afternoon – yellow and white or yellow and green. What did her grandmother think?

Of course Mrs Herriton had an opinion, which she sedately expounded, in spite of Harriet, who said that colours were unnecessary for children, and of Philip, who said that they were ugly. She was getting proud of Irma, who had certainly greatly improved, and could no longer be called that most appalling of things – a vulgar child. She was anxious to form her before her mother returned. So she had no objection to the leisurely movements of the travellers, and even suggested that they should overstay their year if it suited them.

Lilia's next letter was also from Monteriano, and Philip grew quite enthusiastic.

'They've stopped there over a week!' he cried. 'Why! I shouldn't have done as much myself. They must be really keen, for the hotel's none too comfortable.'

'I cannot understand people,' said Harriet. 'What can they be doing all day? And there is no church there, I suppose.'

'There is Santa Deodata, one of the most beautiful churches in Italy.'

'Of course I mean an English church,' said Harriet stiffly. 'Lilia promised me that she would always be in a large town on Sundays.'

'If she goes to a service at Santa Deodata's, she will find more beauty and sincerity than there is in all the Back Kitchens of Europe.'

The Back Kitchen was his nickname for St James's, a small and depressing edifice much patronized by his sister. She always resented any slight on it, and Mrs Herriton had to intervene.

'Now, dears, don't. Listen to Lilia's letter. "We love this place, and I do not know how I shall ever thank Philip for telling me it. It is not only so quaint, but one sees the Italians unspoiled in all their simplicity and charm here. The frescoes are wonderful. Caroline, who grows sweeter every day, is very busy sketching." '

'Everyone to his taste!' said Harriet, who always delivered a platitude as if it was an epigram. She was curiously virulent about Italy, which she had never visited, her only experience of the Continent being an occasional six weeks in the Protestant parts of Switzerland.

'Oh, Harriet is a bad lot!' said Philip as soon as she left the room. His mother laughed, and told him not to be naughty; and the appearance of Irma, just off to school, prevented further discussion. Not only in tracts is a child a peacemaker.

'One moment, Irma,' said her uncle. 'I'm going to the station. I'll give you the pleasure of my company.'

They started together. Irma was gratified; but conversation flagged, for Philip had not the art of talking to the young. Mrs Herriton sat a little longer at the breakfast-table, rereading Lilia's letter. Then she helped the cook to clear, ordered dinner, and started the housemaid turning out the drawing-room, Tuesday being its day. The weather was lovely, and she thought she would do a little gardening, as it was quite early. She called Harriet, who had recovered from the insult to St James's, and together they went to the kitchen-garden and began to sow some early vegetables.

'We will save the peas to the last; they are the greatest fun,' said Mrs Herriton, who had the gift of making work a treat. She and her elderly daughter always got on very well, though they had not a great deal in common. Harriet's education had been almost too successful. As Philip once said, she had bolted all the cardinal virtues and couldn't digest them. Though pious and patriotic, and a great moral asset for the house, she lacked that pliancy and tact which her mother so much valued, and had expected her to pick up for herself. Harriet, if she had been allowed, would have driven Lilia to an open rupture, and, what was worse, she would have done the same to Philip two years before, when he returned full of passion for Italy, and ridiculing Sawston and its ways.

'It's a shame, mother!' she had cried. 'Philip laughs at everything – the Book Club, the Debating Society, the Progressive Whist, the bazaars. People won't like it. We have our reputation. A house divided against itself cannot stand.'

Mrs Herriton replied in the memorable words, 'Let Philip say what he likes, and he will let us do what we like.' And Harriet had acquiesced.

They sowed the duller vegetables first, and a pleasant feeling of righteous fatigue stole over them as they addressed themselves to the peas. Harriet stretched a string to guide the row straight, and Mrs Herriton scratched a furrow with a pointed stick. At the end of it she looked at her watch.

'It's twelve! The second post's in. Run and see if there are any letters.'

Harriet did not want to go. 'Let's finish the peas. There won't be any letters.'

'No, dear; please go. I'll sow the peas, but you shall cover them up – and mind the birds don't see 'em!'

Mrs Herriton was very careful to let those peas trickle evenly from her hand, and at the end of the row she was conscious that she had never sown better. They were expensive too.

'Actually old Mrs Theobald!' said Harriet, returning.

'Read me the letter. My hands are dirty. How intolerable the crested paper is!'

Harriet opened the envelope.

'I don't understand,' she said; 'it doesn't make sense.'

'Her letters never did.'

'But it must be sillier than usual,' said Harriet, and her voice began to quaver. 'Look here, read it, mother; I can't make head or tail.'

Mrs Herriton took the letter indulgently. 'What is the difficulty?' she said after a long pause. 'What is it that puzzles you in this letter?'

'The meaning –' faltered Harriet. The sparrows hopped nearer and began to eye the peas.

'The meaning is quite clear – Lilia is engaged to be married. Don't cry, dear; please me by not crying – don't talk at all. It's more than I could bear. She is going to marry someone she has met in a hotel. Take the letter and read for yourself.' Suddenly she broke down over what might seem a small point. 'How dare she not tell me direct! How dare she write first to Yorkshire! Pray, am I to hear through Mrs Theobald – a patronizing, insolent letter like this? Have I no claim at all? Bear witness, dear' – she choked with passion – 'bear witness that for this I'll never forgive her!'

'Oh, what is to be done?' moaned Harriet. 'What is to be done?'

'This first!' She tore the letter into little pieces and scattered it over the mould. 'Next, a telegram for Lilia! No: a telegram for Miss Caroline Abbott. She, too, has something to explain.'

'Oh, what is to be done?' repeated Harriet, as she followed her mother to the house. She was helpless before such effrontery. What awful thing – what awful person had come to Lilia?

'Someone in the hotel.' The letter only said that. What kind of person? A gentleman? An Englishman? The letter did not say.

'Wire reason of stay at Monteriano. Strange rumours,' read Mrs Herriton, and addressed the telegram to Abbott, Stella d'Italia, Monteriano, Italy. 'If there is an office there,' she added, 'we might get an answer this evening. Since Philip is back at seven, and the eight-fifteen catches the midnight boat at Dover – Harriet, when you go with this, get a hundred pounds in five-pound notes at the bank.'

'But why – what –'

'Go, dear, at once; do not talk. I see Irma coming back; go quickly . . . Well, Irma dear, and whose team are you in this afternoon – Miss Edith's or Miss May's?'

But as soon as she had behaved as usual to her grand-daughter she went to the library and took out the large atlas, for she wanted to know about Monteriano. The name was in the smallest print, in the midst of a woolly-brown tangle of hills which were called the 'Sub-Apennines'. It was not so very far from Siena, which she had learned at school. Past it there wandered a thin black line, notched at intervals like a saw, and she knew that this was a railway. But the map left a good deal to imagination, and she had not got any. She looked up the place in *Childe Harold*, but Byron had not been there. Nor did Mark Twain visit it in the *Tramp Abroad*. The resources of literature were exhausted; she must wait till Philip came home. And the thought of Philip made her try Philip's room, and there she found *Central Italy*, by Baedeker, and opened it for the first time in her life and read in it as follows:

MONTERIANO (pop. 4,800). *Hotels*: Stella d'Italia, moderate only; Globo, dirty. Caffè Garibaldi. Post and Telegraph office in Corso Vittorio Emmanuele, next to Theatre. Photographs at Seghena's (cheaper in Florence). Diligence (1 lira) meets principal trains.

Chief attractions (2–3 hours): Santa Deodata, Palazzo Publico. Sant' Agostino, Santa Caterina, Sant' Ambrogio, Palazzo Capocchi. Guide (2 lire) unnecessary. A walk round the Walls should on no

account be omitted. The view from the Rocca (small gratuity) is
finest at sunset.

History: Monteriano, the Mons Rianus of Antiquity, whose
Ghibelline tendencies are noted by Dante (Purg. xx), definitely
emancipated itself from Poggibonsi in 1261. Hence the distich,
'*Poggibonizzi, fatti in là, che Monteriano si fa città!*' till recently
inscribed over the Siena gate. It remained independent till 1530,
when it was sacked by the Papal troops and became part of the
Grand Duchy of Tuscany. It is now of small importance, and seat of
the district prison. The inhabitants are still noted for their agreeable
manners.

The traveller will proceed direct from the Siena gate to the
COLLEGIATE CHURCH OF SANTA DEODATA, and inspect (5th
chapel on right) the charming Frescoes...

Mrs Herriton did not proceed. She was not one to detect the
hidden charms of Baedeker. Some of the information seemed to
her unnecessary, all of it was dull. Whereas Philip could never
read 'The view from the Rocca (small gratuity) is finest at sunset'
without a catching at the heart. Restoring the book to its place,
she went downstairs and looked up and down the asphalt paths
for her daughter. She saw her at last, two turnings away, vainly
trying to shake off Mr Abbott, Miss Caroline Abbott's father.
Harriet was always unfortunate. At last she returned, hot,
agitated, crackling with bank-notes, and Irma bounced to greet
her, and trod heavily on her corn.

'Your feet grow larger every day,' said the agonized Harriet,
and gave her niece a violent push. Then Irma cried, and Mrs
Herriton was annoyed with Harriet for betraying irritation.
Lunch was nasty; and during pudding news arrived that the cook,
by sheer dexterity, had broken a very vital knob off the kitchen-
range. 'It is too bad,' said Mrs Herriton. Irma said it was three
bad, and was told not to be rude. After lunch Harriet would get
out Baedeker, and read in injured tones about Monteriano, the
Mons Rianus of Antiquity, till her mother stopped her.

'It's ridiculous to read, dear. She's not trying to marry anyone in the place. Some tourist, obviously, who's stopping in the hotel. The place has nothing to do with it at all.'

'But what a place to go to! What nice person, too, do you meet in a hotel?'

'Nice or nasty, as I have told you several times before, is not the point. Lilia has insulted our family, and she shall suffer for it. And when you speak against hotels I think you forget that I met your father at Chamonix. You can contribute nothing, dear, at present, and I think you had better hold your tongue. I am going to the kitchen, to speak about the range.'

She spoke just too much, and the cook said that if she could not give satisfaction she had better leave. A small thing at hand is greater than a great thing remote, and Lilia, misconducting herself upon a mountain in Central Italy, was immediately hidden. Mrs Herriton flew to a registry office, failed; flew to another, failed again; came home, was told by the housemaid that things seemed so unsettled that she had better leave as well; had tea, wrote six letters, was interrupted by cook and housemaid, both weeping, asking her pardon, and imploring to be taken back. In the flush of victory the doorbell rang, and there was the telegram: 'Lilia engaged to Italian nobility. Writing. Abbott.'

'No answer,' said Mrs Herriton. 'Get down Mr Philip's gladstone from the attic.'

She would not allow herself to be frightened by the unknown. Indeed, she knew a little now. The man was not an Italian noble, otherwise the telegram would have said so. It must have been written by Lilia. None but she would have been guilty of the fatuous vulgarity of 'Italian nobility'. She recalled phrases of this morning's letter: 'We love this place – Caroline is sweeter than ever, and busy sketching – Italians full of simplicity and charm.' And the remark of Baedeker, 'the inhabitants are still noted for their agreeable manners', had a baleful meaning now. If Mrs Herriton had no imagination, she had intuition, a more useful quality, and the picture she made to herself of Lilia's fiancé did not prove altogether wrong.

So Philip was received with the news that he must start in half an hour for Monteriano. He was in a painful position. For three years he had sung the praises of the Italians, but he had never contemplated having one as a relative. He tried to soften the thing down to his mother, but in his heart of hearts he agreed with her when she said: 'The man may be a duke or he may be an organ-grinder. That is not the point. If Lilia marries him she insults the memory of Charles, she insults Irma, she insults us. Therefore I forbid her, and if she disobeys we have done with her for ever.'

'I will do all I can,' said Philip in a low voice. It was the first time he had had anything to do. He kissed his mother and sister and puzzled Irma. The hall was warm and attractive as he looked back into it from the cold March night, and he departed for Italy reluctantly, as for something commonplace and dull.

Before Mrs Herriton went to bed she wrote to Mrs Theobald, using plain language about Lilia's conduct, and hinting that it was a question on which everyone must definitely choose sides. She added, as if it was an afterthought, that Mrs Theobald's letter had arrived that morning.

Just as she was going upstairs she remembered that she never covered up those peas. It upset her more than anything, and again and again she struck the banisters with vexation. Late as it was, she got a lantern from the tool-shed and went down the garden to rake the earth over them. The sparrows had taken every one. But countless fragments of the letter remained, disfiguring the tidy ground.

CHAPTER II

WHEN THE BEWILDERED tourist alights at the station of Monteriano, he finds himself in the middle of the country. There are a few houses round the railway, and many more dotted over the plain and the slopes of the hills, but of a town, medieval or otherwise, not the slightest sign. He must take what is suitably termed a *legno* – a piece of wood – and drive up eight miles of excellent road into the Middle Ages. For it is impossible, as well as sacrilegious, to be as quick as Baedeker.

It was three in the afternoon when Philip left the realms of common sense. He was so weary with travelling that he had fallen asleep in the train. His fellow passengers had the usual Italian gift of divination, and when Monteriano came they knew he wanted to go there, and dropped him out. His feet sank into the hot asphalt of the platform, and in a dream he watched the train depart, while the porter who ought to have been carrying his bag ran up the line playing touch-you-last with the guard. Alas! he was in no humour for Italy. Bargaining for a *legno* bored him unutterably. The man asked six lire; and, though Philip knew that for eight miles it should scarcely be more than four, yet he was about to give what he was asked, and so make the man discontented and unhappy for the rest of the day. He was saved from this social blunder by loud shouts, and looking up the road saw one cracking his whip and waving his reins and driving two horses furiously, and behind him there appeared the swaying figure of a woman, holding starfish fashion onto anything she could touch. It was Miss Abbott, who had just received his letter from Milan announcing the time of his arrival, and had hurried down to meet him.

He had known Miss Abbott for years, and had never had much opinion about her one way or the other. She was good, quiet, dull and amiable, and young only because she was twenty-three: there was nothing in her appearance or manner to suggest the fire of youth. All her life had been spent at Sawston with a dull and amiable father, and her pleasant, pallid face, bent on some respectable charity, was a familiar object of the Sawston streets. Why she had ever wished to leave them was surprising; but, as she truly said, 'I am John Bull to the backbone, yet I do want to see Italy, just once. Everybody says it is marvellous, and that one gets no idea of it from books at all.' The curate suggested that a year was a long time; and Miss Abbott, with decorous playfulness, answered him: 'Oh, but you must let me have my fling! I promise to have it once, and once only. It will give me things to think about and talk about for the rest of my life.' The curate had consented; so had Mr Abbott. And here she was in a *legno*, solitary, dusty, frightened, with as much to answer and to answer for as the most dashing adventuress could desire.

They shook hands without speaking. She made room for Philip and his luggage amidst the loud indignation of the unsuccessful driver, whom it required the combined eloquence of the stationmaster and the station beggar to confute. The silence was prolonged until they started. For three days he had been considering what he should do, and still more what he should say. He had invented a dozen imaginary conversations, in all of which his logic and eloquence procured him certain victory. But how to begin? He was in the enemy's country, and everything – the hot sun, the cold air behind the heat, the endless rows of olives, regular yet mysterious – seemed hostile to the placid atmosphere of Sawston in which his thoughts took birth. At the outset he made one great concession. If the match was really suitable, and Lilia were bent on it, he would give in, and trust to his influence with his mother to set things right. He would not have made the concession in England; but here in Italy Lilia, however wilful and silly, was at all events growing to be a human being.

'Are we to talk it over now?' he asked.

'Certainly, please,' said Miss Abbott, in great agitation. 'If you will be so very kind.'

'Then how long has she been engaged?'

Her face was that of a perfect fool – a fool in terror.

'A short time – quite a short time,' she stammered, as if the shortness of the time would reassure him.

'I should like to know how long, if you can remember.'

She entered into elaborate calculations on her fingers. 'Exactly eleven days,' she said at last.

'How long have you been here?'

More calculations, while he tapped irritably with his foot. 'Close on three weeks.'

'Did you know him before you came?'

'No.'

'Oh! Who is he?'

'A native of the place.'

The second silence took place. They had left the plain now and were climbing up the outposts of the hills, the olive-trees still accompanying. The driver, a jolly, fat man, had got out to ease the horses, and was walking by the side of the carriage.

'I understood they met at the hotel.'

'It was a mistake of Mrs Theobald's.'

'I also understand that he is a member of the Italian nobility.'

She did not reply.

'May I be told his name?'

Miss Abbott whispered 'Carella'. But the driver heard her, and a grin split over his face. The engagement must be known already.

'Carella? Conte or Marchese, or what?'

'Signor,' said Miss Abbott, and looked helplessly aside.

'Perhaps I bore you with these questions. If so, I will stop.'

'Oh no, please; not at all. I am here – my own idea – to give all information which you very naturally – and to see if somehow – please ask anything you like.'

'Then how old is he?'

'Oh, quite young. Twenty-one, I believe.'

There burst from Philip the exclamation, 'Good Lord!'

'One would never believe it,' said Miss Abbott, flushing. 'He looks much older.'

'And is he good-looking?' he asked, with gathering sarcasm.

She became decisive. 'Very good-looking. All his features are good, and he is well built – though I dare say English standards would find him too short.'

Philip, whose one physical advantage was his height, felt annoyed at her implied indifference to it.

'May I conclude that you like him?'

She replied decisively again, 'As far as I have seen him, I do.'

At that moment the carriage entered a little wood, which lay brown and sombre across the cultivated hill. The trees of the wood were small and leafless, but noticeable for this – that their stems stood in violets as rocks stand in the summer sea. There are such violets in England, but not so many. Nor are there so many in art, for no painter has the courage. The cart-ruts were channels, the hollows lagoons; even the dry white margin of the road was splashed, like a causeway soon to be submerged under the advancing tide of spring. Philip paid no attention at the time; he was thinking what to say next. But his eyes had registered the beauty, and next March he did not forget that the road to Monteriano must traverse innumerable flowers.

'As far as I have seen him, I do like him,' repeated Miss Abbott, after a pause.

He thought she sounded a little defiant, and crushed her at once.

'What is he, please? You haven't told me that. What's his position?'

She opened her mouth to speak, and no sound came from it. Philip waited patiently. She tried to be audacious, and failed pitiably.

'No position at all. He is kicking his heels, as my father would say. You see, he has only just finished his military service.'

'As a private?'

'I suppose so. There is general conscription. He was in the Bersaglieri, I think. Isn't that the crack regiment?'

'The men in it must be short and broad. They must also be able to walk six miles an hour.'

She looked at him wildly, not understanding all that he said, but feeling that he was very clever. Then she continued her defence of Signor Carella.

'And now, like most young men, he is looking out for something to do.'

'Meanwhile?'

'Meanwhile, like most young men, he lives with his people – father, mother, two sisters, and a tiny tot of a brother.'

There was a grating sprightliness about her that drove him nearly mad. He determined to silence her at last.

'One more question, and only one more. What is his father?'

'His father,' said Miss Abbott. 'Well, I don't suppose you'll think it a good match. But that's not the point. I mean the point is not – I mean that social differences – love, after all – not but what –'

Philip ground his teeth together and said nothing.

'Gentlemen sometimes judge hardly. But I feel that you, and at all events your mother – so really good in every sense, so really unworldly – after all, love – marriages are made in heaven.'

'Yes, Miss Abbott, I know. But I am anxious to hear heaven's choice. You arouse my curiosity. Is my sister-in-law to marry an angel?'

'Mr Herriton, don't – please, Mr Herriton – a dentist. His father's a dentist.'

Philip gave a cry of personal disgust and pain. He shuddered all over, and edged away from his companion. A dentist! A dentist at Monteriano! A dentist in fairyland! False teeth and laughing-gas and the tilting chair at a place which knew the Etruscan League, and the Pax Romana, and Alaric himself, and the Countess Matilda, and the Middle Ages, all fighting and holiness, and the Renaissance, all fighting and beauty! He thought of Lilia no longer. He was anxious for himself: he feared that Romance might die.

Romance only dies with life. No pair of pincers will ever pull it out of us. But there is a spurious sentiment which cannot resist the unexpected and the incongruous and the grotesque. A touch will loosen it, and the sooner it goes from us the better. It was going from Philip now, and therefore he gave the cry of pain.

'I cannot think what is in the air,' he began. 'If Lilia was determined to disgrace us, she might have found a less repulsive way. A boy of medium height with a pretty face, the son of a dentist at Monteriano. Have I put it correctly? May I surmise that he has not got one penny? May I also surmise that his social position is nil? Furthermore –'

'Stop! I'll tell you no more.'

'Really, Miss Abbott, it is a little late for reticence. You have equipped me admirably!'

'I'll tell you not another word!' she cried, with a spasm of terror. Then she got out her handkerchief, and seemed as if she would shed tears. After a silence, which he intended to symbolize to her the dropping of a curtain on the scene, he began to talk of other subjects.

They were among olives again, and the wood with its beauty and wildness had passed away. But as they climbed higher the country opened out, and there appeared, high on a hill to the right, Monteriano. The hazy green of the olives rose up to its walls, and it seemed to float in isolation between trees and sky, like some fantastic ship city of a dream. Its colour was brown, and it revealed not a single house – nothing but the narrow circle of the walls, and behind them seventeen towers – all that was left of the fifty-two that had filled the city in her prime. Some were only stumps, some were inclining stiffly to their fall, some were still erect, piercing like masts into the blue. It was impossible to praise it as beautiful, but it was also impossible to damn it as quaint.

Meanwhile Philip talked continually, thinking this to be great evidence of resource and tact. It showed Miss Abbott that he had probed her to the bottom, but was able to conquer his disgust, and by sheer force of intellect continue to be as agreeable and amusing as ever. He did not know that he talked a good deal of nonsense, and that the sheer force of his intellect was weakened by the sight of Monteriano, and by the thought of dentistry within those walls.

The town above them swung to the left, to the right, to the left again, as the road wound upward through the trees, and the towers began to glow in the descending sun. As they drew near, Philip saw the heads of people gathering black upon the walls, and he knew well what was happening – how the news was spreading that a stranger was in sight, and the beggars were aroused from their content and bid to adjust their deformities; how the alabaster man was running for his wares, and the Authorized Guide running for his peaked cap and his two cards of recommendation – one from Miss M'Gee, Maida Vale, the other, less valuable, from an Equerry to the Queen of Peru; how someone else was running to tell the landlady of the Stella d'Italia to put on her pearl necklace and brown boots and empty the slops from the spare bedroom; and how the landlady was running to tell Lilia and her boy that their fate was at hand.

Perhaps it was a pity Philip had talked so profusely. He had driven Miss Abbott half demented, but he had given himself no time to concert a plan. The end came so suddenly. They emerged from the trees onto the terrace before the walls, with the vision of half Tuscany radiant in the sun behind them, and then they turned in through the Siena gate, and their journey was over. The *dogana* men admitted them with an air of gracious welcome, and they clattered up the narrow dark street, greeted by that mixture of curiosity and kindness which makes each Italian arrival so wonderful.

He was stunned and knew not what to do. At the hotel he received no ordinary reception. The landlady wrung him by the

hand; one person snatched his umbrella, another his bag; people
pushed each other out of his way. The entrance seemed blocked
with a crowd. Dogs were barking, bladder whistles being blown,
women waving their handkerchiefs, excited children screaming
on the stairs, and at the top of the stairs was Lilia herself, very
radiant, with her best blouse on.

'Welcome!' she cried. 'Welcome to Monteriano!' He greeted
her, for he did not know what else to do, and a sympathetic
murmur rose from the crowd below.

'You told me to come here,' she continued, 'and I don't forget
it. Let me introduce Signor Carella!'

Philip discerned in the corner behind her a young man who
might eventually prove handsome and well-made, but certainly
did not seem so then. He was half enveloped in the drapery of a
cold dirty curtain, and nervously stuck out a hand, which Philip
took and found thick and damp. There were more murmurs of
approval from the stairs.

'Well, din-din's nearly ready,' said Lilia. 'Your room's down
the passage, Philip. You needn't go changing.'

He stumbled away to wash his hands, utterly crushed by her
effrontery.

'Dear Caroline!' whispered Lilia as soon as he had gone.
'What an angel you've been to tell him! He takes it so well. But
you must have had a *mauvais quart d'heure*.'

Miss Abbott's long terror suddenly turned into acidity. 'I've
told nothing,' she snapped. 'It's all for you – and if it only takes
a quarter of an hour you'll be lucky!'

Dinner was a nightmare. They had the smelly dining-room
to themselves. Lilia, very smart and vociferous, was at the head
of the table; Miss Abbott, also in her best, sat by Philip, looking,
to his irritated nerves, more like the tragedy confidante every
moment. That scion of the Italian nobility, Signor Carella, sat
opposite. Behind him loomed a bowl of goldfish, who swam
round and round, gaping at the guests.

The face of Signor Carella was twitching too much for Philip to study it. But he could see the hands, which were not particularly clean, and did not get cleaner by fidgeting amongst the shining slabs of hair. His starched cuffs were not clean either, and as for his suit, it had obviously been bought for the occasion as something really English – a gigantic check, which did not even fit. His handkerchief he had forgotten, but never missed it. Altogether, he was quite unpresentable, and very lucky to have a father who was a dentist in Monteriano. And why even Lilia – but as soon as the meal began it furnished Philip with an explanation.

For the youth was hungry, and his lady filled his plate with spaghetti, and when those delicious slippery worms were flying down his throat his face relaxed and became for a moment unconscious and calm. And Philip had seen that face before in Italy a hundred times – seen it and loved it, for it was not merely beautiful, but had the charm which is the rightful heritage of all who are born on that soil. But he did not want to see it opposite him at dinner. It was not the face of a gentleman.

Conversation, to give it that name, was carried on in a mixture of English and Italian. Lilia had picked up hardly any of the latter language, and Signor Carella had not yet learned any of the former. Occasionally Miss Abbott had to act as interpreter between the lovers, and the situation became uncouth and revolting in the extreme. Yet Philip was too cowardly to break forth and denounce the engagement. He thought he should be more effective with Lilia if he had her alone, and pretended to himself that he must hear her defence before giving judgement.

Signor Carella, heartened by the spaghetti and the throat-rasping wine, attempted to talk, and, looking politely towards Philip, said: 'England is a great country. The Italians love England and the English.'

Philip, in no mood for international amenities, merely bowed.

'Italy too,' the other continued a little resentfully, 'is a great country. She has produced many famous men – for example, Garibaldi and Dante. The latter wrote the *Inferno*, the *Purgatorio*, the *Paradiso*. The *Inferno* is the most beautiful.' And, with the complacent tone of one who has received a solid education, he quoted the opening lines –

> Nel mezzo del cammin di nostra vita
> Mi ritrovai per una selva oscura,
> Ché la diritta via era smarrita –

a quotation which was more apt than he supposed.

Lilia glanced at Philip to see whether he noticed that she was marrying no ignoramus. Anxious to exhibit all the good qualities of her betrothed, she abruptly introduced the subject of *pallone*, in which, it appeared, he was a proficient player. He suddenly became shy, and developed a conceited grin – the grin of the village yokel whose cricket score is mentioned before a stranger. Philip himself had loved to watch *pallone*, that entrancing combination of lawn-tennis and fives. But he did not expect to love it quite so much again.

'Oh, look!' exclaimed Lilia, 'the poor wee fish!'

A starved cat had been worrying them all for pieces of the purple quivering beef they were trying to swallow. Signor Carella, with the brutality so common in Italians, had caught her by the paw and flung her away from him. Now she had climbed up to the bowl and was trying to hook out the fish. He got up, drove her off, and, finding a large glass stopper by the bowl, entirely plugged up the aperture with it.

'But may not the fish die?' said Miss Abbott. 'They have no air.'

'Fish live on water, not on air,' he replied in a knowing voice, and sat down. Apparently he was at his ease again, for he took to spitting on the floor. Philip glanced at Lilia, but did not detect her wincing. She talked bravely till the end of the disgusting meal, and then got up saying: 'Well, Philip, I am sure you are ready for bye-bye. We shall meet at twelve o'clock lunch tomorrow, if we don't meet before. They give us *caffè-latte* in our rooms.'

It was a little too impudent. Philip replied, 'I should like to see you now, please, in my room, as I have come all the way on business.' He heard Miss Abbott gasp. Signor Carella, who was lighting a rank cigar, had not understood.

It was as he expected. When he was alone with Lilia he lost all nervousness. The remembrance of his long intellectual supremacy strengthened him, and he began volubly –

'My dear Lilia, don't let's have a scene. Before I arrived I thought I might have to question you. It is unnecessary. I know everything. Miss Abbott has told me a certain amount, and the rest I see for myself.'

'See for yourself?' she exclaimed, and he remembered afterwards that she had flushed crimson.

'That he is probably a ruffian and certainly a cad.'

'There are no cads in Italy,' she said quickly.

He was taken aback. It was one of his own remarks. And she further upset him by adding: 'He is the son of a dentist. Why not?'

'Thank you for the information. I know everything, as I told you before. I am also aware of the social position of an Italian who pulls out teeth in a minute provincial town.'

He was not aware of it, but he ventured to conclude that it was pretty low. Nor did Lilia contradict him. But she was sharp enough to say: 'Indeed, Philip, you surprise me. I understood you went in for equality and so on.'

'And I understood that Signor Carella was a member of the Italian nobility.'

'Well, we put it like that in the telegram so as not to shock dear Mrs Herriton. But it is true. He is a younger branch. Of course families ramify – just as in yours there is your cousin Joseph.' She adroitly picked out the only undesirable member of the Herriton clan. 'Gino's father is courtesy itself, and rising rapidly in his profession. This very month he leaves Monteriano, and sets up at Poggibonsi. And for my own poor part, I think what people *are* is what matters, but I don't suppose you'll agree.

And I should like you to know that Gino's uncle is a priest – the same as a clergyman at home.'

Philip was aware of the social position of an Italian priest, and said so much about it that Lilia interrupted him with, 'Well, his cousin's a lawyer at Rome.'

'What kind of "lawyer"?'

'Why, a lawyer just like you are – except that he has lots to do and can never get away.'

The remark hurt more than he cared to show. He changed his method, and in a gentle, conciliatory tone delivered the following speech:

'The whole thing is like a bad dream – so bad that it cannot go on. If there was one redeeming feature about the man I might be uneasy. As it is I can trust to time. For the moment, Lilia, he has taken you in, but you will find him out soon. It is not possible that you, a lady, accustomed to ladies and gentlemen, will tolerate a man whose position is – well, not equal to the son of the servants' dentist in Coronation Place. I am not blaming you now. But I blame the glamour of Italy – I have felt it myself, you know – and I greatly blame Miss Abbott.'

'Caroline! Why blame her? What's all this to do with Caroline?'

'Because we expected her to –' He saw that the answer would involve him in difficulties, and, waving his hand, continued: 'So I am confident, and you in your heart agree, that this engagement will not last. Think of your life at home – think of Irma! And I'll also say, think of us; for you know, Lilia, that we count you more than a relation. I should feel I was losing my own sister if you did this, and my mother would lose a daughter.'

She seemed touched at last, for she turned away her face and said, 'I can't break it off now!'

'Poor Lilia,' said he, genuinely moved. 'I know it may be painful. But I have come to rescue you, and, book-worm though I may be, I am not frightened to stand up to a bully. He's merely an insolent boy. He thinks he can keep you to your word by threats. He will be different when he sees he has a man to deal with.'

What follows should be prefaced with some simile – the simile of a powder-mine, a thunderbolt, an earthquake – for it blew Philip up in the air and flattened him on the ground and swallowed him up in the depths. Lilia turned on her gallant defender and said:

'For once in my life I'll thank you to leave me alone. I'll thank your mother too. For twelve years you've trained me and tortured me, and I'll stand it no more. Do you think I'm a fool? Do you think I never felt? Ah! when I came to your house a poor young bride, how you all looked me over – never a kind word – and discussed me, and thought I might just do; and your mother corrected me, and your sister snubbed me, and you said funny things about me to show how clever you were! And when Charles died I was still to run in strings for the honour of your beastly family, and I was to be cooped up at Sawston and learn to keep house, and all my chances spoilt of marrying again. No, thank you! No, thank you! "Bully"? "Insolent boy"? Who's that, pray, but you? But, thank goodness, I can stand up against the world now, for I've found Gino, and this time I marry for love!'

The coarseness and truth of her attack alike overwhelmed him. But her supreme insolence found him words, and he too burst forth.

'Yes! And I forbid you to do it! You despise me, perhaps, and think I'm feeble. But you're mistaken. You are ungrateful and impertinent and contemptible, but I will save you in order to save Irma and our name. There is going to be such a row in this town that you and he'll be sorry you came to it. I shall shrink from nothing, for my blood is up. It is unwise of you to laugh. I forbid you to marry Carella, and I shall tell him so now.'

'Do,' she cried. 'Tell him so now. Have it out with him. Gino! Gino! Come in! Avanti! Fra Filippo forbids the banns!'

Gino appeared so quickly that he must have been listening outside the door.

'Fra Filippo's blood's up. He shrinks from nothing. Oh, take care he doesn't hurt you!' She swayed about in vulgar imitation of Philip's walk, and then, with a proud glance at the square shoulders of her betrothed, flounced out of the room.

Did she intend them to fight? Philip had no intention of doing so; and no more, it seemed, had Gino, who stood nervously in the middle of the room with twitching lips and eyes.

'Please sit down, Signor Carella,' said Philip in Italian. 'Mrs Herriton is rather agitated, but there is no reason we should not be calm. Might I offer you a cigarette? Please sit down.'

He refused the cigarette and the chair, and remained standing in the full glare of the lamp. Philip, not averse to such assistance, got his own face into shadow.

For a long time he was silent. It might impress Gino, and it also gave him time to collect himself. He would not this time fall into the error of blustering, which he had caught so unaccountably from Lilia. He would make his power felt by restraint.

Why, when he looked up to begin, was Gino convulsed with silent laughter? It vanished immediately; but he became nervous, and was even more pompous than he intended.

'Signor Carella, I will be frank with you. I have come to prevent you marrying Mrs Herriton, because I see you will both be unhappy together. She is English, you are Italian; she is accustomed to one thing, you to another. And – pardon me if I say it – she is rich and you are poor.'

'I am not marrying her because she is rich,' was the sulky reply.

'I never suggested that for a moment,' said Philip courteously. 'You are honourable, I am sure; but are you wise? And let me remind you that we want her with us at home. Her little daughter will be motherless, our home will be broken up. If you grant my request you will earn our thanks – and you will not be without a reward for your disappointment.'

'Reward – what reward?' He bent over the back of a chair and looked earnestly at Philip. They were coming to terms pretty quickly. Poor Lilia!

Philip said slowly, 'What about a thousand lire?'

His soul went forth into one exclamation, and then he was silent, with gaping lips. Philip would have given double; he had expected a bargain.

'You can have them tonight.'

He found words, and said, 'It is too late.'

'But why?'

'Because –' His voice broke. Philip watched his face – a face without refinement, perhaps, but not without expression – watched it quiver and re-form and dissolve from emotion into emotion. There was avarice at one moment, and insolence, and politeness, and stupidity, and cunning – and let us hope that sometimes there was love. But gradually one emotion dominated, the most unexpected of all; for his chest began to heave and his eyes to wink and his mouth to twitch, and suddenly he stood erect and roared forth his whole being in one tremendous laugh.

Philip sprang up, and Gino, who had flung wide his arms to let the glorious creature go, took him by the shoulders and shook him, and said: 'Because we are married – married – married as soon as I knew you were coming. There was no time to tell you. Oh, oh! You have come all the way for nothing. Oh! And oh, your generosity!' Suddenly he became grave, and said: 'Please pardon me; I am rude. I am no better than a peasant, and I –' Here he saw Philip's face, and it was too much for him. He gasped and exploded and crammed his hands into his mouth and spat them out in another explosion, and gave Philip an aimless push, which toppled him onto the bed. He uttered a horrified 'Oh!' and then gave up, and bolted away down the passage, shrieking like a child, to tell the joke to his wife.

For a time Philip lay on the bed, pretending to himself that he was hurt grievously. He could scarcely see for temper, and in the passage he ran against Miss Abbott, who promptly burst into tears.

'I sleep at the Globo,' he told her, 'and start for Sawston

tomorrow morning early. He has assaulted me. I could prosecute him. But shall not.'

'I can't stop here,' she sobbed. 'I daren't stop here. You will have to take me with you!'

CHAPTER III

OPPOSITE THE VOLTERRA gate of Monteriano, outside the city, is a very respectable whitewashed mud wall, with a coping of red crinkled tiles to keep it from dissolution. It would suggest a gentleman's garden if there was not in its middle a large hole, which grows larger with every rainstorm. Through the hole is visible, firstly, the iron gate that is intended to close it; secondly, a square piece of ground which, though not quite mud, is at the same time not exactly grass; and, finally, another wall, stone this time, which has a wooden door in the middle and two wooden-shuttered windows each side, and apparently forms the façade of a one-storey house.

This house is bigger than it looks, for it slides for two storeys down the hill behind, and the wooden door, which is always locked, really leads into the attic. The knowing person prefers to follow the precipitous mule-track round the turn of the mud wall till he can take the edifice in the rear. Then – being now on a level with the cellars – he lifts up his head and shouts. If his voice sounds like something light – a letter, for example, or some vegetables, or a bunch of flowers – a basket is let out of the first-floor windows by a string, into which he puts his burden and departs. But if he sounds like something heavy, such as a log of wood, or a piece of meat, or a visitor, he is interrogated, and then bidden or forbidden to ascend. The ground floor and the upper floor of that battered house are alike deserted, and the inmates keep to the central portion, just as in a dying body all life retires to the heart. There is a door at the top of the first flight of stairs, and if the visitor is admitted he will find a welcome which is not necessarily cold. There are several rooms, some dark and mostly stuffy – a reception-room adorned with horsehair chairs, woolwork stools, and a stove that is never lit – German bad taste without German domesticity broods over that room; also a living-room, which insensibly glides into a bedroom when the refining influence of hospitality is absent, and real bedrooms; and last, but not least, the loggia, where you can live day and night if you feel inclined, drinking vermouth and smoking cigarettes, with leagues of olive-trees and vineyards and blue-green hills to watch you.

It was in this house that the brief and inevitable tragedy of Lilia's married life took place. She made Gino buy it for her, because it was there she had first seen him, sitting on the mud wall that faced the Volterra gate. She remembered how the evening sun had struck his hair, and how he had smiled down at her, and, being both sentimental and unrefined, was determined to have the man and the place together. Things in Italy are cheap for an Italian, and, though he would have preferred a house in the piazza, or better still a house at Siena, or, bliss above bliss, a house at Leghorn, he did as she asked, thinking that perhaps she showed her good taste in preferring so retired an abode.

The house was far too big for them, and there was a general concourse of his relatives to fill it up. His father wished to make it a patriarchal concern, where all the family should have their rooms and meet together for meals, and was perfectly willing to give up the new practice at Poggibonsi and preside. Gino was quite willing too, for he was an affectionate youth who liked a large home-circle, and he told it as a pleasant bit of news to Lilia, who did not attempt to conceal her horror.

At once he was horrified too; saw that the idea was monstrous; abused himself to her for having suggested it; rushed off to tell his father that it was impossible. His father complained that prosperity was already corrupting him and making him unsympathetic and hard; his mother cried; his sisters accused him of blocking their social advance. He was apologetic, and even cringing, until they turned on Lilia. Then he turned on them, saying that they could not understand, much less associate with, the English lady who was his wife; that there should be one master in that house – himself.

Lilia praised and petted him on his return, calling him brave and a hero and other endearing epithets. But he was rather blue when his clan left Monteriano in much dignity – a dignity which was not at all impaired by the acceptance of a cheque. They took the cheque not to Poggibonsi, after all, but to Empoli – a lively, dusty town some twenty miles off. There they settled down in comfort; and the sisters said they had been driven to it by Gino.

The cheque was, of course, Lilia's, who was extremely generous, and was quite willing to know anybody so long as she had not to live with them, relations-in-law being on her nerves. She liked nothing better than finding out some obscure and distant connection – there were several of them – and acting the lady bountiful, leaving behind her bewilderment, and too often discontent. Gino wondered how it was that all his people, who had formerly seemed so pleasant, had suddenly become plaintive and disagreeable. He put it down to his lady-wife's magnificence, in comparison with which all seemed common. Her money flew apace, in spite of the cheap living. She was even richer than he expected; and he remembered with shame how he had once regretted his inability to accept the thousand lire that Philip Herriton offered him in exchange for her. It would have been a short-sighted bargain.

Lilia enjoyed settling into the house, with nothing to do except give orders to smiling workpeople, and a devoted husband as interpreter. She wrote a jaunty account of her happiness to Mrs Herriton, and Harriet answered the letter saying (1) that all future communications should be addressed to the solicitors; (2) would Lilia return an inlaid box which Harriet had lent her – lent, not given – to keep handkerchiefs and collars in?

'Look what I am giving up to live with you!' she said to Gino, never unwilling to lay stress on her condescension. He took her to mean the inlaid box, and said that she need not give it up at all.

'Silly fellow, no! I mean the life. Those Herritons are very well connected. They lead Sawston society. But what do I care so long as I have my silly fellow!' She always treated him as a boy, which he was, and as a fool, which he was not, thinking herself so immeasurably superior to him that she neglected opportunity after opportunity of establishing her rule. He was good-looking and indolent; therefore he must be stupid. He was poor; therefore he would never dare to criticize his benefactress. He was passionately in love with her; therefore she could do exactly as she liked.

'It mayn't be heaven below,' she thought, 'but it's better than Charles.'

And all the time the boy was watching her, and growing up.

She was reminded of Charles by a disagreeable letter from the solicitors, bidding her disgorge a large sum of money for Irma, in accordance with her late husband's will. It was just like Charles's suspicious nature to have provided against a second marriage. Gino was equally indignant, and between them they composed a stinging reply, which had no effect. He then said that Irma had better come out and live with them. 'The air is good, so is the food; she will be happy here, and we shall not have to part with the money.' But Lilia had not the courage even to suggest this to the Herritons, and an unexpected terror seized her at the thought of Irma or any English child being educated at Monteriano.

Gino became terribly depressed over the solicitors' letter, more depressed than she thought necessary. There was no more to do in the house, and he spent whole days in the loggia leaning over the parapet or sitting astride it disconsolately.

'Oh, you idle boy!' she cried, pinching his muscles. 'Go and play *pallone*.'

'I am a married man,' he answered, without raising his head. 'I do not play games any more.'

'Go and see your friends then.'

'I have no friends now.'

'Silly, silly, silly! You can't stop indoors all day!'

'I want to see no one but you.' He spat onto an olive-tree.

'Now, Gino, don't be silly. Go and see your friends, and bring them to see me. We both of us like society.'

He looked puzzled, but allowed himself to be persuaded, went out, found that he was not as friendless as he supposed, and returned after several hours in altered spirits. Lilia congratulated herself on her good management.

'I'm ready, too, for people now,' she said. 'I mean to wake you all up, just as I woke up Sawston. Let's have plenty of men – and make them bring their womenkind. I mean to have real English tea-parties.'

'There is my aunt and her husband; but I thought you did not want to receive my relatives.'

'I never said such a –'

'But you would be right,' he said earnestly. 'They are not for you. Many of them are in trade, and even we are little more; you should have gentlefolk and nobility for your friends.'

'Poor fellow,' thought Lilia. 'It is sad for him to discover that his people are vulgar.' She began to tell him that she loved him just for his silly self, and he flushed and began tugging at his moustache.

'But besides your relatives I must have other people here. Your friends have wives and sisters, haven't they?'

'Oh yes; but of course I scarcely know them.'

'Not know your friends' people?'

'Why, no. If they are poor and have to work for their living I may see them – but not otherwise. Except –' He stopped. The chief exception was a young lady, to whom he had once been introduced for matrimonial purposes. But the dowry had proved inadequate, and the acquaintance terminated.

'How funny! But I mean to change all that. Bring your friends to see me, and I will make them bring their people.'

He looked at her rather hopelessly.

'Well, who are the principal people here? Who leads society?'

The governor of the prison, he supposed, and the officers who assisted him.

'Well, are they married?'

'Yes.'

'There we are. Do you know them?'

'Yes – in a way.'

'I see,' she exclaimed angrily. 'They look down on you, do they, poor boy? Wait!' He assented. 'Wait! I'll soon stop that. Now, who else is there?'

'The Marchese, sometimes, and the canons of the Collegiate Church.'

'Married?'

'The canons –' he began with twinkling eyes.

'Oh, I forgot your horrid celibacy. In England they would be the centre of everything. But why shouldn't I know them? Would it make it easier if I called all round? Isn't that your foreign way?'

He did not think it would make it easier.

'But I must know someone! Who were the men you were talking to this afternoon?'

Low-class men. He could scarcely recollect their names.

'But, Gino dear, if they're low-class, why did you talk to them? Don't you care about your position?'

All Gino cared about at present was idleness and pocket-money, and his way of expressing it was to exclaim: 'Ouf – pouf! How hot it is in here. No air; I sweat all over. I expire. I must cool myself, or I shall never get to sleep.' In his funny abrupt way he ran out onto the loggia, where he lay full length on the parapet, and began to smoke and spit under the silence of the stars.

Lilia gathered somehow from this conversation that continental society was not the go-as-you-please thing she had expected. Indeed, she could not see where continental society was. Italy is such a delightful place to live in if you happen to be a man. There one may enjoy that exquisite luxury of socialism – that true socialism which is based not on equality of income or character, but on the equality of manners. In the democracy of the *caffè* or the street the great question of our life has been solved, and the brotherhood of man is a reality. But it is accomplished at the expense of the sisterhood of women. Why should you not make friends with your neighbour at the theatre or in the train, when you know and he knows that feminine criticism and feminine insight and feminine prejudice will never come between you! Though you become as David and Jonathan, you need never enter his home, nor he yours. All your lives you will meet under the open air, the only roof-tree of the South, under which he will spit and swear, and you will drop your h's, and nobody will think the worse of either.

Meanwhile the women – they have, of course, their house and their church, with its admirable and frequent services, to which they are escorted by the maid. Otherwise they do not go out much, for it is not genteel to walk, and you are too poor to keep a carriage. Occasionally you will take them to the *caffè* or theatre, and immediately all your wonted acquaintance there desert you, except those few who are expecting and expected to marry into your family. It is all very sad. But one consolation emerges – life is very pleasant in Italy if you are a man.

Hitherto Gino had not interfered with Lilia. She was so much older than he was, and so much richer, that he regarded her as a superior being who answered to other laws. He was not wholly surprised, for strange rumours were always blowing over the Alps of lands where men and women had the same amusements and interests, and he had often met that privileged maniac, the lady tourist, on her solitary walks. Lilia took solitary walks, too, and only that week a tramp had grabbed at her watch – an episode which is supposed to be indigenous in Italy, though really less frequent there than in Bond Street. Now that he knew her better, he was inevitably losing his awe; no one could live with her and keep it, especially when she had been so silly as to lose a gold watch and chain. As he lay thoughtful along the parapet, he realized for the first time the responsibilities of married life. He must save her from dangers, physical and social, for after all she was a woman. 'And I,' he reflected, 'though I am young, am at all events a man, and know what is right.'

He found her still in the living-room, combing her hair, for she had something of the slattern in her nature, and there was no need to keep up appearances.

'You must not go out alone,' he said gently. 'It is not safe. If you want to walk, Perfetta shall accompany you.' Perfetta was a widowed cousin, too humble for social aspirations, who was living with them as factotum.

'Very well,' smiled Lilia, 'very well' – as if she were addressing a solicitous kitten. But for all that she never took a solitary walk again, with one exception, till the day of her death.

Days passed, and no one called except poor relatives. She began to feel dull. Didn't he know the *Sindaco* or the bank-manager? Even the landlady of the Stella d'Italia would be better than no one. She, when she went into the town, was pleasantly received; but people naturally found a difficulty in getting on with a lady who could not learn their language. And the tea-party, under Gino's adroit management, receded ever and ever before her.

He had a good deal of anxiety over her welfare, for she did not settle down in the house at all. But he was comforted by a welcome and unexpected visitor. As he was going one afternoon for the letters – they were delivered at the door, but it took longer to get them at the office – someone humorously threw a cloak over his head, and when he disengaged himself he saw his very dear friend Spiridione Tesi of the custom-house at Chiasso, whom he had not met for two years. What joy! What salutations! So that all the passers-by smiled with approval on the amiable scene. Spiridione's brother was now stationmaster at Bologna, and thus he himself could spend his holiday travelling over Italy at the public expense. Hearing of Gino's marriage, he had come to see him on his way to Siena, where lived his own uncle, lately married too.

'They all do it,' he exclaimed, 'myself excepted.' He was not quite twenty-three. 'But tell me more. She is English. That is good, very good. An English wife is very good indeed. And she is rich?'

'Immensely rich.'

'Blonde or dark?'

'Blonde.'

'Is it possible!'

'It pleases me very much,' said Gino simply. 'If you remember, I always desired a blonde.' Three or four men had collected, and were listening.

'We all desire one,' said Spiridione. 'But you, Gino, deserve your good fortune, for you are a good son, a brave man and a true friend, and from the very first moment I saw you I wished you well.'

'No compliments, I beg,' said Gino, standing with his hands crossed on his chest and a smile of pleasure on his face.

Spiridione addressed the other men, none of whom he had ever seen before. 'Is it not true? Does not he deserve this wealthy blonde?'

'He does deserve her,' said all the men.

It is a marvellous land, whether you love it or hate it.

There were no letters, and of course they sat down at the Caffè Garibaldi, by the Collegiate Church – quite a good *caffè*, that, for so small a city. There were marble-topped tables, and pillars terracotta below and gold above, and on the ceiling was a fresco of the battle of Solferino. One could not have desired a prettier room. They had vermouth and little cakes with sugar on the top, which they chose gravely at the counter, pinching them first to be sure they were fresh. And, though vermouth is barely alcoholic, Spiridione drenched his with soda-water to be sure that it should not get into his head.

They were in high spirits, and elaborate compliments alternated curiously with gentle horse-play. But soon they put up their legs on a pair of chairs and began to smoke.

'Tell me,' said Spiridione – 'I forgot to ask – is she young?'

'Thirty-three.'

'Ah, well, we cannot have everything.'

'But you would be surprised. Had she told me twenty-eight, I should not have disbelieved her.'

'Is she *simpatica*?' (Nothing will translate that word.)

Gino dabbed at the sugar and said after a silence, 'Sufficiently so.'

'It is a most important thing.'

'She is rich, she is generous, she is affable, she addresses her inferiors without haughtiness.'

There was another silence. 'It is not sufficient,' said the other. 'One does not define it thus.' He lowered his voice to a whisper. 'Last month a German was smuggling cigars. The custom-house was dark. Yet I refused because I did not like him. The gifts of such men do not bring happiness. Non era simpatico. He paid for every one, and the fine for deception besides.'

'Do you gain much beyond your pay?' asked Gino, diverted for an instant.

'I do not accept small sums now. It is not worth the risk. But the German was another matter. But listen, my Gino, for I am older than you and more full of experience. The person who understands us at first sight, who never irritates us, who never bores, to whom we can pour forth every thought and wish, not only in speech but in silence – that is what I mean by *simpatico*.'

'There are such men, I know,' said Gino. 'And I have heard it said of children. But where will you find such a woman?'

'That is true. Here you are wiser than I. Sono poco simpatiche le donne. And the time we waste over them is much.' He sighed dolefully, as if he found the nobility of his sex a burden.

'One I have seen who may be so. She spoke very little, but she was a young lady – different to most. She, too, was English, the companion of my wife here. But Fra Filippo, the brother-in-law, took her back with him. I saw them start. He was very angry.'

Then he spoke of his exciting and secret marriage, and they

made fun of the unfortunate Philip, who had travelled over Europe to stop it.

'I regret, though,' said Gino, when they had finished laughing, 'that I toppled him onto the bed. A great tall man! And when I am really amused I am often impolite.'

'You will never see him again,' said Spiridione, who carried plenty of philosophy about with him. 'And by now the scene will have passed from his mind.'

'It sometimes happens that such things are recollected longest. I shall never see him again, of course; but it is no benefit to me that he should wish me ill. And even if he has forgotten, I am still sorry that I toppled him onto the bed.'

So their talk continued, at one moment full of childishness and tender wisdom, the next moment scandalously gross. The shadows of the terracotta pillars lengthened, and tourists, flying through the Palazzo Pubblico opposite, could observe how the Italians wasted time.

The sight of tourists reminded Gino of something he might say. 'I want to consult you since you are so kind as to take an interest in my affairs. My wife wishes to take solitary walks.'

Spiridione was shocked.

'But I have forbidden her.'

'Naturally.'

'She does not yet understand. She asked me to accompany her sometimes – to walk without object! You know, she would like me to be with her all day.'

'I see, I see.' He knitted his brows and tried to think how he could help his friend. 'She needs employment. Is she a Catholic?'

'No.'

'That is a pity. She must be persuaded. It will be a great solace to her when she is alone.'

'I am a Catholic, but of course I never go to church.'

'Of course not. Still, you might take her at first. That is what my brother has done with his wife at Bologna, and he has joined the Freethinkers. He took her once or twice himself,

and now she has acquired the habit and continues to go without him.'

'Most excellent advice and I thank you for it. But she wishes
to give tea-parties – men and women together whom she has
never seen.'

'Oh, the English! They are always thinking of tea. They carry
it by the kilogram in their trunks, and they are so clumsy that
they always pack it at the top. But it is absurd!'

'What am I to do about it?'

'Do nothing. Or ask me!'

'Come!' cried Gino, springing up. 'She will be quite pleased.'

The dashing young fellow coloured crimson. 'Of course I was
only joking.'

'I know. But she wants me to take my friends. Come now!
Waiter!'

'If I do come,' cried the other, 'and take tea with you, this bill
must be my affair.'

'Certainly not; you are in my country!'

A long argument ensued, in which the waiter took part,
suggesting various solutions. At last Gino triumphed. The bill
came to eightpence-halfpenny, and a halfpenny for the waiter
brought it up to ninepence. Then there was a shower of gratitude
on one side and of deprecation on the other, and when courtesies
were at their height they suddenly linked arms and swung down
the street, tickling each other with lemonade-straws as they went.

Lilia was delighted to see them, and became more animated
than Gino had known her for a long time. The tea tasted of
chopped hay, and they asked to be allowed to drink it out of a
wineglass, and refused milk; but, as she repeatedly observed, this
was something like. Spiridione's manners were very agreeable.
He kissed her hand on introduction, and, as his profession had
taught him a little English, conversation did not flag.

'Do you like music?' she asked.

'Passionately,' he replied. 'I have not studied scientific music,
but the music of the heart, yes.'

So she played on the humming piano, very badly, and he sang, not so badly. Gino got out a guitar and sang too, sitting out on the loggia. It was a most agreeable visit.

Gino said he would just walk his friend back to his lodgings. As they went he said, without the least trace of malice or satire in his voice: 'I think you are quite right. I shall not bring people to the house any more. I do not see why an English wife should be treated differently. This is Italy.'

'You are very wise,' exclaimed the other; 'very wise indeed. The more precious a possession the more carefully it should be guarded.'

They had reached the lodging, but went on as far as the Caffè Garibaldi, where they spent a long and most delightful evening.

CHAPTER IV

THE ADVANCE OF regret can be so gradual that it is impossible to say, 'Yesterday I was happy, today I am not.' At no one moment did Lilia realize that her marriage was a failure; yet during the summer and autumn she became as unhappy as it was possible for her nature to be. She had no unkind treatment, and few unkind words, from her husband. He simply left her alone. In the morning he went out to do 'business', which, as far as she could discover, meant sitting in the *farmacia*. He usually returned to lunch, after which he retired to another room and slept. In the evening he grew vigorous again, and took the air on the ramparts, often having his dinner out, and seldom returning till midnight or later. There were, of course, the times when he was away altogether – at Empoli, Siena, Florence, Bologna – for he delighted in travel, and seemed to pick up friends all over the country. Lilia often heard what a favourite he was.

She began to see that she must assert herself, but she could not see how. Her self-confidence, which had overthrown Philip, had gradually oozed away. If she left the strange house there was the strange little town. If she were to disobey her husband and walk in the country, that would be stranger still – vast slopes of olives and vineyards, with chalk-white farms, and in the distance other slopes, with more olives and more farms, and more little towns outlined against the cloudless sky. 'I don't call this country,' she would say. 'Why, it's not as wild as Sawston Park!' And, indeed, there was scarcely a touch of wildness in it – some of those slopes had been under cultivation for two thousand years. But it was terrible and mysterious all the same, and its continued presence made Lilia so uncomfortable that she forgot her nature and began to reflect.

She reflected chiefly about her marriage. The ceremony had been hasty and expensive, and the rites, whatever they were, were not those of the Church of England. Lilia had no religion in her; but for hours at a time she would be seized with a vulgar fear that she was not 'married properly', and that her social position in the next world might be as obscure as it was in this. It might be safer to do the thing thoroughly, and one day she took the advice of Spiridione and joined the Roman Catholic Church, or, as she called it, 'Santa Deodata's'. Gino approved; he, too, thought it safer. And it was fun confessing, though the priest was a stupid old man; and the whole thing was a good slap in the face for the people at home.

The people at home took the slap very soberly; indeed, there were few left for her to give it to. The Herritons were out of the question; they would not even let her write to Irma, though Irma was occasionally allowed to write to her. Mrs Theobald was rapidly subsiding into dotage, and, as far as she could be definite about anything, had definitely sided with the Herritons. And Miss Abbott did likewise. Night after night did Lilia curse this false friend, who had agreed with her that the marriage would 'do', and that the Herritons would come round to it, and then, at the first hint of opposition, had fled back to England, shriek- ing and distraught. Miss Abbott headed the long list of those who should never be written to, and who should never be for- given. Almost the only person who was not on that list was Mr Kingcroft, who had unexpectedly sent an affectionate and inquir- ing letter. He was quite sure never to cross the Channel, and Lilia drew freely on her fancy in the reply.

At first she had seen a few English people, for Monteriano was not the end of the earth. One or two inquisitive ladies, who had heard at home of her quarrel with the Herritons, came to call. She was very sprightly, and they thought her quite uncon- ventional, and Gino a charming boy, so all that was to the good. But by May the season, such as it was, had finished, and there would be no one till next spring. As Mrs Herriton had often observed, Lilia had no resources. She did not like music, or reading, or work. Her one qualification for life was rather blowsy high spirits, which turned querulous or boisterous according to circumstances. She was not obedient, but she was cowardly; and in the most gentle way, which Mrs Herriton might have envied, Gino made her do what he wanted. At first it had been rather fun to let him get the upper hand. But it was galling to discover that he could not do otherwise. He had a good strong will when he chose to use it, and would not have had the least scruple in using bolts and locks to put it into effect. There was plenty of brutality deep down in him, and one day Lilia nearly touched it.

It was the old question of going out alone.

'I always do it in England.'

'This is Italy.'

'Yes, but I'm older than you, and I'll settle.'

'I am your husband,' he said smiling. They had finished their midday meal, and he wanted to go and sleep. Nothing would rouse him up, until at last Lilia, getting more and more angry, said, 'And I've got the money.'

He looked horrified.

Now was the moment to assert herself. She made the statement again. He got up from his chair.

'And you'd better mend your manners,' she continued, 'for you'd find it awkward if I stopped drawing cheques.'

She was no reader of character, but she quickly became alarmed. As she said to Perfetta afterwards, 'None of his clothes seemed to fit – too big in one place, too small in another.' His figure rather than his face altered, the shoulders falling forward till his coat wrinkled across the back and pulled away from the wrists. He seemed all arms. He edged round the table to where she was sitting, and she sprang away and held the chair between them, too frightened to speak or to move. He looked at her with round expressionless eyes, and slowly stretched out his left hand.

Perfetta was heard coming up from the kitchen. It seemed to

wake him up, and he turned away and went to his room without a word.

'What has happened?' cried Lilia, nearly fainting. 'He is ill – ill.'

Perfetta looked suspicious when she heard the account. 'What did you say to him?' She crossed herself.

'Hardly anything,' said Lilia, and crossed herself also. Thus did the two women pay homage to their outraged male.

It was clear to Lilia at last that Gino had married her for money. But he had frightened her too much to leave any place for contempt. His return was terrifying, for he was frightened too, imploring her pardon, lying at her feet, embracing her, murmuring 'It was not I', striving to define things which he did not understand. He stopped in the house for three days, positively ill with physical collapse. But for all his suffering he had tamed her, and she never threatened to cut off supplies again.

Perhaps he kept her even closer than convention demanded. But he was very young, and he could not bear it to be said of him that he did not know how to treat a lady – or to manage a wife. And his own social position was uncertain. Even in England a dentist is a troublesome creature, whom careful people find difficult to class. He hovers between the professions and the trades; he may be only a little lower than the doctors, or he may be down among the chemists, or even beneath them. The son of the Italian dentist felt this too. For himself nothing mattered; he made friends with the people he liked, for he was that glorious invariable creature, a man. But his wife should visit nowhere rather than visit wrongly; seclusion was both decent and safe. The social ideals of North and South had had their brief contention, and this time the South had won.

It would have been well if he had been as strict over his own behaviour as he was over hers. But the incongruity never occurred to him for a moment. His morality was that of the average Latin, and as he was suddenly placed in the position of a gentleman he did not see why he should not behave as such. Of course, had Lilia been different, had she asserted herself and got a grip on his character, he might possibly – though not probably – have been made a better husband as well as a better man, and at all events he could have adopted the attitude of the Englishman, whose standard is higher even when his practice is the same. But had Lilia been different she might not have married him.

The discovery of his infidelity – which she made by accident – destroyed such remnants of self-satisfaction as her life might yet possess. She broke down utterly, and sobbed and cried in Perfetta's arms. Perfetta was kind and even sympathetic, but cautioned her on no account to speak to Gino, who would be furious if he was suspected. And Lilia agreed, partly because she was afraid of him, partly because it was, after all, the best and most dignified thing to do. She had given up everything for him – her daughter, her relatives, her friends, all the little comforts and luxuries of a civilized life – and even if she had the courage to break away there was no one who would receive her now. The Herritons had been almost malignant in their efforts against her, and all her friends had one by one fallen off. So it was better to live on humbly, trying not to feel, endeavouring by a cheerful demeanour to put things right. 'Perhaps,' she thought, 'if I have a child he will be different. I know he wants a son.'

Lilia had achieved pathos despite herself, for there are some situations in which vulgarity counts no longer. Not Cordelia nor Imogen more deserve our tears.

She herself cried frequently, making herself look plain and old, which distressed her husband. He was particularly kind to her when he hardly ever saw her, and she accepted his kindness without resentment, even with gratitude, so docile had she become. She did not hate him, even as she had never loved him; with her it was only when she was excited that the semblance of either passion arose. People said she was headstrong, but really her weak brain left her cold.

Suffering, however, is more independent of temperament, and the wisest of women could hardly have suffered more.

As for Gino, he was quite as boyish as ever, and carried his iniquities like a feather. A favourite speech of his was: 'Ah, one ought to marry! Spiridione is wrong; I must persuade him. Not till marriage does one realize the pleasures and the possibilities of life.' So saying, he would take down his felt hat, strike it in the right place as infallibly as a German strikes his in the wrong place, and leave her.

One evening, when he had gone out thus, Lilia could stand it no longer. It was September. Sawston would be just filling up after the summer holidays. People would be running in and out of each other's houses all along the road. There were bicycle gymkhanas, and on the 30th Mrs Herriton would be holding the annual bazaar in her garden for the C.M.S. It seemed impossible that such a free, happy life could exist. She walked out onto the loggia. Moonlight and stars in a soft purple sky. The walls of Monteriano should be glorious on such a night as this. But the house faced away from them.

Perfetta was banging in the kitchen, and the stairs down led past the kitchen door. But the stairs up to the attic – the stairs no one ever used – opened out of the living-room, and by unlocking the door at the top one might slip out onto the square terrace above the house, and thus for ten minutes walk in freedom and peace.

The key was in the pocket of Gino's best suit – the English check – which he never wore. The stairs creaked and the keyhole screamed; but Perfetta was growing deaf. The walls were beautiful, but as they faced west they were in shadow. To see the light upon them she must walk round the town a little, till they were caught by the beams of the rising moon. She looked anxiously at the house, and started.

It was easy walking, for a little path ran all outside the ramparts. The few people she met wished her a civil goodnight, taking her, in her hatless condition, for a peasant. The walls trended round towards the moon; and presently she came into its light, and saw all the rough towers turn into pillars of silver

and black, and the ramparts into cliffs of pearl. She had no great
sense of beauty, but she was sentimental, and she began to cry;
for here, where a great cypress interrupted the monotony of the
girdle of olives, she had sat with Gino one afternoon in March,
her head upon his shoulder, while Caroline was looking at the
view and sketching. Round the corner was the Siena gate, from
which the road to England started, and she could hear the
rumble of the diligence which was going down to catch the night
train to Empoli. The next moment it was upon her, for the highroad came towards her a little before it began its long zigzag
down the hill.

The driver slackened, and called to her to get in. He did not
know who she was. He hoped she might be coming to the station.

'Non vengo!' she cried.

He wished her goodnight, and turned his horses down the
corner. As the diligence came round she saw that it was empty.

'Vengo . . .'

Her voice was tremulous, and did not carry. The horses
swung off.

'Vengo! Vengo!'

He had begun to sing, and heard nothing. She ran down the
road screaming to him to stop – that she was coming; while
the distance grew greater and the noise of the diligence increased.
The man's back was black and square against the moon, and if
he would but turn for an instant she would be saved. She tried
to cut off the corner of the zigzag, stumbling over the great clods
of earth, large and hard as rocks, which lay between the eternal
olives. She was too late; for, just before she regained the road,
the thing swept past her, thunderous, ploughing up choking
clouds of moonlit dust.

She did not call any more, for she felt very ill, and fainted;
and when she revived she was lying in the road, with dust in her
eyes, and dust in her mouth, and dust down her ears. There is
something very terrible in dust at night-time.

'What shall I do?' she moaned. 'He will be so angry.'

And without further effort she slowly climbed back to captivity, shaking her garments as she went.

Ill-luck pursued her to the end. It was one of the nights when Gino happened to come in. He was in the kitchen, swearing and smashing plates, while Perfetta, her apron over her head, was weeping violently. At the sight of Lilia he turned upon her and poured forth a flood of miscellaneous abuse. He was far more angry but much less alarming than he had been that day when he edged after her round the table. And Lilia gained more courage from her bad conscience than she ever had from her good one, for as he spoke she was seized with indignation and feared him no longer, and saw him for a cruel, worthless, hypocritical, dissolute upstart, and spoke in return.

Perfetta screamed, for she told him everything – all she knew and all she thought. He stood with open mouth, all the anger gone out of him, feeling ashamed, and an utter fool. He was fairly and rightfully cornered. When had husband so given himself away before? She finished; and he was dumb, for she had spoken truly. Then, alas! the absurdity of his own position grew upon him, and he laughed – as he would have laughed at the same situation on the stage.

'You laugh?' stammered Lilia.

'Ah,' he cried, 'who could help it? I, who thought you knew and saw nothing – I am tricked – I am conquered. I give in. Let us talk of it no more.'

He touched her on the shoulder like a good comrade, half amused and half penitent, and then, murmuring and smiling to himself, ran quietly out of the room.

Perfetta burst into congratulations. 'What courage you have!' she cried; 'and what good fortune! He is angry no longer! He has forgiven you!'

Neither Perfetta nor Gino nor Lilia herself knew the true reason of all the misery that followed. To the end he thought that kindness and a little attention would be enough to set things straight. His wife was a very ordinary woman, and why should her ideas differ from his own? No one realized that more than personalities were engaged; that the struggle was national; that generations of ancestors, good, bad or indifferent, forbade the Latin man to be chivalrous to the northern woman, the northern woman to forgive the Latin man. All this might have been foreseen; Mrs Herriton foresaw it from the first.

Meanwhile Lilia prided herself on her high personal standard, and Gino simply wondered why she did not come round. He hated discomfort, and yearned for sympathy, but shrank from mentioning his difficulties in the town in case they were put down to his own incompetence. Spiridione was told, and replied in a philosophical but not very helpful letter. His other great friend, whom he trusted more, was still serving in Eritrea or some other desolate outpost. It would take too long to explain everything to him. And, besides, what was the good of letters? Friends cannot travel through the post.

Lilia, so similar to her husband in many ways, yearned for comfort and sympathy too. The night he laughed at her she wildly took up paper and pen and wrote page after page, analysing his character, enumerating his iniquities, reporting whole conversations, tracing all the causes and the growth of her misery. She was beside herself with passion, and though she could hardly think or see she suddenly attained to magnificence and pathos which a practised stylist might have envied. It was written like a diary, and not till its conclusion did she realize for whom it was meant.

'Irma, darling Irma, this letter is for you. I almost forget I have a daughter. It will make you unhappy, but I want you to know everything, and you cannot learn things too soon. God bless you, my dearest, and save you. God bless your miserable mother.'

Fortunately Mrs Herriton was in when the letter arrived. She seized it and opened it in her bedroom. Another moment, and Irma's placid childhood would have been destroyed for ever.

Lilia received a brief note from Harriet, again forbidding

direct communication between mother and daughter, and concluding with formal condolences. It nearly drove her mad.

'Gently! Gently!' said her husband. They were sitting together on the loggia when the letter arrived. He often sat with her now, watching her for hours, puzzled and anxious, but not contrite.

'It's nothing.' She went in and tore it up, and then began to write – a very short letter, whose gist was 'Come and save me'.

It is not good to see your wife crying when she writes – especially if you are conscious that, on the whole, your treatment of her has been reasonable and kind. It is not good, when you accidentally look over her shoulder, to see that she is writing to a man. Nor should she shake her fist at you when she leaves the room, under the impression that you are engaged in lighting a cigar and cannot see her.

Lilia went to the post herself. But in Italy so many things can be arranged. The postman was a friend of Gino's, and Mr Kingcroft never got his letter.

So she gave up hope, became ill, and all through the autumn lay in bed. Gino was distracted. She knew why: he wanted a son. He could talk and think of nothing else. His one desire was to become the father of a man like himself, and it held him with a grip he only partially understood, for it was the first great desire, the first great passion of his life. Falling in love was a mere physical triviality, like warm sun or cool water, beside this divine hope of immortality: 'I continue.' He gave candles to Santa Deodata, for he was always religious at a crisis, and sometimes he went to her himself and prayed the crude uncouth demands of the simple. Impetuously he summoned all his relatives back to bear him company in his time of need, and Lilia saw strange faces flitting past her in the darkened room.

'My love!' he would say, 'my dearest Lilia! Be calm. I have never loved anyone but you.'

She, knowing everything, would only smile gently, too broken by suffering to make sarcastic repartees.

Before the child was born he gave her a kiss, and said, 'I have prayed all night for a boy.'

Some strangely tender impulse moved her, and she said faintly, 'You are a boy yourself, Gino.'

He answered, 'Then we shall be brothers.'

He lay outside the room with his head against the door like a dog. When they came to tell him the glad news they found him half unconscious, and his face was wet with tears.

As for Lilia, someone said to her, 'It is a beautiful boy!' But she had died in giving birth to him.

CHAPTER V

AT THE TIME of Lilia's death Philip Herriton was just twenty-four years of age – indeed, the news reached Sawston on his birthday. He was a tall, weakly built young man, whose clothes had to be judiciously padded on the shoulder in order to make him pass muster. His face was plain rather than not, and there was a curious mixture in it of good and bad. He had a fine forehead and a good large nose, and both observation and sympathy were in his eyes. But below the nose and eyes all was confusion, and those people who believe that destiny resides in the mouth and chin shook their heads when they looked at him.

Philip himself, as a boy, had been keenly conscious of these defects. Sometimes when he had been bullied or hustled about at school he would retire to his cubicle and examine his features in a looking-glass, and he would sigh and say: 'It is a weak face. I shall never carve a place for myself in the world.' But as years went on he became either less self-conscious or more self-satisfied. The world, he found, made a niche for him as it did for everyone. Decision of character might come later – or he might have it without knowing. At all events he had got a sense of beauty and a sense of humour, two most desirable gifts. The sense of beauty developed first. It caused him at the age of twenty to wear parti-coloured ties and a squashy hat, to be late for dinner on account of the sunset, and to catch art from Burne-Jones to Praxiteles. At twenty-two he went to Italy with some cousins, and there he absorbed into one aesthetic whole olive-trees, blue sky, frescoes, country inns, saints, peasants, mosaics, statues, beggars. He came back with the air of a prophet who would either remodel Sawston or reject it. All the energies and enthusiasms of a rather friendless life had passed into the championship of beauty.

In a short time it was over. Nothing had happened either in Sawston or within himself. He had shocked half a dozen people, squabbled with his sister, and bickered with his mother. He concluded that nothing could happen, not knowing that human love and love of truth sometimes conquer where love of beauty fails.

A little disenchanted, a little tired, but aesthetically intact, he resumed his placid life, relying more and more on his second gift, the gift of humour. If he could not reform the world, he could at all events laugh at it, thus attaining at least an intellectual superiority. Laughter, he read and believed, was a sign of good moral health, and he laughed on contentedly, till Lilia's marriage toppled contentment down for ever. Italy, the land of beauty, was ruined for him. She had no power to change men and things who dwelt in her. She, too, could produce avarice, brutality, stupidity – and what was worse, vulgarity. It was on her soil and through her influence that a silly woman had married a cad. He hated Gino, the betrayer of his life's ideal, and now that the sordid tragedy had come it filled him with pangs, not of sympathy, but of final disillusion.

The disillusion was convenient for Mrs Herriton, who saw a trying little period ahead of her, and was glad to have her family united.

'Are we to go into mourning, do you think?' She always asked her children's advice where possible.

Harriet thought that they should. She had been detestable to Lilia while she lived, but she always felt that the dead deserve attention and sympathy. 'After all she has suffered. That letter kept me awake for nights. The whole thing is like one of those horrible modern plays where no one is in the right. But if we have mourning it will mean telling Irma.'

'Of course we must tell Irma!' said Philip.

'Of course,' said his mother. 'But I think we can still not tell her about Lilia's marriage.'

'I don't think that. And she must have suspected something by now.'

'So one would have supposed. But she never cared for her mother, and little girls of nine don't reason clearly. She looks on it as a long visit. And it is important, most important, that she should not receive a shock. All a child's life depends on the ideal it has of its parents. Destroy that and everything goes – morals, behaviour, everything. Absolute trust in someone else is the essence of education. That is why I have been so careful about talking of poor Lilia before her.'

'But you forget this wretched baby. Waters & Adamson write that there is a baby.'

'Mrs Theobald must be told. But she doesn't count. She is breaking up very quickly. She doesn't even see Mr Kingcroft now. He, thank goodness, I hear, has at last consoled himself with someone else.'

'The child must know some time,' persisted Philip, who felt a little displeased, though he could not tell with what.

'The later the better. Every moment she is developing.'

'I must say it seems rather hard luck, doesn't it?'

'On Irma? Why?'

'On us, perhaps. We have morals and behaviour also, and I don't think this continual secrecy improves them.'

'There's no need to twist the thing round to that,' said Harriet, rather disturbed.

'Of course there isn't,' said her mother. 'Let's keep to the main issue. This baby's quite beside the point. Mrs Theobald will do nothing, and it's no concern of ours.'

'It will make a difference in the money, surely,' said he.

'No, dear; very little. Poor Charles provided for every kind of contingency in his will. The money will come to you and Harriet, as Irma's guardians.'

'Good. Does the Italian get anything?'

'He will get all hers. But you know what that is.'

'Good. So those are our tactics – to tell no one about the baby, not even Miss Abbott.'

'Most certainly this is the proper course,' said Mrs Herriton, preferring 'course' to 'tactics' for Harriet's sake. 'And why ever should we tell Caroline?'

'She was so mixed up in the affair.'

'Poor silly creature. The less she hears about it the better she will be pleased. I have come to be very sorry for Caroline. She, if anyone, has suffered and been penitent. She burst into tears when I told her a little, only a little, of that terrible letter. I never saw such genuine remorse. We must forgive her and forget. Let the dead bury their dead. We will not trouble her with them.'

Philip saw that his mother was scarcely logical. But there was no advantage in saying so. 'Here beginneth the New Life, then. Do you remember, mother, that was what we said when we saw Lilia off?'

'Yes, dear; but now it is really a New Life, because we are all at accord. Then you were still infatuated with Italy. It may be full of beautiful pictures and churches, but we cannot judge a country by anything but its men.'

'That is quite true,' he said sadly. And as the tactics were now settled he went out and took an aimless and solitary walk.

By the time he came back two important things had happened. Irma had been told of her mother's death, and Miss Abbott, who had called for a subscription, had been told also.

Irma had wept loudly, had asked a few sensible questions and a good many silly ones, and had been content with evasive answers. Fortunately the school prizegiving was at hand, and that, together with the prospect of new black clothes, kept her from meditating on the fact that Lilia, who had been absent so long, would now be absent for ever.

'As for Caroline,' said Mrs Herriton, 'I was almost frightened. She broke down utterly. She cried even when she left the house.

I comforted her as best I could, and I kissed her. It is something that the breach between her and ourselves is now entirely healed.'

'Did she ask no questions – as to the nature of Lilia's death, I mean?'

'She did. But she has a mind of extraordinary delicacy. She saw that I was reticent, and she did not press me. You see, Philip, I can say to you what I could not say before Harriet. Her ideas are so crude. Really we do not want it known in Sawston that there is a baby. All peace and comfort would be lost if people came inquiring after it.'

His mother knew how to manage him. He agreed enthusiastically. And a few days later, when he chanced to travel up to London with Miss Abbott, he had all the time the pleasant thrill of one who is better informed. Their last journey together had been from Monteriano back across Europe. It had been a ghastly journey, and Philip, from the force of association, rather expected something ghastly now.

He was surprised. Miss Abbott, between Sawston and Charing Cross, revealed qualities which he had never guessed her to possess. Without being exactly original, she did show a commendable intelligence, and though at times she was gauche and even uncourtly he felt that here was a person whom it might be well to cultivate.

At first she annoyed him. They were talking, of course, about Lilia, when she broke the thread of vague commiseration and said abruptly: 'It is all so strange as well as so tragic. And what I did was as strange as anything.'

It was the first reference she had ever made to her contemptible behaviour. 'Never mind,' he said. 'It's all over now. Let the dead bury their dead. It's fallen out of our lives.'

'But that's why I can talk about it and tell you everything. I have always wanted to. You thought me stupid and sentimental and wicked and mad, but you never really knew how much I was to blame.'

'Indeed, I never think about it now,' said Philip gently. He knew that her nature was in the main generous and upright; it was unnecessary of her to reveal her thoughts.

'The first evening we got to Monteriano,' she persisted, 'Lilia went out for a walk alone, saw that Italian in a picturesque position on a wall, and fell in love. He was shabbily dressed, and she did not even know he was the son of a dentist. I must tell you I was used to this sort of thing. Once or twice before I had had to send people about their business.'

'Yes; we counted on you,' said Philip with sudden sharpness. After all, if she would reveal her thoughts, she must take the consequences.

'I know you did,' she retorted with equal sharpness. 'Lilia saw him several times again, and I knew I ought to interfere. I called her to my bedroom one night. She was very frightened, for she knew what it was about and how severe I could be. "Do you love this man?" I asked. "Yes or no?" She said "Yes." And I said, "Why don't you marry him if you think you'll be happy?"'

'Really – really,' exploded Philip, as exasperated as if the thing had happened yesterday. 'You knew Lilia all your life. Apart from everything else – as if she could choose what would make her happy!'

'Had you ever let her choose?' she flashed out. 'I'm afraid that's rude,' she added, trying to calm herself.

'Let us rather say unhappily expressed,' said Philip, who always adopted a dry satirical manner when he was puzzled.

'I want to finish. Next morning I found Signor Carella and said the same to him. He – well, he was willing. That's all.'

'And the telegram?' He looked scornfully out of the window.

Hitherto her voice had been hard, possibly in self-accusation, possibly in defiance. Now it became unmistakably sad. 'Ah, the telegram! That was wrong. Lilia there was more cowardly than I was. We should have told the truth. It lost me my nerve, at all events. I came to the station meaning to tell you everything then. But we had started with a lie, and I got frightened. And at the end, when you left, I got frightened again and came with you.'

'Did you really mean to stop?'

'For a time, at all events.'

'Would that have suited a newly married pair?'

'It would have suited them. Lilia needed me. And as for him – I can't help feeling I might have got influence over him.'

'I am ignorant of these matters,' said Philip; 'but I should have thought that would have increased the difficulty of the situation.'

The crisp remark was wasted on her. She looked hopelessly at the raw over-built country, and said, 'Well, I have explained.'

'But pardon me, Miss Abbott; of most of your conduct you have given a description rather than an explanation.'

He had fairly caught her, and expected that she would gape and collapse. To his surprise she answered with some spirit, 'An explanation may bore you, Mr Herriton: it drags in other topics.'

'Oh, never mind.'

'I hated Sawston, you see.'

He was delighted. 'So did and do I. That's splendid. Go on.'

'I hated the idleness, the stupidity, the respectability, the petty unselfishness.'

'Petty selfishness,' he corrected. Sawston psychology had long been his speciality.

'Petty unselfishness,' she repeated. 'I had got an idea that everyone here spent their lives in making little sacrifices for objects they didn't care for, to please people they didn't love; that they never learned to be sincere – and, what's as bad, never learned how to enjoy themselves. That's what I thought – what I thought at Monteriano.'

'Why, Miss Abbott,' he cried, 'you should have told me this before! Think it still! I agree with lots of it. Magnificent!'

'Now Lilia,' she went on, 'though there were things about her I didn't like, had somehow kept the power of enjoying herself with sincerity. And Gino, I thought, was splendid, and young, and strong not only in body, and sincere as the day. If they wanted to marry, why shouldn't they do so? Why shouldn't she break with the deadening life where she had got into a groove, and would go on in it, getting more and more – worse than unhappy – apathetic till she died? Of course I was wrong. She only changed one groove for another – a worse groove. And as for him – well, you know more about him than I do. I can never trust myself to judge character again. But I still feel he cannot have been quite bad when we first met him. Lilia – that I should dare to say it! – must have been cowardly. He was only a boy – just going to turn into something fine, I thought – and she must have mismanaged him. So that is the one time I have gone against what is proper, and there are the results. You have an explanation now.'

'And much of it has been most interesting, though I don't understand everything. Did you never think of the disparity of their social position?'

'We were mad – drunk with rebellion. We had no common sense. As soon as you came, you saw and foresaw everything.'

'Oh, I don't think that.' He was vaguely displeased at being credited with common sense. For a moment Miss Abbott had seemed to him more unconventional than himself.

'I hope you see,' she concluded, 'why I have troubled you with this long story. Women – I heard you say the other day – are never at ease till they tell their faults out loud. Lilia is dead and her husband gone to the bad – all through me. You see, Mr Herriton, it makes me specially unhappy; it's the only time I've ever gone into what my father calls "real life" – and look what I've made of it! All that winter I seemed to be waking up to beauty and splendour and I don't know what; and when the spring came I wanted to fight against the things I hated – mediocrity and dullness and spitefulness and society. I actually hated society for a day or two at Monteriano. I didn't see that all these things are invincible, and that if we go against them they will break us to pieces. Thank you for listening to so much nonsense.'

'Oh, I quite sympathize with what you say,' said Philip encouragingly; 'it isn't nonsense, and a year or two ago I should have been saying it too. But I feel differently now, and I hope that you also will change. Society *is* invincible – to a certain degree. But your real life is your own, and nothing can touch it. There is no power on earth that can prevent your criticizing and despising mediocrity – nothing that can stop you retreating into splendour and beauty – into the thoughts and beliefs that make the real life – the real you.'

'I have never had that experience yet. Surely I and my life must be where I live.'

Evidently she had the usual feminine incapacity for grasping philosophy. But she had developed quite a personality, and he must see more of her. 'There is another great consolation against invincible mediocrity,' he said – 'the meeting a fellow victim. I hope that this is only the first of many discussions that we shall have together.'

She made a suitable reply. The train reached Charing Cross, and they parted – he to go to a matinée, she to buy petticoats for the corpulent poor. Her thoughts wandered as she bought them: the gulf between herself and Mr Herriton, which she had always known to be great, now seemed to her immeasurable.

These events and conversations took place at Christmas-time. The New Life initiated by them lasted some seven months. Then a little incident – a mere little vexatious incident – brought it to its close.

Irma collected picture-postcards, and Mrs Herriton or Harriet always glanced first at all that came, lest the child should get hold of something vulgar. On this occasion the subject seemed perfectly inoffensive – a lot of ruined factory chimneys – and Harriet was about to hand it to her niece when her eye was caught by the words on the margin. She gave a shriek and flung the card into the grate. Of course no fire was alight in July, and Irma only had to run and pick it out again.

'How dare you!' screamed her aunt. 'You wicked girl! Give it here!'

Unfortunately Mrs Herriton was out of the room. Irma, who was not in awe of Harriet, danced round the table, reading as she did so, 'View of the superb city of Monteriano – from your lital brother.'

Stupid Harriet caught her, boxed her ears, and tore the post-card into fragments. Irma howled with pain, and began shouting indignantly: 'Who is my little brother? Why have I never heard of him before? Grandmamma! Grandmamma! Who is my little brother? Who is my –'

Mrs Herriton swept into the room, saying: 'Come with me, dear, and I will tell you. Now it is time for you to know.'

Irma returned from the interview sobbing, though, as a matter of fact, she had learned very little. But that little took hold of her imagination. She had promised secrecy – she knew not why. But what harm in talking of the little brother to those who had heard of him already?

'Aunt Harriet!' she would say. 'Uncle Phil! Grandmamma! What do you suppose my little brother is doing now? Has he begun to play? Do Italian babies talk sooner than us, or would he be an English baby born abroad? Oh, I do long to see him, and be the first to teach him the Ten Commandments and the Catechism.'

The last remark always made Harriet look grave.

'Really,' exclaimed Mrs Herriton, 'Irma is getting too tire-some. She forgot poor Lilia soon enough.'

'A living brother is more to her than a dead mother,' said Philip dreamily. 'She can knit him socks.'

'I stopped that. She is bringing him in everywhere. It is most vexatious. The other night she asked if she might include him in the people she mentions specially in her prayers.'

'What did you say?'

'Of course I allowed her,' she replied coldly. 'She has a right to mention anyone she chooses. But I was annoyed with her this morning, and I fear that I showed it.'

'And what happened this morning?'

'She asked if she could pray for her "new father" – for the Italian!'

'Did you let her?'

'I got up without saying anything.'

'You must have felt just as you did when I wanted to pray for the devil.'

'He is the devil,' cried Harriet.

'No, Harriet; he is too vulgar.'

'I will thank you not to scoff against religion!' was Harriet's retort. 'Think of that poor baby. Irma is right to pray for him. What an entrance into life for an English child!'

'My dear sister, I can reassure you. Firstly, the beastly baby is Italian. Secondly, it was promptly christened at Santa Deodata's, and a powerful combination of saints watch over –'

'Don't, dear. And, Harriet, don't be so serious – I mean not so serious when you are with Irma. She will be worse than ever if she thinks we have something to hide.'

Harriet's conscience could be quite as tiresome as Philip's un-conventionality. Mrs Herriton soon made it easy for her daughter to go for six weeks to the Tirol. Then she and Philip began to grapple with Irma alone.

Just as they had got things a little quiet the beastly baby sent another picture-postcard – a comic one, not particularly proper. Irma received it while they were out, and all the trouble began again.

'I cannot think,' said Mrs Herriton, 'what his motive is in sending them.'

Two years before, Philip would have said that the motive was to give pleasure. Now he, like his mother, tried to think of something sinister and subtle.

'Do you suppose that he guesses the situation – how anxious we are to hush the scandal up?'

'That is quite possible. He knows that Irma will worry us about the baby. Perhaps he hopes that we shall adopt it to quiet her.'

'Hopeful indeed.'

'At the same time he has the chance of corrupting the child's morals.' She unlocked a drawer, took out the postcard, and regarded it gravely. 'He entreats her to send the baby one,' was her next remark.

'She might do it too!'

'I told her not to; but we must watch her carefully, without, of course, appearing to be suspicious.'

Philip was getting to enjoy his mother's diplomacy. He did not think of his own morals and behaviour any more.

'Who's to watch her at school, though? She may bubble out any moment.'

'We can but trust to our influence,' said Mrs Herriton.

Irma did bubble out, that very day. She was proof against a single postcard, not against two. A new little brother is a valuable sentimental asset to a schoolgirl, and her school was then passing through an acute phase of baby-worship. Happy the girl who had her quiver full of them, who kissed them when she left home in the morning, who had the right to extricate them from mail-carts in the interval, who dangled them at tea ere they retired to rest! That one might sing the unwritten song of Miriam, blessed above all schoolgirls, who was allowed to hide her baby brother in a squashy place, where none but herself could find him!

How could Irma keep silent when pretentious girls spoke of baby cousins and baby visitors – she who had a baby brother, who wrote her postcards through his dear papa? She had prom-ised not to tell about him – she knew not why – and she told. And one girl told another, and one girl told her mother, and the thing was out.

'Yes, it is all very sad,' Mrs Herriton kept saying. 'My daughter-in-law made a very unhappy marriage, as I dare say you know. I suppose that the child will be educated in Italy. Possibly his grandmother may be doing something, but I have not heard of it. I do not expect that she will have him over. She disapproves of the father. It is altogether a painful business for her.'

She was careful only to scold Irma for disobedience – that eighth deadly sin, so convenient to parents and guardians.

Harriet would have plunged into needless explanations and abuse. The child was ashamed, and talked about the baby less. The end of the school year was at hand, and she hoped to get another prize. But she also had put her hand to the wheel.

It was several days before they saw Miss Abbott. Mrs Herriton had not come across her much since the kiss of reconciliation, nor Philip since the journey to London. She had, indeed, been rather a disappointment to him. Her creditable display of originality had never been repeated; he feared she was slipping back. Now she came about the Cottage Hospital – her life was devoted to dull acts of charity – and though she got money out of him and out of his mother she still sat tight in her chair, looking graver and more wooden than ever.

'I dare say you have heard,' said Mrs Herriton, well knowing what the matter was.

'Yes, I have. I came to ask you: have any steps been taken?'

Philip was astonished. The question was impertinent in the extreme. He had a regard for Miss Abbott, and regretted that she had been guilty of it.

'About the baby?' asked Mrs Herriton pleasantly.

'Yes.'

'As far as I know, no steps. Mrs Theobald may have decided on something, but I have not heard of it.'

'I was meaning, had you decided on anything?'

'The child is no relation of ours,' said Philip. 'It is therefore scarcely for us to interfere.'

His mother glanced at him nervously. 'Poor Lilia was almost a daughter to me once. I know what Miss Abbott means. But now things have altered. Any initiative would naturally come from Mrs Theobald.'

'But does not Mrs Theobald always take any initiative from you?' asked Miss Abbott.

Mrs Herriton could not help colouring. 'I sometimes have given her advice in the past. I should not presume to do so now.'

'Then is nothing to be done for the child at all?'

'It's extraordinarily good of you to take this unexpected interest,' said Philip.

'The child came into the world through my negligence,' replied Miss Abbott. 'It is natural I should take an interest in it.'

'My dear Caroline,' said Mrs Herriton, 'you must not brood over the thing. Let bygones be bygones. The child should worry you even less than it worries us. We never even mention it. It belongs to another world.'

Miss Abbott got up without replying, and turned to go. Her extreme gravity made Mrs Herriton uneasy. 'Of course,' she added, 'if Mrs Theobald decides on any plan that seems at all practicable – I must say I don't see any such – I shall ask if I may join her in it, for Irma's sake, and share in any possible expenses.'

'Please would you let me know if she decides on anything. I should like to join as well.'

'My dear, how you throw about your money! We would never allow it.'

'And if she decides on nothing please also let me know. Let me know in any case.'

Mrs Herriton made a point of kissing her.

'Is the young person mad?' burst out Philip as soon as she had departed. 'Never in my life have I seen such colossal impertinence. She ought to be well smacked, and sent back to Sunday-school.'

His mother said nothing.

'But don't you see – she is practically threatening us? You can't put her off with Mrs Theobald; she knows as well as we do that she is a nonentity. If we won't do anything she's going to raise a scandal – that we neglect our relatives, etc., which is, of course, a lie. Still, she'll say it. Oh, dear, sweet, sober Caroline Abbott has a screw loose! We knew it at Monteriano. I had my suspicions last year one day in the train; and here it is again. The young person is mad.'

She still said nothing.

'Shall I go round at once and give it her well? I'd really enjoy it.'

In a low, serious voice – such a voice as she had not used to him for months – Mrs Herriton said: 'Caroline has been extremely impertinent. Yet there may be something in what she says after all. Ought the child to grow up in that place – and with that father?'

Philip started and shuddered. He saw that his mother was not sincere. Her insincerity to others had amused him, but it was disheartening when used against himself.

'Let us admit frankly,' she continued, 'that after all we may have responsibilities.'

'I don't understand you, mother. You are turning absolutely round. What are you up to?'

In one moment an impenetrable barrier had been erected between them. They were no longer in smiling confidence. Mrs Herriton was off on tactics of her own – tactics which might be beyond or beneath him.

His remark offended her. 'Up to? I am wondering whether I ought not to adopt the child. Is that sufficiently plain?'

'And this is the result of half a dozen idiocies of Miss Abbott?'

'It is. I repeat, she has been extremely impertinent. None the less she is showing me my duty. If I can rescue poor Lilia's baby from that horrible man, who will bring it up either as Papist or infidel – who will certainly bring it up to be vicious – I shall do it.'

'You talk like Harriet.'

'And why not?' said she, flushing at what she knew to be an insult. 'Say, if you choose, that I talk like Irma. That child has seen the thing more clearly than any of us. She longs for her little brother. She shall have him. I don't care if I am impulsive.'

He was sure that she was not impulsive, but did not dare to say so. Her ability frightened him. All his life he had been her puppet. She had let him worship Italy, and reform Sawston just as she had let Harriet be Low Church. She had let him talk as much as he liked. But when she wanted a thing she always got it.

And, though she was frightening him, she did not inspire him with reverence. Her life, he saw, was without meaning. To what purpose was her diplomacy, her insincerity, her continued repression of vigour? Did they make anyone better or happier? Did they even bring happiness to herself? Harriet with her gloomy peevish creed, Lilia with her clutches after pleasure, were after all more divine than this well-ordered, active, useless machine.

Now that his mother had wounded his vanity he could criticize her thus. But he could not rebel. To the end of his days he would probably go on doing what she wanted. He watched with a cold interest the duel between her and Miss Abbott. Mrs Herriton's policy only appeared gradually. It was to prevent Miss Abbott interfering with the child at all costs, and if possible to prevent her at a small cost. Pride was the only solid element in her disposition. She could not bear to seem less charitable than others.

'I am planning what can be done,' she would tell people, 'and that kind Caroline Abbott is helping me. It is no business of either of us, but we are getting to feel that the baby must not be left entirely to that horrible man. It would be unfair to little Irma; after all, he is her half-brother. No, we have come to nothing definite.'

Miss Abbott was equally civil, but not to be appeased by good intentions. The child's welfare was a sacred duty to her, not a matter of pride or even of sentiment. By it alone, she felt, could she undo a little of the evil that she had permitted to come into the world. To her imagination Monteriano had become a magic city of vice, beneath whose towers no person could grow up happy or pure. Sawston, with its semi-detached houses and snobby schools, its book-teas and bazaars, was certainly petty and dull; at times she found it even contemptible. But it was not a place of sin, and at Sawston, either with the Herritons or with herself, the baby should grow up.

As soon as it was inevitable, Mrs Herriton wrote a letter for Waters & Adamson to send to Gino – the oddest letter; Philip saw a copy of it afterwards. Its ostensible purpose was to

complain of the picture-postcards. Right at the end, in a few
nonchalant sentences, she offered to adopt the child, provided
that Gino would undertake never to come near it, and would
surrender some of Lilia's money for its education.

'What do you think of it?' she asked her son. 'It would not
do to let him know that we are anxious for it.'

'Certainly he will never suppose that.'

'But what effect will the letter have on him?'

'When he gets it he will do a sum. If it is less expensive in the
long run to part with a little money and to be clear of the baby,
he will part with it. If he would lose, he will adopt the tone of
the loving father.'

'Dear, you're shockingly cynical.' After a pause she added,
'How would the sum work out?'

'I don't know, I'm sure. But if you wanted to ensure the baby
being posted by return you should have sent a little sum to *him*.
Oh, I'm not cynical – at least I only go by what I know of him.
But I am weary of the whole show. Weary of Italy. Weary, weary,
weary. Sawston's a kind, pitiful place, isn't it? I will go walk in it
and seek comfort.'

He smiled as he spoke, for the sake of not appearing serious.
When he had left her she began to smile also.

It was to the Abbotts' that he walked. Mr Abbott offered him
tea, and Caroline, who was keeping up her Italian in the next
room, came in to pour it out. He told them that his mother had
written to Signor Carella, and they both uttered fervent wishes
for her success.

'Very fine of Mrs Herriton, very fine indeed,' said Mr Abbott,
who, like everyone else, knew nothing of his daughter's
exasperating behaviour. 'I'm afraid it will mean a lot of expense.
She will get nothing out of Italy without paying.'

'There are sure to be incidental expenses,' said Philip cautiously. Then he turned to Miss Abbott and said, 'Do you
suppose we shall have difficulty with the man?'

'It depends,' she replied, with equal caution.

'From what you saw of him, should you conclude that he would make an affectionate parent?'

'I don't go by what I saw of him, but by what I know of him.'

'Well, what do you conclude from that?'

'That he is a thoroughly wicked man.'

'Yet thoroughly wicked men have loved their children. Look at Rodrigo Borgia, for example.'

'I have also seen examples of that in my district.'

With this remark the admirable young woman rose, and returned to keep up her Italian. She puzzled Philip extremely. He could understand enthusiasm, but she did not seem the least enthusiastic. He could understand pure cussedness, but it did not seem to be that either. Apparently she was deriving neither amusement nor profit from the struggle. Why, then, had she undertaken it? Perhaps she was not sincere. Perhaps, on the whole, that was most likely. She must be professing one thing and aiming at another. What the other thing could be he did not stop to consider. Insincerity was becoming his stock explanation for anything unfamiliar, whether that thing was a kindly action or a high ideal.

'She fences well,' he said to his mother afterwards.

'What had you to fence about?' she said suavely. Her son might know her tactics, but she refused to admit that he knew. She still pretended to him that the baby was the one thing she wanted, and had always wanted, and that Miss Abbott was her valued ally.

And when, next week, the reply came from Italy she showed him no face of triumph. 'Read the letters,' she said. 'We have failed.'

Gino wrote in his own language, but the solicitors had sent a laborious English translation, where 'Pregiatissima Signora' was rendered as 'Most Praiseworthy Madam', and every delicate compliment and superlative – superlatives are delicate in Italian – would have felled an ox. For a moment Philip forgot the matter in the manner; this grotesque memorial of the land he had loved moved him almost to tears. He knew the originals of these lumbering phrases; he also had sent 'sincere auguries'; he also had addressed letters – who writes at home? – from the Caffè Garibaldi. 'I didn't know I was still such an ass,' he thought. 'Why can't I realize that it's merely tricks of expression? A bounder's a bounder, whether he lives in Sawston or Monteriano.'

'Isn't it disheartening?' said his mother.

He then read that Gino could not accept the generous offer. His paternal heart would not permit him to abandon this symbol of his deplored spouse. As for the picture-postcards, it displeased him greatly that they had been obnoxious. He would send no more. Would Mrs Herriton, with her notorious kindness, explain this to Irma, and thank her for those which Irma (courteous Miss!) had sent to him?

'The sum works out against us,' said Philip. 'Or perhaps he is putting up the price.'

'No,' said Mrs Herriton decidedly. 'It is not that. For some perverse reason he will not part with the child. I must go and tell poor Caroline. She will be equally distressed.'

She returned from the visit in the most extraordinary condition. Her face was red, she panted for breath, there were dark circles round her eyes.

'The impudence!' she shouted. 'The cursed impudence! Oh, I'm swearing. I don't care. That beastly woman – how dare she interfere – I'll – Philip, dear, I'm sorry. It's no good. You must go.'

'Go where? Do sit down. What's happened?' This outburst of violence from his elegant ladylike mother pained him dreadfully. He had not known that it was in her.

'She won't accept – won't accept the letter as final. You must go to Monteriano!'

'I won't!' he shouted back. 'I've been and I've failed. I'll never see the place again. I hate Italy.'

'If you don't go, she will.'

'Abbott?'

'Yes. Going alone; would start this evening. I offered to write;

she said it was "too late"! Too late! The child, if you please –
Irma's brother – to live with her, to be brought up by her and
her father at our very gates, to go to school like a gentleman, she
paying. Oh, you're a man! It doesn't matter for you. You can
laugh. But I know what people say; and that woman goes to Italy
this evening.'

He seemed to be inspired. 'Then let her go! Let her mess with
Italy by herself. She'll come to grief somehow. Italy's too dangerous, too –'

'Stop that nonsense, Philip. I will not be disgraced by her.
I *will* have the child. Pay all we've got for it. I will have it.'

'Let her go to Italy!' he cried. 'Let her meddle with what she
doesn't understand! Look at this letter! The man who wrote it
will marry her, or murder her, or do for her somehow. He's a
bounder, but he's not an English bounder. He's mysterious and
terrible. He's got a country behind him that's upset people from
the beginning of the world.'

'Harriet!' exclaimed his mother. 'Harriet shall go too. Harriet,
now, will be invaluable!' And before Philip had stopped talking
nonsense she had planned the whole thing and was looking out
the trains.

CHAPTER VI

ITALY, PHILIP HAD always maintained, is only her true self in the height of the summer, when the tourists have left her, and her soul awakes under the beams of a vertical sun. He now had every opportunity of seeing her at her best, for it was nearly the middle of August before he went out to meet Harriet in the Tirol.

He found his sister in a dense cloud five thousand feet above the sea, chilled to the bone, overfed, bored, and not at all unwilling to be fetched away.

'It upsets one's plans terribly,' she remarked, as she squeezed out her sponges, 'but obviously it is my duty.'

'Did mother explain it all to you?' asked Philip.

'Yes, indeed! Mother has written me a really beautiful letter. She describes how it was that she gradually got to feel that we must rescue the poor baby from its terrible surroundings, how she has tried by letter, and it is no good – nothing but insincere compliments and hypocrisy came back. Then she says, "There is nothing like personal influence; you and Philip will succeed where I have failed." She says, too, that Caroline Abbott has been wonderful.'

Philip assented.

'Caroline feels it as keenly almost as us. That is because she knows the man. Oh, he must be loathsome! Goodness me! I've forgotten to pack the ammonia! ... It has been a terrible lesson for Caroline, but I fancy it is her turning-point. I can't help liking to think that out of all this evil good will come.'

Philip saw no prospect of good, nor of beauty either. But the expedition promised to be highly comic. He was not averse to it any longer; he was simply indifferent to all in it except the humours. These would be wonderful. Harriet, worked by her mother; Mrs Herriton, worked by Miss Abbott; Gino, worked by a cheque – what better entertainment could he desire? There was nothing to distract him this time; his sentimentality had died, so had his anxiety for the family honour. He might be a puppet's puppet, but he knew exactly the disposition of the strings.

They travelled for thirteen hours downhill, whilst the streams broadened and the mountains shrank, and the vegetation changed, and the people ceased being ugly and drinking beer, and began instead to drink wine and to be beautiful. And the train which had picked them at sunrise out of a waste of glaciers and hotels was waltzing at sunset round the walls of Verona.

'Absurd nonsense they talk about the heat,' said Philip, as they drove from the station. 'Supposing we were here for pleasure, what could be more pleasurable than this?'

'Did you hear, though, they are remarking on the cold?' said Harriet nervously. 'I should never have thought it cold.'

And on the second day the heat struck them, like a hand laid over the mouth, just as they were walking to see the tomb of Juliet. From that moment everything went wrong. They fled from Verona. Harriet's sketch-book was stolen, and the bottle of ammonia in her trunk burst over her prayerbook, so that purple patches appeared on all her clothes. Then, as she was going through Mantua at four in the morning, Philip made her look out of the window because it was Virgil's birthplace, and a smut flew in her eye, and Harriet with a smut in her eye was notorious. At Bologna they stopped twenty-four hours to rest. It was a *festa*, and children blew bladder whistles night and day. 'What a religion!' said Harriet. The hotel smelt, two puppies were asleep on her bed, and her bedroom window looked into a belfry, which saluted her slumbering form every quarter of an hour. Philip left his walking-stick, his socks and the Baedeker at Bologna; she only left her sponge-bag. Next day they crossed the Apennines with a train-sick child and a hot lady who told them that never, never before had she sweated so profusely. 'Foreigners are a filthy nation,' said Harriet. 'I don't care if there are tunnels; open the window.' He obeyed, and she got another smut in her eye. Nor did Florence improve matters. Eating, walking, even a cross word would bathe them in boiling water. Philip, who was slighter of build, and less conscientious, suffered less. But Harriet had never been to Florence, and between the hours of eight and eleven she crawled like a wounded creature through the streets, and swooned before various masterpieces of art. It was an irritable couple who took tickets to Monteriano.

'Singles or returns?' said he.

'A single for me,' said Harriet peevishly; 'I shall never get back alive.'

'Sweet creature!' said her brother, suddenly breaking down. 'How helpful you will be when we come to Signor Carella!'

'Do you suppose,' said Harriet, standing still among a whirl of porters – 'do you suppose I am going to enter that man's house?'

'Then what have you come for, pray? For ornament?'

'To see that you do your duty.'

'Oh, thanks!'

'So mother told me. For goodness' sake get the tickets; here comes that hot woman again! She has the impudence to bow.'

'Mother told you, did she?' said Philip wrathfully, as he went to struggle for tickets at a slit so narrow that they were handed to him edgeways. Italy was beastly, and Florence station is the centre of beastly Italy. But he had a strange feeling that he was to blame for it all; that a little influx into him of virtue would make the whole land not beastly but amusing. For there was enchantment, he was sure of that; solid enchantment, which lay behind the porters and the screaming and the dust. He could see it in the terrific blue sky beneath which they travelled, in the whitened plain which gripped life tighter than a frost, in the exhausted reaches of the Arno, in the ruins of brown castles which stood quivering upon the hills. He could see it, though his head ached and his skin was twitching, though he was here as a puppet, and though his sister knew how he was here. There was nothing pleasant in that journey to Monteriano station. But nothing – not even the discomfort – was commonplace.

'But do people live inside?' asked Harriet. They had exchanged the railway carriage for the *legno*, and the *legno* had emerged from the withered trees, and had revealed to them their destination.

Philip, to be annoying, answered: 'No.'

'What do they do there?' continued Harriet, with a frown.

'There is a *caffè*. A prison. A theatre. A church. Walls. A view.'

'Not for me, thank you,' said Harriet, after a weighty pause.

'Nobody asked you, miss, you see. Now Lilia was asked by such a nice young gentleman, with curls all over his forehead, and teeth just as white as father makes them.' Then his manner changed. 'But, Harriet, do you see nothing wonderful or attractive in that place – nothing at all?'

'Nothing at all. It's frightful.'

'I know it is. But it's old – awfully old.'

'Beauty is the only test,' said Harriet. 'At least so you told me when I sketched old buildings – for the sake, I suppose, of making yourself unpleasant.'

'Oh, I'm perfectly right. But at the same time – I don't know – so many things have happened here – people have lived so hard and so splendidly – I can't explain.'

'I shouldn't think you could. It doesn't seem the best moment to begin your Italy mania. I thought you were cured of it by now. Instead, will you kindly tell me what you are going to do when you arrive. I do beg you will not be taken unawares this time.'

'First, Harriet, I shall settle you at the Stella d'Italia, in the comfort that befits your sex and disposition. Then I shall make myself some tea. After tea I shall take a book into Santa Deodata's, and read there. It is always fresh and cool.'

The martyred Harriet exclaimed: 'I'm not clever, Philip. I don't go in for it, as you know. But I know what's rude. And I know what's wrong.'

'Meaning –?'

'You!' she shouted, bouncing on the cushions of the *legno* and startling all the fleas. 'What's the good of cleverness if a man's murdered a woman?'

'Harriet, I am hot. To whom do you refer?'

'He. Her. If you don't look out he'll murder you. I wish he would.'

'Tut, tut, tutlet! You'd find a corpse extraordinarily inconvenient.' Then he tried to be less aggravating. 'I heartily dislike the fellow, but we know he didn't murder her. In that letter, though she said a lot, she never said he was physically cruel.'

'He has murdered her. The things he did – things one can't even mention –'

'Things which one must mention if one's to talk at all. And things which one must keep in their proper place. Because he was unfaithful to his wife, it doesn't follow that in every way he's absolutely vile.' He looked at the city. It seemed to approve his remark.

'It's the supreme test. The man who is unchivalrous to a woman –'

'Oh, stow it! Take it to the Back Kitchen. It's no more a supreme test than anything else. The Italians never were chivalrous from the first. If you condemn him for that, you'll condemn the whole lot.'

'I condemn the whole lot.'

'And the French as well?'

'And the French as well.'

'Things aren't so jolly easy,' said Philip, more to himself than to her.

But for Harriet things were easy, though not jolly, and she turned upon her brother yet again. 'What about the baby, pray? You've said a lot of smart things and whittled away morality and religion and I don't know what; but what about the baby? You think me a fool, but I've been noticing you all today, and you haven't mentioned the baby once. You haven't thought about it, even. You don't care. Philip! I shall not speak to you. You are intolerable.'

She kept her promise, and never opened her lips all the rest of the way. But her eyes glowed with anger and resolution. For she was a straight, brave woman, as well as a peevish one.

Philip acknowledged her reproof to be true. He did not care about the baby one straw. Nevertheless, he meant to do his duty, and he was fairly confident of success. If Gino would have sold his wife for a thousand lire, for how much less would he not sell his child? It was just a commercial transaction. Why should it interfere with other things? His eyes were fixed on the towers again, just as they had been fixed when he drove with Miss Abbott. But this time his thoughts were pleasanter, for he had no such grave business on his mind. It was in the spirit of the cultivated tourist that he approached his destination.

One of the towers, rough as any other, was topped by a cross – the tower of the Collegiate Church of Santa Deodata. She was a holy maiden of the Dark Ages, the city's patron saint, and sweetness and barbarity mingle strangely in her story. So holy was she that all her life she lay upon her back in the house of her mother, refusing to eat, refusing to play, refusing to work. The devil, envious of such sanctity, tempted her in various ways. He dangled grapes above her, he showed her fascinating toys, he pushed soft pillows beneath her aching head. When all proved vain he tripped up the mother and flung her downstairs before her very eyes. But so holy was the saint that she never picked her mother up, but lay upon her back through all, and thus assured her throne in Paradise. She was only fifteen when she died, which shows how much is within the reach of any schoolgirl. Those who think her life was unpractical need only think of the victories upon Poggibonsi, San Gimignano, Volterra, Siena itself – all gained through the invocation of her name; they need only look at the church which rose over her grave. The grand schemes for a marble façade were never carried out, and it is brown unfinished stone until this day. But for the inside Giotto was summoned to decorate the walls of the nave. Giotto came – that is to say, he did not come, German research having decisively proved – but at all events the nave is covered with frescoes, and so are two chapels in the left transept, and the arch into the choir, and there are scraps in the choir itself. There the decoration stopped, till in the full spring of the Renaissance a great painter came to pay a few weeks' visit to his friend the Lord of Monteriano. In the intervals between the banquets and the discussions on Latin etymology and the dancing, he would stroll over to the church, and there in the fifth chapel to the right he has painted two frescoes of the death and burial of Santa Deodata. That is why Baedeker gives the place a star.

Santa Deodata was better company than Harriet, and she kept Philip in a pleasant dream until the *legno* drew up at the hotel. Everyone there was asleep, for it was still the hour when only idiots were moving. There were not even any beggars about. The cabman put their bags down in the passage – they had left heavy luggage at the station – and strolled about till he came on the landlady's room and woke her, and sent her to them.

Then Harriet pronounced the monosyllable 'Go!'

'Go where?' asked Philip, bowing to the landlady, who was swimming down the stairs.

'To the Italian. Go.'

'Buona sera, signora padrona. Si ritorna volontieri a Monteriano! (Don't be a goose. I'm not going now. You're in the way, too.) Vorrei due camere –'

'Go. This instant. Now. I'll stand it no longer. Go!'

'I'm damned if I'll go. I want my tea.'

'Swear if you like!' she cried. 'Blaspheme! Abuse me! But understand, I'm in earnest.'

'Harriet, don't act. Or act better.'

'We've come here to get the baby back, and for nothing else. I'll not have this levity and slackness, and talk about pictures and churches. Think of mother; did she send you out for *them*?'

'Think of mother and don't straddle across the stairs. Let the cabman and the landlady come down, and let me go up and choose rooms.'

'I shan't.'

'Harriet, are you mad?'

'If you like. But you will not come up till you have seen the Italian.'

'La signorina si sente male,' said Philip. 'È il sole.'

'Poveretta!' cried the landlady and the cabman.

'Leave me alone!' said Harriet, snarling round at them. 'I don't care for the lot of you. I'm English, and neither you'll come down nor he up till he goes for the baby.'

'La prego – piano – piano – c'è un' altra signorina che dorme –'

'We shall probably be arrested for brawling, Harriet. Have you the very slightest sense of the ludicrous?'

Harriet had not; that was why she could be so powerful. She had concocted this scene in the carriage, and nothing should baulk her of it. To the abuse in front and the coaxing behind she was equally indifferent. How long she would have stood like a glorified Horatius, keeping the staircase at both ends, was never to be known. For the young lady whose sleep they were disturbing awoke, and opened her bedroom door, and came out onto the landing. She was Miss Abbott.

Philip's first coherent feeling was one of indignation. To be run by his mother and hectored by his sister was as much as he could stand. The intervention of a third female drove him suddenly beyond politeness. He was about to say exactly what he thought about the thing from beginning to end. But before he could do so Harriet also had seen Miss Abbott. She uttered a shrill cry of joy.

'You, Caroline, here of all people!' And in spite of the heat she darted up the stairs and imprinted an affectionate kiss upon her friend.

Philip had an inspiration. 'You will have a lot to tell Miss Abbott, Harriet, and she may have as much to tell you. So I'll pay my call on Signor Carella, as you suggested, and see how things stand.'

Miss Abbott uttered some noise of greeting or alarm. He did not reply to it or approach nearer to her. Without even paying the cabman, he escaped into the street.

'Tear each other's eyes out!' he cried, gesticulating at the façade of the hotel. 'Give it her, Harriet! Teach her to leave us alone. Give it her, Caroline! Teach her to be grateful to you. Go it, ladies; go it!'

Such people as observed him were interested, but did not conclude that he was mad. This aftermath of conversation is not unknown in Italy.

He tried to think how amusing it was; but it would not do – Miss Abbott's presence affected him too personally. Either she suspected him of dishonesty, or else she was being dishonest herself. He preferred to suppose the latter. Perhaps she had seen Gino, and they had prepared some elaborate mortification for the Herritons. Perhaps Gino had sold the baby cheap to her for a joke; it was just the kind of joke that would appeal to him. Philip still remembered the laughter that had greeted his fruitless journey, and the uncouth push that had toppled him onto the bed. And, whatever it might mean, Miss Abbott's presence spoiled the comedy: she would do nothing funny.

During this short meditation he had walked through the city, and was out on the other side. 'Where does Signor Carella live?' he asked the men at the *dogana*.

'I'll show you!' cried a little girl, springing out of the ground as Italian children will.

'She will show you,' said the *dogana* men, nodding reassuringly. 'Follow her always, always, and you will come to no harm. She is a trustworthy guide. She is my

$$\begin{cases} \text{daughter.'} \\ \text{cousin.'} \\ \text{sister.'} \end{cases}$$

Philip knew these relatives well; they ramify, if need be, all over the peninsula.

'Do you chance to know whether Signor Carella is in?' he asked her.

She had just seen him go in. Philip nodded. He was looking forward to the interview this time; it would be an intellectual duel with a man of no great intellect. What was Miss Abbott up to? That was one of the things he was going to discover. While she had it out with Harriet, he would have it out with Gino. He followed the *dogana*'s relative softly, like a diplomatist.

He did not follow her long, for this was the Volterra gate, and the house was exactly opposite to it. In half a minute they had scrambled down the mule-track and reached the only practicable entrance. Philip laughed, partly at the thought of Lilia in such a building, partly in the confidence of victory. Meanwhile the *dogana*'s relative lifted up her voice and gave a shout.

For an impressive interval there was no reply. Then the figure of a woman appeared high up on the loggia.

'That is Perfetta,' said the girl.

'I want to see Signor Carella,' cried Philip.

'Out!'

'Out,' echoed the girl complacently.

'Why on earth did you say he was in?' He could have strangled her for temper. He had been just ripe for an interview – just the right combination of indignation and acuteness: blood hot, brain cool. But nothing ever did go right in Monteriano. 'When will he be back?' he called to Perfetta. It really was too bad.

She did not know. He was away on business. He might be back this evening, he might not. He had gone to Poggibonsi.

At the sound of this word the little girl put her fingers to her nose and swept them at the plain. She sang as she did so, even as her foremothers had sung seven hundred years back –

> Poggibonizzi, fatti in là,
> Che Monteriano si fa città!

Then she asked Philip for a halfpenny. A German lady, friendly to the Past, had given her one that very spring.

'I shall have to leave a message,' he called.

'Now Perfetta has gone for her basket,' said the little girl. 'When she returns she will lower it – so. Then you will put your card into it. Then she will raise it – thus. By this means –'

When Perfetta returned, Philip remembered to ask after the baby. It took longer to find than the basket, and he stood perspiring in the evening sun, trying to avoid the smell of the drains and to prevent the little girl from singing against Poggibonsi. The olive-trees beside him were draped with the weekly – or more probably the monthly – wash. What a frightful spotty blouse! He could not think where he had seen it. Then he remembered that it was Lilia's. She had bought it 'to hack about in' at Sawston, and had taken it to Italy because 'in Italy anything does'. He had rebuked her for the sentiment.

'Beautiful as an angel!' bellowed Perfetta, holding out something which must be Lilia's baby. 'But who am I addressing?'

'Thank you – here is my card.' He had written on it a civil request to Gino for an interview next morning. But before he placed it in the basket and revealed his identity he wished to find something out. 'Has a young lady happened to call here lately – a young English lady?'

Perfetta begged his pardon: she was a little deaf.

'A young lady – pale, large, tall.'

She did not quite catch.

'A YOUNG LADY!'

'Perfetta is deaf when she chooses,' said the *dogana's* relative. At last Philip admitted the peculiarity and strode away. He paid off the detestable child at the Volterra gate. She got two nickel pieces and was not pleased, partly because it was too much, partly because he did not look pleased when he gave it to her. He caught her fathers and cousins winking at each other as he walked past them. Monteriano seemed in one vast conspiracy to make him look a fool. He felt tired and anxious and muddled, and not sure of anything except that his temper was lost. In this mood he returned to the Stella d'Italia, and there, as he was ascending the stairs, Miss Abbott popped out of the dining-room on the first floor and beckoned to him mysteriously.

'I was going to make myself some tea,' he said, with his hand still on the banisters.

'I should be grateful –'

So he followed her into the dining-room and shut the door.

'You see,' she began, 'Harriet knows nothing.'

'No more do I. He was out.'

'But what's that to do with it?'

He presented her with an unpleasant smile. She fenced well, as he had noticed before. 'He was out. You find me as ignorant as you have left Harriet.'

'What do you mean? Please, please, Mr Herriton, don't be mysterious; there isn't the time. Any moment Harriet may be down, and we shan't have decided how to behave to her. Sawston was different: we had to keep up appearances. But here we must speak out, and I think I can trust you to do it. Otherwise we'll never start clear.'

'Pray let us start clear,' said Philip, pacing up and down the room. 'Permit me to begin by asking you a question. In which capacity have you come to Monteriano – spy or traitor?'

'Spy!' she answered, without a moment's hesitation. She was standing by the little Gothic window as she spoke – the hotel had been a palace once – and with her finger she was following the curves of the moulding as if they might feel beautiful and strange. 'Spy,' she repeated, for Philip was bewildered at learning her guilt so easily, and could not answer a word. 'Your mother has behaved dishonourably all through. She never wanted the child; no harm in that; but she is too proud to let it come to me. She has done all she could to wreck things; she did not tell you everything; she has told Harriet nothing at all; she has lied or acted lies everywhere. I cannot trust your mother. So I have come here alone – all across Europe; no one knows it; my father thinks

I am in Normandy – to spy on Mrs Herriton. Don't let's argue!'
For he had begun, almost mechanically, to rebuke her for impertinence. 'If you are here to get the child, I will help you; if you
are here to fail, I shall get it instead of you.'

'It is hopeless to expect you to believe me,' he stammered.
'But I can assert that we are here to get the child, even if it costs
us all we've got. My mother has fixed no money limit whatever.
I am here to carry out her instructions. I think that you will
approve of them, as you have practically dictated them. I do
not approve of them. They are absurd.'

She nodded carelessly. She did not mind what he said. All she
wanted was to get the baby out of Monteriano.

'Harriet also carries out your instructions,' he continued.
'She, however, approves of them, and does not know that they
proceed from you. I think, Miss Abbott, you had better take
entire charge of the rescue-party. I have asked for an interview
with Signor Carella tomorrow morning. Do you acquiesce?'

She nodded again.

'Might I ask for details of your interview with him? They
might be helpful to me.'

He had spoken at random. To his delight she suddenly collapsed. Her hand fell from the window. Her face was red with
more than the reflection of evening.

'My interview – how do you know of it?'

'From Perfetta, if it interests you.'

'Who ever is Perfetta?'

'The woman who must have let you in.'

'In where?'

'Into Signor Carella's house.'

'Mr Herriton!' she exclaimed. 'How could you believe her? Do
you suppose that I would have entered that man's house, knowing about him all that I do? I think you have very odd ideas of
what is possible for a lady. I hear you wanted Harriet to go. Very
properly she refused. Eighteen months ago I might have done
such a thing. But I trust I have learned how to behave by now.'

Philip began to see that there were two Miss Abbotts – the
Miss Abbott who could travel alone to Monteriano, and the Miss
Abbott who could not enter Gino's house when she got there.
It was an amusing discovery. Which of them would respond to
his next move?

'I suppose I misunderstood Perfetta. Where did you have your
interview, then?'

'Not an interview – an accident – I am very sorry – I meant
you to have the chance of seeing him first. Though it is your
fault. You are a day late. You were due here yesterday. So I came
yesterday, and, not finding you, went up to the Rocca – you
know that kitchen-garden where they let you in, and there is a
ladder up to a broken tower, where you can stand and see all the
other towers below you and the plain and all the other hills?'

'Yes, yes. I know the Rocca; I told you of it.'

'So I went up in the evening for the sunset; I had nothing to
do. He was in the garden; it belongs to a friend of his.'

'And you talked.'

'It was very awkward for me. But I had to talk; he seemed to
make me. You see, he thought I was here as a tourist; he thinks
so still. He intended to be civil, and I judged it better to be
civil also.'

'And of what did you talk?'

'The weather – there will be rain, he says, by tomorrow evening – the other towns, England, myself, about you a little, and
he actually mentioned Lilia. He was perfectly disgusting; he pretended he loved her; he offered to show me her grave – the grave
of the woman he has murdered!'

'My dear Miss Abbott, he is not a murderer. I have just been
driving that into Harriet. And when you know the Italians as
well as I do you will realize that in all that he said to you he was
perfectly sincere. The Italians are essentially dramatic: they look
on death and love as spectacles. I don't doubt that he persuaded
himself, for the moment, that he had behaved admirably, both
as husband and widower.'

'You may be right,' said Miss Abbott, impressed for the first time. 'When I tried to pave the way, so to speak – to hint that he had not behaved as he ought – well, it was no good at all. He couldn't or wouldn't understand.'

There was something very humorous in the idea of Miss Abbott approaching Gino, on the Rocca, in the spirit of a district visitor. Philip, whose temper was returning, laughed.

'Harriet would say he has no sense of sin.'

'Harriet may be right, I am afraid.'

'If so, perhaps he isn't sinful!'

Miss Abbott was not one to encourage levity. 'I know what he has done,' she said. 'What he says and what he thinks is of very little importance.'

Philip smiled at her crudity. 'I should like to hear, though, what he said about me. Is he preparing a warm reception?'

'Oh no, not that. I never told him that you and Harriet were coming. You could have taken him by surprise if you liked. He only asked after you, and wished he hadn't been so rude to you eighteen months ago.'

'What a memory the fellow has for little things!' He turned away as he spoke, for he did not want her to see his face. It was suffused with pleasure. For an apology, which would have been intolerable eighteen months ago, was gracious and agreeable now.

She would not let this pass. 'You did not think it a little thing at the time. You told me he had assaulted you.'

'I lost my temper,' said Philip lightly. His vanity had been appeased, and he knew it. This tiny piece of civility had changed his mood. 'Did he really – what exactly did he say?'

'He said he was sorry – pleasantly, as Italians do say such things. But he never mentioned the baby once.'

What did the baby matter when the world was suddenly right way up? Philip smiled, and was shocked at himself for smiling, and smiled again. For romance had come back to Italy; there were no cads in her; she was beautiful, courteous, lovable, as of old. And Miss Abbott – she, too, was beautiful in her way, for all her gaucheness and conventionality. She really cared about life, and tried to live it properly. And Harriet – even Harriet tried.

This admirable change in Philip proceeds from nothing admirable, and may therefore provoke the gibes of the cynical. But angels and other practical people will accept it reverently, and write it down as good.

'The view from the Rocca (small gratuity) is finest at sunset,' he murmured, more to himself than to her.

'And he never mentioned the baby once,' Miss Abbott repeated. But she had returned to the window, and again her finger pursued the delicate curves. He watched her in silence, and was more attracted to her than he had ever been before. She really was the strangest mixture.

'The view from the Rocca – wasn't it fine?'

'What isn't fine here?' she answered gently, and then added, 'I wish I was Harriet,' throwing an extraordinary meaning into the words.

'Because Harriet –'

She would not go further, but he believed that she had paid homage to the complexity of life. For her, at all events, the expedition was neither easy nor jolly. Beauty, evil, charm, vulgarity, mystery – she also acknowledged this tangle, in spite of herself. And her voice thrilled him when she broke silence with 'Mr Herriton – come here – look at this!'

She removed a pile of plates from the Gothic window, and they leant out of it. Close opposite, wedged between mean houses, there rose up one of the great towers. It is your tower: you stretch a barricade between it and the hotel, and the traffic is blocked in a moment. Farther up, where the street empties out by the church, your connections, the Merli and the Capocchi, do likewise. They command the Piazza, you the Siena gate. No one can move in either but he shall be instantly slain, either by bows or by cross-bows, or by Greek fire. Beware, however, of the back bedroom windows. For they are menaced by the tower of the Aldobrandeschi, and before now arrows have stuck quivering over the washstand. Guard these windows well, lest there be a repetition of the events of February 1338, when the hotel was surprised from the rear, and your dearest friend – you could just make out that it was he – was thrown at you over the stairs.'

'It reaches up to heaven,' said Philip, 'and down to the other place.' The summit of the tower was radiant in the sun, while its base was in shadow and pasted over with advertisements. 'Is it to be a symbol of the town?'

She gave no hint that she understood him. But they remained together at the window because it was a little cooler and so pleasant. Philip found a certain grace and lightness in his companion which he had never noticed in England. She was appallingly narrow, but her consciousness of wider things gave to her narrowness a pathetic charm. He did not suspect that he was more graceful too. For our vanity is such that we hold our own characters immutable, and we are slow to acknowledge that they have changed, even for the better.

Citizens came out for a little stroll before dinner. Some of them stood and gazed at the advertisements on the tower.

'Surely that isn't an opera-bill?' said Miss Abbott.

Philip put on his pince-nez. ' "*Lucia di Lammermoor*. By the Master Donizetti. Unique representation. This evening." '

'But is there an opera? Right up here?'

'Why, yes. These people know how to live. They would sooner have a thing bad than not have it at all. That is why they have got to have so much that is good. However bad the performance is tonight, it will be alive. Italians don't love music silently, like the beastly Germans. The audience takes its share – sometimes more.'

'Can't we go?'

He turned on her, but not unkindly. 'But we're here to rescue a child!'

He cursed himself for the remark. All the pleasure and the light went out of her face, and she became again Miss Abbott of

Sawston – good, oh, most undoubtedly good, but most appallingly dull. Dull and remorseful: it is a deadly combination, and he strove against it in vain, till he was interrupted by the opening of the dining-room door.

They started as guiltily as if they had been flirting. Their interview had taken such an unexpected course. Anger, cynicism, stubborn morality – all had ended in a feeling of goodwill towards each other and towards the city which had received them. And now Harriet was here – acrid, indissoluble, large; the same in Italy as in England – changing her disposition never, and her atmosphere under protest.

Yet even Harriet was human, and the better for a little tea. She did not scold Philip for finding Gino out, as she might reasonably have done. She showered civilities on Miss Abbott, exclaiming again and again that Caroline's visit was one of the most fortunate coincidences in the world. Caroline did not contradict her.

'You see him tomorrow at ten, Philip. Well, don't forget the blank cheque. Say an hour for the business. No, Italians are so slow; say two. Twelve o'clock. Lunch. Well – then it's no good going till the evening train. I can manage the baby as far as Florence –'

'My dear sister, you can't run on like that. You don't buy a pair of gloves in two hours, much less a baby.'

'Three hours, then, or four; or make him learn English ways. At Florence we get a nurse –'

'But, Harriet,' said Miss Abbott, 'what if at first he was to refuse?'

'I don't know the meaning of the word,' said Harriet impressively. 'I've told the landlady that Philip and I only want our rooms one night, and we shall keep to it.'

'I dare say it will be all right. But, as I told you, I thought the man I met on the Rocca a strange, difficult man.'

'He's insolent to ladies, we know. But my brother can be trusted to bring him to his senses. That woman, Philip, whom you saw will carry the baby to the hotel. Of course you must tip her for it. And try, if you can, to get poor Lilia's silver bangles. They were nice quiet things, and will do for Irma. And there is an inlaid box I lent her – lent, not gave – to keep her handkerchiefs in. It's of no real value; but this is our only chance. Don't ask for it; but if you see it lying about, just say –'

'No, Harriet; I'll try for the baby, but for nothing else. I promise to do that tomorrow, and to do it in the way you wish. But tonight, as we're all tired, we want a change of topic. We want relaxation. We want to go to the theatre.'

'Theatre? Here? And at such a moment?'

'We should hardly enjoy it, with the great interview impending,' said Miss Abbott, with an anxious glance at Philip.

He did not betray her, but said, 'Don't you think it's better than sitting in all the evening and getting nervous?'

His sister shook her head. 'Mother wouldn't like it. It would be most unsuitable – almost irreverent. Besides all that, foreign theatres are notorious. Don't you remember those letters in the *Church Family Newspaper*?'

'But this is an opera – *Lucia di Lammermoor* – Sir Walter Scott – classical, you know.'

Harriet's face grew resigned. 'Certainly one has so few opportunities of hearing music. It is sure to be very bad. But it might be better than sitting idle all the evening. We have no books, and I lost my crochet at Florence.'

'Good. Miss Abbott, you are coming too?'

'It is very kind of you, Mr Herriton. In some ways I should enjoy it; but – excuse the suggestion – I don't think we ought to go to cheap seats.'

'Good gracious me!' cried Harriet, 'I should never have thought of that. As likely as not, we should have tried to save money and sat among the most awful people. One keeps on forgetting this is Italy.

'Unfortunately I have no evening dress; and if the seats –'

'Oh, that'll be all right,' said Philip, smiling at his timorous,

scrupulous womenkind. 'We'll go as we are, and buy the best we
can get. Monteriano is not formal.'

So this strenuous day of resolutions, plans, alarms, battles,
victories, defeats, truces, ended at the opera. Miss Abbott and
Harriet were both a little shamefaced. They thought of their
friends at Sawston, who were supposing them to be now tilting
against the powers of evil. What would Mrs Herriton, or Irma,
or the curates at the Back Kitchen say if they could see the
rescue-party at a place of amusement on the very first day of its
mission? Philip, too, marvelled at his wish to go. He began to
see that he was enjoying his time in Monteriano, in spite of the
tiresomeness of his companions and the occasional contrariness
of himself.

He had been to this theatre many years before, on the occasion of a performance of *La Zia di Carlo*. Since then it had been
thoroughly done up, in the tints of the beetroot and the tomato,
and was in many other ways a credit to the little town. The
orchestra had been enlarged, some of the boxes had terracotta
draperies, and over each box was now suspended an enormous
tablet, neatly framed, bearing upon it the number of that box.
There was also a drop-scene, representing a pink and purple
landscape, wherein sported many a lady lightly clad, and two
more ladies lay along the top of the proscenium to steady a large
and pallid clock. So rich and so appalling was the effect that
Philip could scarcely suppress a cry. There is something majestic
in the bad taste of Italy; it is not the bad taste of a country which
knows no better; it has not the nervous vulgarity of England, or
the blinded vulgarity of Germany. It observes beauty, and
chooses to pass it by. But it attains to beauty's confidence. This
tiny theatre of Monteriano spraddled and swaggered with the
best of them, and these ladies with their clock would have
nodded to the young men on the ceiling of the Sistine.

Philip had tried for a box, but all the best were taken; it was
rather a grand performance, and he had to be content with stalls.
Harriet was fretful and insular. Miss Abbott was pleasant, and

insisted on praising everything; her only regret was that she had
no pretty clothes with her.

'We do all right,' said Philip, amused at her unwonted vanity.

'Yes, I know; but pretty things pack as easily as ugly ones. We
had no need to come to Italy like guys.'

This time he did not reply, 'But we're here to rescue a baby.'
For he saw a charming picture, as charming a picture as he had
seen for years – the hot red theatre; outside the theatre, towers
and dark gates and medieval walls; beyond the walls, olive-trees
in the starlight and white winding roads and fireflies and
untroubled dust; and here in the middle of it all Miss Abbott,
wishing she had not come looking like a guy. She had made the
right remark. Most undoubtedly she had made the right remark.
This stiff suburban woman was unbending before the shrine.

'Don't you like it all?' he asked her.

'Most awfully.' And by this bald interchange they convinced
each other that Romance was here.

Harriet, meanwhile, had been coughing ominously at the
drop-scene, which presently rose on the grounds of Ravens-
wood, and the chorus of Scotch retainers burst into cry. The
audience accompanied with tappings and drummings, swaying
in the melody like corn in the wind. Harriet, though she did
not care for music, knew how to listen to it. She uttered an acid
'Shish!'

'Shut it,' whispered her brother.

'We must make a stand from the beginning. They're talking.'

'It is tiresome,' murmured Miss Abbott; 'but perhaps it isn't
for us to interfere.'

Harriet shook her head and shished again. The people were
quiet, not because it is wrong to talk during a chorus, but
because it is natural to be civil to a visitor. For a little time she
kept the whole house in order, and could smile at her brother
complacently.

Her success annoyed him. He had grasped the principle of
opera in Italy – it aims not at illusion but at entertainment – and

he did not want this great evening party to turn into a prayer-meeting. But soon the boxes began to fill, and Harriet's power was over. Families greeted each other across the auditorium. People in the pit hailed their brothers and sons in the chorus, and told them how well they were singing. When Lucia appeared by the fountain there was loud applause, and cries of 'Welcome to Monteriano!'

'Ridiculous babies!' said Harriet, settling down in her stall.

'Why, it is the famous hot lady of the Apennines,' cried Philip; 'the one who had never, never before –'

'Ugh! Don't. She will be very vulgar. And I'm sure it's even worse here than in the tunnel. I wish we'd never –'

Lucia began to sing, and there was a moment's silence. She was stout and ugly; but her voice was still beautiful, and as she sang the theatre murmured like a hive of happy bees. All through the coloratura she was accompanied by sighs, and its top note was drowned in a shout of universal joy.

So the opera proceeded. The singers drew inspiration from the audience, and the two great sextets were rendered not unworthily. Miss Abbott fell into the spirit of the thing. She, too, chatted and laughed and applauded and encored, and rejoiced in the existence of beauty. As for Philip, he forgot himself as well as his mission. He was not even an enthusiastic visitor. For he had been in this place always. It was his home.

Harriet, like M. Bovary on a more famous occasion, was trying to follow the plot. Occasionally she nudged her companions, and asked them what had become of Walter Scott. She looked round grimly. The audience sounded drunk, and even Caroline, who never took a drop, was swaying oddly. Violent waves of excitement, all arising from very little, went sweeping round the theatre. The climax was reached in the mad scene. Lucia, clad in white, as befitted her malady, suddenly gathered up her streaming hair and bowed her acknowledgements to the audience. Then from the back of the stage – she feigned not to see it – there advanced a kind of bamboo clothes-horse, stuck all over

with bouquets. It was very ugly, and most of the flowers in it
were false. Lucia knew this, and so did the audience; and they
all knew that the clothes-horse was a piece of stage property,
brought in to make the performance go year after year. None the
less did it unloose the great deeps. With a scream of amazement
and joy she embraced the animal, pulled out one or two practicable blossoms, pressed them to her lips, and flung them into her
admirers. They flung them back, with loud melodious cries, and
a little boy in one of the stage-boxes snatched up his sister's carna-
tions and offered them. 'Che carino!' exclaimed the singer. She
darted at the little boy and kissed him. Now the noise became
tremendous. 'Silence! Silence!' shouted many old gentlemen
behind. 'Let the divine creature continue!' But the young men
in the adjacent box were imploring Lucia to extend her civility
to them. She refused, with a humorous expressive gesture. One
of them hurled a bouquet at her. She spurned it with her foot.
Then, encouraged by the roars of the audience, she picked it up
and tossed it to them. Harriet was always unfortunate. The bouquet struck her full in the chest, and a little *billet-doux* fell out
of it into her lap.

'Call this classical?' she cried, rising from her seat. 'It's not even
respectable! Philip! Take me out at once.'

'Whose is it?' shouted her brother, holding up the bouquet in
one hand and the *billet-doux* in the other. 'Whose is it?'

The house exploded, and one of the boxes was violently
agitated, as if someone was being hauled to the front. Harriet
moved down the gangway, and compelled Miss Abbott to follow
her. Philip, still laughing and calling 'Whose is it?' brought up
the rear. He was drunk with excitement. The heat, the fatigue
and the enjoyment had mounted into his head.

'To the left!' the people cried. 'The innamorato is to the left.'

He deserted his ladies and plunged towards the box. A young
man was flung stomach downwards across the balustrade. Philip
handed him up the bouquet and the note. Then his own hands
were seized affectionately. It all seemed quite natural.

'Why have you not written?' cried the young man. 'Why do you take me by surprise?'

'Oh, I've written,' said Philip hilariously. 'I left a note this afternoon.'

'Silence! Silence!' cried the audience, who were beginning to have enough. 'Let the divine creature continue.' Miss Abbott and Harriet had disappeared.

'No! No!' cried the young man. 'You don't escape me now.' For Philip was trying feebly to disengage his hands. Amiable youths bent out of the box and invited him to enter it.

'Gino's friends are ours –'

'Friends?' cried Gino. 'A relative! A brother! Fra Filippo, who has come all the way from England and never written.'

'I left a message.'

The audience began to hiss.

'Come in to us.'

'Thank you – ladies – there is not time –'

The next moment he was swinging by his arms. The moment after he shot over the balustrade into the box. Then the conductor, seeing that the incident was over, raised his baton. The house was hushed, and Lucia di Lammermoor resumed her song of madness and death.

Philip had whispered introductions to the pleasant people who had pulled him in – tradesmen's sons perhaps they were, or medical students, or solicitors' clerks, or sons of other dentists. There is no knowing who is who in Italy. The guest of the evening was a private soldier. He shared the honour now with Philip. The two had to stand side by side in the front, and exchange compliments, whilst Gino presided, courteous, but delightfully familiar. Philip would have a spasm of horror at the muddle he had made. But the spasm would pass, and again he would be enchanted by the kind, cheerful voices, the laughter that was never vapid, and the light caress of the arm across his back.

He could not get away till the play was nearly finished, and Edgardo was singing amongst the tombs of his ancestors. His new friends hoped to see him at the Garibaldi tomorrow evening. He promised; then he remembered that if they kept to Harriet's plan he would have left Monteriano. 'At ten o'clock, then,' he said to Gino. 'I want to speak to you alone. At ten.'

'Certainly!' laughed the other.

Miss Abbott was sitting up for him when he got back. Harriet, it seemed, had gone straight to bed.

'That was he, wasn't it?' she asked.

'Yes, rather.'

'I suppose you didn't settle anything?'

'Why, no; how could I? The fact is – well, I got taken by surprise, but after all, what does it matter? There's no earthly reason why we shouldn't do the business pleasantly. He's a perfectly charming person, and so are his friends. I'm his friend now – his long-lost brother. What's the harm? I tell you, Miss Abbott, it's one thing for England and another for Italy. There we plan and get on high moral horses. Here we find what asses we are, for things go off quite easily, all by themselves. My hat, what a night! Did you ever see a really purple sky and really silver stars before? Well, as I was saying, it's absurd to worry; he's not a pawky father. He wants that baby as little as I do. He's been ragging my dear mother – just as he ragged me eighteen months ago, and I've forgiven him. Oh, but he has a sense of humour!'

Miss Abbott, too, had had a wonderful evening, nor did she ever remember such stars or such a sky. Her head, too, was full of music, and that night when she opened the window her room was filled with warm sweet air. She was bathed in beauty within and without; she could not go to bed for happiness. Had she ever been so happy before? Yes, once before, and here, a night in March, the night Gino and Lilia had told her of their love – the night whose evil she had come now to undo.

She gave a sudden cry of shame. 'This time – the same place – the same thing' – and she began to beat down her happiness, knowing it to be sinful. She was here to fight against this place, to rescue a little soul who was innocent as yet. She was here to champion morality and purity, and the holy life of an English home. In the spring she had sinned through ignorance; she was not ignorant now. 'Help me!' she cried, and shut the window as if there was magic in the encircling air. But the tunes would not go out of her head, and all night long she was troubled by torrents of music, and by applause and laughter, and angry young men who shouted the distich out of Baedeker:

> Poggibonizzi, fatti in là,
> Che Monteriano si fa città!

Poggibonsi was revealed to her as they sang – a joyless, straggling place, full of people who pretended. When she woke up she knew that it had been Sawston.

CHAPTER VII

AT ABOUT NINE o'clock next morning Perfetta went out onto the loggia, not to look at the view, but to throw some dirty water at it. 'Scuse tante!' she wailed, for the water spattered a tall young lady who had for some time been tapping at the lower door.

'Is Signor Carella in?' the young lady asked. It was no business of Perfetta's to be shocked, and the style of the visitor seemed to demand the reception-room. Accordingly she opened its shutters, dusted a round patch on one of the horsehair chairs, and bade the lady do herself the inconvenience of sitting down. Then she ran into Monteriano and shouted up and down its streets until such time as her young master should hear her.

The reception-room was sacred to the dead wife. Her shiny portrait hung upon the wall – similar, doubtless, in all respects to the one which would be pasted on her tombstone. A little piece of black drapery had been tacked above the frame to lend a dignity to woe. But two of the tacks had fallen out, and the effect was now rakish, as of a drunkard's bonnet. A coon song lay open on the piano, and of the two tables one supported Baedeker's *Central Italy*, the other Harriet's inlaid box. And over everything there lay a deposit of heavy white dust, which was only blown off one memento to thicken on another. It is well to be remembered with love. It is not so very dreadful to be forgotten entirely. But, if we shall resent anything on earth at all, we shall resent the consecration of a deserted room.

Miss Abbott did not sit down, partly because the antimacassars might harbour fleas, partly because she had suddenly felt faint, and was glad to cling onto the funnel of the stove. She struggled with herself, for she had need to be very calm; only if she was very calm might her behaviour be justified. She had broken faith with Philip and Harriet: she was going to try for the baby before they did. If she failed she could scarcely look them in the face again.

'Harriet and her brother,' she reasoned, 'don't realize what is before them. She would bluster and be rude; he would be pleasant and take it as a joke. Both of them – even if they offered money – would fail. But I begin to understand the man's nature: he does not love the child, but he will be touchy about it – and that is quite as bad for us. He's charming, but he's no fool; he conquered me last year; he conquered Mr Herriton yesterday, and if I am not careful he will conquer us all today, and the baby will grow up in Monteriano. He is terribly strong; Lilia found that out, but only I remember it now.'

This attempt, and this justification of it, were the results of the long and restless night. Miss Abbott had come to believe that she alone could do battle with Gino, because she alone understood him; and she had put this, as nicely as she could, in a note which she had left for Philip. It distressed her to write such a note, partly because her education inclined her to reverence the male, partly because she had got to like Philip a good deal after their last strange interview. His pettiness could be dispersed, and as for his 'unconventionality', which was so much gossiped about at Sawston, she began to see that it did not differ greatly from certain familiar notions of her own. If only he would forgive her for what she was doing now, there might perhaps lie before them a long and profitable friendship. But she must succeed. No one would forgive her if she did not succeed. She prepared to do battle with the powers of evil.

The voice of her adversary was heard at last, singing fearlessly from his expanded lungs, like a professional. Herein he differed from Englishmen, who always have a little feeling against music, and sing only from the throat, apologetically. He padded upstairs, and looked in at the open door of the reception-room without seeing her. Her heart leapt and her throat was dry when he turned away and passed, still singing, into the room opposite. It is alarming not to be seen.

He had left the door of this room open, and she could see into it, right across the landing. It was in a shocking mess. Food, bedclothes, patent-leather boots, dirty plates and knives, lay strewn over a large table and on the floor. But it was the mess that comes of life, not of desolation. It was preferable to the charnel-chamber in which she was standing now, and the light in it was soft and large, as from some gracious noble opening.

He stopped singing, and cried, 'Where is Perfetta?'

His back was turned and he was lighting a cigar. He was not speaking to Miss Abbott. He could not even be expecting her. The vista of the landing and the two open doors made him both remote and significant, like an actor on the stage, intimate and unapproachable at the same time. She could no more call out to him than if he was Hamlet.

'You know!' he continued. 'But you will not tell me. Exactly like you.' He reclined on the table and blew a fat smoke-ring. 'And why won't you tell me the numbers? I have dreamt of a red hen – that is two hundred and five, and a friend unexpected – he means eighty-two. But I try for the *terno* this week. So tell me another number.'

Miss Abbott did not know of the *tombola*. His speech terrified her. She felt those subtle restrictions which come upon us in fatigue. Had she slept well she would have greeted him as soon as she saw him. Now it was impossible. He had got into another world.

She watched his smoke-ring. The air had carried it slowly away from him, and brought it out intact upon the landing.

'Two hundred and five – eighty-two. In any case I shall put them on Bari, not on Florence. I cannot tell you why; I have a feeling this week for Bari.' Again she tried to speak. But the ring mesmerized her. It had become vast and elliptical, and floated in at the reception-room door.

'Ah! you don't care, if you get the profits. You won't even say,

"Thank you, Gino." Say it, or I'll drop hot, red-hot ashes on you. "Thank you, Gino –" '

The ring had extended its pale blue coils towards her. She lost self-control. It enveloped her. As if it was a breath from the pit, she screamed.

There he was, wanting to know what had frightened her, how she had got here, why she had never spoken. He made her sit down. He brought her wine, which she refused. She had not one word to say to him.

'What is it?' he repeated. 'What has frightened you?'

He, too, was frightened, and perspiration came starting through the tan. For it is a serious thing to have been watched. We all radiate something curiously intimate when we believe ourselves to be alone.

'Business –' she said at last.

'Business with me?'

'Most important business.' She was lying, white and limp, in the dusty chair.

'Before business you must get well; this is the best wine.'

She refused it feebly. He poured out a glass. She drank it. As she did so she became self-conscious. However important the business, it was not proper of her to have called on him, or to accept his hospitality.

'Perhaps you are engaged,' she said. 'And as I am not very well –'

'You are not well enough to go back. And I am not engaged.'

She looked nervously at the other room.

'Ah, now I understand,' he exclaimed. 'Now I see what frightened you. But why did you never speak?' And taking her into the room where he lived, he pointed to – the baby.

She had thought so much about this baby, of its welfare, its soul, its morals, its probable defects. But, like most unmarried people, she had only thought of it as a word – just as the healthy man only thinks of the word death, not of death itself. The real thing, lying asleep on a dirty rug, disconcerted her. It did not stand for a principle any longer. It was so much flesh and blood, so many inches and ounces of life – a glorious, unquestionable fact, which a man and another woman had given to the world. You could talk to it; in time it would answer you; in time it would not answer you unless it chose, but would secrete, within the compass of its body, thoughts and wonderful passions of its own. And this was the machine on which she and Mrs Herriton and Philip and Harriet had for the last month been exercising their various ideals – had determined that in time it should move this way or that way, should accomplish this and not that. It was to be Low Church, it was to be high-principled, it was to be tactful, gentlemanly, artistic – excellent things all. Yet now that she saw this baby, lying asleep on a dirty rug, she had a great disposition not to dictate one of them, and to exert no more influence than there may be in a kiss or in the vaguest of the heartfelt prayers.

But she had practised self-discipline, and her thoughts and actions were not yet to correspond. To recover her self-esteem she tried to imagine that she was in her district, and to behave accordingly.

'What a fine child, Signor Carella. And how nice of you to talk to it. Though I see that the ungrateful little fellow is asleep! Seven months? No, eight; of course eight. Still, he is a remarkably fine child for his age.'

Italian is a bad medium for condescension. The patronizing words came out gracious and sincere, and he smiled with pleasure.

'You must not stand. Let us sit on the loggia, where it is cool. I am afraid the room is very untidy,' he added, with the air of a hostess who apologizes for a stray thread on the drawing-room carpet. Miss Abbott picked her way to the chair. He sat near her, astride the parapet, with one foot in the loggia and the other dangling into the view. His face was in profile,, and its beautiful contours drove artfully against the misty green of the opposing hills. 'Posing!' said Miss Abbott to herself. 'A born artist's model.'

'Mr Herriton called yesterday,' she began, 'but you were out.'

He started an elaborate and graceful explanation. He had gone for the day to Poggibonsi. Why had the Herritons not written to him, so that he could have received them properly? Poggibonsi would have done any day; not but what his business there was fairly important. What did she suppose that it was?

Naturally she was not greatly interested. She had not come from Sawston to guess why he had been to Poggibonsi. She answered politely that she had no idea, and returned to her mission.

'But guess!' he persisted, clapping the balustrade between his hands.

She suggested, with gentle sarcasm, that perhaps he had gone to Poggibonsi to find something to do.

He intimated that it was not as important as all that. Something to do – an almost hopeless quest! 'E manca questo!' He rubbed his thumb and forefinger together, to indicate that he had no money. Then he sighed, and blew another smoke-ring. Miss Abbott took heart and turned diplomatic.

'This house,' she said, 'is a large house.'

'Exactly,' was his gloomy reply. 'And when my poor wife died –' He got up, went in, and walked across the landing to the reception-room door, which he closed reverently. Then he shut the door of the living-room with his foot, returned briskly to his seat, and continued his sentence. 'When my poor wife died I thought of having my relatives to live here. My father wished to give up his practice at Empoli; my mother and sisters and two aunts were also willing. But it was impossible. They have their ways of doing things, and when I was younger I was content with them. But now I am a man. I have my own ways. Do you understand?'

'Yes, I do,' said Miss Abbott, thinking of her own dear father, whose tricks and habits, after twenty-five years spent in their company, were beginning to get on her nerves. She remembered, though, that she was not here to sympathize with Gino – at all events, not to show that she sympathized. She also reminded herself that he was not worthy of sympathy. 'It is a large house,' she repeated.

'Immense; and the taxes! But it will be better when – Ah! but you have never guessed why I went to Poggibonsi – why it was that I was out when he called.'

'I cannot guess, Signor Carella. I am here on business.'

'But try.'

'I cannot; I hardly know you.'

'But we are old friends,' he said, 'and your approval will be grateful to me. You gave it me once before. Will you give it now?'

'I have not come as a friend this time,' she answered stiffly. 'I am not likely, Signor Carella, to approve of anything you do.'

'Oh, signorina!' He laughed, as if he found her piquante and amusing. 'Surely you approve of marriage?'

'Where there is love,' said Miss Abbott, looking at him hard. His face had altered in the last year, but not for the worse, which was baffling.

'Where there is love,' said he, politely echoing the English view. Then he smiled on her, expecting congratulations.

'Do I understand that you are proposing to marry again?'

He nodded.

'I forbid you, then!'

He looked puzzled, but took it for some foreign banter, and laughed.

'I forbid you!' repeated Miss Abbott, and all the indignation of her sex and her nationality went thrilling through the words.

'But why?' He jumped up, frowning. His voice was squeaky and petulant, like that of a child who is suddenly forbidden a toy.

'You have ruined one woman; I forbid you to ruin another. It is not a year since Lilia died. You pretended to me the other day that you loved her. It is a lie. You wanted her money. Has this woman money too?'

'Why, yes!' he said irritably. 'A little.'

'And I suppose you will say that you love her.'

'I shall not say it. It will be untrue. Now my poor wife –'

He stopped, seeing that the comparison would involve him in difficulties. And indeed he had often found Lilia as agreeable as anyone else.

Miss Abbott was furious at this final insult to her dead acquaintance. She was glad that after all she could be so angry with the boy. She glowed and throbbed; her tongue moved nimbly. At the finish, if the real business of the day had been completed, she could have swept majestically from the house. But the baby still remained, asleep on a dirty rug.

Gino was thoughtful, and stood scratching his head. He respected Miss Abbott. He wished that she would respect him. 'So you do not advise me?' he said dolefully. 'But why should it be a failure?'

Miss Abbott tried to remember that he was really a child still – a child with the strength and the passions of a disreputable man. 'How can it succeed,' she said solemnly, 'where there is no love?'

'But she does love me! I forgot to tell you that.'

'Indeed.'

'Passionately.' He laid his hand upon his own heart.

'Then God help her!'

He stamped impatiently. 'Whatever I say displeases you, signorina. God help you, for you are most unfair. You say that I ill-treated my dear wife. It is not so. I have never ill-treated anyone. You complain that there is no love in this marriage. I prove that there is, and you become still more angry. What do you want? Do you suppose she will not be contented? Glad enough she is to get me, and she will do her duty well.'

'Her duty!' cried Miss Abbott, with all the bitterness of which she was capable.

'Why, of course. She knows why I am marrying her.'

'To succeed where Lilia failed! To be your housekeeper, your slave, your –' The words she would like to have said were too violent for her.

'To look after the baby, certainly,' said he.

'The baby –?' She had forgotten it.

'It is an English marriage,' he said proudly. 'I do not care about the money. I am having her for my son. Did you not understand that?'

'No,' said Miss Abbott, utterly bewildered. Then for a moment, she saw light. 'It is not necessary, Signor Carella. Since you are tired of the baby –'

Ever after she remembered it to her credit that she saw her mistake at once. 'I don't mean that,' she added quickly.

'I know,' was his courteous response. 'Ah, in a foreign language (and how perfectly you speak Italian) one is certain to make slips.'

She looked at his face. It was apparently innocent of satire.

'You meant that we could not always be together yet, he and I. You are right. What is to be done? I cannot afford a nurse, and Perfetta is too rough. When he was ill I dare not let her touch him. When he has to be washed, which happens now and then, who does it? I. I feed him, or settle what he shall have. I sleep with him and comfort him when he is unhappy in the night. No one talks, no one may sing to him but I. Do not be unfair this time; I like to do these things. But nevertheless' (his voice became pathetic) 'they take up a great deal of time, and are not all suitable for a young man.'

'Not at all suitable,' said Miss Abbott, and closed her eyes wearily. Each moment her difficulties were increasing. She wished that she was not so tired, so open to contradictory impressions. She longed for Harriet's burly obtuseness or for the soulless diplomacy of Mrs Herriton.

'A little more wine?' asked Gino kindly.

'Oh no, thank you! But marriage, Signor Carella, is a very serious step. Could you not manage more simply? Your relatives, for example –'

'Empoli! I would as soon have him in England!'

'England, then –'

He laughed.

'He has a grandmother there, you know – Mrs Theobald.'

'He has a grandmother here. No, he is troublesome, but I must have him with me. I will not even have my father and mother too. For they would separate us,' he added.

'How?'

'They would separate our thoughts.'

She was silent. This cruel, vicious fellow knew of strange refinements. The horrible truth, that wicked people are capable of love, stood naked before her, and her moral being was abashed. It was her duty to rescue the baby, to save it from contagion, and she still meant to do her duty. But the comfortable sense of virtue left her. She was in the presence of something greater than right or wrong.

Forgetting that this was an interview, he had strolled back into the room, driven by the instinct she had aroused in him. 'Wake up!' he cried to his baby, as if it was some grown-up friend. Then he lifted his foot and trod lightly on its stomach.

Miss Abbott cried, 'Oh, take care!' She was unaccustomed to this method of awakening the young.

'He is not much longer than my boot, is he? Can you believe that in time his own boots will be as large? And that he also –'

'But ought you to treat him like that?'

He stood with one foot resting on the little body, suddenly musing, filled with the desire that his son should be like him, and should have sons like him, to people the earth. It is the strongest desire that can come to a man – if it comes to him at all – stronger even than love or the desire for personal immortality. All men vaunt it, and declare that it is theirs; but the hearts of most are set elsewhere. It is the exception who comprehends that physical and spiritual life may stream out of him for ever. Miss Abbott, for all her goodness, could not comprehend it, though such a thing is more within the comprehension of women. And when Gino pointed first to himself and then to his baby, and said 'Father – son,' she still took it as a piece of nursery prattle, and smiled mechanically.

The child, the first-fruits, woke up and glared at her. Gino did not greet it, but continued the exposition of his policy.

'This woman will do exactly what I tell her. She is fond of children. She is clean; she has a pleasant voice. She is not beautiful; I cannot pretend that to you for a moment. But she is what I require.'

The baby gave a piercing yell.

'Oh, do take care!' begged Miss Abbott. 'You are squeezing it.'

'It is nothing. If he cried silently then you may be frightened. He thinks I am going to wash him, and he is quite right.'

'Wash him!' she cried. 'You? Here?' The homely piece of news seemed to shatter all her plans. She had spent a long half-hour in elaborate approaches, in high moral attacks; she had neither frightened her enemy nor made him angry, nor interfered with the least detail of his domestic life.

'I had gone to the *farmacia*,' he continued, 'and was sitting there comfortably, when suddenly I remembered that Perfetta had heated water an hour ago – over there, look, covered with a cushion. I came away at once, for really he must be washed. You must excuse me. I can put it off no longer.'

'I have wasted your time,' she said feebly.

He walked sternly to the loggia and drew from it a large earthenware bowl. It was dirty inside; he dusted it with a table-cloth. Then he fetched the hot water, which was in a copper pot. He poured it out. He added cold. He felt in his pocket and brought out a piece of soap. Then he took up the baby, and, holding his cigar between his teeth, began to unwrap it. Miss Abbott turned to go.

'But why are you going? Excuse me if I wash him while we talk.'

'I have nothing more to say,' said Miss Abbott. All she could do now was to find Philip, confess her miserable defeat, and bid him go in her stead and prosper better. She cursed her feebleness; she longed to expose it, without apologies or tears.

'Oh, but stop a moment!' he cried. 'You have not seen him yet.'

'I have seen as much as I want, thank you.'

The last wrapping slid off. He held out to her in his two hands a little kicking image of bronze.

'Take him!'

She would not touch the child.

'I must go at once,' she cried; for the tears – the wrong tears – were hurrying to her eyes.

'Who would have believed his mother was blonde? For he is brown all over – brown every inch of him. Ah, but how beautiful he is! And he is mine; mine for ever. Even if he hates me he will be mine. He cannot help it; he is made out of me; I am his father.'

It was too late to go. She could not tell why, but it was too late. She turned away her head when Gino lifted his son to his lips. This was something too remote from the prettiness of the nursery. The man was majestic; he was a part of Nature; in no ordinary love scene could he ever be so great. For a wonderful physical tie binds the parents to the children; and – by some sad, strange irony – it does not bind us children to our parents. For if it did, if we could answer their love not with gratitude but with equal love, life would lose much of its pathos and much of its squalor, and we might be wonderfully happy. Gino passionately embracing, Miss Abbott reverently averting her eyes – both of them had parents whom they did not love so very much.

'May I help you to wash him?' she asked humbly.

He gave her his son without speaking, and they knelt side by side, tucking up their sleeves. The child had stopped crying, and his arms and legs were agitated by some overpowering joy. Miss Abbott had a woman's pleasure in cleaning anything – more especially when the thing was human. She understood little babies from long experience in a district, and Gino soon ceased to give her directions, and only gave her thanks.

'It is very kind of you,' he murmured, 'especially in your beautiful dress. He is nearly clean already. Why, I take the whole morning! There is so much more of a baby than one expects. And Perfetta washes him just as she washes clothes. Then he screams for hours. My wife is to have a light hand. Ah, how he kicks! Has he splashed you? I am very sorry.'

'I am ready for a soft towel now,' said Miss Abbott, who was strangely exalted by the service.

'Certainly! Certainly!' He strode in a knowing way to a cup-board. But he had no idea where the soft towel was. Generally he dabbed the baby on the first dry thing he found.

'And if you had any powder.'

He struck his forehead despairingly. Apparently the stock of powder was just exhausted.

She sacrificed her own clean handkerchief. He put a chair for her on the loggia, which faced westward, and was still pleasant and cool. There she sat, with twenty miles of view behind her, and he placed the dripping baby on her knee. It shone now with health and beauty; it seemed to reflect light, like a copper vessel. Just such a baby Bellini sets languid on his mother's lap, or Signorelli flings wriggling on pavements of marble, or Lorenzo di Credi, more reverent but less divine, lays carefully among flowers, with his head upon a wisp of golden straw. For a time Gino contemplated them standing. Then, to get a better view, he knelt by the side of the chair, with his hands clasped before him.

So they were when Philip entered, and saw, to all intents and purposes, the Virgin and Child, with Donor.

'Hallo!' he exclaimed; for he was glad to find things in such cheerful trim.

She did not greet him, but rose up unsteadily and handed the baby to his father.

'No, do stop!' whispered Philip. 'I got your note. I'm not offended; you're quite right. I really want you; I could never have done it alone.'

No words came from her, but she raised her hands to her mouth, like one who is in sudden agony.

'Signorina, do stop a little – after all your kindness.'

She burst into tears.

'What is it?' said Philip kindly.

She tried to speak, and then went away, weeping bitterly.

The two men stared at each other. By a common impulse they ran onto the loggia. They were just in time to see Miss Abbott disappear among the trees.

'What is it?' asked Philip again. There was no answer, and somehow he did not want an answer. Some strange thing had happened which he could not presume to understand. He would find out from Miss Abbott, if ever he found out at all.

'Well, our business,' said Gino, after a puzzled sigh.

'Our business – Miss Abbott has told you of that.'

'No.'

'But surely –'

'She came for business. But she forgot about it; so did I.'

Perfetta, who had a genius for missing people, now returned, loudly complaining of the size of Monteriano and the intricacies of its streets. Gino told her to watch the baby. Then he offered Philip a cigar, and they proceeded to the business.

CHAPTER VIII

'MAD!' SCREAMED HARRIET – 'absolutely stark, staring, raving mad!'

Philip judged it better not to contradict her.

'What's she here for? Answer me that. What's she doing in Monteriano in August? Why isn't she in Normandy? Answer that. She won't. I can: she's come to thwart us; she's betrayed us – got hold of mother's plans. Oh, goodness, my head!'

He was unwise enough to reply: 'You mustn't accuse her of that. Though she is exasperating, she hasn't come here to betray us.'

'Then why has she come here? Answer me that.'

He made no answer. But fortunately his sister was too much agitated to wait for one. 'Bursting in on me – crying and looking a disgusting sight – and says she has been to see the Italian. Couldn't even talk properly; pretended she had changed her opinions. What are her opinions to us? I was very calm. I said: "Miss Abbott, I think there is a little misapprehension in this matter. My mother, Mrs Herriton –" Oh, goodness, my head! Of course you've failed – don't trouble to answer – I know you've failed. Where's the baby, pray? Of course you haven't got it. Dear sweet Caroline won't let you. Oh yes, and we're to go away at once and trouble the father no more. Those are her commands. Commands! COMMANDS!' And Harriet also burst into tears.

Philip governed his temper. His sister was annoying, but quite reasonable in her indignation. Moreover, Miss Abbott had behaved even worse than she supposed.

'I've not got the baby, Harriet, but at the same time I haven't exactly failed. I and Signor Carella are to have another interview this afternoon, at the Caffè Garibaldi. He is perfectly reasonable and pleasant. Should you be disposed to come with me, you would find him quite willing to discuss things. He is desperately in want of money, and has no prospect of getting any. I discovered that. At the same time, he has a certain affection for the child.' For Philip's insight, or perhaps his opportunities, had not been equal to Miss Abbott's.

Harriet would only sob, and accuse her brother of insulting her; how could a lady speak to such a horrible man? That, and nothing else, was enough to stamp Caroline. Oh, poor Lilia!

Philip drummed on the bedroom window-sill. He saw no escape from the deadlock. For though he spoke cheerfully about his second interview with Gino he felt at the bottom of his heart that it would fail. Gino was too courteous; he would not break off negotiations by a sharp denial; he loved this civil, half-humorous bargaining. And he loved fooling his opponent, and did it so nicely that his opponent did not mind being fooled.

'Miss Abbott has behaved extraordinarily,' he said at last; 'but at the same time –'

His sister would not hear him. She burst forth again on the madness, the interference, the intolerable duplicity of Caroline.

'Harriet, you must listen. My dear, you must stop crying. I have something quite important to say.'

'I shall not stop crying,' said she. But in time, finding that he would not speak to her, she did stop.

'Remember that Miss Abbott has done us no harm. She said nothing to him about the matter. He assumes that she is working with us; I gathered that.'

'Well, she isn't.'

'Yes; but if you're careful she may be. I interpret her behaviour thus: she went to see him, honestly intending to get the child away. In the note she left me she says so, and I don't believe she'd lie.'

'I do.'

'When she got there, there was some pretty domestic scene between him and the baby, and she has got swept off in a gush of sentimentalism. Before very long, if I know anything about psychology, there will be a reaction. She'll be swept back.'

'I don't understand your long words. Say plainly –'

'When she's swept back, she'll be invaluable. For she has made quite an impression on him. He thinks her so nice with the baby. You know, she washed it for him.'

'Disgusting!'

Harriet's ejaculations were more aggravating than the rest of her. But Philip was averse to losing his temper. The access of joy that had come to him yesterday in the theatre promised to be permanent. He was more anxious than heretofore to be charitable towards the world.

'If you want to carry off the baby, keep your peace with Miss Abbott. For if she chooses she can help you better than I can.'

'There can be no peace between me and her,' said Harriet gloomily.

'Did you –?'

'Oh, not all I wanted. She went away before I had finished speaking – just like those cowardly people! – into the church.'

'Into Santa Deodata's?'

'Yes; I'm sure she needs it. Anything more unchristian –'

In time Philip went to the church also, leaving his sister a little calmer and a little disposed to think over his advice. What had come over Miss Abbott? He had always thought her both stable and sincere. That conversation he had had with her last Christmas in the train to Charing Cross – that alone furnished him with a parallel. For the second time, Monteriano must have turned her head. He was not angry with her, for he was quite indifferent to the outcome of their expedition. He was only extremely interested.

It was now nearly midday, and the streets were clearing. But the intense heat had broken, and there was a pleasant suggestion of rain. The Piazza with its three great attractions – the Palazzo Pubblico, the Collegiate Church, and the Caffè Garibaldi: the intellect, the soul, and the body – had never looked

more charming. For a moment Philip stood in its centre, much
inclined to be dreamy, and thinking how wonderful it must feel
to belong to a city, however mean. He was here, however, as an
emissary of civilization and as a student of character, and, after
a sigh, he entered Santa Deodata's to continue his mission.

There had been a *festa* two days before, and the church still
smelt of incense and of garlic. The little son of the sacristan was
sweeping the nave, more for amusement than for cleanliness,
sending great clouds of dust over the frescoes and the scattered
worshippers. The sacristan himself had propped a ladder in the
centre of the Deluge – which fills one of the nave spandrels –
and was freeing a column from its wealth of scarlet calico. Much
scarlet calico also lay upon the floor – for the church can look as
fine as any theatre – and the sacristan's little daughter was trying
to fold it up. She was wearing a tinsel crown. The crown really
belonged to St Augustine. But it had been cut too big: it fell
down over his cheeks like a collar – you never saw anything so
absurd. One of the canons had unhooked it just before the *festa*
began, and had given it to the sacristan's daughter.

'Please,' cried Philip, 'is there an English lady here?'

The man's mouth was full of tin-tacks, but he nodded cheerfully towards a kneeling figure. In the midst of this confusion
Miss Abbott was praying.

He was not much surprised; a spiritual breakdown was quite
to be expected. For though he was growing more charitable
towards mankind he was still a little jaunty, and too apt to
stake out beforehand the course that will be pursued by the
wounded soul. It did surprise him, however, that she should
greet him naturally, with none of the sour self-consciousness
of a person who had just risen from her knees. This was indeed
the spirit of Santa Deodata's, where a prayer to God is thought
none the worse of because it comes next to a pleasant word to
a neighbour. 'I am sure that I need it,' said she; and he, who
had expected her to be ashamed, became confused, and knew
not what to reply.

'I've nothing to tell you,' she continued. 'I have simply changed straight round. If I had planned the whole thing out, I could not have treated you worse. I can talk it over now; but please believe that I have been crying.'

'And please believe that I have not come to scold you,' said Philip. 'I know what has happened.'

'What?' asked Miss Abbott. Instinctively she led the way to the famous chapel, the fifth chapel on the right, wherein Giovanni da Empoli has painted the death and burial of the saint. Here they could sit out of the dust and the noise, and proceed with a discussion which promised to be important.

'What might have happened to me – he has made you believe that he loves the child.'

'Oh yes; he has. He will never give it up.'

'At present it is still unsettled.'

'It will never be settled.'

'Perhaps not. Well, as I said, I know what has happened, and I am not here to scold you. But I must ask you to withdraw from the thing for the present. Harriet is furious. But she will calm down when she realizes that you have done us no harm, and will do none.'

'I can do no more,' she said. 'But I tell you plainly I have changed sides.'

'If you do no more, that is all we want. You promise not to prejudice our cause by speaking to Signor Carella?'

'Oh, certainly. I don't want to speak to him again; I shan't ever see him again.'

'Quite nice, wasn't he?'

'Quite.'

'Well, that's all I wanted to know. I'll go and tell Harriet of your promise, and I think things'll quiet down now.'

But he did not move, for it was an increasing pleasure to him to be near her, and her charm was at its strongest today. He thought less of psychology and feminine reaction. The gush of sentimentalism which had carried her away had only made her more alluring. He was content to observe her beauty and to profit by the tenderness and the wisdom that dwelt within her.

'Why aren't you angry with me?' she asked, after a pause.

'Because I understand you – all sides, I think – Harriet, Signor Carella, even my mother.'

'You do understand wonderfully. You are the only one of us who has a general view of the muddle.'

He smiled with pleasure. It was the first time she had ever praised him. His eyes rested agreeably on Santa Deodata, who was dying in full sanctity, upon her back. There was a window open behind her, revealing just such a view as he had seen that morning, and on her widowed mother's dresser there stood just such another copper pot. The saint looked neither at the view nor at the pot, and at her widowed mother still less. For lo! she had a vision: the head and shoulders of St Augustine were sliding like some miraculous enamel along the roughcast wall. It is a gentle saint who is content with half another saint to see her die. In her death, as in her life, Santa Deodata did not accomplish much.

'So what are you going to do?' said Miss Abbott.

Philip started, not so much at the words as at the sudden change in the voice. 'Do?' he echoed, rather dismayed. 'This afternoon I have another interview.'

'It will come to nothing. Well?'

'Then another. If that fails I shall wire home for instructions. I dare say we may fail altogether, but we shall fail honourably.'

She had often been decided. But now behind her decision there was a note of passion. She struck him not as different, but as more important, and he minded it very much when she said:

'That's not doing anything! You would be doing something if you kidnapped the baby, or if you went straight away. But that! To fail honourably! To come out of the thing as well as you can! Is that all you are after?'

'Why, yes,' he stammered. 'Since we talk openly, that is all I am after just now. What else is there? If I can persuade Signor Carella to give in, so much the better. If he won't, I must report the failure to my mother, and then go home. Why, Miss Abbott, you can't expect me to follow you through all these turns –'

'I don't! But I do expect you to settle what is right and to follow that. Do you want the child to stop with his father, who loves him and will bring him up badly, or do you want him to come to Sawston, where no one loves him, but where he will be brought up well? There is the question put dispassionately enough even for you. Settle it. Settle which side you'll fight on. But don't go talking about an "honourable failure", which means simply not thinking and not acting at all.'

'Because I understand the position of Signor Carella and of you, it's no reason that –'

'None at all. Fight us if you think us wrong. Oh, what's the use of your fairmindedness if you never decide for yourself? Anyone gets hold of you and makes you do what they want. And you see through them and laugh at them – and do it. It's not enough to see clearly; I'm muddle-headed and stupid, and not worth a quarter of you, but I have tried to do what seemed right at the time. And you – your brain and your insight are splendid. But when you see what's right you're too idle to do it. You told me once that we shall be judged by our intentions, not by our accomplishments. I thought it a grand remark. But we must intend to accomplish – not sit intending on a chair.'

'You are wonderful!' he said gravely.

'Oh, you appreciate me!' she burst out again. 'I wish you didn't. You appreciate us all – see good in all of us. And all the time you are dead – dead – dead. Look, why aren't you angry?' She came up to him, and then her mood suddenly changed, and she took hold of both his hands. 'You are so splendid, Mr Herriton, that I can't bear to see you wasted. I can't bear – she has not been good to you – your mother.'

'Miss Abbott, don't worry over me. Some people are born not to do things. I'm one of them; I never did anything at school or at the Bar. I came out to stop Lilia's marriage, and it was too late. I came out intending to get the baby, and I shall return an "honourable failure". I never expect anything to happen now, and so I am never disappointed. You would be surprised to know what my great events are. Going to the theatre yesterday, talking to you now – I don't suppose I shall ever meet anything greater. I seem fated to pass through the world without colliding with it or moving it – and I'm sure I can't tell you whether the fate's good or evil. I don't die – I don't fall in love. And if other people die or fall in love they always do it when I'm not there. You are quite right: life to me is just a spectacle, which – thank God, and thank Italy, and thank you – is now more beautiful and heartening than it has ever been before.'

She said solemnly, 'I wish something would happen to you, my dear friend; I wish something would happen to you.'

'But why?' he asked, smiling. 'Prove to me why I don't do as I am.'

She also smiled, very gravely. She could not prove it. No argument existed. Their discourse, splendid as it had been, resulted in nothing, and their respective opinions and policies were exactly the same when they left the church as when they had entered it.

Harriet was rude at lunch. She called Miss Abbott a turncoat and a coward to her face. Miss Abbott resented neither epithet, feeling that one was justified and the other not unreasonable. She tried to avoid even the suspicion of satire in her replies. But Harriet was sure that she was satirical because she was so calm. She got more and more violent, and Philip at one time feared that she would come to blows.

'Look here!' he cried, with something of the old manner, 'it's too hot for this. We've been talking and interviewing each other all the morning, and I have another interview this afternoon. I do stipulate for silence. Let each lady retire to her bedroom with a book.'

'I retire to pack,' said Harriet. 'Please remind Signor Carella, Philip, that the baby is to be here by half-past eight this evening.'

'Oh, certainly, Harriet. I shall make a point of reminding him.'

'And order a carriage to take us to the evening train.'

'And please,' said Miss Abbott, 'would you order a carriage for me too?'

'You going!' he exclaimed.

'Of course,' she replied, suddenly flushing. 'Why not?'

'Why, of course you would be going. Two carriages, then. Two carriages for the evening train.' He looked at his sister hopelessly. 'Harriet, what ever are you up to? We shall never be ready.'

'Order my carriage for the evening train,' said Harriet, and departed.

'Well, I suppose I shall. And I shall also have my interview with Signor Carella.'

Miss Abbott gave a little sigh.

'But why should you mind? Do you suppose that I shall have the slightest influence over him?'

'No. But – I can't repeat all that I said in the church. You ought never to see him again. You ought to bundle Harriet into a carriage, not this evening, but now, and drive her straight away.'

'Perhaps I ought. But it isn't a very big "ought". Whatever Harriet and I do, the issue is the same. Why, I can see the splendour of it – even the humour. Gino sitting up here on the mountain top with his cub. We come and ask for it. He welcomes us. We ask for it again. He is equally pleasant. I'm agreeable to spend the whole week bargaining with him. But I know that at the end of it I shall descend empty-handed to the plains. It might be finer of me to make up my mind. But I'm not a fine character. And nothing hangs on it.'

'Perhaps I am extreme,' she said humbly. 'I've been trying to run you, just like your mother. I feel you ought to fight it out with Harriet. Every little trifle, for some reason, does seem incalculably important today, and when you say of a thing that "nothing hangs on it" it sounds like blasphemy. There's never any knowing – how am I to put it? – which of our actions, which of our idlenesses won't have things hanging on it for ever.'

He assented, but her remark had only an aesthetic value.

He was not prepared to take it to his heart. All the afternoon he rested – worried, but not exactly despondent. The thing would jog out somehow. Probably Miss Abbott was right. The baby had better stop where it was loved. And that, probably, was what the fates had decreed. He felt little interest in the matter, and he was sure that he had no influence.

It was not surprising, therefore, that the interview at the Caffè Garibaldi came to nothing. Neither of them took it very seriously. And before long Gino had discovered how things lay, and was ragging his companion hopelessly. Philip tried to look offended, but in the end he had to laugh. 'Well, you are right,' he said. 'The affair *is* being managed by the ladies.'

'Ah, the ladies – the ladies!' cried the other, and then he roared like a millionaire for two cups of black coffee, and insisted on treating his friend, as a sign that their strife was over.

'Well, I have done my best,' said Philip, dipping a long slice of sugar into his cup, and watching the brown liquid ascend into it. 'I shall face my mother with a good conscience. Will you bear me witness that I've done my best?'

'My poor fellow, I will!' He laid a sympathetic hand on Philip's knee.

'And that I have –' The sugar was now impregnated with coffee, and he bent forward to swallow it. As he did so his eyes swept the opposite side of the Piazza, and he saw there, watching them, Harriet. 'Mia sorella!' he exclaimed. Gino, much amused, laid his head upon the little table, and beat the marble humorously with his fists. Harriet turned away and began gloomily to inspect the Palazzo Pubblico.

'Poor Harriet!' said Philip, swallowing the sugar. 'One more wrench and it will all be over for her; we are leaving this evening.'

Gino was sorry for this. 'Then you will not be here this evening as you promised us. All three leaving?'

'All three,' said Philip, who had not revealed the secession of Miss Abbott; 'by the night train; at least, that is my sister's plan. So I'm afraid I shan't be here.'

They watched the departing figure of Harriet, and then entered upon the final civilities. They shook each other warmly by both hands. Philip was to come again next year, and to write beforehand. He was to be introduced to Gino's wife, for he was told of the marriage now. He was to be godfather to his next baby. As for Gino, he would remember some time that Philip liked vermouth. He begged him to give his love to Irma. Mrs Herriton – should he send her his sympathetic regards? No; perhaps that would hardly do.

So the two young men parted with a good deal of genuine affection. For the barrier of language is sometimes a blessed barrier, which only lets pass what is good. Or – to put the thing less cynically – we may be better in new clean words, which have never been tainted by our pettiness or vice. Philip, at all events, lived more graciously in Italian, the very phrases of which entice one to be happy and kind. It was horrible to think of the English of Harriet, whose every word would be as hard, as distinct and as unfinished as a lump of coal.

Harriet, however, talked little. She had seen enough to know that her brother had failed again, and with unwonted dignity she accepted the situation. She did her packing, she wrote up her diary, she made a brown paper cover for the new Baedeker. Philip, finding her so amenable, tried to discuss their future plans. But she only said that they would sleep in Florence, and told him to telegraph for rooms. They had supper alone. Miss Abbott did not come down. The landlady told them that Signor Carella had called on Miss Abbott to say goodbye, but she, though in, had not been able to see him. She also told them that it had begun to rain. Harriet sighed, but indicated to her brother that he was not responsible.

The carriages came round at a quarter past eight. It was not raining much, but the night was extraordinarily dark, and one of the drivers wanted to go slowly to the station. Miss Abbott came down and said that she was ready, and would start at once.

'Yes, do,' said Philip, who was standing in the hall. 'Now that we have quarrelled we scarcely want to travel in procession all the way down the hill. Well, goodbye; it's all over at last; another scene in my pageant has shifted.'

'Goodbye; it's been a great pleasure to see you. I hope that won't shift, at all events.' She gripped his hand.

'You sound despondent,' he said, laughing. 'Don't forget that you return victorious.'

'I suppose I do,' she replied, more despondently than ever, and got into the carriage. He concluded that she was thinking of her reception at Sawston, whither her fame would doubtless precede her. What ever would Mrs Herriton do? She could make things quite unpleasant when she thought it right. She might think it right to be silent, but then there was Harriet. Who could bridle Harriet's tongue? Between the two of them Miss Abbott was bound to have a bad time. Her reputation, both for consistency and for moral enthusiasm, would be lost for ever.

'It's hard luck on her,' he thought. 'She is a good person. I must do for her anything I can.' Their intimacy had been very rapid, but he too hoped that it would not shift. He believed that he understood her, and that she, by now, had seen the worst of him. What if after a long time – if after all – he flushed like a boy as he looked after her carriage.

He went into the dining-room to look for Harriet. Harriet was not to be found. Her bedroom, too, was empty. All that was left of her was the purple prayerbook which lay open on the bed. Philip took it up aimlessly, and saw – 'Blessed be the Lord my God, who teacheth my hands to war, and my fingers to fight.' He put the book in his pocket, and began to brood over more profitable themes.

Santa Deodata gave out half past eight. All the luggage was on, and still Harriet had not appeared. 'Depend upon it,' said the landlady, 'she has gone to Signor Carella's to say goodbye to her little nephew.' Philip did not think it likely. They shouted all over the house and still there was no Harriet. He began to be uneasy. He was helpless without Miss Abbott; her grave kind face had cheered him wonderfully, even when it looked displeased. Monteriano was sad without her; the rain was thickening; the scraps of Donizetti floated tunelessly out of the wineshops, and of the great tower opposite he could only see the base, fresh papered with the advertisements of quacks.

A man came up the street with a note. Philip read: 'Start at once. Pick me up outside the gate. Pay the bearer. H. H.'

'Did the lady give you this note?' he cried.

The man was unintelligible.

'Speak up!' exclaimed Philip. 'Who gave it you – and where?'

Nothing but horrible sighings and bubblings came out of the man.

'Be patient with him,' said the driver, turning round on the box. 'It is the poor idiot.' And the landlady came out of the hotel and echoed: 'The poor idiot. He cannot speak. He takes messages for us all.'

Philip then saw that the messenger was a ghastly creature, quite bald, with trickling eyes and grey twitching nose. In any other country he would have been shut up; here he was accepted as a public institution, and part of Nature's scheme.

'Ugh!' shuddered the Englishman. 'Signora padrona, find out from him; this note is from my sister. What does it mean? Where did he see her?'

'It is no good,' said the landlady. 'He understands everything, but he can explain nothing.'

'He has visions of the saints,' said the man who drove the cab.

'But my sister – where has she gone? How has she met him?'

'She has gone for a walk,' asserted the landlady. It was a nasty evening, but she was beginning to understand the English. 'She has gone for a walk – perhaps to wish goodbye to her little nephew. Preferring to come back another way, she has sent you this note by the poor idiot and is waiting for you outside the Siena gate. Many of my guests do this.'

There was nothing to do but to obey the message. He shook hands with the landlady, gave the messenger a nickel piece, and drove away. After a dozen yards the carriage stopped. The poor idiot was running and whimpering behind.

'Go on,' cried Philip, 'I have paid him plenty.'

A horrible hand pushed three soldi into his lap. It was part of the idiot's malady only to receive what was just for his services. This was the change out of the nickel piece.

'Go on!' shouted Philip, and flung the money into the road. He was frightened at the episode; the whole of life had become unreal. It was a relief to be out of the Siena gate. They drew up for a moment on the terrace. But there was no sign of Harriet. The driver called to the *dogana* men. But they had seen no English lady pass.

'What am I to do?' he cried; 'it is not like the lady to be late. We shall miss the train.'

'Let us drive slowly,' said the driver, 'and you shall call her by name as we go.'

So they started down into the night, Philip calling 'Harriet! Harriet! Harriet!' And there she was, waiting for them in the wet, at the first turn of the zigzag.

'Harriet, why don't you answer?'

'I heard you coming,' said she, and got quickly in. Not till then did he see that she carried a bundle.

'What's that?'

'Hush –'

'What ever is that?'

'Hush – sleeping.'

Harriet had succeeded where Miss Abbott and Philip had failed. It was the baby.

She would not let him talk. The baby, she repeated, was asleep, and she put up an umbrella to shield it and her from the rain. He should hear all later. So he had to conjecture the course of the wonderful interview – an interview between the South Pole and the North. It was quite easy to conjecture: Gino crumpling up suddenly before the intense conviction of Harriet; being told, perhaps, to his face that he was a villain; yielding his only son, perhaps for money, perhaps for nothing. 'Poor Gino,' he thought. 'He's no greater than I am, after all.'

Then he thought of Miss Abbott, whose carriage must be descending the darkness some mile or two below them, and his easy self-accusation failed. She, too, had conviction; he had felt its force; he would feel it again when she knew this day's sombre and unexpected close.

'You have been pretty secret,' he said; 'you might tell me a little now. What do we pay for him? All we've got?'

'Hush!' answered Harriet, and dandled the bundle laboriously, like some bony prophetess Judith, or Deborah, or Jael. He had last seen the baby sprawling on the knees of Miss Abbott, shining and naked, with twenty miles of view behind him, and his father kneeling by his feet. And that remembrance, together with Harriet, and the darkness, and the poor idiot, and the silent rain, filled him with sorrow and with the expectation of sorrow to come.

Monteriano had long disappeared, and he could see nothing but the occasional wet stem of an olive, which their lamp illumined as they passed it. They travelled quickly, for this driver did not care how fast he went to the station, and would dash down each incline and scuttle perilously round the curves.

'Look here, Harriet,' he said at last, 'I feel bad; I want to see the baby.'

'Hush!'

'I don't mind if I do wake him up. I want to see him. I've as much right in him as you.'

Harriet gave in. But it was too dark for him to see the child's face. 'Wait a minute,' he whispered, and before she could stop him he had lit a match under the shelter of her umbrella. 'But he's awake!' he exclaimed. The match went out.

'Good ickle quiet boysey, then.'

Philip winced. 'His face, do you know, struck me as all wrong.'

'All wrong?'

'All puckered queerly.'

'Of course – with the shadows – you couldn't see him.'

'Well, hold him up again.' She did so. He lit another match. It went out quickly, but not before he had seen that the baby was crying.

'Nonsense,' said Harriet sharply. 'We should hear him if he cried.'

'No, he's crying hard; I thought so before, and I'm certain now.'

Harriet touched the child's face. It was bathed in tears. 'Oh, the night air, I suppose,' she said, 'or perhaps the wet of the rain.'

'I say, you haven't hurt it, or held it the wrong way, or anything; it is too uncanny – crying and no noise. Why didn't you get Perfetta to carry it to the hotel instead of muddling with the messenger? It's a marvel he understood about the note.'

'Oh, he understands.' And he could feel her shudder. 'He tried to carry the baby –'

'But why not Gino or Perfetta?'

'Philip, don't talk. Must I say it again? Don't talk. The baby wants to sleep.' She crooned harshly as they descended, and now and then she wiped up the tears which welled inexhaustibly from the little eyes. Philip looked away, winking at times himself. It was as if they were travelling with the whole world's sorrow, as if all the mystery, all the persistency of woe were gathered to a single fount. The roads were now coated with mud, and the carriage went more quietly but not less swiftly, sliding by long zigzags into the night. He knew the landmarks pretty well: here was the cross-road to Poggibonsi; and the last view of Monteriano, if they had light, would be from here. Soon they ought to come to that little wood where violets were so plentiful in spring. He wished the weather had not changed; it was not cold, but the air was extraordinarily damp. It could not be good for the child.

'I suppose he breathes, and all that sort of thing?' he said.

'Of course,' said Harriet, in an angry whisper. 'You've started him again. I'm certain he was asleep. I do wish you wouldn't talk; it makes me so nervous.'

'I'm nervous too. I wish he'd scream. It's too uncanny. Poor Gino! I'm terribly sorry for Gino.'

'Are you?'

'Because he's weak – like most of us. He doesn't know what he wants. He doesn't grip onto life. But I like that man, and I'm sorry for him.'

Naturally enough, she made no answer.

'You despise him, Harriet, and you despise me. But you do us no good by it. We fools want someone to set us on our feet. Suppose a really decent woman had set up Gino – I believe Caroline Abbott might have done it – mightn't he have been another man?'

'Philip,' she interrupted, with an attempt at nonchalance, 'do you happen to have those matches handy? We might as well look at the baby again if you have.'

The first match blew out immediately. So did the second. He suggested that they should stop the carriage and borrow the lamp from the driver.

'Oh, I don't want all that bother. Try again.'

They entered the little wood as he tried to strike the third match. At last it caught. Harriet poised the umbrella rightly, and for a full quarter-minute they contemplated the face that trembled in the light of the trembling flame. Then there was a shout and a crash. They were lying in the mud in darkness. The carriage had overturned.

Philip was a good deal hurt. He sat up and rocked himself to and fro, holding his arm. He could just make out the outline of the carriage above him, and the outlines of the carriage cushions and of their luggage upon the grey road. The accident had taken place in the wood, where it was even darker than in the open.

'Are you all right?' he managed to say. Harriet was screaming, the horse was kicking, the driver was cursing some other man.

Harriet's screams became coherent. 'The baby – the baby – it slipped – it's gone from my arms! I stole it!'

'God help me!' said Philip. A cold circle came round his mouth, and he fainted.

When he recovered, it was still the same confusion. The horse was kicking, the baby had not been found, and Harriet still screamed like a maniac: 'I stole it! I stole it! I stole it! It slipped out of my arms!'

'Keep still!' he commanded the driver. 'Let no one move. We may tread on it. Keep still.'

For a moment they all obeyed him. He began to crawl through the mud, touching first this, then that, grasping the cushions by mistake, listening for the faintest whisper that might guide him. He tried to light a match, holding the box in his teeth and striking at it with the uninjured hand. At last he succeeded, and the light fell upon the bundle which he was seeking.

It had rolled off the road into the wood a little way, and had fallen across a great rut. So tiny it was that had it fallen lengthways it would have disappeared, and he might never have found it.

'I stole it! I and the idiot – no one was there.' She burst out laughing.

He sat down and laid it on his knee. Then he tried to cleanse the face from the mud and the rain and the tears. His arm, he supposed, was broken, but he could still move it a little, and for the moment he forgot all pain. He was listening – not for a cry, but for the tick of a heart or the slightest tremor of breath.

'Where are you?' called a voice. It was Miss Abbott, against whose carriage they had collided. She had re-lit one of the lamps, and was picking her way towards him.

'Silence!' he called again, and again they obeyed. He shook the bundle; he breathed into it; he opened his coat and pressed it against him. Then he listened, and heard nothing but the rain and the panting horses, and Harriet, who was somewhere chuckling to herself in the dark.

Miss Abbott approached, and took it gently from him. The face was already chilly, but thanks to Philip it was no longer wet. Nor would it again be wetted by any tear.

CHAPTER IX

THE DETAILS OF Harriet's crime were never known. In her illness she spoke more of the inlaid box that she had lent to Lilia – lent, not given – than of recent troubles. It was clear that she had gone prepared for an interview with Gino, and, finding him out, she had yielded to a grotesque temptation. But how far this was the result of ill-temper, to what extent she had been fortified by her religion, when and how she had met the poor idiot – these questions were never answered, nor did they interest Philip greatly. Detection was certain: they would have been arrested by the police of Florence or Milan, or at the frontier. As it was, they had been stopped in a simpler manner a few miles out of the town.

As yet he could scarcely survey the thing. It was too great. Round the Italian baby who had died in the mud there centred deep passions and high hopes. People had been wicked or wrong in the matter; no one save himself had been trivial. Now the baby had gone, but there remained this vast apparatus of pride and pity and love. For the dead, who seem to take away so much, really take with them nothing that is ours. The passion they have aroused lives after them, easy to transmute or to transfer, but well-nigh impossible to destroy. And Philip knew that he was still voyaging on the same magnificent, perilous sea, with the sun or the clouds above him, and the tides below.

The course of the moment – that, at all events, was certain. He and no one else must take the news to Gino. It was easy to talk of Harriet's crime – easy also to blame the negligent Perfetta or Mrs Herriton at home. Everyone had contributed – even Miss Abbott and Irma. If one chose, one might consider the catastrophe composite or the work of fate. But Philip did not so choose. It was his own fault, due to acknowledged weakness in his own character. Therefore he, and no one else, must take the news of it to Gino.

Nothing prevented him. Miss Abbott was engaged with Harriet, and people had sprung out of the darkness and were conducting them towards some cottage. Philip had only to get into the uninjured carriage and order the driver to return. He was back at Monteriano after a two hours' absence. Perfetta was in the house now, and greeted him cheerfully. Pain, physical and mental, had made him stupid. It was some time before he realized that she had never missed the child.

Gino was still out. The woman took him to the reception-room, just as she had taken Miss Abbott in the morning, and dusted a circle for him on one of the horsehair chairs. But it was dark now, so she left the guest a little lamp.

'I will be as quick as I can,' she told him. 'But there are many streets in Monteriano; he is sometimes difficult to find. I could not find him this morning.'

'Go first to the Caffè Garibaldi,' said Philip, remembering that this was the hour appointed by his friends of yesterday.

He occupied the time he was left alone not in thinking – there was nothing to think about; he simply had to tell a few facts – but in trying to make a sling for his broken arm. The trouble was in the elbow-joint, and as long as he kept this motionless he could go on as usual. But inflammation was beginning, and the slightest jar gave him agony. The sling was not fitted before Gino leapt up the stairs, crying –

'So you are back! How glad I am! We are all waiting –'

Philip had seen too much to be nervous. In low, even tones, he told what had happened; and the other, also perfectly calm, heard him to the end. In the silence Perfetta called up that she had forgotten the baby's evening milk; she must fetch it. When she had gone Gino took up the lamp without a word, and they went into the other room.

'My sister is ill,' said Philip, 'and Miss Abbott is guiltless. I should be glad if you did not have to trouble them.'

Gino had stooped down by the rug, and was feeling the place where his son had lain. Now and then he frowned a little and glanced at Philip.

'It is through me,' he continued. 'It happened because I was cowardly and idle. I have come to know what you will do.'

Gino had left the rug, and began to pat the table from the end, as if he was blind. The action was so uncanny that Philip was driven to intervene.

'Gently, man, gently; he is not here.'

He went up and touched him on the shoulder.

He twitched away, and began to pass his hands over things more rapidly – over the table, the chairs, the entire floor, the walls, as high as he could reach them. Philip had not presumed to comfort him. But now the tension was too great – he tried.

'Break down, Gino; you must break down. Scream and curse and give in for a little; you must break down.'

There was no reply, and no cessation of the sweeping hands.

'It is time to be unhappy. Break down, or you will be ill like my sister. You will go –'

The tour of the room was over. He had touched everything in it except Philip. Now he approached him. His face was that of a man who has lost his old reason for life and seeks a new one.

'Gino!'

He stopped for a moment; then he came nearer. Philip stood his ground.

'You are to do what you like with me, Gino. Your son is dead, Gino. He died in my arms, remember. It does not excuse me; but he did die in my arms.'

The left hand came forward, slowly this time. It hovered before Philip like an insect. Then it descended and gripped him by his broken elbow.

Philip struck out with all the strength of his other arm. Gino fell to the blow, without a cry or a word.

'You brute!' exclaimed the Englishman. 'Kill me if you like! But just you leave my broken arm alone.'

Then he was seized with remorse, and knelt beside his adversary and tried to revive him. He managed to raise him up, and propped his body against his own. He passed his arm round him. Again he was filled with pity and tenderness. He awaited the revival without fear, sure that both of them were safe at last.

Gino recovered suddenly. His lips moved. For one blessed moment it seemed that he was going to speak. But he scrambled up in silence, remembering everything, and he made not towards Philip, but towards the lamp.

'Do what you like; but think first –'

The lamp was tossed across the room, out through the loggia. It broke against one of the trees below. Philip began to cry out in the dark.

Gino approached from behind and gave him a sharp pinch. Philip spun round with a yell. He had only been pinched on the back, but he knew what was in store for him. He struck out, exhorting the devil to fight him, to kill him, to do anything but this. Then he stumbled to the door. It was open. He lost his head and, instead of turning down the stairs, he ran across the landing into the room opposite. There he lay down on the floor between the stove and the skirting-board.

His senses grew sharper. He could hear Gino coming in on tiptoe. He even knew what was passing in his mind, how now he was at fault, now he was hopeful, now he was wondering whether after all the victim had not escaped down the stairs. There was a quick swoop above him, and then a low growl like a dog's. Gino had broken his fingernails against the stove.

Physical pain is almost too terrible to bear. We can just bear it when it comes by accident or for our good – as it generally does in modern life, except at school. But when it is caused by the malignity of a man, full-grown, fashioned like ourselves, all our control disappears. Philip's one thought was to get away from that room at whatever sacrifice of nobility or pride.

Gino was now at the farther end of the room, groping by the little tables. Suddenly the instinct came to him. He crawled quickly to where Philip lay and had him clean by the elbow.

The whole arm seemed red-hot, and the broken bone grated in the joint, sending out shoots of the essence of pain. His other arm was pinioned against the wall, and Gino had trampled in behind the stove and was kneeling on his legs. For the space of a minute he yelled and yelled with all the force of his lungs. Then this solace was denied him. The other hand, moist and strong, began to close round his throat.

At first he was glad, for here, he thought, was death at last. But it was only a new torture; perhaps Gino inherited the skill of his ancestors – the childlike ruffians who flung each other from the towers. Just as the windpipe closed the hand fell off, and Philip was revived by the motion of his arm. And just as he was about to faint, and gain at least one moment of oblivion, the motion stopped, and he would struggle instead against the pressure on his throat.

Vivid pictures came dancing through the pain – Lilia dying some months back in this very house, Miss Abbott bending over the baby, his mother at home, now reading evening prayers to the servants. He felt that he was growing weaker; his brain wandered; the agony did not seem so great. Not all Gino's care could indefinitely postpone the end. His yells and gurgles became mechanical – functions of the tortured flesh rather than true notes of indignation and despair. He was conscious of a horrid tumbling. Then his arm was pulled a little too roughly, and everything was quiet at last.

'But your son is dead, Gino. Your son is dead, dear Gino. Your son is dead.'

The room was full of light, and Miss Abbott had Gino by the shoulders, holding him down in a chair. She was exhausted with the struggle, and her arms were trembling.

'What is the good of another death? What is the good of more pain?'

He too began to tremble. Then he turned and looked curiously at Philip, whose face, covered with dust and foam, was visible by the stove. Miss Abbott allowed him to get up, though she still held him firmly. He gave a loud and curious cry – a cry of interrogation it might be called. Below there was the noise of Perfetta returning with the baby's milk.

'Go to him,' said Miss Abbott, indicating Philip. 'Pick him up. Treat him kindly.'

She released him, and he approached Philip slowly. His eyes were filling with trouble. He bent down, as if he would gently raise him up.

'Help! Help!' moaned Philip. His body had suffered too much from Gino. It could not bear to be touched by him.

Gino seemed to understand. He stopped, crouched above him. Miss Abbott herself came forward and lifted her friend in her arms.

'Oh, the foul devil!' he murmured. 'Kill him! Kill him for me.'

Miss Abbott laid him tenderly on the couch and wiped his face. Then she said gravely to them both, 'This thing stops here.'

'Latte! Latte!' cried Perfetta, hilariously ascending the stairs.

'Remember,' she continued, 'there is to be no revenge. I will have no more intentional evil. We are not to fight with each other any more.'

'I shall never forgive him,' sighed Philip.

'Latte! Latte freschissimo! Bianco come neve!' Perfetta came in with another lamp and a little jug.

Gino spoke for the first time. 'Put the milk on the table,' he said. 'It will not be wanted in the other room.' The peril was over at last. A great sob shook the whole body, another followed, and then he gave a piercing cry of woe, and stumbled towards Miss Abbott like a child and clung to her.

All through the day Miss Abbott had seemed to Philip like a goddess, and more than ever did she seem so now. Many people look younger and more intimate during great emotion. But some there are who look older, and remote, and he could not think that there was little difference in years, and none in composition, between her and the man whose head was laid upon her breast. Her eyes were open, full of infinite pity and full of majesty, as if they discerned the boundaries of sorrow, and saw unimaginable tracts beyond. Such eyes he had seen in great pictures but never in a mortal. Her hands were folded round the sufferer, stroking him lightly, for even a goddess can do no more than that. And it seemed fitting, too, that she should bend her head and touch his forehead with her lips.

Philip looked away, as he sometimes looked away from the great pictures where visible forms suddenly become inadequate for the things they have shown to us. He was happy; he was assured that there was greatness in the world. There came to him an earnest desire to be good through the example of this good woman. He would try henceforward to be worthy of the things she had revealed. Quietly, without hysterical prayers or banging of drums, he underwent conversion. He was saved.

'That milk,' said she, 'need not be wasted. Take it, Signor Carella, and persuade Mr Herriton to drink.'

Gino obeyed her, and carried the child's milk to Philip. And Philip obeyed also and drank.

'Is there any left?'

'A little,' answered Gino.

'Then finish it.' For she was determined to use such remnants as lie about the world.

'Will you not have some?'

'I do not care for milk; finish it all.'

'Philip, have you had enough milk?'

'Yes, thank you, Gino; finish it all.'

He drank the milk, and then, either by accident or in some spasm of pain, broke the jug to pieces. Perfetta exclaimed in bewilderment. 'It does not matter,' he told her. 'It does not matter. It will never be wanted any more.'

CHAPTER X

'HE WILL HAVE to marry her,' said Philip. 'I heard from him this morning, just as we left Milan. He finds he has gone too far to back out. It would be expensive. I don't know how much he minds – not as much as we suppose, I think. At all events there's not a word of blame in the letter. I don't believe he even feels angry. I never was so completely forgiven. Ever since you stopped him killing me, it has been a vision of perfect friendship. He nursed me, he lied for me at the inquest, and at the funeral, though he was crying, you would have thought it was my son who had died. Certainly I was the only person he had to be kind to; he was so distressed not to make Harriet's acquaintance, and that he scarcely saw anything of you. In his letter he says so again.'

'Thank him, please, when you write,' said Miss Abbott, 'and give him my kindest regards.'

'Indeed I will.' He was surprised that she could slide away from the man so easily. For his own part, he was bound by ties of almost alarming intimacy. Gino had the southern knack of friendship. In the intervals of business he would pull out Philip's life, turn it inside out, remodel it, and advise him how to use it for the best. The sensation was pleasant, for he was a kind as well as a skilful operator. But Philip came away feeling that he had not a secret corner left. In that very letter Gino had again implored him, as a refuge from domestic difficulties, 'to marry Miss Abbott, even if her dowry is small'. And how Miss Abbott herself, after such tragic intercourse, could resume the conventions and send calm messages of esteem, was more than he could understand.

'When will you see him again?' she asked. They were standing together in the corridor of the train, slowly ascending out of Italy towards the St Gotthard tunnel.

'I hope next spring. Perhaps we shall paint Siena red for a day or two with some of the new wife's money. It was one of the arguments for marrying her.'

'He has no heart,' she said severely. 'He does not really mind about the child at all.'

'No; you're wrong. He does. He is unhappy, like the rest of us. But he doesn't try to keep up appearances as we do. He knows that the things that have made him happy once will probably make him happy again.'

'He said he would never be happy again.'

'In his passion. Not when he was calm. We English say it when we are calm – when we do not really believe it any longer. Gino is not ashamed of inconsistency. It is one of the many things I like him for.'

'Yes; I was wrong. That is so.'

'He's much more honest with himself than I am,' continued Philip, 'and he is honest without an effort and without pride. But you, Miss Abbott, what about you? Will you be in Italy next spring?'

'No.'

'I'm sorry. When will you come back, do you think?'

'I think never.'

'For whatever reason?' He stared at her as if she were some monstrosity.

'Because I understand the place. There is no need.'

'Understand Italy!' he exclaimed.

'Perfectly.'

'Well, I don't. And I don't understand you,' he murmured to himself, as he paced away from her up the corridor. By this time he loved her very much, and he could not bear to be puzzled. He had reached love by the spiritual path: her thoughts and her goodness and her nobility had moved him first, and now her whole body and all its gestures had become transfigured by them.

The beauties that are called obvious – the beauties of her hair and her voice and her limbs – he had noticed these last; Gino, who never traversed any path at all, had commended them dispassionately to his friend.

Why was she so puzzling? He had known so much about her once – what she thought, how she felt, the reasons for her actions. And now he only knew that he loved her, and all the other knowledge seemed passing from him just as he needed it most. Why would she never come to Italy again? Why had she avoided himself and Gino ever since the evening that she had saved their lives? The train was nearly empty. Harriet slumbered in a compartment by herself. He must ask her these questions now, and he returned quickly to her down the corridor.

She greeted him with a question of her own. 'Are your plans decided?'

'Yes. I can't live at Sawston.'

'Have you told Mrs Herriton?'

'I wrote from Monteriano. I tried to explain things; but she will never understand me. Her view will be that the affair is settled – sadly settled since the baby is dead. Still, it's over; our family circle need be vexed no more. She won't even be angry with you. You see, you have done us no harm in the long run. Unless, of course, you talk about Harriet and make a scandal. So that is my plan – London and work. What is yours?'

'Poor Harriet!' said Miss Abbott. 'As if I dare judge Harriet! Or anybody.' And without replying to Philip's question she left him, to visit the other invalid.

Philip gazed after her mournfully, and then he looked mournfully out of the window at the decreasing streams. All the excitement was over – the inquest, Harriet's short illness, his own visit to the surgeon. He was convalescent, both in body and spirit, but convalescence brought no joy. In the looking-glass at the end of the corridor he saw his face haggard, and his shoulders pulled forward by the weight of the sling. Life was greater than he had supposed, but it was even less complete. He had seen the need for strenuous work and for righteousness. And now he saw what a very little way those things would go.

'Is Harriet going to be all right?' he asked. Miss Abbott had come back to him.

'She will soon be her old self,' was the reply. For Harriet, after a sharp paroxysm of illness and remorse, was quickly returning to her normal state. She had been 'thoroughly upset,' as she phrased it, but she soon ceased to realize that anything was wrong beyond the death of a poor little child. Already she spoke of 'this unlucky accident', and 'the mysterious frustration of one's attempts to make things better'. Miss Abbott had seen that she was comfortable, and had given her a kind kiss. But she returned feeling that Harriet, like her mother, considered the affair as settled.

'I'm clear enough about Harriet's future, and about parts of my own. But I ask again, What about yours?'

'Sawston and work,' said Miss Abbott.

'No.'

'Why not?' she asked, smiling.

'You've seen too much. You've seen as much and done more than I have.'

'But it's so different. Of course I shall go to Sawston. You forget my father; and even if he wasn't there I've a hundred ties: my district – I'm neglecting it shamefully – my evening classes, the St James's –'

'Silly nonsense!' he exploded, suddenly moved to have the whole thing out with her. 'You're too good – about a thousand times better than I am. You can't live in that hole; you must go among people who can hope to understand you. I mind for myself: I want to see you often – again and again.'

'Of course we shall meet whenever you come down; and I hope that will mean often.'

'It's not enough; it'll only be in the old horrible way, each with a dozen relatives round us. No, Miss Abbott; it's not good enough.'

'We can write at all events.'

'You will write?' he cried, with a flush of pleasure. At times his hopes seemed so solid.

'I will indeed.'

'But I say it's not enough – you can't go back to the old life if you wanted to. Too much has happened.'

'I know that,' she said sadly.

'Not only pain and sorrow, but wonderful things: that tower in the sunlight – do you remember it, and all you said to me? The theatre, even. And the next day – in the church; and our times with Gino.'

'All the wonderful things are over,' she said. 'That is just where it is.'

'I don't believe it. At all events, not for me. The most wonderful things may be to come –'

'The wonderful things are over,' she repeated, and looked at him so mournfully that he dare not contradict her. The train was crawling up the last ascent towards the Campanile of Airolo and the entrance of the tunnel.

'Miss Abbott,' he murmured, speaking quickly, as if their free intercourse might soon be ended, 'what is the matter with you? I thought I understood you, and I don't. All those two great first days at Monteriano I read you as clearly as you read me still. I saw why you had come, and why you changed sides, and afterwards I saw your wonderful courage and pity. And now you're frank with me one moment, as you used to be, and the next moment you shut me up. You see, I owe too much to you – my life, and I don't know what besides. I won't stand it. You've gone too far to turn mysterious. I'll quote what you said to me: "Don't be mysterious; there isn't the time." I'll quote something else: "I and my life must be where I live." You can't live at Sawston.'

He had moved her at last. She whispered to herself hurriedly, 'It is tempting –' And those three words threw him into a tumult of joy. What was tempting to her? After all, was the greatest of things possible? Perhaps, after long estrangement, after much tragedy, the South had brought them together in the end. That laughter in the theatre, those silver stars in the purple sky, even the violets of a departed spring, all had helped, and sorrow had helped also, and so had tenderness to others.

'It is tempting,' she repeated, 'not to be mysterious. I've wanted often to tell you, and then been afraid. I could never tell anyone else, certainly no woman, and I think you're the one man who might understand and not be disgusted.'

'Are you lonely?' he whispered. 'Is it anything like that?'

'Yes.' The train seemed to shake him towards her. He was resolved that though a dozen people were looking he would yet take her in his arms. 'I'm terribly lonely, or I wouldn't speak. I think you must know already.' Their faces were crimson, as if the same thought was surging through them both.

'Perhaps I do.' He came close to her. 'Perhaps I could speak instead. But if you will say the word plainly you'll never be sorry; I will thank you for it all my life.'

She said plainly, 'That I love him.' Then she broke down. Her body was shaken with sobs, and lest there should be any doubt she cried between the sobs for Gino! Gino! Gino!

He heard himself remark: 'Rather! I love him too! When I can forget how he hurt me that evening. Though whenever we shake hands –' One of them must have moved a step or two, for when she spoke again she was already a little way apart.

'You've upset me.' She stifled something that was perilously near hysterics. 'I thought I was past all this. You're taking it wrongly. I'm in love with Gino – don't pass it off – I mean it crudely – you know what I mean. So laugh at me.'

'Laugh at love?' asked Philip.

'Yes. Pull it to pieces. Tell me I'm a fool or worse – that he's a cad. Say all you said when Lilia fell in love with him. That's the help I want. I dare tell you this because I like you – and because you're without passion; you look on life as a spectacle; you don't enter it; you only find it funny or beautiful. So I can trust you to cure me. Mr Herriton, isn't it funny?' She tried to laugh herself, but became frightened and had to stop. 'He's not a gentleman, nor a Christian, nor good in any way. He's never flattered me nor honoured me. But because he's handsome, that's been enough. The son of an Italian dentist, with a pretty face.' She repeated the phrase as if it was a charm against passion. 'Oh, Mr Herriton, isn't it funny!' Then, to his relief, she began to cry. 'I love him, and I'm not ashamed of it. I love him and I'm going to Sawston, and if I mayn't speak about him to you sometimes, I shall die.'

In that terrible discovery Philip managed to think not of himself but of her. He did not lament. He did not even speak to her kindly, for he saw that she could not stand it. A flippant reply was what she asked and needed – something flippant and a little cynical. And indeed it was the only reply he could trust himself to make.

'Perhaps it is what the books call "a passing fancy"?'

She shook her head. Even this question was too pathetic. For, as far as she knew anything about herself, she knew that her passions, once aroused, were sure. 'If I saw him often,' she said, 'I might remember what he is like. Or he might grow old. But I dare not risk it, so nothing can alter me now.'

'Well, if the fancy does pass, let me know.' After all, he could say what he wanted.

'Oh, you shall know quick enough.'

'But before you retire to Sawston – are you so mighty sure?'

'What of?' She had stopped crying. He was treating her exactly as she had hoped.

'That you and he –' He smiled bitterly at the thought of them together. Here was the cruel antique malice of the gods, such as they once sent forth against Pasiphaë. Centuries of aspiration and culture – and the world could not escape it. 'I was going to say – what ever have you got in common?'

'Nothing except the times we have seen each other.' Again her face was crimson. He turned his own face away.

'Which – which times?'

'The time I thought you weak and heedless, and went instead of you to get the baby. That began it, as far as I know the beginning. Or it may have begun when you took us to the theatre, and I saw him mixed up with music and light. But I didn't understand till the morning. Then you opened the door – and I knew why I had been so happy. Afterwards, in the church, I prayed for us all; not for anything new, but that we might just be as we were – he with the child he loved, you and I and Harriet safe out of the place – and that I might never see him or speak to him again. I could have pulled through then – the thing was only coming near, like a wreath of smoke; it hadn't wrapped me round.'

'But through my fault,' said Philip solemnly, 'he is parted from the child he loves. And because my life was in danger you came and saw him and spoke to him again.' For the thing was even greater than she imagined. Nobody but himself would ever see round it now. And to see round it he was standing at an immense distance. He could even be glad that she had once held the beloved in her arms.

'Don't talk of "faults". You're my friend for ever, Mr Herriton, I think. Only don't be charitable and shift or take the blame. Get over supposing I'm refined. That's what puzzles you. Get over that.'

As she spoke she seemed to be transfigured, and to have indeed no part with refinement or unrefinement any longer. Out of this wreck there was revealed to him something indestructible – something which she, who had given it, could never take away.

'I say again, don't be charitable. If he had asked me, I might have given myself body and soul. That would have been the end of my rescue-party. But all through he took me for a superior being – a goddess. I who was worshipping every inch of him, and every word he spoke. And that saved me.'

Philip's eyes were fixed on the Campanile of Airolo. But he saw instead the fair myth of Endymion. This woman was a goddess to the end. For her no love could be degrading: she stood outside all degradation. This episode, which she thought so sordid, and which was so tragic for him, remained supremely beautiful. To such a height was he lifted that without regret he could now have told her that he was her worshipper too. But what was the use of telling her? For all the wonderful things had happened.

'Thank you,' was all that he permitted himself. 'Thank you for everything.'

She looked at him with great friendliness, for he had made her life endurable. At that moment the train entered the St Gotthard tunnel. They hurried back to the carriage to close the windows lest the smuts should get into Harriet's eyes.

APPENDIX

An Exchange between
Forster and R. C. Trevelyan

(R. C. Trevelyan was an author who wrote under the name 'Bob Trevy'. The original letter from him to Forster has been lost.)

Forster to Trevelyan, 28 October 1905

Your letter was rather what I expected, and very much what I feel about my book myself, though on the whole I am less severe, and inclined, I think, to view my work too complacently. The object of the book is the improvement of Philip, and I did really want the improvement to be a surprise. Therefore in chapters 1–2 I never hinted at the possibility, but at the same time did not demonstrate the impossibility, or did not mean to. In ch. 5 he has got into a mess, through trying to live only by a sense of humour and by a sense of the beautiful. The knowledge of the mess embitters him, and this is the improvement's beginning. From that time I exhibit new pieces of him – pieces that he did not know of, or at all events had never used. He grows large enough to appreciate Miss Abbott, and in the final scene he exceeds her.

All this is what I intended.

But I do begin to think (– I will say 'to fear' for it is a pity it should be so –) that this 'surprise' method is artistically wrong, and that from the first one must suggest the possibility, not merely the non-impossibility, of improvement. I disliked and do dislike finger posts, and couldn't bear in the earlier scenes the thought of inserting 'Philip has other things in him besides these: watch him', however well the insertion had been made.

And, when I wrote Monteriano I pushed this dislike to an extreme and should have felt the suggestion that a book must have one atmosphere to be pedantic. Life hasn't any, and the hot and cold of its changes are fascinating to me. I determined to imitate in this and let the result be artistic if it liked. Naturally it did not like.

I too would like to have a talk, and can't get what I want to say on paper. You can gather however that I know I am not a real artist, and at the same time am fearfully serious over my work and willing to sweat at atmosphere if it helps me to [achieve??] what I want. What I want, I think, is the sentimental, but the sentimental reached by no easy beaten track – I cannot explain myself properly, for you must remember (I forget it myself) that though 'clever' I have a small and cloudy brain, and cannot clear it by talking or reading philosophy. In fact my equipment is frightfully limited, but so good in parts that I want to do with it what I can.

Miss Abbott comes to grief for archaeological reasons. She was originally meant to turn out smaller and different. About the scene between Philip and Gino I don't, however, quite concur. (Less important than the death of the baby, which is the real crisis.) P. is a person who has scarcely ever felt the physical forces that are banging about in the world, and he couldn't get good and understand by spiritual suffering alone. Bodily punishment, however unjust superficially, was necessary too: in fact the scene – to use a heavy word, and one that I have only just thought of – was sacramental. Nor do I lose interest in Gino after it: here the possibility was hinted at during his intercourse with Lilia.

If you are good enough to write again, I wish you'd tell me on which pages I am unduly facetious. That is an awful evil, and only you have warned me against it. And I wish, if it was only two or three lines, you would say something about my style. It is scarcely fair though, after all your goodness, to bother you again. You're the only person who has troubled to criticize me in any detail.

Trevelyan to Forster, undated

... Your letter was very interesting, and made me feel I had been too severe in my strictures, even from my point of view. But though I exaggerated my objections, I still feel them to be real. It is largely no doubt, as you suggest, a question of atmosphere, whatever exactly that vaguest of words may mean. The story no doubt necessitated several different atmospheres, Sawston and the various other non-Sawston atmospheres, i.e. Philip's, Gino's, Miss Abbott's. But I think you should have contrasted Philip and Miss Abbott more with Sawston from the beginning, and made one feel that however much they were *in* Sawston for the time being, they were yet not *of* it, and would eventually rise superior to it. This would at once have gained them our sympathies, and our interest in Philip's development, besides making Sawston more amusing, as seen through Philip's gradually enlightened eyes. But this won't help you much, and I don't feel sure I am right either. No doubt what I suppose one must call style is at the bottom of much that I object to. In the more comic parts it is often right enough, and, in much of the more serious parts, at any rate unobjectionable. But I find it often far too conversational and even slangy, e.g. p. 301, where 'beastly Italy' is merely beastly indeed, and what you gain in expressiveness does not compensate for what you lose in something far more important. For the purely narrative part of a story, where the author himself speaks, should surely keep throughout a certain sameness of quality, and also a certain dignity, and if possible, beauty, even in a slight or comic narrative, at least it does in all the books I really care about. The dialogue, if necessary, should be more unequal, either in the emotional or the slangy direction, or in any other direction. This is why I also do not like p. 300, the whole paragraph from 'They travelled' down to 'Verona' with its 'people ceasing being ugly' etc., and its '*waltzing* train *picking* them out etc.' Besides I think you ought always to try deliberately to write beautifully, I do not mean poetically

– all beauty is not poetry, and Jane Austin [*sic*] and Petronius are often quite beautiful, to say nothing of Apuleius and Cervantes, in their most sublimely amusing moments. Turgenef [*sic*], being when at his best a great sentimentalist, has to be beautiful in the most deliberate way, and when you are sentimental, you will find you have to be so no less. What beauty of style consists in, who can say. But no doubt simplicity and economy of expression are negative elements, as well as the almost complete avoidance of jarring modern notes, and journalistic idiom, which to my mind partly spoils the writing of even such skilful writers as Mac-Carthy and Roger Fry. The positive elements each must find out for himself by practice; no doubt the rhythm of the sentences, which should be both beautiful in themselves, and as expressive as possible, and also the perfect choice and placing of expressive words, that must be neither exaggerated nor weak nor ugly – these things and many others are what make up style now, just as they did in the time of the Greeks: but you know all these things as well as I do, and practise them too; only, it seems to me, not uncompromisingly enough as yet. To take another instance of a different kind, I do not think p. 242 succeeds. You seem to have felt rightly that the scene, as it was beautiful, should be described beautifully, but your method seems to me ingenious where it should be simple. The elaborate metaphor of the sea and rocks is surely not appropriate to convey the emotion, and is too much in the nature of an Elizabethan or Henry-Jacobean conceit. Tourgenef [*sic*] would have made it a thing one could never forget; but he would not have talked of 'Art' and 'painter's courage'. That is conversation, not art, and even the writing of modern novels is an art, and may be a very great one, though MacCarthy to my amazement tells me it can never be so. Yet I am very glad indeed that MacCarthy liked your book, for his judgement is very valuable, and he never likes anything without very good reasons, and is the best critic of modern novels I know. To be that, one should be rather more modern than I am, and less enamoured of the classics; and I should not have ventured on these long lectures, if I had not thought you wished it, and if I did not like your work a great deal already. I am glad people appreciate it as much as it seems they do, as it is so much more interesting than other people's in that line, at least so it seems to me. We have just been to Cambridge and seen Dickinson, Kanes (*sic*?), and Dent, who all liked your book a great deal . . .

This book is set in GARAMOND, the first typeface in
the ambitious programme of matrix production
undertaken by the Monotype Corporation
under the guidance of Stanley Morrison
in 1922. Although named after the
great French royal typographer,
Claude Garamond (1499–
1561), it owes much to
Jean Jannon of Sedan
(1580–1658).